Blue Shoe

*Also by Anne Lamott
in Large Print:*

Traveling Mercies

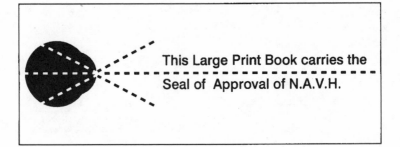

This Large Print Book carries the
Seal of Approval of N.A.V.H.

Blue Shoe

Anne Lamott

The author gratefully acknowledges permission to quote: "I Am Not I," from *Lorca and Jiménez* by Robert Bly. Copyright © 1973, 1977 Robert Bly. Reprinted by permission of Beacon Press, Boston. Lines from "Hope," from *The Collected Poems of Langston Hughes.* Copyright © 1994 by The Estate of Langston Hughes.

Published in 2003 by arrangement with Riverhead Books, a member of Penguin Putnam Inc.

Wheeler Large Print Hardcover Series.

The text of this Large Print edition is unabridged.
Other aspects of the book may vary from the original edition.

Set in 16 pt. Plantin by Myrna S. Raven.

Printed in the United States on permanent paper.

Library of Congress Cataloging-in-Publication Data

Lamott, Anne.
    Blue shoe / Anne Lamott.
      p. cm.
    ISBN 1-58724-362-8 (lg. print : hc : alk. paper)
    1. San Francisco (Calif.) — Fiction. 2. Mothers and daughters — Fiction. 3. Female friendship — Fiction.
4. Divorced women — Fiction. 5. Single mothers — Fiction.
6. Large type books. I. Title.
PS3562.A4645 B57 2003
   813'.54—dc21   2002190761

THIS BOOK IS DEDICATED TO

Douglas Foster
and
Steven Barclay

I am not I.
  I am this one
walking beside me whom I do not see,
whom at times I manage to visit,
and whom at other times I forget;
who remains calm and silent while I talk,
and forgives, gently, when I hate,
who walks where I am not,
who will remain standing when I die.

                    Juan Ramón Jiménez

acknowledgments

I am so grateful to David Talbot, who published some of this material in slightly different form, at salon.com. Over the years, he has offered me the ideal space in which to try out new work, and I greatly value his friendship, and his magazine.

It would be hard to capture my gratitude to Sarah Chalfant and Andrew Wylie, my agents. Sarah's constancy and faith in this book were the small campfire at which I warmed myself whenever I was afraid. Sonesh Chainani at the Wylie agency was always there for me, working too hard and making me laugh.

Cindy Spiegel, my editor at Riverhead, took a huge chance on me, and I greatly value her work on this book. My copy editor, Anna Jardine, was dogged and brilliant: together she and Cindy saved me from my gravest writerly defects. Cindy's assistant, Venetia van Kuffeler, is a marvel.

Doug Foster worked with me every step of the way, as editor and birth coach. This book would not exist without his contributions.

Neshama Franklin, Mark Childress, and Robyn Posin, so wise, smart, and funny, helped me more than I can say.

I could not get by without the tenderness and

direction of the congregation of St. Andrew Presbyterian Church, Marin City, California, the Reverend Ms. Veronica Goines, pastor.

And I want to say a special thanks to Pat Gomez, of Tiburon, California, who in 1982 took me in for a year and a half, when I was drunk and sad and lonelier than I had ever been before, and with whom I discovered a little blue shoe.

one

The world outside the window was in flames. The leaves on the pistachio trees shone fire-red and orange. Mattie studied the early-morning light. She was lying on the side of the bed where her husband should have been sleeping. Those trees were one reason she'd moved back into her parents' old home after leaving Nicholas, these trees and the sloping grassy hillside behind the house. Also, there was no mortgage: her parents had paid it off during the course of their marriage. She and her brother, Al, had grown up playing on the hill and in the buckeyes with their low, broad branches; her six-year-old, Harry, played there now, and her daughter, Ella, two, would also climb one day soon. The leaves of the delicate Japanese maple between Mattie's window and the wobbly fence were still green, but elsewhere in the garden were russets and butterscotch-oranges, other trees giddy with color, almost garish, like gypsy dresses. When she strained to listen, she could imagine them saying, We gave you shade, and now we'll give you a little kick-ass beauty before we die. A choir of chickadees and finches sang above the sounds of a quiet neighborhood waking up, the cars of people heading to work and school, the clatter and thumps of the recycling truck, a dog barking, leaves rustling in a gentle wind, silence. A moment later she heard the rats in the walls begin to stir.

Her mother, Isa (it rhymed with "Lisa"), who still owned the house, had failed to mention that there were rats in the walls. Rats, and the green rug in the master bedroom that for many years had been peed on by Isa's cats. A faint odor of urine clung to it despite Mattie's every effort at eradication. Isa had been planning to sell the house as a fixer-upper in the wildly inflated San Francisco Bay area real estate market, but a month after she'd reached the top of the waiting list for The Sequoias, a retirement community where she hoped to grow old, she'd moved out. She had some money socked away from her husband Alfred's small life insurance policy, which, coupled with Social Security, was enough to pay for her expenses in the new apartment.

Her unwanted stuff was still on the shelves, and in the garage and attic. The house looked much as it always had, or at least for the nearly twenty years Isa had lived there alone, after Mattie and Al had moved out and Alfred had died. Isa had taken one couch with her to the new apartment, a few chairs, a dresser, and Al's old twin bed, and had sent the rest of her furniture to the dump or Goodwill. There were mirrors in every room of the house. Isa had always liked to look at herself, striking movie star poses. Mattie avoided the mirrors whenever possible. What she saw when she did glance at her reflection was chestnut-brown hair, which she usually wore in a braid; tired eyes, so dark that the pupils didn't show; fair English skin and a broad snub nose from her mother; black lashes and brows from her dad, as well as his big teeth; and full lips, set off nicely by a white ring of scar on her chin from a rock Al had thrown at her when they were young.

Isa had left her house vacant for six months at Mattie's request, while Mattie got up the nerve to leave her husband. She'd been planning to break away from Nicky in spring, because she'd had it with his mammoth inconsistency — his hilarious and brilliant conversations, interspersed with brooding narcissism; his charming and amiable contributions to the business of raising children together, wedged in between immobilization and depression, for which he would not seek help; his inexhaustible interest in her thoughts about the world, progressive politics, and the arts, marbled into the slow, cold gaze with which he looked up from his secret phone calls when she entered his study; the silent, wounding way he stopped making love to her for weeks at a time, right after nights of hot, tender sex. Then, in March, when the world was wild and green, full of blossom and fragrance and mud, Mattie's best friend, Angela, had told her gently that she was moving to Los Angeles, to live with Julie, the woman she'd recently fallen for.

"But you're my only real friend!" Mattie wept, and Angela had cried too. They had been talking in different kitchens for years now, ever since the night they met over a stranger's stove during a party for Nicky, when the College of Marin made him an assistant professor of literature. Minutes after meeting, the two women broke off entirely from the others. They sat on the kitchen floor and talked like teenagers about their mothers and their bodies and God, to whom they were both devoted, and their pets, to whom they were also devoted, and Nicky, about whom they were both ambivalent. Angela worked with him at the college, where she read and graded papers for the entire English department, and while she enjoyed his sense of humor, she disliked his elitism. He liked to discuss books and politics; he had no patience for stories of real people trying to get through the day. Angela and Mattie started getting together several times a week, to hike or cook or help each other around the house. Nicky accused Mattie of being in love, of going gay. At the same time, he had dropped hints that he didn't think Angela was a real lesbian: she just hadn't met the right man yet, it was a phase, and would pass. And a few years ago, Angela noticed that Nicky had taken off after classes with of one of his students, a beautiful twenty-two-year-old black woman. Mattie was six months pregnant with Ella at the time. Several years before, he had had an affair that nearly ended the marriage, although he had never given Mattie further cause to doubt his fidelity. But one day after she and Mattie had become inseparable friends, Angela followed Nicky and the young woman to the Tamalpais Motel, and then she told Mattie. Mattie confronted Nicky, and he broke off the affair, and while Mattie eventually forgave him, without forgetting, Nicky never forgave Angela, and Angela never forgave Nicky.

Angela sometimes wore her short honey-colored hair in two vertical tufts, like velvet giraffe horns. Her wide eyes were steel-blue. She was Jewish, expansive and yeasty and uncontained, as if she had a birthright for outrageousness. She knew things. Mattie couldn't live without her.

The smell of wet soil, blossoms, and grass wafted through the kitchen window as Mattie heard Angela's news. "But you're not going to have to live without me," Angela said, crying. "We'll talk every day, and I'll come up every chance I can."

Mattie went back into therapy to deal with the devastation of losing Angela. The therapist pointed out gently that some of her grief must be related to her deteriorating marriage. In some ways, losing Angela was harder. It was like the death some years before of Mattie's old cat, who had loved her the way her parents were supposed to have loved her: purely, without conditions. In any case, for a few months Mattie didn't have the strength to bear both her friend's departure and the end of her marriage. And then one day, she did.

When the leaves began to blaze and the days grew shorter, she brought her children and their things to the house she had grown up in. She brought some furniture, their dog, two cats, a couple of porno movies stolen from Nicky, and his bottle of Valium. He did not ask her about them. It was assumed that the children would live with her, and visit him on the weekends. He adored them but would not have been willing or able to share custody, even if Mattie had been willing. As it was, he took them most weekends, often late Saturday morning, then dropped them off Sunday nights with an air of weary heroism, like a firefighter returning the engine to the firehouse after a particularly difficult outing. The children were grief-stricken that he did not live with them anymore. Mattie prayed with them every night, then prayed separately for their hearts to heal, even prayed for Nicky's happiness and half meant it. After a month of weekend visits with Nicky, the children's distress lessened.

Mattie hadn't worried so much about Ella, who had ways of comforting herself and a generally sunny disposition. But Harry was sad and concerned. He was erratic, like Nicky: sometimes he acted so mean to Mattie and Ella that Mattie wanted to strike him, and at other times he could be utterly charming, especially with his sister. He'd carry her around from room to room as if she were an animated grocery sack, making faces and wisecracks to amuse her. Mattie saw how much he wanted Ella to disappear sometimes, but that he also listened for her when she was in her crib. He put his face right into hers to make her laugh, and she chortled, pleased that something was so grabbably close. Then he'd pinch her and make her cry. He took things from her, and she wailed, while he looked blank and innocent. He hugged her too tightly, he loved her too much, he hated all the same things he loved about her — her ineptitude, her cuteness, her messiness, her smells.

Mattie stopped seeing the therapist, and paid for Harry to go instead.

It helped; time's passing helped. Nothing really helped. And the house — it had been a mistake to move back in. It was falling apart, revealing mold and memories and ghosts. Mattie's beloved father had died of a heart attack in the laundry room, twenty years before. He was fifty-one and had never looked better than in the moments before his death. He had looked a lot like Mattie's brother Al did now, but trimmer, tall, with thicker brown hair, and the huge teeth that hardly fit in his mouth. Everyone had loved her father, including, about half the time, Isa. Still, it had been a miserable marriage, a shifting, malignant lava-lamp of a marriage, although it always looked great from the outside, two tall handsome parents well-known in the town for their willingness to serve on the city council, the school board, liberals who agitated for the poor, who had an air of being with it, hikers in the days when knapsacks were avant-garde. They were people to whom others turned for advice. But inside the house, which they had bought for $20,000 in 1963, slammed doors and loud silences filled the spaces between exquisite meals and good California wine.

Mattie had thought she was getting such a great deal when she moved back in — free rent on a house with a bedroom for each of her children. But it didn't take long to notice the secrets and memories tiptoeing around, holding their highballs, debonair and amused at first, then hissing in the master bedroom as her mother had when her father returned from his monthly trips to Washington, D.C. Harry was now sleeping in the bedroom where Al had grown up, where at fifteen he had started doing drugs while Isa and Alfred pretended he was doing homework; Ella slept in Mattie's old room, the one with the slanted ceiling and eaves, behind which all manner of nightmares had waited quietly.

The laundry room where her father had died looked almost exactly the same as before, with its old washer-dryer from Sears, lots of sunlight and trees outside the window, and space to move around. Isa had spent hours here, pawing through her husband's clothes, looking for clues to his absences, searching her teenage son's pockets. What did she think she would find — needles, bindles, a treasure map? She'd searched her daughter's clothes here too, for cigarettes and birth control pills, which she'd found and seized like a customs inspector.

Why, in the current crisis of divorce and bottomless loss, had Mattie run back to the past, to her parents' home, her husband's side of the bed? She hadn't known where else to go. It was free and it was familiar.

"Where else can I go? Nicky owned that house before we got married. It's his. Otherwise, he doesn't have much money, I don't make much. He'll help us, but I can't afford to rent anything as nice as this. With a yard."

When Mattie moved in, Angela, who called herself a Newj, for New Age Jew, flew up to perform an exorcism, a deep-smoke smudge with Native American herbs that made the house smell for days as if the Grateful Dead had been practicing in the garage.

After the first autumn rains, Mattie discovered just how much damage her mother had been disguising over the years with paint and caulking and cabinets. Isa had evidently installed cabinets wherever rot or cracks or mold had appeared. So there were cabinets everywhere, which was great for storage. But if you removed even one section, you discovered that behind the shelves were moldy patches of

17

Sheetrock, exposed live wires in broken sockets, ugly swatches of bore beetle infestation. Mattie shuddered to think what was behind the cabinets in the damper areas — the garage and laundry room.

The rats' scratching grew louder. She asked her mother to pay for an exterminator. Mattie was barely getting by with child support and a little extra from Nicky and the money she made as a fit model for Sears: she was a perfect size 12. But she had forgotten to get an education.

"Oh, for Chrissakes," Isa had said when Mattie asked her for the money. "What is it with you? Why don't you count your blessings for a change?" Mattie did count her blessings, all the time. She always had. She'd always believed in a freelance God, but kept it to herself, as her parents and brother were devout atheists. A few years into her marriage, she'd found a church nearby, where she staggered like Monsieur Hulot into a relationship with Jesus. And she had come out of the closet as a believer. Her brother referred to it as her blind spot. Her mother refused to discuss it, as if Mattie believed in pyramid power. Mattie didn't care. She thanked God several times a day for what she had, and trusted Him for what she needed. She thanked Him for two healthy children, for her church, for a house with a yard. She thanked God for helping her finally get out of her marriage, and for helping her more or less survive the pain of Angela's leaving. She even thanked God for giving her such a difficult mother, because she believed that while it had been nearly life-threatening to survive Isa's mothering, the price she and Al had paid was exactly what it cost to become who they were. She thanked God, and her mother, for giving her Al. And she prayed to accept and believe that she had everything she needed. But she also had rats.

Ella lay in her crib one afternoon playing with her belly button, in the room where Mattie had grown up. Ella had just woken from the nap she took every day after a vigorous morning at day care. Mattie couldn't take her eyes off Ella — her blond hair, pudgy limbs, sweet and self-sufficient character. When Ella was born, she'd been colicky and had to suckle all the time; when she wasn't nursing, she'd needed to suck on Mattie's fingers. She'd graduated to a pacifier for a while, then found her thumb. The discovery of her belly button at a year and a half had marked the start of a new relationship, one of pleasure and comfort.

Whenever her shirt and pants gaped open, she'd put her finger inside. She twiddled the belly button, played it as if thumping the twangy connection between her and her mother, her belly a guitar.

Her belly button was an extra sense organ: if something had a nice texture, if it was slippery, say, or warm, she put it against her tummy; her voice would grow thick and furry, and she would say clearly, as if there could be any mistake, "My belly." Mattie had to make sure she had access through her clothes so she could find it. When she did, her whole body went soft and she let out a sigh.

Mattie reached down in the crib and lifted Ella out. "Let's go make something with blocks. Harry will be home soon, and we'll have grilled cheese sandwiches." Both of them missed Harry when he was at school — he had just started first grade — but life was much more peaceful in the hours when he was gone. Harry was busy, and loud, and lived in movement. He took life by the throat and shook it. He had his father's temper, his gift for instilling fear in others. He'd made an instant friend of the boy who lived next door, right after they'd arrived in the house. While she walked one afternoon with Ella and Harry, Mattie had noticed a towheaded boy, a year or so younger than Harry, in costume chain mail, a wooden sword dangling from his belt, in the yard next door. He'd been watering a hydrangea bush, as his blonde mother watched from the back step with a dish towel draped over her shoulder. Mattie stopped and waved to the mother, and the boy had whipped around, still holding the hose, so that Ella and Mattie had been sprayed. The mother had come running, with everyone laughing but Ella. Mattie wiped Ella's face with her T-shirt while Ella tried to decide whether to cry, and the boy's mother handed Mattie the dish towel. The two boys faced off, staring at each other as if seeing themselves in a mirror.

The mother's name was Margrethe. She was from Denmark, but had only a faint accent. The boy was named Stefan, and he only whispered. He could hardly contain himself; he had something marvelous hidden in his fist behind his back. His mother urged him to share it.

"No, no, is my little itty tro," he said with great pleased worry.

"Show Harry your itty tro," said the mother. Mattie was alarmed to see the agitation on Harry's face. He seemed to be in a battle to restrain himself from knocking the boy over, as if he was about to say, "I'm going to shoot it out of your hand, boy."

Stefan peered into the opening of his fist.

"Is my itty tro," he chirped. "My little itty tro."

"But what is it?" asked Harry. "What do you do with it?"

Stefan moved his fist through the air like a toy plane. "Zah! Zah!"

Mattie reached for Harry, who was breathing hard now. She felt heat spreading through his T-shirt, and his heart pounding beneath her hand.

"What is his little itty tro?" Mattie asked as nicely as possible.

"I don't know, this is the first I've heard of it," said the mother.

"Is my itty tro!" Stefan proclaimed, and flew his fist through the air. "Zah zah zah!"

Harry studied Stefan in a hard, bored way. Then he said, quietly, too quietly, "Give me the itty tro."

Stefan looked at him, worried as a kitten, and took one step back.

"Give me the itty tro!" Harry said. Stefan made a quiet strangled sound, like the sound a hurt deer might make. Harry raised his fist, and Stefan opened his own hand to reveal a feather.

Somehow they ended up best friends. They played together nearly every day.

Mattie now held Ella in her arms. The rats in the walls were squeaking. God, they had gotten so loud. The scratching had been bad enough, but the squeaks sounded like a mob was assembling back there, lighting torches. Beams and rafters were being nibbled into battering rams. Mattie scurried out, carrying Ella, and went to call her mother.

Isa answered right away, but as usual she was running out the door. "I'll call you later, darling," she said.

"No, Mom. We've waited long enough. The rats are getting worse and worse, and I really need you to pay for an exterminator."

"Oh, for Chrissakes, this can't wait till I get home? Two hours?"

Mattie sighed. Of course it could wait two hours, but with Isa, two hours could turn into two months or two years. "Call me later," Mattie said, and hung up. "Ees go?" Ella asked. Mattie nodded: Isa go, always go, going, going, gone. She was in her prime at seventy-one, an inspiration to everyone in town, beautiful like an aging model in a vitamin commercial, elegant, lively, opinionated. Mattie was in awe of her energy and drive. Her sharp corners had been sanded over the years, and she'd mellowed slightly along the way, was gentler now, sometimes even able to listen.

Mattie wondered, looking at Ella, how different she herself would have been if Isa had been this way thirty years before, instead of so anxious and critical. Mattie could see that Angela's best qualities — her spiritual thirst, her soulfulness, her equal capacity for playfulness and grief — were the direct result of having had a tense and neglectful mother like Isa. Angela had suggested that Isa's gift had been as a foil: looking at her charming unhappiness all those years, Mattie could see exactly who she didn't want to be when she grew up. Either you became like that, as Mattie and Angela hadn't, or you became the antidote for the mother's poison. What you needed you invented, and then gave away, so there would be some of it in your world. What would Ella decide to become — or not? Mattie saw herself and Angela as the trees that grew out of cliffs and boulders above the ocean near Monterey — evergreen creatures, windswept, magnificent,

23

twisty, gnarled pines growing out of the layers of rock, where maybe there had once been some nutrition, maybe there had once been soil from which the trees had sprung, but then the soil had blown away, and they still grew.

Mattie and Ella sat on the floor in front of the fireplace, eating crackers, building a castle, still waiting for Harry. Their aging Cavalier King Charles spaniel, Marjorie, lay beside them. She had soulful brown eyes and a creamy white coat dappled with reddish-brown. She was old and sick. "Marjorie," Mattie said, "will you pay for an exterminator?" Like the Little Red Hen trying to get someone to help her with the wheat.

Harry wept when he got home that afternoon and overheard Mattie tell Al on the phone that she was going to have the rats poisoned. "All they want is a chance to live and take care of their tiny families," Harry cried in protest. So she abandoned the idea for a time. She took the children to the hardware store and bought some Have-a-Heart traps.

She baited and set them, but it turned out that Have-a-Heart traps were called Have-a-Heart because they didn't actually trap rats. They did just the opposite, in fact; they seemed to provide the rats with a lovely late-night snack of cheese.

Now she was afraid again all the time.

She wasn't particularly afraid of mice, but rats were more like snakes — snakes in bad fur coats.

In bed alone at night with no husband or best friend within range to protect her, a snail between two shells, she listened to the mewling of the rats. Sometimes there was an awful soft slithering sound, as if a rat was slowly drawing its tail across the wall behind her bed, and when that happened she went and got Harry and brought him into her bed. Having him in bed with you was about as peaceful as sleeping with a monkey, but better than being alone with the rats.

By mid-November, darkness had truly arrived, like the darkness that had been inside her for many months now. Go to bed, put on some thick socks, the cold weather said, and she did. She knew she was not going to get the lift she'd gotten used to from October's sun, so she looked for domestic sun: candles, lamplight, fires in the fireplace.

The storms of winter began, tossed down by towering clouds and marked by sudden shifts of light. The stark changes helped: she felt less stuck because the sky wasn't *ever* stuck. It grew dark and threatening, and then the sun came out and lit up the leaves. The leaves shone back. Darkness descended again, but through the dark and dreary skies, sunbeams slanted, bright and operatic. She'd had days like this when she'd first met Nicky — dark, bright, dreary, operatic. He had been a lecturer of English at San Francisco State; she was the manager of a restaurant on Shattuck. She had bummed around the country for a while after college, with a boyfriend she expected to marry. He went to live in Spain and she had joined him for a couple of years, but he drank too much and they fought, and she had returned to California without him. She slept in her old room at Isa's until her mother's frantic schedule and wild mood swings started to drive her nuts. Mattie moved out, rented a cheap studio in San Francisco. She went to work as a manager in a waterfront dive, and finally decided to study literature at San Francisco State. She was exhausted by her workload at the restaurant and school, feeling half dead, until she met Nicky. He reached down and pulled her to her feet, made her laugh again, took her dancing, took her to bed, took her to Paris. How had her marriage gone from there, the glorious place where it began, to this ugly end?

Somehow the arithmetic had stopped working. For a long time, the marriage worked like a mostly reliable car. He had been unfaithful to her once, with a student, and she'd almost left him. But they patched things back together, and then she got pregnant with Harry. Harry changed everything, for a while. And then Nicky began to withdraw, and she thought he was having more affairs, although he'd never admit it, and she wanted to leave with Harry, but then she got pregnant again, with Ella. Things were sweeter again briefly, and then horrible when he had the affair with the twenty-two-year-old, then better again after Ella's birth. Then they grew apart again. She added up the columns every few months, and the positive column won, even if only by a tiny margin. Then one day she added things up, and she was short. And then she was short more often than not. Children, and the house, and the life they'd put together — hikes, walks on the beaches of West Marin, dinners with friends, mostly from the college, work for left-wing causes and candidates — were no longer enough of an excuse to stay together. Nothing worked consistently anymore, not the illusion or the self-made glue that had held them together, not even the armature of habit. For years, when she was scared enough, she made it a point not to hang out with the hollowness and dead spots in her heart. She made the dog of doubt go lie under the bed and stop sniffing around so much. And the physical pieces had fit, until the end. At bedtime they'd still snuggled and made love. They might lie down grim, but their limbs found themselves in old habits soon enough.

Angela and Al had advised Mattie to leave, but she stayed on. Finally the machine of the marriage broke down, and she said to herself, "If I stay, I'm going to the bottom." She was more afraid of this than of leaving, and so she left.

The rats were the first thing she heard one morning as she woke up, even before the songbirds and the artillery of the recycling truck. She bolted awake, then lay listening miserably. Rat tails were so naked, like bone.

Mattie called Evergreen Pest Control. They would charge two hundred dollars for the first visit, and the check from Nicky wasn't due for another two weeks, but she went ahead and made the appointment.

She'd thought about asking Nicky if he would split the cost with Isa — the rats were, after all, in the house where his children lived — but when she called, Nicky's new girlfriend answered and Mattie hung up. He insisted that he had started seeing Lee only after Mattie filed for divorce, but this young blonde Scottish woman, two years out of college, had sprung so instantly into being his serious girlfriend that Mattie knew he must have been seeing her even before the separation. All of a sudden one day in October he was routinely referring to a girlfriend, and the children came back from a weekend with him reporting that she had been there overnight Saturday, and in the kitchen making pancakes when they woke up the next morning.

Lee was tall and thin and had the thick blond hair of a Breck girl. Mattie's hair was growing thin, while her waist grew thick. She wanted to murder both of them in Nicky's bed. Lee was at least ten years younger than Mattie. For months after they split up, Mattie and Nicky fought about the children, schedules, money — everything except Lee. They never said her name. Eventually there was improvement the size of a ladybug in their relationship, and then improvement the size of a tadpole. Mattie felt ill only some of the time. Her automotive hypochondria decreased and she only intermittently heard axles about to drop, tires about to blow. After hours of prayers and reading Scripture and endless talks with Angela and Al and her pastor, Mattie could talk to Lee, if Lee happened to answer the phone at Nicky's, without feeling like hanging herself.

So she called Nicky's house that night after making the Evergreen appointment, and he answered. He said that he would be glad to pay. He'd bring her a check the next afternoon.

When he came over for lunch the next day, they had a beer or two and talked about the rats, and the children. Then they went to bed. She had not planned on this, although it had been her idea to take him to the bedroom so he could hear the rats himself. "Oh, baby," he said, with a look of compassionate misery on his suave, gypsy face. She looked out the window at the persimmons on the tree across the street, hanging like little orange Japanese lanterns. Their neighbor had given them a basketful. Mattie had baked persimmon puddings. She could almost smell them now. She looked back at Nicky.

A few days later he came by, looking for insurance papers she had accidentally packed up, and then, the day before the exterminator's appointment, he dropped the children off late on a Sunday night, read them to sleep after their baths, and one thing led to another.

Mattie remembered the apostle Paul, crying out that he did all the things he was desperate not to do, and so few of the things he knew he ought to do. She promised herself she would never do it again.

She might not have, either, if Evergreen Pest Control hadn't postponed the appointment until the end of the week. They were so sorry for the cancellation that they offered to take ten percent off the bill. Nicky called that night to see if the rats had been taken care of. She told him about the delay. He came over to console her.

The evening before the rescheduled exterminator's appointment, Mattie was sitting in the garden with Harry and Ella. The early-December dusk was juicy and brisk, with an ache of diminishing light, and it made her feel both pensive and relieved; the days were so short now. She was yearning for bedtime when she heard the phone ring inside. It was Isa, calling to say that she was bringing a friend's two grandchildren by for the night. Their house had burned down earlier that day, and the parents were in the hospital for observation. They were going to be fine, but Isa needed to stay with them at the hospital. This was so Isa: Isa the hero, Mattie the chambermaid to her mother's need to do big, visible good deeds. But Mattie smiled; it was a role she loved.

Just before eight, Mattie and the kids heard Isa pull up in her Volkswagen bug. They ran outside to greet her. Under the streetlight, Isa's bumper glowed with decals like Girl Scout badges, the alphabet soup of her days — decals for UNICEF, of which she was regional director for the Halloween collection; the NAACP, under whose auspices she tutored a teenage girl and registered voters; the ACLU, for which she did clerical work for death penalty appeals; AARP, which she had only recently joined; NOW, for which she did fundraising; and AAA, her auto club, which she didn't need, because men of all ages jockeyed to work on her car.

Two black boys sat solemnly on top of ACLU literature in the backseat, wrapped in one bright green blanket, so that they floated like a pair of sea otter babies swaddled in kelp while their parents went looking for food.

On the passenger seat sat a panting bug-eyed pug.

"Oh darling, I'm so sorry to do this to you,"

Isa said, unfolding herself from the cramped front seat like a long-legged bird. "But what else could I have done?" She indicated the children, then the dog. "And we couldn't leave the dog behind, the kitchen has no roof, the plastic is all melted."

"It's okay, Mom. Really. They'll be fine. You can go now."

But Isa came in with the boys, Alfie and Rue. She helped them get set up in the living room with Harry and Ella, and blocks, colored pencils, glasses of chocolate milk. Their awful pug, who had perhaps been tense even before the fire, ran around the living room and peed.

Isa let Mattie clean up the pee, and then the pellets, which popped out of the dog like bullets. Harry and Ella and Marjorie sat quietly on the oversize easy — Marjorie's chair, it was called — watching all the commotion, while Isa bustled about, running command central, calling friends of the family and hospital personnel.

After Isa left, Mattie played with the kids — drew, built with blocks, read — and at ten put them to bed on the living room floor. At one, she heard her mother's car pull up in front of the house. Wrapping herself in a quilt, she went outside. Isa rolled down her window. A handsome black man sat in the passenger seat. Isa introduced him as the children's father, and he got out of the car to fetch his sons. Mattie offered to accompany him, but when he declined her help she simply told him where they were sleeping.

In the streetlight, Isa looked like a skeleton in a cheap wig, a figurine from the Mexican Day of the Dead. Mattie reached out to stroke her bony arm.

"I don't know where we'd have been without your mother," the man told Mattie when he returned, a sleeping child over one shoulder and the other boy walking beside him. People had been telling Mattie this since she was four or five. She shook her head and smiled at the ground. Somehow the man shoehorned the children into the backseat of the car without waking the younger boy. The man got in, and the dog sat on his lap. Mattie went to the driver's side to kiss her mother good-bye, and they exchanged tired smiles. "You were a hero," said Isa, and they gazed at each other, until she put the car in first and inched forward. The moon glowed like a porthole seen from the inside of a ship, looking out into an ocean of light.

Mattie could not fall asleep that night. She was too keyed up, and the rats had never been louder. She spent half the night trying, through force of will, to keep them from getting out and finding her children. She imagined them nosing Ella with their sharp furry snouts. Mattie could imagine one digging into her stomach, clutching at her aorta, trying to tear it loose. A rat was the only animal that would actually crawl over your head, as if you were a corpse, or a crop it was checking, and it might come back in a week to see how you were doing. Rats owned the night.

Mattie dragged herself out of bed at seven and got the children ready for day care and school. She made them breakfast, packed their lunches, got them dressed. Then she and Ella walked Harry to the bus stop at the corner, waited to see him get on the bus, and continued on to Ella's day-care center. Mattie lumbered home feeling like a crabby, bloated robot, and called the men at Evergreen to see what time they were coming. When she found out not until the afternoon, she almost went back to bed. But there were boxes to unpack in the garage, and she had promised herself she would try to unpack one or two every day. She hadn't returned calls from the week before, and she went around feeling as if she was several weeks behind on her housework all the time. There always seemed to be another batch of dishes in the sink, bottomless baskets of laundry.

She went out to the garage and opened a box at random. It contained her framed photographs. This gave Mattie a brief lift. She could set them out on the mantel. She unwrapped each photograph like a present. Isa looked up at her from forty years before, all soft waves and painted eyebrows. One side of her lips was turned up as though in a moment she might smile, and the other was turned down in prim disgust, like a person of nobility trying to suppress the horror of finding herself standing next to you. Mattie covered the disgusted side of Isa's face with her hand, smiled at nice Isa with her crinkly brown eyes. The next picture she unwrapped was of Isa at age nine, not long after her father had died. She wore a dress, and ribbons in her hair, but looked as desperate and hungry as the wild child found in the forests of France. While looking at this picture with Mattie, her father had said that when you're eating in the wild, you eat when the food is there. If you wait, someone might grab the potato out of your paws. "That's the reason your mother is the way she is," he'd said. "Starving. That's how she gets so much done."

When she found a photo of her brother at four, Mattie reached out to touch the scar on his forehead, which he'd gotten by falling onto the coffee table, soon after Mattie was born. He'd fallen a lot as a child; he'd had poor coordination and terrible vision. He was an angry kid, and no one knew exactly why. He wept whenever Alfred went away on business. He wept when his parents brought Mattie home from the hospital, and told them to give her to the neighbors down the street — Isa loved to tell this story. He sometimes punched Mattie in the arm, and wrecked her things. He was unfriendly to Isa and Alfred's frequent dinner guests, which made Isa madder than anything. He was often sent to his room without dinner, and Mattie sneaked him oranges and saltines and boxes of Jell-O.

His parents sent him to a psychiatrist when he was twelve, after the counselors at school said they could not welcome him back the next year if his aggression was unchecked. He was often sick in the mornings during those early adolescent years. When he was ten, he'd hurt a neighbor's cat (although not badly, as Isa was quick to point out, as if the cat had over-reacted). He'd caused a child to have a biking accident, started a fire in a neighbor's garage, blown up Mattie's dollhouse in the backyard. Isa had insisted on the therapy, after the family had moved from an apartment into the house.

After he turned thirteen, Al's troubles grew more serious. He started smoking, and stealing hubcaps. Then he took to dressing like Illya Kuryakin on *The Man from U.N.C.L.E.* and stealing spotlights off people's roofs. He stole a slingshot from a friend's father, and staked out neighbors' houses for days, planning his assaults; he hurled good-size rocks through their windows. Late one night, after a few beers at a dance, he shot at a neighbor's upstairs window. The man was cut by a big shard of glass and needed treatment, but first he called the cops, and they caught Al and threatened to send him to juvenile hall.

His psychiatric appointments increased to two a week. There went Mattie's ballet lessons and family vacations. And Alfred started picking fights with Isa: Wasn't one session a week enough, at eighty dollars an hour — for Christ's sake? Did she think that money grew on *trees?* Alfred was a lawyer at a small firm in San Rafael and worked as a legal advisor to congressional committees on civil liberties and welfare, and Isa worked part-time, running an office at a furniture warehouse, but they barely got by.

Isa soldiered on, though, signing on as an office temp to pay for the second appointment. So she grew even more impossible.

Next Al was drawn to the fast cars of older boys. He continued to see his therapist, and to smoke and drink and take LSD with his longhaired friends from high school. Mattie tried to save her family, by being good and helpful, trying to need almost nothing, willing to give all she had. She danced with her father, rubbed his feet, helped her mother with the cooking and cleaning. She remembered the first time Isa took Al to the therapist, leaving her alone in the house on a Saturday morning when Alfred was away in Washington. Mattie had been only eight. She'd walked around the house, feeling its hugeness, and its boundary — like standing inside a tree's hollowed stump. She'd felt that if she made a sound, it would echo, and so she sat motionless in the rocking chair holding her cat for dear life.

Mattie loved her big brother, even though — or because — he didn't seem to love her very much, or at any rate, very often. She understood why he never seemed to want to come home, hanging out down at the boardwalk, smoking, into the early evenings: home was hard. Alfred and Isa were unhappy, silently most of the time, but sometimes exploding. Mattie felt it was somehow her fault: she imagined they had all been happy before she was born. Alfred was often looped, Isa was always cleaning, or updating precinct lists, or baking bread, or putting stamps on mailers, or folding UNICEF boxes for trick-or-treaters, and Al found it hard to be there. Mattie felt she had to stick around, because it always cheered up her father to see her.

Occasionally, Al and Mattie shared joints in his bedroom and listened to the Grateful Dead on his stereo, and these were memories she savored. He went to the therapist for years, and eventually stopped ruining and stealing Mattie's things, her 45's, her babysitting money, all the things Isa let him get away with, maybe because she would have liked to do them herself, and then Al even started liking school, a little hippie school in San Francisco. He learned to drive his father's Volkswagen bus, and he'd always give Mattie a ride, anywhere, anytime, just to get to drive. When he was not withdrawn or grounded or mad at the world, he and Mattie could make each other laugh. Then he'd gotten a scholarship to Cal, and as soon as he moved out of the family home, he finally began to love Mattie, confiding in her, listening to her tell him her problems with boys. He stayed at Cal until he had a graduate degree in political science. Al gave a lot of credit to Isa. He remained ferociously loyal to her, even though, as he'd put it once, "First she keeps me from totally losing my mind, then she seems to *try* and drive me crazy."

"Al!" Mattie said out loud now, and went to the phone to call him. He was teaching, though. The secretary said she'd give him the message.

Al looked both like their father and like Harry, except that he had gained weight in his face and stomach. Both he and Mattie had two huge front teeth, not especially white, which had required two years of braces for each of them. Neither of them had been able to close their mouths until after the braces, but they ended up with the shy, pleasant smiles of the formerly bucktoothed. Al taught addicted public high school students in a program called Smith and Wilson High, after AA's founders. He'd been sober himself for a long time now. In his late twenties, no longer using drugs but drunk most nights, he realized he was deteriorating faster than he could lower his standards, and he quit. Now he lived in a glade at the edge of a twenty-acre estate owned by a local actor who'd hit it big. It was in the country, across a dirt road from the estate, inside a giant ring of fallen logs. Al had converted a chicken coop on the property into a real cabin, snug and warm, with illegal plumbing, and plants everywhere.

Sometimes his girlfriend, Katherine, lived with him, a lanky woman of forty who looked like an overgrown girl. She was out of town a lot, a social worker who traveled to poor communities around the country and helped set up medical clinics. She had a cabin of her own in Fairfax. Mattie was very fond of her. Katherine was so shy that it was hard to imagine her telling doctors and nurses and community leaders what to do. When she sat down, she curled around herself, wrapping one leg around the other as if she were made out of pipe cleaners. She had short glossy black hair, and was allergic to cats — she took medicine before visiting Mattie's house or Isa's. She and Al split up every six months or so — she wanted to have children, and he was not ready, and her time was running out. But they worked things out, and had stayed together for six years now.

Isa was not particularly taken with Katherine. "I find her rather — blah," Isa told Mattie. "Al with that marvelous sense of humor, and Katherine a bit of a bump on a log, don't you think? Not someone to show off to your friends."

★ ★ ★

Mattie drove to pick Ella up at the day-care center at one. She felt too tired to walk the four blocks. They lay down for a nap together when they got home, but the phone beside Mattie's bed rang almost immediately. "Oh, what's the matter? You sound so sleepy," Angela said on the other end.

"I was up all night. I hate my life. The only good part is the kids. Do you have any sarin gas?"

"I'll go look as soon as we get off the phone."

"Why did I leave Nicky, again? I'm so lonely, and so broke."

"Because he was a total shit," Angela said. "He used to look at you with contempt. Most of his friends were old girlfriends, and he wore them around his waist like a belt of shrunken heads, and shook them at you from time to time."

"Oh, now I remember."

"He's just a mean guy."

"But now I have rats."

"It's a good trade. Poor Mattie. Let me tell you the big difference between Nicky and God, okay?"

"Okay."

"God doesn't ever think He's Nicky."

Nicky was like the shipwrecked Professor on *Gilligan's Island*, constantly coming up with ingenious inventions made of foliage, generators made from coconut husks, ice chests made

41

from seashells, yet apparently never getting around to repairing the *SS Minnow*.

Mattie wished the man from Evergreen would show up. She was hungry. Maybe she should make Ella and herself a nice grilled cheese sandwich. But there was no bread. She'd been trying to remember bread for days. One of the last arguments she and Nicky had had before she left was over bread. He had called from the college to see if they needed anything, and she'd said bread, for toast and Harry's lunches, and he had come home with a bag of fancy sourdough rolls, and she'd cried out, "Bread. I said 'bread.' Bread-bread." And he'd looked at her pityingly because she was so clearly crazy — disgusting and petty. The children loved the rolls. Still, Nicky continued to look at Mattie with such dead meanness, such smugness in his eyes as they tore into the buns, that she knew in that instant she could leave. The next day she'd told him the marriage was over. She'd found him in the bedroom, in his special chair by the huge window, the one place inside where he was allowed to smoke, if the window was open. He was smoking, as usual, with the cigarette down in the webbing of his fingers instead of up at the top, as if he were at the Village Vanguard listening to Thelonious Monk and smoking a Gauloise Blonde instead of a Merit Ultra Light menthol. "It's over," she said quietly. He smirked, and took a long drag on his cigarette.

Free at last, free at last. And going down the tubes.

Ella turned to the sound of the doorbell. Marjorie barked from the other room. The Evergreen man was here.

two

When Mattie opened the front door, Ella in her arms, she found a woeful longhaired man in a brown jumpsuit on the front step. The Evergreen Pest Control patch above his pocket was not filled in with a name. He appeared to be in his mid-to-late thirties, with a fuzzy brown ponytail, long straight nose, black goatee, and closely set brown eyes that made him look like an incompetent bird of prey.

"So you have rats," he said. When she nodded, he shuddered.

She thought he was joking, but the worried expression stayed on his face.

"I'm Mattie," she said, "and this is Ella." Ella burrowed into her neck.

"I'm Daniel," he replied, staring at his feet. So Mattie stared at hers. Ella peered down at all four feet, as if looking over a cliff.

"Do you want to come in?"

"No, thank you. I'm going to start in the garage and the yard. I'll set some traps, with bait in them for the rats to eat. That drives them out with a terrible thirst, in search of water."

She imagined rats all over her yard, pulling themselves along on their bellies like thirsty men in cartoon deserts. "Is it safe for my animals?"

"Yep." He sighed and stood straight.

"How long is this going to take?"

"An hour, maybe less. I'll come back when I'm done."

"Okay," Mattie said, and closed the door. She sat on the living room floor with Ella and began playing with wooden blocks. They were building a castle with many windows.

After ten minutes the doorbell rang and the door opened. Daniel poked his head in. Mattie looked up from the floor.

"Do you need something?" she asked.

"Look, I'm going to be honest," he said. "I don't have the stomach for this job."

"Pardon me?"

"This was my first day." He pointed to the blank Evergreen patch. "My wife and I need the money. I'm a carpenter, but there's not much work right now. I thought I'd have what it took to be an Evergreen rat man."

She stared at him perplexed.

"If I can use the phone, I'll explain that I just quit, and that they need to send someone else over as soon as possible."

She looked at him. "That's fine."

"Could I have a drink of water?" he asked.

"All right," she said. By the time she returned to the living room with a glass of water, he was already sitting on the floor working on the castle with Ella and talking on the cordless phone. "Great," he was saying. Mattie sat down nearby, feeling suddenly shy. Ella was at her most engaging. Mattie listened to her making grunty sounds while adding to the castle, and to Daniel talking on the phone. She stared through the window at the persimmon tree across the street, still heavily laden with its fruit, a Renaissance color, like gilded borders, giving off warm light.

"They'll send someone tomorrow," he announced. "I don't suppose you have any other work for me, do you?"

"What do you mean?"

"Things where I don't have to kill anything — like carpentry, or electrical repairs."

"Like odd jobs?" she asked. Daniel nodded. Ella handed him a yellow cone. He studied the castle and slid the cone carefully into an open window, as if it were a candle flame.

Mattie looked out the window. "Isn't the world orange right now?" she asked. She sounded, even to herself, like a fruitcake.

But looking up from his work, Daniel said, "Orange keeps us warm." This time Mattie nodded. "I'm cold," he said, like a child.

"Would you like a cup of tea instead of water?"

He had large hands and long fingers. He filled the windows of the castle with colored cones and blocks and figurines that lay all over the rug — warriors, dinosaurs, sea creatures. Then, suddenly, he leapt to his feet.

"What is it?" she asked.

"I'm late for my next appointment. I have to go."

Mattie frowned. "But you just quit your job."

He thought about this. "Good point." He inhaled loudly. Ella handed him a green wooden triangle. He used it to stab himself in the head. "I have to make some money today. I promised my wife. Thank you for the tea and for letting me play," he said to Ella. Mattie felt afraid — she imagined Daniel as having killed the real Evergreen rat man, stolen his uniform, stuffed him into the trunk of his car so he could worm his way into her house. But a bigger part of her was desperate for him to stay. Daniel's eyes were quiet and kind.

"Do you want to chop firewood? I could pay fifteen dollars an hour," Mattie blurted out. She wanted him to stay. She'd come up with the money.

"Really? Sure."

She took him out to the backyard, showed him a pile of logs Isa had bought long before, her father's hatchet, and an old stump slashed with hatchet blows her father and Al had made over the years.

Inside, Mattie and Ella listened to the sound of splitting wood. Ella looked down at her belly button for the answer, as if it were a mailbox. They worked on the castle until Harry and Stefan burst through the door. "Do you boys want something to eat?" Mattie called. Without answering, they walked toward Harry's room with the oddest possible gait, as if they were squeezing the cheeks of their bottoms tightly together. And when Mattie followed them to Harry's room, she discovered they did have the cheeks of their bottoms squeezed tight, to hold Band-Aids in place, as Harry explained. They had each put an unwrapped Band-Aid in the crack of their bottoms in case they got hurt while playing. The two boys twisted yogically to extract the Band-Aids from their under-pants.

"It's okay," Mattie said. "It's good to be pre-pared. But go do that in the bathroom. Throw those in the trash. Why didn't you carry them in your pockets?" she asked.

"Because we're spies."

Stefan was courtly with Ella, and stopped to admire her castle on his way to the bathroom, but Harry sidestepped her reach as you would the family octopus. "Who's the guy in the back chopping up our wood?" he called to Mattie.

"He used to be the Evergreen man. Now he's — well, I don't know what he is now. He needed work, we needed wood for the fire."

The days got shorter and darker, and there was the beginning of a ruddy sunset when Isa came over for late tea a week later. She wore pleated black linen pants, a gray wool sweater, and a periwinkle scarf, and moved like a woman balancing a tray on her head. She brought a perfect gift, beautifully wrapped, for

48

everyone. For Mattie, a green serving plate with "Plate" written with a finger in the clay by the handicapped person who'd made it at the foundation on whose board Isa served. For Harry a set of fancy felt-tip pens, for Ella a stuffed bear with hair you could braid. "What's the occasion?" Mattie asked. Isa sat on the floor and helped Ella braid the bear's hair. Harry lay beside them petting Marjorie, the package of pens shoved into the pocket of his jeans. Although he was always drawing meticulous tiny figures, frightful animals, detailed buildings, he would not open it for days. He preferred the perfect look of brand-new things to the things themselves, loved the brief suspended moments before the inevitable depreciation of dulled tips and chewed caps.

"Your mother has a nice new man in her life," Isa told Mattie. "But that's all I'm going to say." Isa zipped her lips as though Mattie were a three-year-old. Poor guy, thought Mattie. Watching her play with Ella, she tried to imagine her mother sitting with her and Al on the floor, and knew it had never happened. Her mother had always been so busy. She had always arrived home from work just minutes before Mattie and Al got home from school. She'd greet them warmly, still dressed for the office, and then turn on the TV. Sometimes she turned on the radio too, as if trying to create a little party with lots of voices. Her role was spokesperson for both parents: Clear the dishes, clean your rooms, study harder — in Al's case, study at all. Commitment and routines: homework, showers, dental appointments.

Mattie's father took the joyful parts. He drank and danced, stood at his bookcases looking up a poem that he loved, or stared off into space after putting the needle down on a new album on the hi-fi. There was always music on when he was home, and he was always trying to get Isa to dance. But she would never have anything to do with him after dinner, there was too much work, and so he settled for Mattie, dancing around on the wall-to-wall carpet, first with her on his shoes like three-dimensional Arthur Murray footprints, then on her own feet, dipping, twirling, looking up to meet his eyes. He'd collapse on the couch with his drink and try to get Mattie to take off his garters and rub his feet, while Al hid in his room and Isa sterilized their living quarters. Isa would have put the house in an autoclave if she could have.

Watching Isa with Ella — they were both named Isabella — Mattie felt a pang of admiration for her mother. She had kept the family together all those years, with a husband who was gone every month, and a troubled son; she was always committed to her causes, and had even been jailed once after a mass protest at a nuclear power site. In her early seventies she was still quite beautiful. Mattie hoped she would age as gracefully as her mother. Isa had perfectly smooth silver hair, pearly dentures, crinkly eyes. Something dormant had woken in her when Harry was born. She seemed curious about the world again, no longer completely rooted to her routines and efficiency. This was the blessing of being a grandmother. She was no longer so hurried and paranoid.

Mattie felt jealous: when she was little, Isa had seen threats everywhere, things to fear and protect oneself and one's children from — strangers, germs, dogs and dog shit, the Russians. But when Harry came along, and then Ella, Isa had relaxed, opened entirely to their love, holding their soft, warm bodies close, all that skin so fresh and new, not loaded with shame, not guarded against her or anyone else. Their heads were like fountains at which she might finally drink.

Isa looked up at Mattie, self-conscious now. "What?" she demanded.

"Oh, nothing," Mattie said, looking away so that Isa could go back to her granddaughter's sweet smells — her breath, her baby hair. Then it went on too long: Mattie pursed her lips and wanted to break it up, like a cop nudging someone slumped over at a bar. These were her babies, and she loved them more than anything — the delicious smells of their heads, so visceral, vibrational, intoxicating: all of it, all those baptisms, tears and soppy diapers, leaky breast milk, spilled formula, baths in the sink. Isa had had her chance.

Harry ran off with Ella's bear, and Ella howled. Mattie yelled at him to come back, and he did. He picked up Ella and lugged her around the room as if she were the legless pencil man outside Macy's. She sniffed back tears. "Chicken alert!" he shouted, and she started cracking up. "Chicken alert!" he shouted again, and she squawked.

One morning when the sky was moody and dark, Mattie found herself thinking of Daniel while she was folding laundry. It had been a couple of weeks since he'd come to kill her rats. The tiny mole on his bottom lid had made him seem smart and watchful as a whale. She entertained the fantasy of calling him up and asking him over, to play with the blocks, or chop more wood, or maybe watch one of Nicky's nice movies with her. *Andrea's Big Day* was a good one. Very tasteful. *Rear Entry* was equally tender.

At last, she was sleeping again. The rats were gone. Another man from Evergreen had come the day after Daniel's visit, enthusiastically placed the poison in plastic tubs, and wiped out her rats. She tried to imagine what kind of wife Daniel would have, someone quiet, she believed, a little plain perhaps. He certainly wasn't much to look at, but something about him had stirred things up inside her.

She called the Evergreen number and told the receptionist that Daniel had left something at her house; was there a way they could let him know? The receptionist sounded skeptical. "He left something there a couple weeks ago? Like what?" she asked. Like his panty hose, Mattie wanted to say.

The next morning she found him on her doorstep, a loaf of homemade bread in his hands. He was squinting at her.

"Did I really leave something here?" he asked. Mattie shook her head. She could hardly breathe. She hated being caught in a lie.

"I had some more odd jobs I hoped you could do, and I didn't want Evergreen to know I was giving you work."

"Oh," Daniel said. "Well, great. Here. My wife and I baked bread this morning. I grabbed you a loaf on my way out."

He fixed the drip under the kitchen sink, replaced a porch light fixture, went to the hardware store and got a new splatter guard for the garbage disposal, replaced the doorknob in Harry's room, cut up more firewood, stacked it, washed down the walkway to the house with diluted bleach to remove the slime, repaired a hole in the fence where Marjorie had gotten out. He worked for four hours straight, and when he was done, she gave him eighty dollars.

"This is too much," he said.

"No, no," she insisted. "It's fine. I just got paid."

Mattie made them tea, and toast from the bread he had brought. She wanted to ask if he had a church. Asking the question was a habit of hers that used to make Nicky furious; he said it made him feel he was married to a Jehovah's Witness. As hard as she tried not to say anything, she blurted it out.

"No, I don't. My wife's not a believer, but I am. More or less. Do you go to church?" he asked.

"Oh, yeah."

"Is the music nice?"

"You've got to come sometime," she replied. It gave her a lift just to think of it. She loved how ragged the music sounded some days. The church was racially integrated, with more women than men, fifty to sixty in all most Sundays, plus twenty children from infants to teens. It was the only place where she could sing. She loved the big proud bodies of the women in the choir, and how they could swing, and how planted on the earth they seemed, with no apology for taking up so much space. It was as if they assumed they were beautiful, and only needed to decide what color to dress the beauty in. "Corner of Drake and First. Services at eleven every Sunday."

And the very next Sunday, Daniel was there, sitting by himself near the door.

Mattie didn't even see him at first. She was

54

greeting her friends, helping the older people find seats, checking what songs they'd be singing, when she noticed him flipping through a hymnal. She caught his eye while the choir filed in, and blinked out hello in Morse code. He bowed in greeting, and now it was her turn to look down.

The choir sang her favorite songs, "Just As I Am" and "Softly and Tenderly." Mattie heard the desperation and generosity beneath the notes. She listened with her eyes closed to the sermon, which was about letting God into your worst drawers and closets, and how healing could not happen if you let God into a living room that had been cleaned for the occasion. If you wanted the healing, you had to show God the mess.

"I loved it," Daniel told her afterward. "Can I come again?"

"Hey, cutie," a man said over static when she picked up the phone the next day. For a brief moment she thought it was Daniel, and her heart jumped. She flushed when she realized it was her brother.

"How are you?" she asked.

"Well, I'm fine, honey chile," Al said, "but you're not going to believe what I saw this morning. I found Daddy's old car, our old VW."

"No you didn't. That car doesn't exist any-more."

"Yes I did, miss. It passed me in front of the library. A-I-M eight-five-two."

"Holy cow." Hearing the license plate number triggered the adrenaline in her — A-I-M, Alfred or Al, Isa, Mattie, 852.

"Did it . . . recognize you?"

"Yes, I think it did. I think it gave me a furtive little wave."

Mattie quieted her mind. "Didn't Dad sell it to Neil?" Neil Grann had been her father's best friend when Mattie and Al were growing up. He lived out near the coast with his only child, Abby, who was about Mattie's age, and his girlfriend, Yvonne Lang. They hosted afternoon gatherings every few weeks, with wine and the newest jazz recordings, and people always brought their kids, who played in the woodsy backyard while the grown-ups drank and talked.

"He sold it to Abby for a thousand dollars, the year he bought the Mazda. After Neil died. A-I-M eight-five-two. Abby smashed it up almost immediately, and that's the last I'd heard."

Mattie saw the car herself a few days later, in the parking lot at Albertsons. She waited for the driver to come out, not knowing what she would say if he did. No one came during the fifteen minutes she waited. But not long afterward, while she was crossing the street from the post office, she saw the Volkswagen begin to pull away in front of her, and she'd pounded on

56

the side. The driver stopped.

She stepped to the window, smiling at the shaggy old man behind the wheel. He rolled down the window.

"This is my old family car," she said. "I learned to drive in it."

"I'll be damned." The man patted the steering wheel. "This is the best car I ever owned. I bought it from Sam Ray back in the seventies, after Neil Grann's daughter nearly totaled it."

"Abby."

"Right, Abby," the man said. "Wait, let me pull over." He eased the Volkswagen to the curb, and Mattie walked slowly over. She remembered Abby so well, running like a colt behind Neil's ramshackle house. She had long reddish-blond hair and smooth fair skin, delicate features, long legs, knobby knees, a quick mind. Neil, Yvonne, Alfred, and other friends sat on the porch drinking when it was warm, or around the fire in winter, listening to jazz on the hi-fi, dancing when they were inside, reading poems aloud, planning revolution and saying sexy things, laughing so loud at their own stories you could hear from the fort the children would be building behind the house, until one of the women, usually Yvonne, would call everyone in for dinner.

"Wait, which one was your dad?" the man asked.

"Alfred Ryder. Did you know him? Dark

shaggy hair, kind of handsome? With big, slightly buck teeth?"

"I never actually met him. But when the guy undented the glove box, I found a few odds and ends, some IDs of your father's, a library card, an old registration. There was a bracelet, a funny little blue rubber shoe, a paint-can key, like, you know, you'd pry open the lid off a can of paint with? My wife made me save it all in a Ziploc bag. I'm sure we still have it somewhere. Here's my number, if you ever want the stuff."

Mattie handed Al the paint-can key. It was flecked with dried paint, winter-sky blue. The daisy bracelet was one she had made twenty-five years before, lavender and light blue, with a rose border, her favorite colors, and she put it on now, while Al turned the splattered key over in his hand. Their father's signature on the library card and car registration made Al double over with only slightly exaggerated grief — those small, precise letters, straight up and down like fence slats. There was a bottle opener from the bait shop in Marshall, the kind Alfred called a church key. And the odd blue shoe, an inch and a half long, soft rubber, a turquoise high-top sneaker with finely detailed laces, complete with a toe guard. The blue shoe fit perfectly in the space where her fingers met the palm of her hand. She curled her fingers around it and held on. Mattie and Al looked at each other.

★ ★ ★

She asked if she could keep the shoe, and he said, "Of course you can." Maybe she was just missing her dad, maybe she was losing her mind, but for whatever reason she found herself unable to put it down. She held it while pushing the shopping cart with Ella in the front; she shoved it in her pocket when she thought someone might see her, but then took it out and made sure not to wash it with the laundry. She kept it overnight on the mantel above the fireplace and in the mornings stuffed it back in her pocket when she walked Harry to the bus stop and Ella to day care. She took it out when she got home. She had it all the way through December, her least favorite month. She took it when she went Christmas shopping, placed it on the mantel on Christmas Eve while she filled the children's stockings with chocolates and trinkets and tangerines, had it in the pocket of her jeans when she handed the kids over to Nicky at lunchtime — he and Lee got the children for Christmas dinner. Al and Katherine, Isa and Lewis came to Mattie's that night, bearing side dishes to eat with the turkey she had cooked, the blue shoe beside the cutting board like a tiny enchanted creature from the Brothers Grimm. She held the shoe inside the crook of her fingers while she pushed the vacuum cleaner around, held it when she talked on the phone, unfurling her fingers to take in the intricate details, the laces, the toe guard.

She hid it in her fist when Nicky stopped by for the children, and it made her feel powerful again, as if there were parts of her he didn't know about. Nicky looked at her curiously these days, and she smiled, as mysteriously as she could, back at him, at his beautiful eyes, his thick, curly hair. She no longer ached to see him, no longer hoped he would stay over. She bustled Harry and Ella off with exuberant kisses when he came to pick them up, calling out that she loved them, would see them the next day, and then she'd go inside, to putter or put away things that were still unpacked, or stretch on the couch with whatever she was reading. No matter what she was doing, she almost always held the little shoe in her hand. It felt good to have something to hold on to.

She'd read somewhere that after World War II ended in Europe, lost children wandered around until they were gathered in camps run by the Allies. There they were fed and cared for while relatives were located or new families found who could take them in. In one camp it was discovered that none of the children was sleeping well. Their nerves were shot, the memories fresh and haunting. Then a social worker determined that if the children were each given a piece of bread to hold at night, they could fall asleep. This was not bread to eat — there was plenty of that when the children were hungry. No, this piece of bread was just to hold on to, to reassure the children through the night that

60

they were safe now, that there would be bread to eat in the morning.

She saw Daniel at church the following Sunday and asked if he could come work again. When he came by two days later, she showed him the little shoe.

"Very interesting," he said. He had brought her more bread, black with seeds, still warm.

"When do I get to meet Pauline?" Mattie asked. She felt she should meet his wife.

"She's picking me up today at five. My car's in the shop."

Pauline was beautiful. Mattie was amazed. Daniel had never mentioned this. She was small and slight on top, with a large, round bottom, and her features were too big for her frame — her long nose, lips, hazel eyes, chin, her cheekbones. Ropes and tendrils of curly blond hair were piled high on her head. She wore rings on every finger, a silver anklet, a velvet skirt, and an antique lace blouse. She spoke in warm, vigorous tones. She moved like a dancer, and in fact had trained for ballet until college, when it became clear she would never be great. She had a lovely laugh, and paid very close attention whenever anyone spoke, actually cocking her head to listen.

Mattie had a puzzling and immediate aversion to her.

Ella fell instantly in love, with the velvet and lace, the apricot nail polish, the tinkling of all

61

that silver. Within minutes, Pauline was dandling her on her knees, asking her questions about the cats, who milled around the floor at her feet as if Ella were their queen.

"Did you like her? What's she like?" Al asked Mattie on the phone that night.

"She looks like an aging teenage hooker."

"Would you give her my number?" he asked.

Mattie considered, smiling. "Where's Katherine?"

Al paused too. "She's in Vermont. She went to see her parents, and decided to stay for a few weeks. She's sort of mad at me."

"The bad news for you is that Pauline clearly adores Daniel. She's a bit dramatic for my blood. She told me she's in therapy twice a week. So maybe she's cuckoo. Like I should talk."

Mattie still felt shaky these days. She was okay in church, or doing certain things with the children — playing with blocks was helpful, and reading to them in bed was even better — but her head was often filled with terrible thoughts, sadistic and vengeful, usually directed at her mother, or Nicky, or his girlfriend, cute little Scottish Lee. Mattie had dented her own car twice, and then gouged the fender on a rental; she told Al and Isa that if they saw her coming, they should pull off the road and assume the crash position. Mattie didn't know who was still friends with her since the divorce — the couples Nicky had introduced her to from the college were mostly his friends now, friendly to her but belonging to him. She wasn't in the mood to make new ones. Encounters of more than a few minutes made her long to be home with the kids and the animals. Other people grated on her nerves. Life grated on her nerves. She was getting a little funny. She felt out of body, drifting and alone, with only the children and her mother and Al to tether her to the dock.

Lee, pretty enough to be an actress, liked to drop mentions of auditions and movie roles into her infrequent conversations with Mattie. "And what would some of your bigger credits include?" Mattie wanted to ask. Lee had a straight nose, dark eyes, good teeth, and the beautiful Scottish accent. It was all too much. "I want to kill myself," Mattie told Angela one night on the phone. "And then get on with my life."

"Honey," Angela replied, "you don't know yourself well enough right now to commit suicide. So it would be considered a homicide."

One Saturday, Lee showed up to get the kids. Mattie smiled warmly as she opened the door for her, but inwardly, a vile kaleidoscope of feelings spun slowly — pangs of shame, even though Lee had almost certainly slept with Nicky while Mattie was still married to him, and then calm, erotic power, and then hatred for Nicky, and then hatred for herself. Ella began to cry when she saw Lee. Mattie carried her into the kitchen, and Lee followed. Ella needed to be held in Mattie's arms at the table for a few minutes before she would agree to leave. Lee tried to interest her in all the marvelous things they would be doing that day — they'd go to the park until Nicky was done with his meeting, and then drive to Olema. But Ella wasn't having any of it. She rocked back and forth in her mother's arms, rubbing her cheek against Mattie's sweater, Mattie nuzzling the top of her head. Harry said hello to Lee in a high, earnest voice, but sat next to Mattie at the table, holding the package of pens Isa had given him. He arranged them gravely in the order in which they'd first arrived, the spectrum of the rainbow, while Lee looked to Mattie for help. Harry dug in, putting each pen's stamped logo into alignment inside the plastic sleeve.

Mattie hated the idea that her kids would wake up with Nicky and Lee, when the children would be at their sleepiest and sweetest, unarmored and snuggly. She prayed, but it was hopeless. When she wasn't in bed with him — and sometimes when she was — she wished Nicky would die, badly. Cancer, murder, even — right after he had left late one night — Lou Gehrig's disease. She buried her face in her hands at stoplights and prayed for healing, and then she'd imagine a torrid movie of Nicky and

Lee in bed, screaming first in erotic joy, then in terror when Mattie appeared in their doorway to toss a rattlesnake at them. Nicky thrived, grew handsomer, while Mattie looked wizened. She did not believe she would ever stop hating Nicky and Lee, until her pastor told her that when God was going to do something wonderful, it started with something hard, and when God was going to do something exquisite, He or She started with an impossibility.

Daniel called her every few days, or she called him. It was fun to have a new friend. He met her at church every Sunday, and it seemed natural that they would start driving there together. One afternoon they went for a walk out to the beach on the Tennessee Valley Trail. Mattie had made a point of inviting Pauline along.

"I'm not a hiker, Mattie," Pauline told her. "But Daniel loves to. You go without me."

And so Mattie and Daniel had gone for a walk alone.

"My bedroom smells like cat pee," she said as they walked toward the salt and roar of the ocean. "My mother had a cat disorder. I've tried everything. Odormute. Nature's Miracle. I even rented a steam cleaner."

"We may have to pull up the whole rug," he said. "And toss it."

"I would pay you fifteen bucks an hour."

"You can if you want, but you don't need to," he said.

The following weekend they carried the mattress together into the living room, the mattress as boneless as a drunk, so that they staggered under its weight. It buckled in half and they tripped, but they managed to lug it out through two doorways and onto the floor by the fireplace. In her mind she saw them flop down on the mattress and lie there breathless, staring at the ceiling, catching their breath, and then growing still, like in the movies. But in the visible world, they dusted off their hands and returned to the bedroom for the night tables, the dresser, the bookshelf. Pauline called a couple of hours into their work, and Daniel talked to her warmly for a few minutes. Mattie strained to listen.

When everything was out of the room, they took X-acto knives, chisels, and screwdrivers and pried up sections of rug. Mattie felt as embarrassed as if she herself had peed on the rug over the years, but when she alluded to this, Daniel shrugged and said, "Let's just do it. We'll get this monstrosity up and figure out what we have on our hands. Then we'll take it from there." They listened to CDs, and talked about their marriages, Pauline's depressions, Mattie's children. It took hours to pull up the carpet and padding, tufts embedded in all the staples on the floorboards. There were urine stains on the boards, and Daniel said, "We'll pry these up too."

When Pauline called again, Daniel held his

hand over the receiver and asked Mattie if they could take a ten-minute break. "Sure," she said enthusiastically, and he sprawled on the floor and asked his wife about her day.

Later, while they removed staples from the floor and cleaned away fibers and dust like smudges off a child's face, Daniel looked so happy and proud that Mattie was reminded of someone. It took a while for her to remember who it was he reminded her of. Finally she recalled a magazine photograph she had torn out and saved because she loved it so: the picture of a joyful East Indian, with rocks tied up in a net hanging from his penis. He shone with the power of the weight, and of bearing the weight, and he didn't need more power than that.

She worked as long as she could, but her eyelids grew heavy and she couldn't fight her exhaustion. "I didn't sleep last night," she said. "I have to go lie down."

She dropped off to sleep for an hour on Ella's bed.

Daniel was still at work when she got up. "Now what?" she asked.

"Now we clean up, and figure out how to buy some new flooring."

She got them cold glasses of apple juice, and they sat on the bare wood side by side. "So. Tell me how you met Pauline," she said.

Daniel smiled. "I met her at a party. It was at her house, on her twenty-fifth birthday. Some mutual friends brought me along. They wanted us to meet, although they warned me she was coming out of a bad depression. So I went with them to dinner at her house the following weekend. I liked the way she looked. I was so sick of these skinny girls who wouldn't eat with me — and boy, Pauline would eat with me. And then — this is what did me in — her cat came in, this big orange male, and she took him in her lap and began stroking him, kneading him, working him over, and he was slavering, and she just worked him, like she'd been sent over from the escort service. And I thought, Boy, I'd love to let her have a go at me."

"So now what?"

"Now we do the best we can. Some days go better than others."

"I mean, how do we get money for a floor?"

Daniel turned red. "Oh!" They looked away from each other. "We can do it cheaply — put in parquet. We'll have a garage sale next weekend," he said. "It'll give us all a chance to clean our closets."

And they did. They held it in front of Daniel and Pauline's house, and raised nearly three hundred dollars, which they split. Mattie bought some cheap parquet. She and Daniel put it down over several days when Harry was at school and Ella at day care. Mattie borrowed a hundred dollars from Isa to give to Daniel.

The new floor transformed Mattie, both the look of it and the marvelous absence of cat urine. Now there were sweet new smells, flowers from her garden in a vase, fresh air wafting through the windows. It looked and smelled like a miracle. Mattie decided to celebrate. It was time for a housewarming party: they had been here long enough.

Angela said, "I know a guy who can play the didgeridoo."

"You make that sound like a good thing," said Mattie. But she ended up hiring him anyway to play at the party, which would be in late January.

She invited Al and Katherine, her mother, and the new boyfriend, Lewis, a dapper old man from the South who lived in the same retirement community. He was half black, cocoa brown with a spray of moles across his cheeks and a film of near-blindness over his black eyes. She invited Daniel and Pauline, Angela and Julie, some friends from church, and some friends of Nicky's and hers from before the divorce.

Curiously, Mattie's spirits began to rise, even though many days in a row brought cold rain. Some mornings the sun hauled itself up reluctantly, rolling like a slow bowling ball across the sky. As Mattie started to come out of her funk, everyone else grew depressed; she called Angela one night and found her grumpy and withdrawn.

"I've been so down too," said Mattie. "But

for no reason, a few days ago I woke up feeling lighter inside. As if help was on the way. Someday soon, the light will return. That was the message of Advent, right? And Hanukkah. I was thinking we could have a little retroactive ritual at my party."

"Ix-nay, ix-nay," Angela said.

"Come on — a ceremony with candles?"

"No, no, no."

"Look — you're Reform, right?"

"Of course I'm Reform. I've got a crucifix on my front door."

"Well, what if we made it a party for the depressed?"

"Listen, Mattie, I left you alone when you were down. Can you call me tomorrow when the drugs wear off?"

Al was in a bad mood too, and said he wouldn't come to the party if there was a ceremony, unless it was a small-animal sacrifice. Pauline was depressed as well, but then, as Mattie had learned, Pauline was often depressed. One Sunday, Mattie had made her some soup and tried to talk her into going to church, but she had not been interested.

"I'm a dancer," she said, as if this explained anything.

Daniel and Mattie went to church without Pauline. They sat together whispering before the service began. Their shoulders touched. They shared a hymnal when they stood to sing. The sermon was on forgiveness, not one of

Mattie's strong suits. She asked Daniel if he could fix the porch light after church, and he said sure.

Mattie made them lunch when he was done, quesadillas and homemade salsa and lemonade.

"Daniel? Has there ever been anyone you couldn't forgive?"

He thought about this. "Yeah, there was this guy, it took me three or four years. It was a man Pauline had danced with, when she was a dancer, in her twenties. He was very handsome, and they'd been together before she and I hooked up. She was always on the phone with him, and I hated this guy. *Hated* him. But I prayed for him anyway. One morning I woke up, and the first thing I did was to feel around for my hostility toward him, like for my wallet, and in that instant, I saw that I had become his jailer. But being his jailer was making me his prisoner."

"Then what happened?" Mattie felt glum. He was telling her the story of her and Nicky.

"When I got out of the loop, their friendship fell apart. Pauline fell apart too. She had what I guess you'd call a minor breakdown."

"And now she's okay?"

"Yeah, she's fine."

I'm Nicky's jailer, Mattie said to herself. The mole on Daniel's bottom eyelid was no bigger than the head of a pin. It hung suspended near his iris like a star.

71

So she did exactly what Daniel had done. She went around praying for Nicky and Lee, and when one of them called, she made herself be sweet. She didn't sleep with Nicky for a while, claiming, whenever he hinted, to have a cold. She let the machine pick up when he called late at night, and she silently repeated, a dozen times a day, "I pray for you both to have everything that will make you happy." She did it even though she really felt no peace, just hatred and jealousy and self-loathing. Then one morning she woke up in the cold and the dark, and the ugly feelings were gone.

Now when Mattie thought of Nicky or Lee or heard their voices, the needle didn't always move to the right or the left. She had to pinch herself to make sure she wasn't dreaming. An infected splinter had worked itself loose, risen to the surface. Quirky blessings began to arrive. A family with a girl Ella's age moved in down the block, and then their cat had a single kitten, a calico, which Ella and Harry talked Mattie into taking; so now they had three cats. But the best development of all came one Saturday morning when Mattie was having toast with Daniel and Pauline in the breakfast nook and Lee arrived to get the children. The three of them had been celebrating when Lee arrived, because all three had been working lately. Mattie had had a few weeks' work at Sears; if she sucked in her stomach, she was still a perfect size 12. Pauline had been assisting at dance classes at a local theater. And Daniel was doing carpentry, and odd jobs, including the delivery of a sandwich he'd invented to the best delis in town — Daniel's Chopped Salad Sandwich. The sandwich was good, with lettuce, tomato, artichoke heart, avocado, water chestnuts, and a lemony aïoli, on thick slices of white bread that Pauline baked every day. Mattie sometimes helped make the sandwiches, and Pauline gave her a third of the profits when she did, often a hundred dollars a week for a few hours' work a day in their light-filled kitchen.

Lee knocked on the kitchen door that Saturday morning. "Come in," Mattie said, and called for the children. She smiled and introduced Lee to Pauline and Daniel, and then Pauline cocked her head to listen.

"You have such a pretty voice," she told Lee, "all trills and burrs. But I can't quite put my finger on your accent. Are you from Glasgow?"

Lee smiled sheepishly. "Well, actually," she admitted, "I'm from Oregon. But my parents are both Scottish, and I guess that influenced me when I was learning to speak."

Mattie's face broke into a smile, and she wanted to crow, but instead said, "Ahh!" warmly. It was too good to be true: Lee had been faking her cute little accent. Her little burrs, her little itty tro! Mattie couldn't stop beaming, beaming at Harry when he burst into the kitchen. He burrowed up against his mother loyally, and Mattie hummed and

73

imagined Lee in a kilt, blowing away on bag-
pipes.

A dozen people came to the housewarming
party, the last Saturday in January. Angela had
flown up alone the day before, and she and
Mattie stayed up all night cooking: jambalaya,
fried chicken, bell peppers fried with mustard
seed, chocolate mousse.

Al and Katherine were the first to arrive. He
was wearing a tie-dyed Rastafarian T-shirt, and
dribbling a basketball he'd brought for Harry.
Katherine wore her usual organic medley of
cotton and suede and silk, with the brown
shoes that Al called her frogstompers. She
brought Mattie a jar of pumpkin butter. She
tried to peer into the living room to see who
else might be there, like a girl at her first boy-
girl party.

Isa arrived next. "Are you getting a little fat,
Al?" she asked after exchanging kisses with him
and Katherine, as if this were the wittiest possible thing to say. She'd come with Lewis, who
doffed his brown fedora the moment he
stepped inside. A few old friends trickled in, all
wonderfully dressed.

Daniel wore a dark green silk shirt tucked
into black pleated pants, and the kind of sandals men wear in advertisements for Puerto
Rican rum. He had twisted his wiry hair into
short dreadlocks, and had never looked better.
Pauline's thick curls were piled high and loose

on top of her head. She had gained weight because of the new antidepressant she was on. Mattie wanted to ask, "Would you mind coming into the bathroom and hopping up on the scales for me?" Then she began to worry Pauline was pregnant. People had babies so late nowadays. Pauline was coming up on forty. It pleased Mattie to think that Pauline was older than she and Daniel were. Daniel fluttered around her, bringing her plates of food from the table set up outdoors beneath an umbrella. Mattie kept noticing Pauline's hands resting on the swell of her belly under a simple stylish black linen dress and found herself growing more anxious. She prayed to have a moment of clarity, and by God, she did. It was that she was mad as a hatter. That's okay, she said, patting her own shoulder. All your better people were.

"You look wonderful," Mattie told Pauline, and that was true — she looked stunning. Two other women were wearing simple black linen shifts similar to Pauline's, but they were poised and lean and busy, darting around as if trying to catch something they could put to use, while Pauline just sat there, regally. Finally she got slowly to her feet, and said, loudly enough that anyone nearby could hear, "Is there Tampax in your bathroom?"

Mattie nodded kindly, flooded with relief.

She hadn't seen some of her guests since before she and Nicky had split up. She'd forgotten how much she enjoyed them, but she felt shy too. She sat with Daniel, Pauline, and Lewis on the periphery of the group. They all grilled Lewis as if he were a teenage boy who wanted to date their daughter. He held up to scrutiny, telling the story of his coming to live in California. He'd moved from Alabama during World War II to work in the Sausalito boatyards, then stayed on in Marin City afterward. He had been a welder by trade, but was retired since 1980, when his vision began to fail.

"Marin City — that's where we go to church," Mattie said, meaning herself and Daniel.

"Really, which one?" When Mattie told him, Lewis clapped his hands to his cheeks. "Would you consider bringing me along?" he asked. "We lost our pastor at New Hope Baptist, and I don't like his replacement at all."

Mattie made plans to pick him up at The Sequoias on her way to Daniel's the next day. This made Isa look as if she might put her finger down her throat. Mattie ignored her.

"How much can you see?" Mattie asked Lewis.

"The outline of you, and the palette of you. Not much else."

"Why don't you leave him alone? Let the poor man eat in peace."

"Isa, darling," Lewis said. "This is how people get to know one another."

Mattie wanted to make a bullhorn of her hands and bellow, "*Run! For the love of God, run while you can*," but Isa was now wrapping her silky strings of touch and attention around Lewis, gripping his hand with reassurance, smoothing a crumb of food from beside his mouth.

Guests came over to pay their respects to Isa as if she was the Godfather. It was quite touching to hear them lay their lives out like smorgasbords. Oh, Isa, this is so tasty, and I think you'll like this, it will make you proud of me, and Here's an interesting morsel. And Isa would taste it, and say with her kind face, You've made such a good banquet. Oh, these are such delicious dishes.

Nicky honked when he pulled up in front of the house. Harry and Ella poured out of the backseat, dressed in their best clothes: Harry in cords and a white dress shirt, Ella in a black velvet party dress trimmed with lace. Harry picked her up like a sack of potatoes and carried her over to Mattie. After hugging and kissing Mattie, Angela, Isa, and Al, he hauled her off toward the sandbox.

Mattie listened to songbirds over people's voices, the tinkle of glasses and ice cubes, the clink of forks on plates, and then, all at once, to her son's sharp cries from the sandbox. Red-faced, Harry was weeping, clutching at one of his eyes like the Cyclops, while Ella looked on with horror and people streamed over to help. "What is it?" Mattie asked, bending in close. "Let me see."

Katherine came over and squatted beside Harry. "Take your hand away, sweetheart," she said. She opened his eye with her long pale fingers. "You've got a little sand in your eye," she said. "Will you come inside and let me flush it out?"

"I've torn my cornea," Harry sobbed. "As if you even care."

"Harry, you can watch your tone," said Mattie.

"Will you come inside with me?" Katherine asked again.

"No, I want my mom to do it."

Katherine shrugged at Mattie.

Mattie put her arm around Harry's shoulders and looked into his eyes. She wondered whether she had known the word *cornea* at six years old. When he didn't stop crying, she sighed quietly, took him by the hand, and said, "Come on, honey. Let's go flush out your eye."

He looked as if someone had splashed acid in his face. In the bathroom, she tried to wash out whatever it was with water, and when that didn't work, she plopped down on the toilet to think.

"The crying will wash it out," she said, pulling him into her lap. He tore at his eye, rubbed hard, whimpered, and she cooed and patted him with mounting hostility. The sand did not dislodge, but if it was indeed sand, the crying would wash his eyes for him. What would Jesus do? Roll his eyes and growl softly, as she was doing? She pictured Jesus and the men He lived with, whiny bachelors all — "Can I be first?" "What about me, Lord?" — and saw Him sigh and head back up the mountain. Where could she go?

Her child sobbed in her arms, and she held him. Boy, she thought, when Jesus said we must become as little children to enter the kingdom of heaven, He was definitely not referring to Harry. Maybe He had been misquoted. Maybe He did not say you must be like little children, but that you should eat little children — with a little butter and garlic. She exhaled softly, and Harry heard. He lurched out of her lap and tried to figure out whether she was mocking him. With his hand cupped over his eye as if to keep it from spilling out of its socket, he careened around the bathroom. "Stop!" she wanted to cry. "It's sand in your eye, not napalm!" She did not believe he was in any real distress, and her heart refused to budge, to give, to breathe. She did not like children. She should not have had any. This one was already ruined.

"I want to go to the hospital," he said, reedy, imperious, blaming.

"I'm having a party!" she implored. He was gasping for breath now, but she persuaded him to take off his clothes and step under the shower. She watched him through the glass door. "Open your eyes!" she called to him. Open your heart, she heard in silent reply; but she couldn't. So she did what she could: she opened her own eyes instead.

And under the torrent of water she saw a hunched and miserable boy, skinny, lonely, exiled — a refugee camp of one. "Honey?" she said. He stared up at the spray with his eyes open, looking demented. She tapped the glass. He looked over at her, and she was softened by his bleary agony. Suffering was suffering. She opened the door and reached gently inside for him, holding out a towel. "Honey, let's get you some help."

"Who could help us?"

"I don't know." Harry didn't say anything, and she toweled him off. When she finished with his hair, she draped the towel over him like a drop cloth over an old lamp. She lifted one corner and peered into his wild face. "What's going on?" she whispered.

"Daddy's going to have a baby," he wailed.

"What?" The news knocked the wind out of her.

"Daddy and Lee are going to have a baby!"

Heat rose in her. "They are?"

Harry nodded. "I heard her tell it on the phone." He gasped for breath, quavering. "Daddy didn't tell me." They sat together on the toilet while he wept. Finally he grew quiet and fell asleep. Amazing that he was so like her.

She held him sprawled across her lap.

She listened to him sleep, and to the sounds of the party. After a while she carried him to his bedroom, where she laid him on his bed. She dressed him in a T-shirt and Power Rangers underpants, and covered him with a blanket. She went to the kitchen, found the little blue shoe on the counter, put it in her pocket, and walked back outside.

Lewis turned his head toward her, but his eyes looked up, as if to the hills, from the shelter of his brows and deep folds of skin. His eyes were as black and round as knots in a tree. He was eating jambalaya with great pleasure, his loud digestion surprising them all from time to time. Mattie offered him the shoe and he turned it over in his hand. "It was my father's," she said when he gave it back.

"Of course it was not your father's," Isa insisted from beside him.

"It was, Mom," said Al. "It was in the old VW bus."

"Why on earth would your father have had such a preposterous gewgaw? I'm sure it was not Alfred's."

Mattie felt she would burst with resentment. "Why are you being so mean today?"

"It's simply idiotic, Mattie." Isa waved her away. Al growled. Katherine patted him on the knee.

"Why would you call me an idiot at my own party?" Mattie cried.

"Oh, for Chrissakes," Isa exclaimed, sounding genuinely distressed. "I only meant, what do you think you'll find by poking around Alfred's old things? It's gruesome."

Mattie went inside to compose herself. She sat at the kitchen table and closed her eyes. She was thinking of a line from a poem by Rumi, "Through love, all pain will turn to medicine," and in her mind she flicked the poem like holy water onto Isa's haughty face.

The didgeridoo player arrived just in time, as Isa was trying to persuade Lewis to throw away his brown fedora. When Ella saw the musician carrying the long instrument over his shoulder, she ran to greet him. Al went inside to wake Harry. The musician set up in the garden, near the food table, and soon began to play. Out came a low, windy moan, an eerie dirge. Isa drew back and looked at Lewis with horror. "Oh, for Chrissakes," she said, laughing. Mattie covered her eyes to block out her mother. She sensed someone sitting down on the bench beside her — Pauline. Mattie felt a stir of affection for her, and took her hand. Ella climbed into Mattie's lap. Al stepped into sight, with Harry gripping his new basketball in his arms. They sat down on the ground together, Al crossing his legs Indian style, enveloping Harry.

The voice of the didgeridoo was a call from far away, from centuries back. If you pressed your ear to the ground, Mattie thought, this was the tone the earth would make. The music resonated like an ancient god, or what desert winds must have sounded like to the first ears on earth. She closed her eyes again. She felt doomed, and lumpy, fat and old. She tried to recall the women from church, their triumphant wideness, centered and vigorous, and this helped. Ella clung to her like a baby koala. Mattie nuzzled her, snorfled her neck. The didgeridoo sounded like an enormous animal panting at the end of its life. Mattie looked up and found Daniel standing before her, lifting her daughter into his arms. He held her in front of his chest, his long hands knitted together effortlessly to make a seat in which round, rosy Ella perched, somewhat worried, but curious. "Want to dance?" he asked her. "I'm probably the only person you know who can dance to the didgeridoo." Ella thought this over, tugging on her chin like an alchemist.

Mattie opened her fingers slowly so she could peek in at the little rubber shoe, as if examining a poker hand. Harry and Al were talking, and Daniel still held Ella in his arms, turning in slow circles. Mattie watched, listened, breathed in deep and slow: if the sound of the didgeridoo was a color, it would be rich and earthy, plant purple, like eggplant with light behind it.

three

It was the rainiest May ever. A sense of ordinary life had established itself by late winter, had risen from the chaos and comfort of schedules and lazy weekends, school and vacations, colds and flus and dentist appointments, long sleepy Saturday mornings of drawing together in Mattie's bed. In early spring, they threw off their jackets and tore outside. The garden was in full crazy bloom and the children were growing like Topsy too, as Isa always said. They now spent three weekends a month with Nicky and Lee, so that Mattie could bring them to church one Sunday, piled into the car with Daniel and Lewis. She was just getting by financially: she had a lot of work at Sears, Nicky had increased her child support by one hundred dollars a month, the sandwich-making business continued to thrive.

Al had lost ten pounds since Christmas. He and Daniel were playing tennis once a week now. They were equally terrible, but fascinating to watch. Al struck frozen poses before hitting each return, as if a stream of water might pour from the statuary of his head; Daniel moved with the herky-jerk robot steps of someone in ski boots. Harry had his seventh birthday, Ella her third. Although she was both bright and watchful, she was still not talking very much. Mattie could see that she communicated brilliantly in other ways, but Nicky insisted on taking her to the doctor. Some people were just naturally quieter than others, the doctor said. Isa sometimes tried to badger Ella into conversing with her, and if Ella resisted, Isa would demand, "Cat gotcher tongue?" until Mattie would threaten her with a raised fist. The animals were fine, the kitten growing into a real cat and less of a holy terror. Marjorie was slowing down more. Isa and Lewis were together all the time: Isa seemed amused by this late-in-life affair. Lewis always smiled at her gently, and came to church with Mattie and Daniel on Sundays.

A storm woke Mattie at dawn. She lay in the dark room and listened to Marjorie snore, more like a bear than a sick dog. Two cats were asleep on the bed, the third on the chair. She had promised to take the children to Samuel P. Taylor Park today, even in the rain. She did not mind this weather, and certainly preferred it to the tyranny of a bright blue day, when old voices told you to get off your duff and go outside. Hours after a storm passed, the wet enlivening grayness — a watercolor brush on wet paper — made the wind and the howl all worthwhile.

She got up to make coffee. The animals sprinted to the kitchen at her heels like hungry

Secret Service agents, so she fed them before putting the water on to boil. It was only seven. The paper was on the front step. She heard old man Buell across the street putting out his empty bottles for recycling, and Kathy Brock next door shaking a bag of kibble like maracas to summon her playboy cat. Ella would be getting glasses today, and then they could go to the park. Mattie hoped Al and Isa would come too. With Nicky and Lee's wedding around the corner, the baby on the way, all that amniotic fluid drawing the children out of their gravitational orbits, they had to pull together now.

But Al called at eight, sounding worried. "Something strange has happened, and I don't know what to make of it. The woman from The Sequoias just called to say that Mom was found this morning over by Safeway, wandering around in her pajamas."

"What? What'd you just say?"

"It's strange. She was apparently sleepwalking. Someone from Safeway stopped to help her, and walked her back home. He said she was fine as soon as he shook her. But the woman at the front desk was worried. I should take her in to the Saturday clinic at Kaiser."

Isa refused to see the doctor. Al called Mattie later in the morning to report that he was at Isa's and she had all but put the dresser up against the door to keep him out. She had eventually let him in, made him toast, and they had looked through an old photo album together. She seemed fine. He stopped by Mattie's at lunchtime, and she made him beans and dirty rice; he played fairies in the rain with Ella.

It was two weeks more before they made it to the park, on another rainy day. The children rode in the back of the car, Isa next to Mattie. They sang along to Peter, Paul and Mary as they drove past green meadows and pastures carpeted with lupine, furnished with horses and sheep and cows, colts, lambs, calves.

After a while Harry whined, "Why are we going out there in the rain? We could be home drinking cocoa."

"Oh, don't be a poop," said Isa.

"But this is dangerous to be driving around in the rain, with alcoholics driving around so fastly in their cars."

"Why are you such an old worrywart?" Isa demanded.

The weather grew worse. When they got out of the car at the park, the children shielded their faces as they raced ahead toward their tree. Isa was walking tentatively, and Mattie spotted her as if she were on a balance beam.

"You okay, Mom?"

Isa nodded.

Harry and Ella burst into the opening of a tree, the same one that Mattie and Al had burst into when they were little, and Isa and Mattie followed. The tree was called a family-circle redwood, a great mother tree with several trunks around her, grown into her, and a tepee-shaped space inside. Half of the mother trunk was charred, perhaps from a lightning strike, and smelled like campfire; the unburnt parts were russet.

Mattie spread an oilcloth on the ground, deep wine-red against the duff, and they all sat down with their backs against the trunk. She poured paper cups of cocoa from a thermos. When the children had finished drinking, they asked to go outside. Mattie sat close to her mother, picking out her faint almond scent amid the smell of trees and burnt wood.

Inside the tree were slits and clefts and openings to another world within. The bark above them was more male, testicular, as Mattie pointed out to Isa. They laughed.

"Speaking of which, how are things with Lewis?" Mattie asked.

Isa yelped with indignation. "You get your head out of the gutter," she cried, hitting Mattie on the shoulder with an imaginary purse, blushing but pleased.

The hollow rose high inside the tree. Much had burned away, but more was left than had been taken, so the tree had kept growing.

Mattie went to bed again with Nicky in June, two weeks before the wedding. This was a new low. She prayed to God to help her say no when Nicky called, asked for the strength to call him back and cancel. But she didn't cancel, and he came. Maybe the reasons she so wanted to stop sleeping with him — the secrecy, the sinfulness, the disgust — were also the things that pulled her into bed with him. Sleeping with Nicky helped kill the desire, for weeks at a time, to get back together with him. But there was a sweetness this time too, a quiet familiarity. Their bodies still fit so wonderfully in motion, like hands rubbing lotion into each other.

"It's hard to imagine giving this up," Nicky said. "I suppose we ought to, though."

"Yes, of course," she replied. "It's not good for the kids, and the baby you're going to have. Or Lee. Or us. But other than that . . ."

They were quiet awhile. "Remember when we were in Idaho, when you were pregnant with Harry?" Nicky asked. She nodded in the dark. She remembered the scent of the lodgepole pines, and the river at night where the salmon were spawning. How they thrashed and splashed, like sharks in the starlight. "Then a few weeks after we got home, Harry was born. That was when life really began for me." She started to cry. He could not stay long enough to console her.

After Nicky left, she put on her robe and went out to stand in the drizzle. It was cold but the water felt good, like punctuation. The rain got inside her robe, and she walked around the garden feeling wet and silvery.

In the morning, while she made breakfast,

the children stood at the window in the kitchen, hypnotized by the drops of rain on the glass. Ella's white-blond hair, mussed with sleep, was the brightest thing in the room. Harry, with his brown skin and dark hedgehog brush cut, glowed like wood. Mattie stood next to them while the eggs fried, watching the rain on the window. It was like watching ants march in a line to their colony, from many into one. The kids tracked drops that threaded their way down the glass, and Harry, endlessly competitive, cheered on rivals in a horse race of water beads, shoving Ella when she tapped on the window and interfered with one drop's natural course. "People don't shove people, Harry," she cried.

Mattie went back to the stove to flip the eggs. Harry, now drawing faces on the steamy glass, said, "Mom? How will you and Daddy get back together if he marries Lee?"

Her heart sank.

"Daddy and I aren't going to get back together. We are never going to be married again. Lee is going to be your stepmother."

"Should we call her Mom too?"

Mattie spun around and jabbed at the air with her spatula. "Don't you dare."

Harry considered her. Then his face darkened. "So will Lee die at the same time as me and Ella? Or just you?"

"What?"

"Won't you and I die at the exact same

time?" he asked in rising panic.

Mattie placed food on the table. "No, honey. Where did you hear that?"

"From Stefan. He and his mom are dying at the exact same second."

"No, they're not, darling. And besides, I'm thirty years older than you. So you and Ella — and Stefan — will probably live much longer."

Harry gaped at her. He pushed his eggs away. Then he covered his face with his hands and began to sob, which got Ella started too. "If I had known that," he cried, running back to the window, "I would never have agreed to be born."

The sun returned and poured through the kitchen and bedroom windows, but the living room remained dreary, because it had only one window. Mattie wanted to install a bigger window, but she had no money, and the windows Daniel inherited at work sites were single-paned, like the one in the already drafty living room.

Then Pauline called one day to say she'd had a brainstorm. "Let's find a mirror to put above the fireplace."

"There are already too many mirrors in this house. Anyway, I need a real window in the living room, not a mirror." Mattie was suspicious of Pauline's kindness. "I want to look at myself less, not more. Plus, they must be very expensive."

"First of all, mirrors are a kind of window," Pauline said. "They bring light and the outside world to a wall that doesn't have an opening in it. They can be an opening of light. You don't have one in the living room. And you can buy a fancy, beautiful one at a junk shop."

So Mattie went to a used-furniture store with the bedside tables she had bought with Nicky, and traded them for a big mirror with a white ropy wooden frame around it. And it did let in the world, the garden and the sky, it did let in the light, and the darkness. The only thing Mattie didn't like about it was having to see her own tired reflection, the tinsel of gray in her hair.

When Nicky came by to pick up the children on the afternoon before his wedding, Mattie tried to act both as harried and as nonchalant as she could. She was wearing a sleeveless blouse that she'd meant to change, as she was sweaty from cleaning. She raced about, getting Ella ready. Lee had picked out the children's wedding finery. Mattie could not remember having felt so phony and smiley, so unfine, in her entire life. She was with Ella in her bedroom when the doorbell rang. "Oh, there's your daddy now," Mattie said, and Ella clung to her. They walked to the kitchen and Mattie called for Harry, but he did not come, and when they opened the door, they found Nicky there looking chagrined.

"Hey," he said to Mattie. "Are you okay?"

"I'm fine," she replied, with enormous hostility.

He reached for Ella, who stuck to Mattie like a bandage.

"Come on in," Mattie told him. "We're not quite together yet." She handed him the children's overnight bag, and sat at the table with Ella.

"Where's Harry?"

"I don't know. He's here somewhere." Ella put her thumb in her mouth and sucked, and Mattie nuzzled her hair. Ella ducked her head.

"Honey, don't suck your thumb," Nicky wheedled, and Mattie glowered at him. He winced, and got up to look for Harry.

Mattie looked fondly at the expanse of chubby belly between Ella's pants and her T-shirt. After a moment Ella peered down too, as if over the side of a low bridge. She slowly inserted her thumb in her belly button and pushed it in, making contact after a moment with something deep inside. "My belly," she whispered to Mattie.

"Yes."

Ella pushed her thumb deeper into her belly button. Her gaze lost focus and she began to relax in Mattie's arms. Nicky, looking grim, appeared in the doorway to say he couldn't find Harry. Mattie went to search, and found him in a corner of the laundry room, holding Marjorie tightly.

When Nicky and the children finally left, Mattie went to cry in the bathroom. She cried so hard that she threw up. Then she sat on the couch in the dark living room and cried even more. The three cats gathered around her like physicians, and Marjorie crawled onto her lap. In the dark, the new mirror looked like an underground tunnel.

After a few hours she went to get the little blue shoe, which was now in an empty sugar bowl on the kitchen table. She took out an album of family photographs and looked at pictures of her father — as a young groom, and then with baby Al in his arms; on the porch at Neil Grann's with his arm around Yvonne, Neil's girlfriend; with Mattie on his shoulders, him holding on tight to her skinny ankles. She checked the messages on her answering machine. Angela had called twice, and Isa had called to invite her to a Meg Ryan movie — leave it to Isa to have the world's worst solutions for grief. Al had called to say he and Katherine would come over if Mattie just gave the word. Mattie did not feel like being around a couple. Daniel had called to say that he and Pauline were going to the ballet and sent their love, and Harry had left a message, in a tiny voice, that he wanted to ask her a question about the sky. Mattie really listened, as if he were there: "When does what you smell become the sky? When is it not just the air right around you? Like when would the smell of

94

grass that was coming up from the dirt be the bottom of the sky?"

Daniel and Pauline took her to the movies the next day. Nicky and Lee would be at City Hall about then. Mattie sat in the aisle seat with Daniel beside her. Pauline handed her some Kleenex across Daniel's lap. Mattie felt better when the movie was over, because that meant the wedding was over too. Pauline invited her for dinner, but she wanted to be alone, with her pets, and maybe a small cheese pizza. In a perfect world, she would have had Daniel over alone. It was not a perfect world. She ate pizza, drank beer, took a Valium, and read herself to sleep.

Al called the next day and announced, "I think we're going to have to put Mom in a loony bin."

"Okay," Mattie said.

There was silence. "You're supposed to ask why."

"Oh, I'm sorry. Why do we have to put Mom in the bin?"

"Because she has ten bags of cat food in the cabinet next to the stove, all opened, none of them even half empty. And she has three bowls of kibble on a placemat, all the same brand and flavor, for the one cat."

"I've noticed that, but it's not so bad. It's not like sleepwalking to Safeway."

"I don't think she should be driving. I mean, do you let an old person drive until they kill somebody, or crash into a parked car?"

"I don't know. I don't actually have an owner's manual for Isa."

When Nicky dropped the children off that night, he poked his head in long enough to say that everything had gone fine. The children ran into her arms. Harry smelled as sweet and pungent as sawdust, Ella as deliciously odd as puppy breath. The touch of their skin, the smells, made her whole again, like an animal lost in the wilds that finds its mother.

She looked up to see Nicky watching them, and she tried to appear elegant and maternal and spiritual, but inside she thought, Nyaah-nyaah, our children don't do this with you!

Soon after the wedding, she decided to remodel her bedroom. It was dark and ugly, with walnut paneling from the fifties. Daniel and Pauline's bedroom looked like a solarium for honeymooners, cozy and sweet and filled with light and a nice view. She asked Daniel if he'd help her.

"Yeah! Let's tear down that horrible paneling. And maybe put in more windows. I'd love to, it would be fun. A great project."

He asked her if the walls had insulation; she didn't know. "Let's take off one or two panels and see," he suggested, but she didn't want to do it; she was afraid of what might be underneath.

"How bad could it be?" Daniel asked blithely. "No offense to your father — this paneling was a popular look from the pages of *Argosy* at that time. We had it too. It was just as ugly at our house, with everything but antlers and a mounted moose head."

"Okay," she said. Daniel took a chisel from her tool box and pried off a board. Underneath was the absence not just of insulation, but of anything. There was only framing. "Oops," said Daniel. "They forgot to put up walls."

Mattie examined the void between the two-by-fours. "What can we do?"

"We need to put in some insulation, some drywall, then prime it, and paint. And then this room will be bright and warm."

That night she asked her mother for the money, and called Daniel with the good news, but got Pauline instead. They talked and then she asked to speak to Daniel. He wasn't home. "He's delivering sandwiches," Pauline said. "Can I give him a message?"

"Tell him I have the Sheetrock money. And Saturday would be great."

After a pause, Pauline said, "Saturday's not going to work for us." Mattie felt a flicker of anxiety. "I got tickets for Mark Morris, and I'm hoping to spend the day in the city with Daniel. That is, if you can spare him." Mattie held her breath. The kitchen grew silent except for the

97

buzz of a light. "Can't you do it Sunday?"

"No, we've got church."

"I don't think Daniel will be at church. We'll be in the city overnight."

Mattie stammered. She had been put back in her place. But as it turned out, Daniel did want to work the next weekend.

"I don't want to see Mark Morris," he said to Mattie later over the phone. "I already told Pauline that. We just had a terrible fight about it, and she left. I couldn't have been clearer — I told her I'd go with her, but not for the whole day, and not overnight — but she made plans for us to stay with a friend of hers who I hate, and I'm not going. I want to spend the day working on your house. And I want to go to church on Sunday."

Mattie thought about calling Pauline to straighten things out. Instead she called Angela, who advised her to keep her nose out of it. "This is really none of your business," she said. Mattie waited to see how things worked out, and on Friday, Daniel called saying he would be there first thing in the morning.

"Is Pauline still mad?" Mattie asked.

"Oh, yeah. Big-time." Daniel cleared his throat. A bracing warmth flushed through Mattie, like the first sip of a martini.

Pauline went to the city by herself, and Daniel came over in a subdued and distracted mood. He and Mattie took up all the walnut paneling and piled it into his truck. They hauled it to the dump in San Rafael, ate hamburgers at Wendy's, and went to the hardware store in town. They bought a roll of insulation, and Sheetrock, then worked through the afternoon. By nightfall, they had half of the insulation stapled up.

"I should've gone with Pauline," Daniel said when they were finished. "I should've arranged to meet her in the city. And gone to see Mark Morris with her. I don't even know if she'll come back in the morning now. Once when she got mad, she stayed away for days."

"Where did she stay?" Mattie asked.

"I don't know. But I felt sick the whole time she was gone."

His color was terrible, as if he had a stomachache. Mattie felt better than she had in quite a while. Today was the tomorrow she'd been worrying about before Nicky's wedding, but now, thanks partly to Daniel, she was okay. She went and got the blue shoe from the kitchen, and pressed it into Daniel's hand. "Here," she said. "Hold on to this. You need it more than I do."

He looked at it. "Wow." He closed his long fingers around it and jammed his hand into his pants pocket.

Daniel couldn't go to church the next morning. Mattie was surprised by how disappointed she was. She had picked up Lewis, and they drove together. At church they sat near the choir, to be enveloped by all that singing.

Mattie battled against a rubbery, numb sensation when she thought about Daniel rushing after Pauline, and she got a little sick when she thought of Nicky's joy in Lee's pregnancy. But this is where I am, Lord, she prayed, this is how it is with me right now. She felt her own brokenness deeply, a longing to come clean and be helped, a signal going out from her. Yet she also found herself wishing she hadn't given Daniel the blue shoe. Having the shoe meant that he would come through; he and Pauline would make up. Mattie realized, with a start, that she didn't want them to make up. When she got home, she found a message from Daniel on the answering machine: He had gone to the city and would be back the next day to finish the job.

He couldn't come the next day, though, or the next, and on Wednesday she had a fitting gig with Sears. This was fine with her; she was still a perfect size 12, her one claim to fame, and she liked being needed, by grown-ups, at least for the moment, at least by Sears.

Daniel came over on Thursday. They finished stapling the insulation and began hammering the Sheetrock, but they didn't talk much. He had another job on Friday, so they finished on Saturday. He showed her how to smear the Sheetrock with something he called mud.

And then he gave her a report about the previous Saturday night. He had gone to the city that night, to the Marines Memorial Theatre, dressed in his best clothes, and waited outside to spot Pauline and her friends. He'd bought a scalped ticket for one hundred dollars, which she ended up being mad about, because she'd given his ticket away and now they were out a hundred dollars and didn't even get to watch the performance together. He stayed overnight with her at her friend Adrienne's, the one he hated, and Pauline had forgiven him. Mattie said how glad she was.

On Monday, Mattie and Daniel painted the walls and ceiling Navajo white. What had been a cold, dark, blotchy room was now warm and full of light. Mattie felt as if a big cleansing wind had swept through both the room and her soul, blowing the ghosts of her parents away.

A few days later, Al came over, and stretched out on the couch to relax. Within five minutes, he was reading the kids a book one of them had thrust at him. He was like a jukebox: Harry or Ella made a selection and then nudged the machine to get it to play the song. Each time he finished a book, Al made a great show of exhaustion, crying out, "That's it! No more." The children would titter and glance at each other, and run off to find another book.

Al escaped, for a moment, to the kitchen. Mattie was cutting paper-thin slices of Parmesan, laying each slice on a piece of buttered sourdough baguette. He picked one up and dis-

101

patched it in a bite. "Hmmph," she said, and continued slicing. He picked up another and ate it too. "Al!" she cried.

"I'm as hungry as a dog." Hearing the word "dog," Marjorie clicked into the kitchen, and Al fed her a few chunks of bread.

"How come Katherine gets so mad at me?" Al asked. "At cute old me?"

"Maybe because you don't want to have babies with her."

"I don't want to have babies with anyone. I have Harry and Ella already."

"And she wants her own."

"But I was such an unhappy kid," Al said. "How many other people do you know who had therapists back then when we were kids? None. You had to be really far gone. And I was. I was blowing things up at, like, eight. Me and my friends stole purses from old ladies. We stole beer from the Corner Market when we were ten. I had huge problems at school. And Daddy *still* didn't want to spend money on a therapist, till I started with this hand-washing thing. That got his attention."

"Why do you think you were so unhappy?"

"Why do you think *you* were?"

Mattie thought about this. "Because I was raised by screwed-up, unhappy people in a bad marriage. Daddy had some kind of secret life, in Washington, and Mom was sort of — what's the word? — pathological."

Al lifted the lid off the Wedgwood sugar bowl

102

and looked in. He took out the paint-can key and began to clean his nails with it.

"Don't do that, Al. You'll chip the paint off."

"Mattie!"

"I just want to keep it the way it was when we got it. Like evidence."

Al laughed. "Evidence of what? There's a room painted blue somewhere. Or not. So what?"

He walked the saltshaker over to the paint-can key, and smashed it into the key, grimly, like the boy he had been once, when he'd pushed little toy metal cars and plastic army men around this same table. He looked up at her now with such affection that she blushed. He stood beside her while she diced an apple, and tugged her braid. "Toot-toot," he said.

Pauline came along with Daniel one afternoon, bringing a gift — a bread machine. Mattie saw it as a peace offering: they had not spoken since the Mark Morris weekend. The bread machine was the same kind Pauline used. She had kept it in her garage for a while and thought Mattie might like it. Mattie gushed over it, even though she did not want a bread machine. She was so tired as it was all the time; when would she bake bread? But Pauline wanted her to have it, and Mattie wanted to get back on good terms with her. She could always put it in the garage next to Isa's ice cream machine. They could be roommates.

"This is great," Mattie assured Pauline, who looked quite pleased with herself.

"The smell of dough makes you proud to be an animal," Pauline said. "An animal that sniffs things and gives off smells, salty or sweet or yeasty." Mattie nodded. It was actually true.

After Pauline and Daniel left, Mattie found three aprons and she and the children began to make their first loaf. Harry measured flour, Ella measured salt.

"When I was a child, Isa made bread all the time, white bread, can you imagine? This was before she became a health food nut. White bread, black bread, Danish pastry for your uncle Al." She remembered Isa kneading dough, like a masseuse, wiping at her damp furrowed brow with the back of her sleeve, punching the dough down — Whap! Take that! And so, wafting through the tension in the house, a house full of books, the best hi-fi equipment, great jazz albums, fine food and expensive booze, were comforting smells from a world of gingham aprons.

Isa called and Mattie told her to stop by. When she arrived, the children jumped up and down and screamed, and dragged their grandmother to the kitchen to see the great new machine and the rising dough. Isa made a great fuss over it while they were within earshot. But when they left the room, she made a face of disapproval.

"What?" Mattie asked.

"A bread-making machine? Why on earth would you need a machine to make bread? Isn't that the whole point? The mixing and the kneading and the slapping and the shaping?"

"Yeah, you're right. But Pauline really wants us to have it, and you saw how happy it makes the kids." Mattie rolled her eyes. "Let's have a drink."

"It's going to end up in the garage with the ice cream maker," Isa predicted. Mattie smiled, and made old-fashioneds for them both. Isa looked worn. Even the bright African fabric of her pants and tunic couldn't disguise how dull and perplexed she seemed. The tan foundation on her face ended in pasty dewlaps, and she'd taken to painting eyeliner on her lower lid, so that her eyes would show up within all those folds.

"Are you okay?" Mattie asked, and Isa said, yeah, sure, maybe a little tired. She launched into stories about the losers at The Sequoias, the space cadets, the terminally ill, and the nuts on the third floor, as if to demonstrate that she was as sharp as ever. There *was* a floor where the nuttier people lived, Isa insisted. They were slackers, complainers, troublemakers. They'd gotten Revi, her favorite housecleaner, fired. Mattie listened. Listening was love, somebody had once said. Her mother was all too much, too many words, too much makeup, too much frenzy. But when Isa brought out a folded-up copy of a letter she'd written to The Sequoias' director, protesting Revi's firing, asserting that it was outrageous and possibly racist, that neither she nor any of the other residents would rest until justice was served, Mattie felt a rush of love for her mother. Isa had demanded that Revi be reinstated at his ten-dollar-an-hour job. How deeply she fought for underdogs. Her whole life she had shown up and protested, written letters, phoned in fresh troops, agitated for the rights of those who she felt had been treated poorly, who couldn't speak up for themselves. There were framed photos all over the house of her parents in hard hats, with shovels, placards, paintbrushes.

But there was also such denseness and hostility in Isa, the need to manipulate and goad, the need for reassurances to which she would not admit, greediness, grabbiness, contempt. "Let's have another old-fashioned," Mattie said.

Isa cast a skeptical, prying eye at her. "Darling, do you drink more than you used to?"

"God, Mom! Of course not."

"I worry. I have always worried, about you and Al, and maybe watched you a little carefully, because of your father's binges."

"Binges? You mean those weekends at Neil's? Wine with dinner?" Mattie felt an uncomfortable stirring.

"I'm going to go," Isa said, and she rose. "Talk to Al. He knows."

"Daddy didn't have binges, Mom. And Al would have told me."

"Okay, fine." Isa held up her hands: I come in peace. She smiled a self-satisfied smile.

Mattie went right to the phone. "Al. Maybe I'm going crazy. Mom was just here and she bombed me. She said to ask you about Daddy's binges. That you've known all along."

Al groaned. "That's all such bullshit — so Isa. I mean, Alfred drank with his buddies on weekends. He had a cocktail with Mom every night. And wine with dinner." He stopped talking. Mattie could hear the line buzz.

"Tell me what else you know." She'd expected far more protest, a more reassuring set of memories. The long silence terrified her. "Say something! You're scaring me."

Al didn't talk for a moment. "I don't know much, Mattie. I did use to see him out in West Marin, when I was a teenager. I was out there a lot with my friends. And I'd see him with Yvonne, from time to time, but Neil wouldn't be with them. I saw him once at the Bolinas Fourth of July parade, and he was pretty loaded, even though it was only nine in the morning.

"But everyone was getting high then, you know? Once I was in San Francisco on a Saturday, when Daddy was supposed to be away on one of his trips. I thought he was in Washington. Me and my friends were going to a tribal stomp in Golden Gate Park. We had to go down Lombard, because someone had a connection there for great acid. And I was sitting in the car with Matt Gold, while Jeanie went in to buy the acid, and I saw Daddy in the doorway of a pizza joint. I could tell he was trying to duck out of sight. But he pretended to be thrilled to see me."

Mattie took this in. Did she want to know what came next? "Alone?"

"No."

"Was he with a woman?"

"No, well, that was the thing — he was with Abby Grann. She was just a girl, around your age, right? They both looked upset, and then Daddy started waving at me. He asked where I was going, and I told him. I said, 'I thought you were away on business,' and he said that the flight had been canceled, he wasn't leaving till that afternoon. And he'd happened just that moment to have run into Abby.

"I was so relieved not to get busted that I didn't really think much about it then. He was definitely loaded that time. He asked if I needed some money, which I did. He gave me twenty bucks, and then put his arm around my shoulders. Then he said good-bye to Abby too, and walked away from us both."

Mattie and the children put the risen dough in a bread pan and then into the bread machine. It sat on the kitchen counter, a squat

108

robot. Ella closed the lid, Mattie plugged it in, Harry turned it on.

Almost immediately they heard a loud ticking. The bread machine sounded like it had a bomb inside. "What is it?" Harry cried out, his face red with worry and pain, while Ella moaned. Mattie turned off the machine, unplugged it, then reached her hand down through the dough to the blade and tightened it. She turned the machine back on and tiptoed away, but the ticking started again.

"I don't think I can handle this," Harry fumed, and he pushed Ella brusquely on his way out of the kitchen.

"People don't do that to people, Harry," Ella cried.

"You draw with your sister," Mattie told him, and set the children up in the living room. She returned to tinker with the machine and finally figured out what was wrong: the bread pan was not pushed down onto the heating coils. She adjusted it, and soon the machine was making a low hum.

"Crisis averted," she said to herself, and went into the living room. But minutes later there was a new noise, a thunk and rumble, like the sound of unbalanced laundry in the washer, followed by a crash.

Harry raced out of the living room. Mattie lifted Ella into her arms and ran for the kitchen too, where they found the bread machine lying on its side on the floor, the pan nearby, a round blob of dough like a rejected organ beside it. It looked as if the machine had committed suicide.

"Oh, God!" Harry looked at Mattie wide-eyed.

"What should I do?" she said.

"Maybe it'll still work," Harry said. Mattie put the machine back on the counter and tried to fit the lid on. The lid was bent, badly askew, and she loosened screws and tried to realign it. When she found she couldn't, she closed the lid, and even though the machine still looked broken, she decided to try again.

Two hours later they had a perfect loaf of golden-brown bread. You could have put it on the cover of a magazine. God, it was amazing: you took a pile of flour, some water and sugar and salt and yeast, what looked like ash, and then not too much later, you had food for your family.

It turned out to be terrible-tasting, though, with a texture like sawdust. The children loved it anyway. They wanted slices one inch thick, slathered with butter and honey. They ate so much bread that night that Ella almost threw up and Harry passed out on the living room floor. But it was great to toast your own bread, even if it didn't quite turn out: it was a little rough, but comforting, like a soft beard.

Daniel's dreadlocks were nearly an inch long now, the light brown of his eyes. She sat with him and Lewis at church. Lewis had his black bowler, but during the service he held it in his lap. Mattie sneaked glances at the nappy dreads springing from Daniel's head. Daniel smelled of beeswax candles.

When they dropped Lewis off at The Sequoias, Mattie said, "I wonder where Mom is. Her car's gone."

"Probably at the store," said Lewis. "She shops for us on Sunday."

"Tell her to call me when she gets back, will you?"

Lewis doffed his bowler in reply.

Isa didn't get home that day. Instead she called in a rage from a police station, where she was being held. "Jesus Christ!" she fumed. "They wouldn't have brought me in if I were younger. This is ageism! Call the ACLU. Call AARP."

"Mom! What happened?"

It all tumbled out too fast. "What happened was, goddamn Caltrans had their machinery parked illegally by the side of the road. And I veered to the right because someone was making an unsafe lane change, and it startled me, I suppose, and I pulled over to the right and the next thing I knew, there's a crashing smashing ripping sound, and it's their goddamn machinery gouging my passenger door like a can opener."

"You drove up on the shoulder of the highway?"

"I told you. I pulled over because another person was making a lane change, and Caltrans had abandoned some machinery there. . . ."

"Excuse me, ma'am." Mattie heard a male voice. "You cannot tie up the phone. Do you or don't you want me to talk to your daughter?"

"I want you to leave me the hell alone, young man."

"I'm afraid I'm going to have to insist on having the phone."

"What are you, the Gestapo?"

After a few more words were exchanged, a man came on and introduced himself as the arresting officer.

"The what?" said Mattie.

"Your mother hit some Caltrans machinery that was parked on the shoulder near the Strawberry exit, machinery that was clearly marked with a flashing sign. And then she kept driving."

"*Mein Kommandant!*" Isa called out in the background.

"Your mother destroyed the sign, and her car door."

"*Ja, ja ja,*" Isa shouted.

Mattie went with Al to pick up Isa at the police station. She was pale and fluttery, clearly unnerved, and the officer behind the front desk glared at all of them as they passed by. Mattie and Al had already examined the passenger door of her VW in the parking lot on their way in: it was crumpled and torn. "We're sorry," Al told the officer in his most placating voice. The man threw his hands up and wouldn't speak to them. Al drove Isa's car to Mattie's, the door secured with a bungee cord.

Mattie took Isa to see the doctor. When Dr. Brodkey asked Isa to describe the accident, Isa looked at Mattie with pleading eyes, like someone who did not speak the language.

"Well, my God, it was absolutely reckless endangerment," she cried. "I intend to sue for damages."

"Mom, why didn't you just stop? Why did you keep going? That's where the trouble came from."

"Caltrans left machinery on the road!"

"On the shoulder of the road!" Mattie said.

"Shhhh," Dr. Brodkey soothed. "Mattie's concerned, Isa. To tell you the truth, I'm concerned too. I'm hearing a faint murmur I've never noticed before." She tilted her head to listen again. "I'm going to schedule an echocardiogram. Otherwise, you seem fine. You can get dressed now."

Mattie and her mother did not look at each other after the doctor left. Isa gazed around the room in slow motion, as if toward a mysterious sound. When Mattie approached with her camisole, Isa squinted as if Mattie were far away, or in bright light or shadow.

"Stay with us tonight," said Mattie. "So I can keep an eye on you."

"Oh, great," Isa replied. "Just what I always wanted."

A week later Mattie and Lewis took Isa in for her echocardiogram. In the waiting room Lewis kept them all talking, distracted and connected. Mattie smiled at the clarity of his gaze that saw so little, the spray of small moles on his cheekbones, the crosshatching of his brow. He sat upright like a rock, the essence of a benevolent old man, not truculent or ashamed like so many old white men she'd known. When it was time for the test, Isa gripped Mattie's hand so tightly as they walked that Mattie's fingertips turned purple; still Mattie let her hold on. The technician, a woman, sat in front of a bank of machines and instructed Isa to take off her sweater and bra, then hop up on the table.

Mattie took her mother's purse and turned to help her out of her clothes. Isa lifted her arms like a child, and Mattie pulled the sweater over her head. Isa had a slightly sour smell. And she had on the same camisole that she'd worn the week before. It was soiled, as though she'd been using it as an apron.

The sight of her mother's body still shocked Mattie whenever she saw it, the withered breasts otherwise so like her own, moles everywhere, bad-looking ones on her back, along her bra line.

Mattie helped Isa onto the table, where she

stretched on her back and stared like a corpse at the ceiling.

"Okay, darling, now lie on your side," said the technician, and the kindness in her voice shamed Mattie.

Watching Isa's heart was like watching the sonogram of Harry when he was still inside, a baby floating in sepia-colored clouds in a fan-shaped frame. Isa's heart valves opened and shut like the mouth of a baby bird, a gaping beak opening and closing. Isa lay stiffly on her side, as if it hurt when the technician moved the apparatus around on her chest.

"You okay, Mom?"

Isa nodded, staring straight ahead. Mattie took her hand, and again Isa held it tight. On the screen, the light wavered like sun filtering down through the surface of a pool. Mattie thought: My mother's heart!

"Am I okay?" Isa asked.

"I'm just taking movies for the doctor," said the technician.

"But do you see anything wrong?"

"You have to talk to your doctor. This is what all hearts look like, darling. There's nothing to be afraid of."

"What a trip," Mattie said. The technician nodded.

"I'm lighting it so we can see the direction of the blood flow." On the screen were flashes of fire, explosions, patches of cool blue ice.

"It looks like aerial spy photography now," Mattie told her mother. "And now it looks like the surface of Mars!"

"But does it look like everything is okay?" Isa asked again.

"Yes, Mom. To me it does. It looks like everything's fine."

And everything was fine, at least with her heart. The doctor left a message on both their answering machines. On Isa's she said that the results of the echocardiogram were terrific, no abnormalities, she must have been hearing things when she thought she heard a murmur, all the walking over the years and watching her diet that Isa had done had paid off. On Mattie's she said this also. But she added that she was concerned about something else.

"I can't quite put my finger on it," Dr. Brodkey said. "I know that when I saw her, she was shaken by the accident, and yet she still didn't seem like her old self. I sense there's something going on in there, and I'm going to order a few tests. I'll tell her they're all routine."

Al came for dinner that night. Isa made a half-hearted effort to join in the dinner-table conversation, chastised Harry to sit up straight, cut Ella's chicken off the bone for her, and then absentmindedly began eating off her plate. Ella watched anxiously as the food disappeared. "Thank you, Mom," Mattie said enthusiastically, moving the plate back onto Ella's placemat, and

Isa slowly looked around for her own, which was right in front of her. "Mattie?" she said in a small voice. "I think I'm ready for bed."

Mattie helped her out of her chair. Everyone said good night, and she took Mattie's arm to steady herself. Mattie put her to bed in her own bedroom, after helping her into a nightie, which hung on Isa. Mattie sat beside her on the bed, rubbing her back and shoulder blades as she did Harry's and Ella's, until Isa drifted off; Mattie would make up the sofa bed in the living room for herself.

Al, meanwhile, tried to get the children into a bubble bath but they raced away. Finally he caught Ella and carried her like a rolled-up rug under his arms. "People don't carry people, Al," she cried, but he paid her no attention. Harry got Al to put her down and chase him, by calling him a doo-doo butthead. Mattie scooped Ella up and buried her nose in her daughter's neck. She smelled like a flower bed, dirt and petals.

When everyone else was asleep, Mattie and Al sat with Marjorie in the yard, a clear, starry sky overhead. Through the thick lower branches of the towering redwood tree, she saw a star flicker, a light as sharp and bright as a diamond. She pointed it out to her brother. How could that be? The branches were so dense, and yet a glittering pinprick of light had shone through, like a tiny ornament on the inner branches of the tree.

four

Lee and Nicky had their baby in early July, a big, blond, hunky, chunky boy, named Alexander. Mattie came outside in the postapocalyptic heat to admire him in his infant car seat not long after his birth, one day when Nicky came to pick up the children. This was the most divorced Mattie had ever felt. After he drove off with his three children, she lumbered back inside, hearing the sucking sound of her thighs. She spent the morning cleaning the house like a domestic robot, and the afternoon shopping. She bought several new lipsticks, skin cream that cost what she spent on food every week, art supplies for the children, saltwater sandals for Ella, new luggage for traveling nowhere in particular, and a two-pound box of Godiva truffles.

It was too hot. The days were endless and too bright and there was nowhere to hide until it got dark, and the dark was too short. Mattie felt as if she were in a torture chamber with her eyes taped open.

In the following weeks, Nicky glowed with an inner light, an angel revealing himself to unbelievers. Mattie tried to think spiritual thoughts, but instead found herself fantasizing about dashing Drano into his face. She had all the symptoms of meningitis, and then her hip went out. She limped around like Walter Brennan. Angela tried to convince her that this was a blessing; she had no choice but to move really consciously, so each step had meaning. Secretly, though, Mattie believed she was dying. Harry began having nightmares, crying out in the night for Mattie to come to him, or silently climbing into her bed. She did her best to comfort him. Who was supposed to comfort her? He kicked all night. Ella developed a new habit, nuzzling a sore she had caused on her wrist by chewing on herself, holding her wrist as if it were sprained, and nibbling at the skin. Mattie worried about the sore, and about appearances — what would other mothers think? That her daughter was cannibalizing herself? She tried to move her daughter's wrists away from those small, perfect white teeth, but Ella always resumed with a look of satisfaction: I can do something for me that you can't do. There must have been comfort in the pain, and in the stopping of the pain — a circuit: she got to cause the tingle, and she got to release it.

Earlier in the summer, Isa had fainted near the mailboxes at The Sequoias, but she had come to quickly. At first Dr. Brodkey thought Isa had suffered a minor stroke, but she decided to wait until the problem presented itself again. She put Isa on vitamins, and Isa improved. When Mattie picked Lewis up for church on Sundays now, he stressed how much

Isa had done that week, how far she was walking, as if without these assurances Mattie might pop her into a home.

Then Marjorie began to decline, retiring to the dark, cool space beneath Mattie's bed.

Mattie lost ten pounds in the months after Alexander was born, and looked both chic and gaunt. When she went in for a fitting at Sears, it turned out she was no longer a perfect size 12. Sears had no choice but to let someone else fill in until Mattie gained the weight back. The fittings manager, a perfect size 18, obviously felt terrible as she delivered the news. But Mattie was euphoric. She almost quit forever right then. She felt a wholeness in being thin, pride in firmer thighs and an orphan's face. Anyone would want to comfort her, encourage and feed her — not that she would eat someone's vile food. Yet she worried about how she would pay the bills. She bought a coffee milk shake on the way home, and one the next day too. A month later she was able to work again.

For a number of weeks, she and Nicky did not sleep together. It was too hot and the days were longer than necessary. Summer meant too much sunlight and not enough moon, but the break from Nicky brought relief to her mind, and it settled, like a pond. The children improved. Harry slept in his own bed again, and Ella stopped eating her wrist. Then in August, Daniel and Pauline flew off to Florida to visit her parents, and Lee drove baby Alexander to

Carmel to see her parents and sister for the weekend. That night Nicky called after the children were asleep. Mattie told him about Marjorie, and they cried together on the phone. The next thing she knew, he was in her living room stroking Marjorie. A stiff scotch later he was stroking Mattie.

She was hungover in the morning. She felt caught in a permanent moment of separation, the letdown of having had sex with someone she no longer loved; of having had sex to get further away. She tried to pray and feel genuine contrition but could not, and she told Jesus, I have to trust that you still like me this morning. You said you would never leave me, and I am holding you to your word. She made the children blueberry pancakes. Harry was sleepy, cross and disorganized as usual, Ella rather dopey. Mattie missed Daniel and wondered if he missed her. She imagined Pauline at the Florida shore, in a bikini, flaunting that big lasagna ass, saying poetic things to Daniel about the surf.

When Daniel and Pauline returned from Florida, Mattie invited them out to Samuel P. Taylor Park. But Pauline wanted to stay home and putter. "You have him today," she said to Mattie, as if they were Mormon wives.

Mattie and Daniel sat alone inside the circle of tree. "The wood in here is the color of a hawk," he said quietly.

121

Mattie watched spiders and bugs. "It reminds me of organ music," she said. "It's pulsing, and deep and swelling and rhythmic."

Daniel closed his eyes. "You're right. It's like sitting in a big organ pipe."

They sorted the earth through their fingers like children, the dirt and the feathery needles, leaves, bony twigs, soft heathery moss, bits and bones and stones. Their knees touched once but mostly they kept them in. Mattie tucked herself into a corner. It hid her, although it filled her with vigor too. "This is a space out of the world," Daniel said. Mattie moved her hand in a circular motion over the bark. The wood beneath her palm had been burned. It was soft and almost furry, like a horse's neck and flanks.

That week Harry's nightmares began again and he returned to her bed. She hated to admit it, but she enjoyed the company. The cats woke up when Harry came in. When he slept, the two younger cats leapt on his feet if he tossed, and the old cat, who slept near the pillows, washed his face and eyes at his slightest movement.

Ella was working her sores once more, nuzzling and nibbling the red abraded spots, like someone discovering fire and then trying to keep it alive. One spot was on her left wrist, where she would wear a watch one day. She looked at the wrist with constant longing, as if to see what time it was, to see whether it was

122

time to eat her arm again.

One morning Mattie found bloody dog stools on the living room floor. The vet said it was just a matter of time. How could the end of the world be just a matter of time? The children cried off and on, and lay with Marjorie beneath Mattie's bed.

There was no time that summer for Mattie or Al to pursue the trail of the paint-can key, or the little blue shoe. Al wanted to, but Mattie no longer felt sure they had even belonged to Alfred. The kids were with her more since the baby had been born, at least every other weekend, and Isa called too often — sometimes seven or eight times in a day. She usually got the answering machine and left increasingly hostile messages, as if Mattie were there but avoiding her. Mattie made the rounds, taking the children to their stations — friends' houses, parks, movies, swimming pools — trying on clothes at Sears when there was work, shopping for Isa and Lewis, helping Pauline and Daniel make or deliver sandwiches, and she returned home to listen to the record of her mother's disapproval. Isa needed rides now everywhere too, as her doctor had finally persuaded her to stop driving, and Lewis needed the rides that Isa could no longer offer. Mattie felt she had two more children, big, slow, old children. At one point Isa grew muzzy and dazed again, and Mattie took her to the doctor's. After a thorough going-over, the doctor administered a test, called a mini-mental, to check for dementia. Isa counted back by sevens from one hundred, and repeated a string of words that the doctor recited at the beginning of the test: "Red, wheel, rose, Colorado." She aced the test, and looked over at Mattie as if she might stick her tongue out: Told you so.

Isa called Mattie the next morning to say, "Red, wheel, rose, Colorado." Mattie laughed and shook her head.

Nicky gained weight along with the baby. It was the first time Mattie had seen him chubby, and it made her happy to know that he hated his new soft belly and fat cheeks. There was no time for him to go to the gym anymore. There were only slow hikes on the weekends, with Alexander in a Snugli, Harry and Ella walking alongside in expensive hiking boots. Afterward Harry did impersonations for Mattie of Nicky on these hikes — wide-eyed and jovial and pretentious: "Oh, Zander, look at the birdie! That's a little flycatcher. See the yellowthroat? Hi, birdie! Can you wave, Zander? Want to know what its eggs look like? Oh, where's the birdie going? Oh, don't cry, honey — Mean birdie! Don't cry, honey." Mattie would laugh at Harry's renditions, but she also remembered their own walks three years earlier, Harry trotting along beside Nicky with Ella in the baby-pack, learning about the dotted blue-gray eggs of cedar waxwings.

Harry's posture was terrible. It had worsened

since Mattie and Nicky had separated, but she did not nag him about it. Harry had enough to deal with. He could be funny and sweet, but then he would make Ella cry with whispered songs about worms and graves. He grabbed colored pencils out of her hands, punched her arms when she wouldn't obey him. And sometimes he was such a whiner. Where had Mattie gone wrong? His friends' mothers said he was the most polite child they knew — Mattie believed that good manners covered a multitude of sins — but at home he hurt Ella and some days what came out of his mouth were only complaints: "I hate this cereal, you knew that." "You look stupid in that shirt, like a hippie." "You read this book all wrong, Daddy reads it funnier."

When Mattie talked to Daniel about this, he told her a joke to console her, about a new monk in a silent monastery, who was allowed to speak only two words every five years. The first time he came before the elders, he said, "Cold floors." Five years later, permitted to speak again, he said, "Terrible food." And five years later, "I quit."

The elders looked at one another, and then turned to the monk with contempt. "I'm not surprised," one said. "You haven't done anything since you got here but complain."

Harry's body was filled with complaint too — rashes, diarrhea, and two cavities in his teeth, although he flossed and brushed every night. It was Angela who recommended counseling again. Mattie made an appointment for them to see her therapist.

But when the day came, Harry refused to go. He escaped Mattie's grip, diving under her bed, where Marjorie lay sleeping. "We need to get you help for these nightmares," Mattie said, peering in at her son and dog.

Harry looked at her. "You already know what it is," he whispered.

Flooded with heat and too many heartbeats, she stared back.

"I heard Daddy be here that night. Another night, too. Why?"

A spinning wheel inside her tossed silken lies into the air. "Oh honey," she said, "you're right, your daddy was here, but he came to get some insurance papers, files, things he needed for his work that got mixed up in my stuff. I'll show you the files, they're in boxes on the top shelf of my closet. Come out, I'll show you." He did, and she pointed out boxes filled with shoes she no longer wore, high on the shelves of her closet, and he looked at them with relief.

Mattie went to see the therapist alone that morning, the last day of August. She told Dr. Nolan about sleeping with Nicky, and Harry's nightmares, and then sat fidgeting miserably as if she'd been sent to the principal's office. "I'm not here to absolve you," Dr. Nolan said kindly. "That's not my job. But I can tell you a couple of things. One is something we used to talk about a lot — that when you feel disgust for yourself, it keeps hope alive. It means that somehow your relationship with Nicky is still current, that your dad is still alive, giving that look of disgust to Isa. It's home! Home is still intact. So that's the vocabulary of being involved with him — disgust with yourself."

"What do I do?"

"What if you put your children's pain ahead of your own needs?"

After their session, Mattie sat on the front step of the therapist's building, crying. The sun was a sheet-metal disk in the deep-blue sky. The lawns in the neighborhood were brown. She thought about driving out to the beach to walk in the surf. There might be fog at the beach. Fog was the moon's cousin, like nurses with cool compresses for her temples, and she drove out to Point Reyes, and there was fog, and it was good.

A few days later she went to talk to her pastor, to confess that until recently she had been an adulterer, who slept with her ex-husband, lied to her children, mocked her mother. She wanted to start over, she cried.

He listened kindly. He must have been about her age, but seemed older, wore horn-rimmed glasses and lace-up Hush Puppies, geeky, wise, and sweet. "That's wonderful, then. Your new twenty-four hours starts whenever you decide it does. I'll tell you what's most amazing to me,"

127

the pastor said. "That Jesus comes to people like us. Cowards, liars — even mother-mockers! And entrusts us with the kingdom of God, with carrying the message of peace. We get that peace too, when we surrender to the horrible belief that God loves us anyway. Surrender, or just plain run out of bullets."

Marjorie lived longer than anyone expected, but right after school started, Harry in second grade, Ella in nursery, she began having seizures. Katherine often came by to sit with her, and said encouraging things, as if the dog were a toddler lying miserably under the table.

One day she took a biscuit out of her pocket and fed it to Marjorie. She turned sadly to Mattie. "She doesn't look great. I would get some prednisone from your vet, to make her more comfortable. That's what Al and I did when our dog was dying."

The prednisone did help, and Marjorie got better for a while. Her appetite was good, and Mattie and the children took her for walks every day, and she walked along sniffing the deep smells of fall, of hibernation and holiday. " 'O Death,' " Daniel said during one walk with Mattie and Marjorie, quoting Dorothy Parker, " 'O Death, where is thy sting-a-ling-a-ling?' " And indeed, life and Marjorie both continued along.

The leaves changed color again, red, orange, yellow, and purple, and flew like flags. Almost a year had passed since she'd opened her front door and found Daniel standing there, staring down at his feet.

Mattie was so aware of the darkness in the fall. She put lights up everywhere, candles, white Christmas tree lights, a string of plastic fish lights that Al gave her. She loved the shorter days, frowning, lowering, Heathcliff days, and she liked the early nights, the wintery rawness in the air. Someone kept taking the snow globe and giving it a good shake, so you went from sunlight piercing through the moody day, to wind and rain and storm, storms that drove you inside to the fire. Another shake of the globe, and you woke to the blush and slash of a winter sunrise.

Isa had a disturbing episode on Thanksgiving. She was holding a gravy boat out toward Lewis at Mattie's dinner table, when suddenly the gravy boat began to tilt. It all happened in slow motion, people turning to watch Isa pour a stream of gravy into Lewis's lap, Lewis taking the gravy boat from her hands.

Again, the doctor was not overly concerned. Isa seemed fine during an examination, steady and clear. Meds adjusted, she began walking two miles a day with Lewis on the path that ran along the salt marsh beside The Sequoias.

December seemed like it would never end. Each day was so short, and yet lasted forever. Mattie hated December. If God would only make her His West Coast representative, she would cancel the whole month. Everyone was mentally ill, frantic and tired. To make matters worse this year, Harry and Ella spent their first Christmas Eve away, with Nicky and Lee and little Ratzo, as Al called Alexander, now almost six months old. Mattie spent Christmas Eve with Isa and Lewis, Al and Katherine, and went to the movies Christmas Day until it was time to pick up the children. She ached with missing them, ached with missing her father. She remembered one Christmas Eve at Neil Grann's, she must have been ten or so, when all the adults were thoroughly bombed by dusk. Her mother had stayed home with the flu. Somehow no one had quite gotten dinner together at the Granns'. Mattie, Al, Abby, and a few other kids had played outside in the freezing cold, until finally Yvonne thought to make them grilled cheese sandwiches. Mattie remembered waking up Christmas morning and knowing her parents had had a fight. Her father smelled hungover at breakfast. Isa had made bacon and cinnamon buns. "That Yvonne Lang is *crazy*," Alfred had declared, by way of placating Isa. "Absolutely mad," he'd said with amusement, although Mattie kept thinking, But she was the only one who remembered to *feed* us.

Mattie, Harry, and Ella tried to stay up until midnight on New Year's Eve, but they were all asleep by ten o'clock, on blankets in front of the fire, Marjorie and the cats curled up with

them. The morning brought a sense of brisk-
ness and new beginnings, brilliant green grass
breaking through the earth. Mattie had everyone over for black beans and rice: Isa and
Lewis, both bright and excited to be at a party
during the day; Daniel and Pauline, pale and
hungover; Katherine and Al. Katherine was all
in blue — light-blue cap with bugle beads,
light-blue leggings, a gray-blue turtleneck. She
looked like a nurse for herons. She mulled
cider on the stove, filling the house with the
scent of cloves and apples and cinnamon with
cinnamon sticks as stirrers. Mattie lit her candles, the Christmas tree lights, the bass fish
lights, to celebrate that the year had turned. It
was going to whap them around for a while,
but it was marching toward more light.

They walked through town after lunch, Marjorie along beside them. They faced into wind
and drizzle. Mattie felt goaty in her walk.

The next time Mattie walked into town,
Marjorie couldn't make it home and Mattie
had to carry her. The vet had run out of good
ideas. Mattie found her mind breaking up like
a bad cell phone connection. She had felt this
way as a teenager, but her father had always
been there to see her through. She went to
look for him in the attic, where his boxes were
stored. But she found only white powder over
everything, fluffed out from the insulating material around the pipes in the attic, glittering

in the flashlight beam like asbestos.

She called Daniel to tell him that she and the children had been breathing asbestos dust all this time and would surely die. Daniel came right over. He found her crying at the kitchen table because the children had black lung disease.

Daniel got out the ladder and disappeared for a time. He came back to report that there was no asbestos in the attic. He took her into town for a hot fudge sundae, and she could breathe again.

Mattie told Al she'd been plunged into a panic over their father. They were sitting at the kitchen table, and Mattie was turning the paint-can key over and over in her hand. "I don't know why I'm missing Daddy right now," she said. "I just feel like if he was around, we would be okay. He'd help us when we were broke, he'd be in charge of taking care of Isa, that wouldn't be on us anymore. He'd be our dad. We'd be people in the world with a dad. It would be like having a president there for you, caring for you. And if you had that, you'd feel safe."

Al rubbed his eyes. "Mattie. That's a fantasy dad. Right now, I'm not even sure who Daddy was. We need to poke around, maybe see if we can shed some light on how we all got so — lost."

"What's that going to get us?" Mattie said.

"Maybe just more pain and disillusionment."

"Maybe, maybe not. And besides, disillusionment is good."

"But even if I wanted to be more disillusioned, we have nothing to go on."

"Sure we do," Al said. "First of all, we have memories, and photos. We've got boxes of stuff in the attic, details, clues. And we have the desire to pursue this. Plus, there were all those things in the glove box of the Volkswagen, right? There was the daisy bracelet. That was yours. There was the library card, which belonged to him, his car registration, the bottle opener from the bait shop in Marshall. So all that stuff was his. It could be telling us some kind of story. A story about our father; about our family. It intrigues me — this little blue shoe, this nothingness little blue shoe, and a paint-can key. He opened a can of blue paint with it one day. What did he paint? We never had a light-blue room."

Later that afternoon, when Harry was at Stefan's and Ella was down for a nap, Al took out the ladder and set it up under the crawl space, climbed the steps, and pushed the door over onto the floor of the attic. Mattie followed. She felt terribly afraid and teetered on the stepladder with her head poking through the passage.

She pulled herself up with a hand from Al, and they stood hunched over, breathing in the

133

fusty smell of things moldering in boxes, stuff Isa and Alfred hadn't wanted to see anymore. That was why you put things in attics. Mattie smelled mice, mold, moths. Al switched on the light.

There was old familiar furniture with limb problems. "Oh," she could imagine her father saying, "this would take me five minutes to fix," but he had never gotten around to it. The floor joists and ancient electrical wires were lit by a dusty, greasy bare bulb. Mattie turned her flashlight on and started reading the sides of boxes. They were actually labeled: "Hats," "Artwork," "Children Misc.," "School Papers," "Alfred."

She imagined her parents bringing their things up here, and the illusion that if it's there in your attic, it will be held, and it will be whole, in a museum: memory will not flee, and so neither will you.

She sensed the mice, quicksilver, furtive, hallucinatory.

Al lifted one corner of an old oilcloth. It had become a mouse nest, covered with droppings, sawdust, bits of insulation. Mattie recoiled, holding one hand to her heart like an elderly aunt.

They walked around in a crablike Quasimodo crouch; they scrabbled.

"Wow," said Al, looking around at the boxes, the plastic garment bags hanging from a wooden pole, the hobbled furniture, the wrapped pipes. "Where do we even start? I guess with the Alfred boxes."

Mattie felt they'd been returned to childhood, spying on their parents, holding their breath. They were looking at their parents' insides — at their mother's handbag collection, their father's uniform from the Navy, which had been eaten by moths.

"God, this is such a trip, Mat. I am running on so much adrenaline."

"This is Mom and Dad, saved in boxes. Mummified. It's as close to ancient Egypt as we're ever going to get."

Mattie closed her eyes and inhaled the smell of wood, hot wood, insulation, and dust, looked up at the pipes, wrapped like mummies. There was something exposed here that wanted her and Al out; something trapped. Once there had been framing and open space and fresh air flowing over the wood, and you could stand right here on a ladder and see for a distance in every direction. But the carpenters had closed it up. Now it felt tiny and sealed off, breathing only its own stale air.

In one of the boxes marked "Alfred" were things that should have gone in the "Children Misc." boxes: filigreed, speckled drawings Mattie and Al had made in elementary school, diplomas from kindergarten and high school, report cards, which they pored over. Mattie had gotten all A's every year, Al had gotten C's and D's, an occasional B-minus. He fumed over old injustices. "That fucking bitch Mrs. Hauser, I should have gotten a B-minus in fifth-grade math. I was robbed. That's why I turned out the way I did."

There were the love letters Alfred had written to Isa from his naval post in Germany, letters Mattie and Al had written from camp, letters from Neil Grann. There were letters Alfred's parents and grandparents had written to him when he was in the Navy and in college. There were letters from his brother and sister, postcards from everywhere.

They worked in silence, opening the topmost letters, reading snippets to each other, carefully refolding the letters and putting them back in envelopes. Some of the letters simply could not be opened, almost turning to dust in their hands.

Neil's letters were in a manila folder, like a manuscript. Only one of them was still in its envelope, at the very back of the folder, the return address being the Cove, which was just north of Marshall — one of the nearly deserted coastal towns between Stinson and Mendocino. There was a restaurant there called Nick's Cove, with two mounted deer heads on the wall, a great old pier that fishermen still used, three rickety huts on stilts attached to the restaurant. Alfred used to take the family to the restaurant on Sunday afternoons, for barbecued oysters and deep-fried-seafood platters, or just past it, to parties at Neil and Yvonne's.

Neil had wanted to write. Actually, Neil had wanted to be a famous writer, although he did not seem to write very much. Mattie remembered, over the years, hearing him describe a novel he'd been working on forever, which he never seemed to finish and which in fact seemed to decrease in pages over time. It concerned the latest drunken marriage of a reclusive bon vivant, who had beatnik friends in their own unhappy marriages. "It's just dreadful," Alfred had confided to Mattie.

"Am building a separate floor for Abby, Ryder," Neil wrote in a nearly illegible scrawl on a piece of plain paper. "She has become impossible. So it's this, or a private school for bad girls in Switzerland. Her mother can't or won't take her. Her mother's *insane*. Abby's safer here with me. At any rate, I'm getting ready to hoist four 6 x 14 x 28-foot Douglas fir beams ten feet in the air, the slightest misjudgment of which will render me akin to a frog on wet pavement."

"Ryder," he wrote in another letter, "Absolutely terrible weekend with Kiernan and his new lady. I can only think of it as a go-for-broke effort to outrage and violate the concept of 'host' and that of 'guest.' Also such peripheral things as 'friendship' and 'reasonably good manners.' Won't bother with the details, except for the one which goes that they spent eighteen of their twenty-four hours grousing about the guest house, keeping the sliding door shut tight against the mild fall weather, the birds, the water, the trees, the . . . ah, shit. Yvonne hung in with me the whole time. Ladies are mostly O.K.-to-delightful, unless you are espoused to them. But Yvonne is gold."

They got to the second-to-last letter. Mattie let Al read it while she went to get Ella up from her nap. When she came out of Ella's room, her sleepy red-faced daughter draped over her shoulder, she heard Al call from the kitchen. He had come down from the attic too, and now stood by the table, holding up a finger.

"Listen," he said.

He took a deep breath as Mattie sat down beside him. Ella wandered off, whispering for the kitties. " 'Abby has moved out to live with a friend's family,' " Al read. " 'Abby calls sometimes, loaded, to say hello, but we end up in fights. Yvonne says to tell you she found a place for her friend, so not to worry, cheap and remote, run-down, needs repairs. Saw two ospreys fishing this a.m. Many ospreys here.' "

"Huh," Mattie said. "Why is it so interesting to you?"

" 'Run-down,' " he read. "See? Maybe it needed a fresh coat of paint."

"Oh, for Chrissakes, Al." She widened her eyes. "God, I just sounded exactly like Isa."

Al took the last letter out of the envelope, unfolded it, and began to read. He handed Mattie the letter. "Fuck you, Alfred," was all it said. "You're dead to me."

Mattie stared at the words on the page.

There was no date on the letter. She handed it to Al. He held the letter to the light, as if a watermark might appear with further instructions.

There was no time in the new year to do any more sleuthing. Driving, laundry and homework, gardening, trips to doctors and the vet all got in the way. Ella's wrists were better again, Harry loved his second-grade teacher, whom he planned to marry one day. Al and Katherine were doing well. She was gone a lot, once to Appalachia, once to see her parents in Vermont again — her father had heart disease — but when she was around, she watched and listened to Al with amused affection. And Mattie didn't sleep with Nicky once.

She and Nicky had grown into some kind of friendship. Mattie had held Alexander for the first time. She hadn't meant to. Lee and Nicky had both made sure to leave him home when either of them came to pick up Ella and Harry, but finally a day came when Lee needed to bring Alex with her. He had grown into a big, solid, jolly boy, who looked like Nicky, or a fair, chubby version of Harry, and smelled like baby shampoo. Mattie felt sick to see Harry in the face of her replacement's child. She reeled and could hardly breathe. But all she could do was smile at him and say hello. He threw himself into Mattie's arms. Mattie felt his wiggly toughness for a moment, and then he stopped, stared into her stranger's face, saw that he'd made a terrible error in judgment, and bellowed for Security.

Mattie asked Isa casually one night if she and Alfred had ever painted any of their rooms light blue. "Oh, for Chrissakes, of course not," Isa brayed. "We would never have painted any of our rooms anything but white." When it came out that Mattie was asking because of the paint-can key, Isa cried out — in what seemed like real rage — that Mattie would be the death of her if this insanity, this chasing of rainbows, kept up.

Marjorie declined more quickly all of a sudden, spent more and more time under Mattie's bed. She had bloody stools again. Her tender longhaired vet said she would have to be put to sleep soon. One night when the kids were with Nicky, Mattie started crying and couldn't stop: How was she going to survive this? She called Daniel and Pauline. Pauline was in the city. Daniel offered to come over with Chinese take-out.

They ate with the TV on in the living room. *Suddenly, Last Summer* was on the classic movie channel.

"This will be just the thing," Daniel announced. They watched in silence for a while, spaced out but together. "I'm going to faint in this heat," Daniel kept saying in a southern voice, exactly like Elizabeth Taylor fanning herself. "I'm going to faint."

"Thank you for coming over so quickly," Mattie told him, sniffling.

"I'm going to faint," Daniel trilled. Mattie looked at him out of the corners of her eyes, and smiled. She turned back to the movie. She started to feel that she could go on.

"Why did Elizabeth Taylor's son get eaten again?" she asked.

"I don't remember. I think the other guys were angry with him."

She smiled but her heart felt infected with sadness about Marjorie.

"Tennessee Williams must have figured out that you really get people's attention if you have someone eat somebody else," he said.

"Yeah, well. It certainly got mine."

Marjorie's gas got so bad that it hurt their eyes, but Ella still crawled under the bed and lay with her in the cool dark. She took stuffed animals along for company and made up stories for Marjorie about fairies and field mice. Mattie peered under the bed one morning and found Ella sucking her thumb, which seemed like progress. At least she was not gnawing at her skin. She was stroking Marjorie's back with her other hand. Mattie crawled down beside them, while Ella tended to Marjorie like a candy striper, stroking her dark shape. Mattie lay on her back and stared at the slats of the bed from below. It was like being in a cage, or

141

inside the ribs of Jonah's whale.

Harry called Nicky at work that day, crying about Marjorie, and Nicky came over for dinner that night. He sat at the table with the children while Mattie cooked roast beef and Yorkshire pudding, which he loved. Marjorie lay at their feet.

"We have been so lucky to have such a perfect dog, haven't we?" Nicky asked, and the children nodded. Tears streamed down Harry's face. "There's no way around the awfulness of this part of it, though." He took a sip of red wine. Mattie diced carrots for the salad on a cutting board, feeling grateful for his help, for his having shown up. "I never even heard the name Cavalier King Charles spaniel till I met Marjorie. In fact, I thought Cavalier meant they didn't care — like, 'Oh, so another cat got run over on Maple, well, fuck it.' " Harry gasped, and Ella clapped a hand over her mouth.

"Nicky!" Mattie cried, but she laughed too.

"Where did we get her again?" Harry asked.

"I'd always wanted a little dog," Mattie said, as they started to eat. "So I answered an ad in the newspaper. This woman had a Cavalier King Charles spaniel, but the woman was nuts. She grilled me over the phone for an hour.

"Then there was a follow-up call. I arranged to meet Marjorie. It was an awful scene. She was jailed in a crate underneath a birdcage in the woman's living room. There were feathers floating down on her head, which startled her every time they hit. But for me, it was love at first sight. She was so gentle and elegant.

"I asked the woman why she was giving her away. I couldn't believe it. The nutcase told me she had too many children and too many pets. And she couldn't give away the children.

"So I got to take the dog home. She climbed onto my chest and sprawled there like a bearskin rug. She stared at me without blinking, all the way home. It was like she was trying to communicate with me telepathically, but I wasn't enough on the ball to make the connection.

"Then your dad fell in love with Marjorie too." After dinner Nicky lay with Marjorie in the cool darkness on the floor beneath Mattie's bed, with Harry and Ella beside him, while Mattie washed the dishes and cried.

She took Ella to the pediatrician, a kindly man with fluffy silver hair named Dr. Silver, who asked Ella if she thought she could find an alternative to chewing on her wrist. She told him, to Mattie's surprise, shyly, yes, she could. And what was that alternative?

"M&M's," Ella said.

Dr. Silver wrote her a prescription for a large bag of M&M's. Mattie got it filled.

Marjorie stayed alive. It was an amazing, if gassy, miracle. The flatulence was terrible. Al said it smelled like air wafting up from bloated corpses in Civil War photographs, but Marjorie hung on.

Then during an uncharacteristically hot week in late February, she took a turn for the worse. She stopped eating almost entirely. Angela flew up to be with Mattie and the children. It was over. Mattie called the vet and asked if he would come to put Marjorie to sleep at the house. Mattie asked Isa to take care of the children. Mattie and Angela sat with the sick dog in the kitchen, an oscillating fan on the counter, and drank lemonade while they sweltered and panted, and Marjorie kept farting from under the table. Angela peered down at the dog and said, "Woo-wee, honey. That is some serious situation you've got going on down there." She fanned the air, but then gamely climbed under the table.

Ella came in and joined Marjorie and Angela, and each time Mattie peeked, Ella was gazing at Marjorie with wide, round eyes of grief, taking surreptitious bites on her sore. Then Harry came home. He stormed into the kitchen and sized up the situation, bellowed in pain, and climbed into Mattie's lap. Over the sound of the fan, Marjorie's breathing was loud and labored.

"What's the matter with Marjorie's breathing?" Harry asked. Mattie shrugged. He got under the table with Ella and Angela. Mattie went to join them. Marjorie's chest rose with a gasp that accompanied each breath.

"She's very sick, Harry. We're going to have to put her down."

Ella's wide eyes brimmed with tears. She bent her head to her wrist with a balletic grace and nibbled at the sore place.

Mattie located Harry in the bathroom, behind a locked door. "What will we do?" he bawled. He cried out in grief and pounded the door. "What can we do? I'm so afraid!"

"Please let me in, darling," Mattie pleaded.

"No — no way. If I do, you'll talk to me about God."

"I promise not to."

"I don't believe in God. I think when you die you go blank. I won't go to church anymore if Marjorie dies. I don't like anyone at church, I don't even know their names, they don't mean anything to me."

"I promise not to talk about God," Mattie repeated, and he let her in.

She sat on the floor near the toilet, Harry on the rug in front of the sink. He cried with his head buried in his arms, and shook off her attempts to touch him. When he seemed done, he looked at her, his eyes lined in red, and asked if they could have Marjorie frozen.

"Like cryogenics, where they freeze you and bring you back someday?"

"Yeah, when they find a cure. Stefan's mom told us about it."

"Well, no one knows if it works. No *real* scientists think it does. And they don't freeze dogs. It costs a fortune."

"But wouldn't you try to get the money, if it was me?"

"Honey?"

"Mommy! I don't want to die. I'm so afraid." He started crying again.

"But darling, you probably won't die for eighty years."

"I don't even want to die in eighty years."

"We're almost too sad about Marjorie to go on, aren't we?"

Harry didn't answer. Mattie handed him a box of Kleenex. He wiped his nose on his sleeve and then shredded a tissue. He shredded another. A snowdrift grew while she thought of what to do.

"What do you believe in?" she asked. "I thought you believed in Jesus."

"I do, I just believe in all the other gods too."

"Oh," Mattie said nicely. "What other gods?"

"The Greek and Roman gods."

The snowdrift of Kleenex grew higher.

The pastor had said once that when people could not imagine surviving physical death, he told them that the bulb could not conceive of the flower it would become. Mattie tried passing this along to Harry. He moaned, butting his nose against the shoulder of her T-shirt, like a horse trying to get you to give it the lump of sugar. She found this touching, until she realized he was wiping his nose on her sleeve.

146

"Eewwhh," she said.

Harry lay on the bathroom rug, and Mattie gave him a backrub. He was tight and stiff. The red faded from his face, and she rubbed his shoulders until he yawned. "I'm going to fall asleep," he said.

"Right here?"

"Uh-huh."

She stretched out on a small portion of the rug, and Harry moved closer so she could hold him. "I just really want to be frozen when I die," he whispered.

"Okay," she said. "You can be frozen."

They fell asleep on the bathroom rug. The cats sat in the doorway, watchful, appalled.

While Angela drove the weeping children over to Isa's, Al arrived at Mattie's with Katherine, whose eyes were red. She brought wildflowers from their glade, in a makeshift vase of wet napkins and tinfoil. Daniel came alone, with a loaf of bread Pauline had made for the mourners. He hugged Mattie and slid the little blue shoe into her hand. "Oh my God," she whispered. She jammed it in her pocket. She called Nicky, who began to sniffle and said he'd be there soon.

Everyone lay on the floor with Marjorie and did a laying on of hands. They turned over onto their backs to look at the underside of the table, as if they were out beneath the stars.

Kafka said that the point of life is that it

ends, and Mattie supposed that to some extent this was true. She and Angela watched Marjorie, whose eyes stared at nothing, who struggled for breath. "She's been getting ready to leave for a while," Mattie said.

They made a bed for her under the table, with a fluffy blue baby blanket. Marjorie looked again at Mattie, weak and sweet and trusting. Nicky arrived and climbed under the table with them, and Marjorie wagged her tail. Mattie and Angela sat up, and Nicky turned to Mattie and hugged her, and then Angela, their first hug in years, and they all waited for the vet.

He arrived at a little after six, with his brown bag, and joined the crowd under the table. Mattie offered the vet a glass of wine, but he declined the offer. He scratched Marjorie behind the ears. "There are going to be great cat butts in heaven to sniff," he told her in a priestly tone. Marjorie wagged her tail at the sound of his voice. Mattie and Nicky stroked her, telling her over and over, "You are a sweet girl, such a sweet girl," and everyone was teary except the vet, who looked sad and tired. Marjorie wagged her tail to the end, but without much life force, like windshield wipers on a car with a nearly dead battery. She was making a soft, muffled peeping and cooing that baby dolphins might make the first moments after they were born. The vet gave her an injection in the leg, and a few seconds later, while Mattie stroked her head, she breathed in and then out for the last time, like a sigh.

Isa insisted that she and the children be there for the burial that night. "They need to say good-bye. There will be grief, but it's going to be there anyway. It's better to see it. This way, they can remember how alive she was, but this is what happened, and they can say good-bye." Mattie knew that her mother was right.

Mattie carried Marjorie's body, still in the blanket, to the backyard, near the ranunculus, where she was to be buried. The flowers were jaunty and brawny, like their muscular name, in stained-glass colors.

Mattie had shown Nicky where to dig the hole. It was harder work than he had expected. His shovel kept hitting rocks.

The children wept and moaned when they saw Marjorie's body on the light-blue blanket. Ella threw herself into Mattie's arms, while Harry fell to his knees beside the dog and wailed piteously. It was absurd and cathartic, and Mattie could see that he was weeping for everything, all that he had lost so far, all the sad things that were still to come. Isa sent Mattie inside for a box, and when she protested, Isa snapped at her. "Oh, for Chrissakes, Mattie, of course you need a box. We always used a box." Mattie remembered that this was true, all those birds and field mice she and Al had buried in this yard so many years before, old cats, and once a litter of dead kittens, always in a shoe box. Isa had believed that children should bury the family pets, just as she insisted that Mattie and Al watch each litter of kittens and puppies be born.

Harry and Ella had buried birds before, and mice that the cats had killed. They seemed to like burying things. They knew to make a bed for Marjorie with the blanket, in the box Mattie found, and they tucked her in while Nicky dug deeper. Angela picked rocks out of the growing pile of dirt.

The light was fading. Pauline arrived and lingered on the patio away from the others. Finally the hole was big enough for the box, and the children placed Marjorie in her box inside. Nicky shoveled dirt on top, and the children pushed in dirt too, and when the box was covered, they patted the dirt down hard with their fists, as if punching down bread dough. They decorated the grave with everything they could find, a ring of rocks, flowers, wood, crayons, plastic figurines. Daniel made a cross from two twigs tied with a bit of dirty string, and Mattie went inside for a black Magic Marker so they could write Marjorie's name on the cross. That's who was there, and everyone should know. That lump in the ground was our pet, she would say, if anyone were to ask, and this was her name.

five

One rainy morning in mid-March, Ella sat at the window staring like a cat at the snakes of water that raced down the pane. Mattie stood beside her chair so that they could watch the storm together. She traced the back of Ella's ear with the tip of her nose, and listened to Harry playing out in the rain. A few boys from Harry's class were over at Stefan's today. One was handsome and blond and cherubic. This gave him enormous power and leverage. Another was doughy and tense, like an incompetent guard in the yard at San Quentin. When the sun shone through the rain, Mattie thought the storm might be nearly over, but then the sun slid back behind the scrim of clouds, and the rain kept coming down.

She was glad for the rain. After pummeling and pricking for days, the wind had stopped and the rain began to fall. March was a teaser, so springlike and soft and warm and bright, the hills lush and green and dotted with wildflowers, but as soon as your soul relaxed in the balminess, then whoosh! A horrible cold stepped forth, worse than in winter because the days had been promising something and then reneged.

"How can you do this to me?" Harry cried

one day at the biting wind.

"I can do anything I want, because I'm March," said Mattie.

Mattie was depressed, and agitated. She felt paranoid and personally betrayed. The spiky wind seemed crueler than in other months because she'd put her winter coat away during those hot days in February, and she felt silly making a fire in springtime.

She was banking on the vernal equinox, comforting herself with the belief that on that day, when the darkness ebbed and the light returned, all sorts of things would fall into place. She needed to get out more, she thought, otherwise how would she meet a man? If she met a man, she would never have to sleep with Nicky anymore. It would help her forgive Nicky, and Lee, and Alexander. One day she thought she was getting there, until she saw Harry watching his father and Alex together out on the lawn, through the window of his bedroom, and Harry looked like someone who had just discovered his new lawn turned to Swiss cheese by gophers. Mattie's heart grew harder.

Harry was having problems in school. His grades were only part of it. His homework came home wadded up, as if he had given up before he'd even started. His homework said, I hate this! He said out loud, "I hate this!" too, and he fought with Mattie. Forty minutes of homework took him two hours. Mattie called the teacher and left protest messages on the machine: "When are these children supposed to have their childhoods? My kid only weighs fifty pounds," she said in despair. Sometimes Mattie had to iron his papers before they could be handed in. It seemed to hurt him physically to write, but there was no money for a tutor.

Nicky started coming over twice a week to help with homework. He sat with Harry in the kitchen and worked on math and spelling, and she listened from the living room to Harry's endless excuses. "The teacher is sexist, she hates all the boys." He preyed on his parents' ambivalence toward so much homework. Still, they made him do it, and Mattie was amazed that Nicky kept at it. He stayed till their bedtime to snuggle with his children and read them to sleep, and one night, after a particularly rough bout with Harry, he straggled into the living room and collapsed in a chair across from Mattie.

"What do we do?" he asked her, massaging his neck.

Mattie shook her head. "I don't know. Thanks for being in it with me." Nicky shrugged. "He's starting to learn the material. I want to save him, and I want to smack him. You want a drink?"

"Yeah," he said. "Sure. Let me do the honors."

He sat down across from Mattie. She swirled her scotch like it was brandy, or dice. When she finally looked up, he was rubbing his eyes. He leaned his forehead against his hand, and appeared to fall asleep. After a while, he lifted the bottom of his faded black T-shirt and wiped his glasses clean. She caught a glimpse of his stomach, soft and brown. He set his glasses on the coffee table and looked at her. She looked back. "He's such a sweet boy," he said. His gaze was heavy-lidded and sustained. Mattie could have looked into her lap and shielded herself, but she saw something like a rueful smirk forming on his lips, and felt it on her own.

Getting back into bed with Nicky again after all that time both relieved the anxieties that it was not related to, and created new ones. She was momentarily released from her worries about Isa, and about whether or not Harry would pass second grade. He did, thanks largely to Nicky's help. On the last day of school, Harry tore through the front door shouting for Mattie, holding his report card up like the Olympic flame.

Isa had improved physically by the beginning of summer. Her face grew lightly tanned and rosy from her daily walks beside the salt marsh with Lewis, and she was steadier on her feet. She ate a healthy diet, watched the nightly news, went swimming with Mattie and the children at the community pool; but she called too often now, and then did not remember having called even an hour before. She began referring to Katherine as Kathleen or Caroline. It occurred to Mattie that this might be hostility rather than forgetfulness.

Sometimes she was fine, almost her old self. One hot afternoon, she and Mattie drove out to the woods near Samuel P. Taylor Park, and went for a short walk in the sun, beneath hills that looked like animals, big old beasts. The light was crisp and dry, casting hard shadows because there was no moisture in the air, and Isa was clear as a bell. They walked more slowly than they would have a year before, but steadily, as if they had chosen to slow down so they might enjoy the time. They talked about the old times and old movies as they walked. When they found a redwood grove, they stepped into its shade. Mattie got the canteen of water out of her knapsack, and Isa, tipping it back to take a swig, looked positively Austrian with rude good health. It was dark and moist under the redwoods, it was a cathedral.

Two days later when Mattie stopped by Isa's with groceries, she found her mother on all fours in her bedroom, trying to pick up the shadows of leaves from her rug.

The roses in Mattie's garden were in full bloom, the purple hibiscus was thriving, but many of the flowers were dead. The bulbs were long gone, and all the plants that had shot out of the earth like rockets in spring had spluttered, were dead and played out. The light at dusk was discreet.

Harry enjoyed Isa's company, their long talks about science programs they watched together on TV, her interest in his friends, his opinions. And Isa adored him, reviving in his presence. It was clear that she preferred his company to Ella's. She cuddled with Ella, and drew, and played fairies with her on the couch, but Harry was full of questions and theories and comments, while Ella remained so quiet. Besides, Isa had always preferred the company of men, especially handsome men, and Harry was growing quite handsome. His permanent teeth were in, the same huge, slightly buck ones — so big his mouth could hardly contain them — that Mattie and Al had inherited from Alfred. He too would need braces one day.

Harry's love for Isa touched Mattie deeply. A new creation had emerged from the woman Isa had been when Mattie was little, the damaged, betrayed woman who did such good works in the world: manic and wronged, trying not to sulk, because if she did, Alfred might leave. Mattie could still sense the coiled wire inside Isa, the terror and rage that tried to push their way out of her chest. Mattie had spent her childhood trying to help Isa feel good about the coils — They're so pretty! So shiny! But Harry had a knack for getting her to do things she loved, that benefited him at the same time:

bake cookies, sew clothing for the puppets he made with Popsicle sticks and pipe cleaners, tell stories about how naughty Al had been when he was a little boy.

Isa doted on Harry, and to a lesser degree, on Ella, and in the early fall, the doting turned into a fierce dotage.

Dr. Brodkey could find nothing wrong. "She's just getting old," she told Mattie.

"But so quickly," Mattie protested.

"Believe me, there's still a lot of life in the old girl."

However, when Isa got sick with a virulent stomach flu and had to spend a week in the medical center at The Sequoias, she did not rebound. Lewis spent all day every day in the chair beside her bed, reading the newspaper to her, watching whatever she liked on TV, napping in his seat when she napped. Mattie arranged nursing care for Isa when she was released to her apartment, using Isa's meager savings. It was that, or have her come stay with them, which Mattie nearly decided to do. Al talked her out of it. Isa had lost ten pounds and several inches in height over just six months. She had been as tall as Mattie; now Mattie towered over her.

Harry made drawings and clay figurines for Isa, and visited when Mattie could bring him over. One afternoon they found Isa hooked up to an IV of saline and vitamins. She looked as if she were dying, but a light went on when she saw her grandson.

That night at dinner, when he would not eat, Mattie asked Harry if he was worried about Isa, because she looked so sick and old.

He nodded. "At first I thought it was a sick other woman," he said.

"How did that make you feel?"

"Well, I felt great after I could see that it was her."

"How come you felt so great?"

"Because I got to be with *Isa*."

One day while fidgeting with the paint-can key and worrying about Isa's condition, Al had an inspiration. He and Mattie had tried, unsuccessfully, to look up Abby's and Yvonne's numbers in the West Marin phone book, but now Al wondered whether the Cove, where Neil had lived, was just far enough north past Marshall to be included in the Petaluma listings. And indeed, when he looked in the phone book, he found Abby listed.

When they called, the phone just rang and rang. Mattie began phoning obsessively, at various hours, early in the morning, late at night, but no one answered. She and Al considered driving to the Cove for the day, to look around, ask questions. Everybody had known Neil. Someone would know something that would lead to something else. He had been famous in these parts for his parties, his looks, the poets and painters he counted as friends: Allen

Ginsberg, Wendell Berry, W. S. Merwin.

But Mattie and Al had a hard time finding a day when they were both free. The children grew like weeds, Isa was holding her own, the days passed in a flash. When Mattie went to write checks she was shocked that it was October. It should have been March 23.

One night Mattie came across a photograph of Abby she'd never seen, in an album of Isa's that was jammed into a section of cookbooks on her shelf. She and Al and Katherine and the children had brought Isa a dinner of roasted chicken. Lewis, whose stomach was acting up, stopped by briefly to say hello, and to ask the children over after dinner. Al and Katherine prepared plates for everyone in the kitchen, while Isa and Mattie looked through the photo album. Mattie found it impossible to imagine her mother as the young beauty in the photographs, long and leggy, her handsome husband's arm around her shoulders in so many photos, both inevitably smoking, her children on her knees, Isa in the latest fashions, bright Asian silk blouses with butterfly clasps, Guatemalan blouses over dungarees, crisp floral blouses with capri pants. In one photo, Isa and Alfred sat on the beach in Inverness near tar-daubed pilings. An egret stood in the surf almost out of the frame, a bottle of wine rested in a hole in the sand, surrounded by pebbles and keyhole limpets as if by ice in a silver bucket. And there, a little ways away in the sand, building a sand castle with Mattie and Al, was Abby Grann.

All three of the children were topless, surrounded in the sand by constellations of shells, Abby a girl by Fra Angelico, porcelain skin and delicate features except for long wide lips, her hair streaming loose down her back, crowned by sunlight. Mattie glanced sideways at Isa, who looked stricken, and Mattie felt a rush. Maybe the answers to all her questions could be gotten the easy way, right here.

"Look at Abby," Mattie said.

"I don't want a picture of Abby in with my things!" Isa cried.

"But why not? I thought you liked Neil."

"I loathed him. All the Granns. Especially that awful Abby. Jesus."

"God, Mom. She was just a little girl."

"You don't know anything." Isa turned her head away.

"Tell me, then," Mattie said softly. The air was charged with their held breath, and Mattie felt meanness flicker inside her. It shocked her, this cold sense of pleasure in making Isa squirm. She reached for Isa's hand — Mommy, Mommy! — but by then it was too late. Isa shook her off. She peeled back the sheet of plastic that clung to the photographs, grabbed the picture of Abby, and tore it in half. Mattie protested, and Isa tore it again.

"It's my picture," Isa cried. "Mine! And I don't want it anymore." She got up and stalked to the kitchen, stopping to throw the pieces of the picture into a metal can painted with cheerful gold pears.

Mattie sat stiffly on the couch, holding something invisible in her lap, a potted plant of shame. Why couldn't you even ask your mother questions without feeling like one of the Weathermen? These photos were of people Mattie had grown up with. She and Al had smoked their first cigarettes with Abby. Abby had brought Mattie Kotex when Mattie started her first period, when she'd been trapped out at Neil's for the weekend with only their fathers. Abby had given Mattie clean underpants to put on after a shower, had thrown out the bloody pair in a paper bag.

Mattie went to the kitchen. Isa turned away. Mattie felt deeply contrite. "I'm so sorry, Mom," she wailed. Isa looked past her, and Al shot Mattie sympathetic looks.

After ten icy minutes and a glass of wine, Isa began to soften. "Would you please not foist pictures of my enemies at me?" she said to Mattie. "Neil was a playboy," Isa said, "everyone knew it. And Abby was a slut and everyone knew that too." Mattie hung her head to show her surrender and contrition. Harry and Ella lifted their faces to Isa's dark light, grimacing with the hope that she would forgive their mother. They were the children of the bad person. Isa inhaled deeply, and smiled on the exhale. She held her head high and looked back and forth between the young children as if trying to decide between two desserts. Finally she leaned sideways so that Mattie could kiss her on the cheek. She patted her daughter like the queen's naughty dog. A great passing of plates commenced, a bucket brigade of salad, chicken, and rice. The fire had been extinguished. When the children were excused from the table, they ran down the hall to find Lewis.

Harry was drawing at Lewis's table when Mattie went to retrieve the children. Ella was asleep on the couch, covered with a faded afghan. Lewis's old dog, Precious, snored beside her. His studio was clean, except for an easy chair of beige velour with stained armrests and a cushion that seemed to have had a stroke.

Mattie knew life had been strained for Lewis's family. One of his sons had done time in Leavenworth, and no one knew where one of his daughters had ended up. A niece was raising his grandchildren; his wife had died at fifty. Isa was supposed to have been some kind of solution: late love. But what a mess. Maybe this was why he kept his temple so clean. The kitchen area was filled with cleaning utensils, brooms, dustpan, mop. Even Precious looked like a duster of some sort. Clean clothes hung on hangers on the walls. There were photographs in cheap-looking frames on every available surface — his wife and parents, his wedding, him in his welder's gear from his days at Marin Ship during the war, his sons and daughters, nieces and nephews, and babies everywhere, dark little faces shining in bassinets and studio holiday props from Sears.

Mattie kissed Lewis and crossed to the table to admire the children's artwork. Ella had drawn cats in dresses and tiaras, Harry was just finishing a battle scene, with knights and swords and bleeding soldiers and dragons with pointy teeth. Mattie looked around at all the lamps, all of them on, fighting against the darkness of Lewis's failing sight. There were ornamental plates on the walls, painted with the faces of Coretta Scott King and JFK; grandchildren's handprints in clay.

"How does my mom seem to you, Lewis?" Mattie asked.

"Not so good." He looked toward his window. "She's getting so old, so quickly."

Mattie sat beside him. She searched his aged face, dark and sprayed with those tiny moles, the face of an old baby. "Her mind is going," he said. "It's muddied, and she's afraid. She's standing on a ledge that has gotten too small for her. It's breaking my heart. She walks around trying to remember what she's walking around looking for."

"We all do it, Lewis. I do it all the time."

"Well, oh my gosh, me too. But when Isa does it, she's lost." His eyes had filled with

163

tears, and he dabbed at his nose. "She gets lost and then truly worried, like she's hearing a siren in the night." Mattie felt strangely relieved that someone besides her and Al felt so sad about Isa. Lewis made her less afraid, less hard and dry, with his tears and watered words.

"Mom?" She was on the phone to Isa the next day. "It's me."

"Hi, Me. How are you?"

"Good. Dr. Brodkey just called. She said your phone has been busy, so she left a message with me to let you know you have an appointment next Tuesday. At nine-thirty. I'll pick you up at nine." This was not quite true. Mattie had approached Dr. Brodkey: Please look at my mother. Help us figure out what to do.

There was a long silence. Mattie could hear Isa's grandfather clock chime.

"Then do I get to drive again?" Isa demanded. "Answer me, Mattie. You know, you're not in charge of me."

Dr. Brodkey gave Isa a thorough exam, and another mini-mental, which she aced again. The doctor rather apologetically pronounced her healthy as a horse.

"Then can I drive again?" Isa asked.

"Your children are worried, because you may be having little strokes."

"The children are not in charge of me," Isa cried.

"Would you agree not to drive until our next appointment?"

Isa sulked coquettishly, arms crossed, but she nodded.

Mattie felt that time was playing with her; whole weeks passed like stones skipping over water. The vigor and weirdness of Halloween gave birth to November, stately and ponderous, the dramatic darkening in the days. She rested, and tried to dig a deep hole for herself, pull in her soul's cloak around her. The light of December was pinched, and it hung down, glowering and tight, and then rushed toward the winter solstice. The surface tension broke. January had a wonderful sloppiness, trees in bloom, daffodils and tulips, lush intensity. I'll tease you with the light, said the days: Chicken alert!

An early spring arrived, with skies of faded-workshirt blue. Ella would be five, amazingly. She would start kindergarten in the fall. Harry would be nine. Some days it was so beautiful outside: nature had lured the ants and the birds and the bears, blinking their eyes in the sunlight. But then the barbed wind returned, and everyone froze and huddled and crawled into bed.

Thoughts of Daniel were like a salt lick where Mattie comforted herself. He always called when she most needed a friend, called to ask her if she wanted work as a carpenter's apprentice when he had some to offer. He called to point out stories in the paper, he called with words of wisdom.

"Tell me the secret of life," she asked him one day over the phone.

He thought for a moment. "Take Ella to the park."

"And then I'll be all well?"

"Yep."

Daniel invited her to go to the movies with him and Pauline that night.

You should ditch her, Mattie wanted to say, her sad-sack, bad-mood, big-butt self. And just you and me go to the movies, to cuddle.

"That sounds great," she said. She cradled her head in her hands after she hung up the phone, and prayed. Please help me stop coveting Daniel. Please help me love Pauline. Can't you send me someone of my own? And then she heard the sound of soft footsteps padding toward the kitchen. Ella stepped in, bleary from sleep, her hair in a feathery white-blond knot on top of her head, so fair and moonlit that she might start speaking in Norwegian.

They snuggled in the kitchen. Sunshine washed in through the windows. Ella described a long dream about horses, and Mattie listened to the rills in the stream of her daughter's words, and then they went to find her glasses so she could practice reading.

Mattie and Ella stood in the garden staring at

the six-foot stretch of fence that now lay nearly flat on the ground. Everything was blooming, an absurdity of blossoms. Some were delicate and demure and Asian, others like popcorn, and there was an apricot tree with testosterone near the rotted planks of the original fence.

Mattie used to stand on the two-by-fours near the base of the fence when she was little, peeking over at the life of the street, dogs walking by as if on the way to work, children on foot or bike, cars and strangers and fire trucks. Now anyone nearby could see her standing there, and she felt as if her pants had fallen to the ground.

She always felt guilty when she began a construction project with Daniel. He was like a practice husband to her: This is what it would be like to have someone who would help you when things broke down, someone to go to the movies with, someone to whom you could hand off the plates you had just washed for a quick rinse and stacking in the dish rack. This is what it would feel like to sit at church with a partner, to go for a drive and have someone besides the children with whom to talk.

Pauline lay on the couch at home much of the time now, according to Daniel, resting her back, sleepy from a new antidepresssant. One Sunday when Mattie had stopped by to pick Daniel up for church, Pauline came into the living room in her bathrobe, sleepy and sexy and insolent, and Daniel told Mattie that he'd be staying home today. He was sorry he hadn't called and saved her the trip. Pauline said he should go anyway.

"Oh, no, I want to be with you," he said.

"Daniel, I want you to go, don't you understand?" she said sharply.

Daniel looked crushed. Pauline hung her head. Mattie felt unhappiness flowing between them like an air current, and was ashamed to find her own mood soaring.

"You should do whatever you want," Pauline told him. "Stay, if you want to. I'm going to go lie down." She turned and limped back to the bedroom.

Daniel looked blank. Mattie held her breath, desperately wanting him to come with her. "Can I still go with you?" he asked.

"Yes, of course."

He tore around getting ready, looking for his glasses, ironing a shirt. Then he grabbed his worn Bible, and they walked to the car together.

Pauline was making nice when they went to the movies together that night. This put Mattie in an extremely sour mood. She and the kids had been late picking up Daniel and Pauline, because Harry would not wear anything over his T-shirt, although the night was cold, and it was hard for Mattie to stop trying to goad him or jerk him, because she was freezing. Pauline stood up for Harry when Mattie tried to blame him for their lateness. She said, "Whether Harry wants a sweater or not is really none of your business. He's a big boy now," and Harry sighed with gratitude. Ella had dressed up in her parka with a furry hood.

Mattie wanted to grab Pauline by the throat, but she settled for two boxes of bonbons. She sat with Ella on one side, Pauline on the other. Daniel sat on the other side of Pauline. Mattie kept herself from leaning across Pauline to talk to Daniel all through the movie, and comforted herself with the knowledge that they could talk later, in the car. She tried to lose herself in the movie, about a little girl on a farm and her fierce, loving old grandmother, all earth force and hardwood and velvet. All of a sudden Mattie sensed motion, and looked around to see Pauline turning in her seat, beaming at her. Mattie smiled and went back to watching the movie, but ten minutes later, she felt more ducking and bobbing, and looked over to discover Pauline grinning at her again, in an odd combination of threatening and submissive expressions. Stop looking at me, Mattie wanted to cry — why are you looking at me! She pulled her shoulders in more closely and glared at the screen. More ducking, bobbing, and Pauline's little head up too close again, covering her mouth as if she'd made a faux pas, a tiny belch. This time Mattie refused to look back. She moved imperceptibly closer to Ella and stared at the screen while Pauline stared at her.

This went on for more than an hour, Mattie trying to hide in the magic of the movie, Pauline tapping shyly at the sides, wanting in. Mattie, trying not to be penetrated, missed much of the movie.

"She is so annoying," Mattie complained to Angela on the phone that night, after putting the children to bed.

"Oh, boy. How does Daniel react?"

"I couldn't see him. God. I am so lonely that I'm going to vomit. I'm never going to have a boyfriend. How do you find people to date? I don't even have the right underwear. It's all hopeless."

"You listen here," Angela replied. "God is about to put a guy onto your conveyor belt. He's assembling him right now, doing a complete workup on him. You're going to be doing errands, and this guy is going to emerge from the conveyor belt of the luggage bin. And you just have to lift him up like a duffel bag. And he'll be single, and available."

"Why does Daniel love her? And why was I mean to her tonight?"

"She's so invasive. It's like some simultaneous need for revenge and connection, like Isa getting close enough to stick the knife in. Then saying, 'Look how close we are now!' "

Outside, the day was balmy and crisp and sparkling, and inside, church seemed warm and muscular as a heart. During the first hymn, she felt the weight of the choir lift her, carry her. She was sitting, as usual, between Lewis and Daniel. Lewis looked older now, but so much soul shone through his tiredness it didn't really matter. He was as excited as a birthday boy because the pastor had asked him to give the children's sermon on the Gloria Patri. Lewis was using a walker today, and he wore a black suit and blue shirt for the occasion. After confession, the pastor held his hand out toward him, as if inviting him to dance. Lewis made his way to the front, smacking his walker on the floor with every step. He stood before the congregation with his brown face held upward, as if being inspected by a mother with a washcloth.

He appeared to have fallen asleep standing. The children fidgeted in their chairs. After a moment, he addressed the semicircle of children. "Glory!"

They looked at him nervously.

"Say that with me: Glory! That's what we're here to say."

"Glory," the children whispered.

He began to sing the Gloria Patri, so slowly that Mattie held her breath. Each word echoed back into itself. The sound pierced her, got into her deepest places with oxygen, without the plink of piano or the distraction of the correct notes. Lewis sang loud and off-key. You could hear the roughness, and in the silence between notes you could hear a baby snoring in his mother's arms. Lewis quavered on, and you could hear the elegance of dusty endings, an old man singing near a snoring baby boy.

Mattie had high hopes for the vernal equinox, and the new fence. The equinox was going to bring a man, and the fence would keep Nicky out.

One Friday, she and Daniel walked along the planks of the fence to where the rot stopped, then back to where the latch would be placed once there was healthy wood to attach it to; from where the fence had to end, to where it could begin, so they would know how many planks to buy. Daniel came over before dinner and dug the first hole, a foot deep, and then poured Quikrete on a board. Harry held the hose on it while Daniel stirred everything with a shovel. Then Harry held the post in place while Daniel poured in the Quikrete. They held the post while it set. They slapped five. Harry did a chicken dance of joy.

The next morning she and Daniel and Harry tore down the part of the fence that was going to be replaced. This immediately improved things — now there was air and light and view and space, instead of just collapse. When the debris was cleared away, the area to be framed became apparent. They put in three more posts, and leveled them carefully.

Daniel showed Harry and Ella how to make sure the wood was straight, when the bubble rose to the center of the level. "Now that we know these posts are level and true, everything can be measured from them. Once you know where true is, it defines everything else that has to happen."

He nailed in braces, one near the top of the posts, one near the bottom, to hold the two-by-fours they put in next. Then they hammered in the planks. Daniel hammered in the first two, and set Harry up with a hammer at the third. He arranged planks for Harry to nail in. He set Ella up at the first plank, so she could practice hammering. Daniel nailed in planks with a few manly strokes, while Mattie nailed with a girly rat-a-tat woodpecker style. Harry nailed angrily, Ella as if she were a holistic nurse and the fence needed a gentle energy treatment with her hammer. When they ran out of wood, they looked through the planks from the old fence. The salvageable ones filled the remaining space exactly.

After lunch, Daniel got out his power tools and put in a latch. He worked with such humility. Right after Mattie had moved into the house, she asked Nicky to come over one afternoon to shorten the legs on her bedside table. He swaggered in under his heavy belt of tools, all but tipping his hat, and flipped the little table over like a heifer he was about to brand.

Daniel's work made a great fence, solid and true, with hilarious charm.

"If we had had to make a perfect fence,"

Daniel said, "we would not have had to start with what we had on our hands, which was part of a fence to build on and not much money. But that's what we did have to work with."

"Today we arrested entropy," she told Nicky when he happened to call that night. "We pushed it back fifteen feet."

"Can I come see it?" he asked, and she tried to say no but after a moment said okay. She wanted to get laid, but she also wanted to lie in bed afterward and talk, about nothing in particular. He would hold her close, and he always made her laugh. The moon shone on the new wood, as they stood together admiring the fence she had helped build, to keep him out.

She kept praying for a man of her own. Some nights she lay in bed and imagined gazing into Daniel's eyes. One night she even made out with the back of her hand, like a teenager. She remembered lines she loved from a T. S. Eliot poem: "I said to my soul, be still, and wait without hope, / For hope would be hope for the wrong thing." But still, she hoped. Sometimes when the phone rang she thought, Oh, maybe that's him, a man the universe has selected, calling to introduce himself. But it was usually Isa, forgetting she had just called a few moments before.

Mattie did not want to be the parent to her

parent, but who'd asked? You just did it, like you did the dishes all those years, because the dishes needed doing. She tried to bear witness to her mother's decline as lovingly as she could. Some days went better than others.

Sometimes she could keep her heart open even when Isa was being mean and bossy. Other times she imagined running her mother down in the parking lot. When she felt like this, but acted humanely, it seemed to repair something inside herself. It gave her a sense of how she might have felt if she hadn't had Isa for a mother. It was not facing what life dealt that made you crazy, but rather trying to set life straight where it was unstraightenable.

Isa came over one morning to watch the children while Mattie did errands. When Mattie returned, she found that Isa had apparently gone snooping in her desk. Isa held Neil's letters up, like a reprimand. "Is that what you wanted?"

Mattie put her groceries away, turned from her mother. "I just want to know more about my dad."

Isa sneered. "This is about Neil, not your father."

"I just want to know the truth."

Isa's face was grim and cloudy. "Oh, you want a little truth?" she asked malevolently. Mattie wanted to run and hide in her bedroom, as she used to, when Isa looked at Alfred in that way, breathing hard like a bull. "Here's a nice Neil story, Mattie. One year he taught at Squaw Valley at the writing conference, and he invited us along. Abby was with him. Neil brought her up to the mountains to get her away from bad influences, right? But he was the worst influence for miles. What a joke! He stood with your father and me on a balcony overlooking a barbecue, pointing to the women and girls he'd slept with so far that week. 'I got her,' he'd say. Then point to another. 'And her. I may get her tonight.' Your dad laughed, by the way."

Mattie could not take her eyes off her mother, her sudden strength, her passion. "God, Mom," she managed finally. "That's pretty bad."

"Want more truth? I can give you more. That awful Yvonne Lang, I loathed that woman. Why Neil ditched his first wife for that cow, I'll never know. Now, Nancy was a real lady. She went to *Smith*. I don't even think Yvonne went to junior college. She's why Abby ran away."

"Why?" Mattie's voice broke like a little girl's. She remembered Yvonne as the only adult in their circle who paid any attention to the children. "She was always kind to us kids."

"She let herself go. All that ridiculous ethnic jewelry. She looked like a medicine man." Isa moved forward in her chair as if she was about to stand but instead kept falling forward until she slid out of her chair, unconscious, onto the floor. Mattie ran to her side.

Isa awoke right away, and looked into Mattie's frightened eyes. Mattie fussed, but Isa shushed her. "Just help me up, and give me a hand to my bed."

"You're at my house, Mom," Mattie reminded her. Isa lay on the floor with her daughter crouched beside her, and looked at the floor as if she were an astronaut, and the air above the blue linoleum were outer space, rolling out in every direction as far as you could see.

The doctor told Isa that she was fine, it had just been a little spell, but she called Mattie later to say it was almost definitely a small stroke. She didn't know what to try next. As it was, she ordered more tests, new medicine, but Isa had more episodes.

It was like watching her play Red Light, Green Light, moving forward until made to freeze for an instant. Each time she started again, there was less of her working. Her steps were more tentative. Gone was the stride of the bossy woman. Now as often as not she wanted to hold on to Mattie's arm, and she moved much more slowly. One day she might seem her old self, the next day a version ten years older. The complaints never ceased, and the new theme was that Mattie and Al came to her house only to take her on errands; she never got to go anywhere nice with them. If they did something fun, they did it with each other. She was right to some extent: what made most outings fun was that Isa wasn't there. So on the spur of the moment one Saturday, they decided to take her along with the kids to the beach.

Al had shown up at Mattie's early that morning and announced that today was the day. They were going out to find Abby. Mattie resisted. "We'll do it another day. I promised Mom I'd take her somewhere nice."

"We'll take her to the beach at the Cove instead," Al insisted. "She can play with the kids. We'll be close by. She doesn't need to know what we're up to. One of us can go into town to look for Abby. The other can stay behind and babysit Mom."

The fog burned away before their eyes. Isa and the children began a secret project at the north end of the beach. Mattie and Al stood out of earshot. They walked along past heaps of seaweed deposited by the tide like pieces of wet and tangled fabric, fabulous after the rain, so many colors and textures that something inside Mattie's soul wanted to sort them out, at least the lovely cream- and rose-colored ones, hang them up to dry, or lay them neatly in piles — let someone else deal with the dark, oily greens.

She had been surprised that morning to find the blue shoe still in the pocket of the jeans she was wearing when they built the fence, and she had been rubbing it ever since. It fit so perfectly in her fingers; she felt for the slight rise of the laces. They could still see Isa and the children near a great rock, building a house of twigs and stones and seaweed.

Mattie was the first to notice what looked like a piece of driftwood in the surf ten feet from the shore, a blob caught in the random violence of the waves. Then a head, a bird's head, lifted out of the water and was gone, lost, submerged. The bird's wing rose a moment later, flapping.

"Look," she said to Al. They stopped, and Al made a strangled cry, as if there were a person in the waters, but suddenly the bird was gone again. Nearby, sandpipers, gulls, and murres scrabbled and pecked for food in the sand. In the surf, the wing rose like the arm of a swimmer on his last few breaths, rose again, fell, and the bird was pushed closer to shore.

"Should we try to save it?" Al asked.

Mattie held her palms up. "I think we should sit down and be still."

Eventually the bird washed onto the sand and the waves poured over its broken wings, marbled brown and gray and white. It was barely able to lift its head, sloe eyes full of exhaustion. It was dying, this was clear. All of its tail feathers were gone; it was a raggedy garbage bird whose body you'd find in the seaweed. The waves came back for it, washed it back into the surf.

"We have to try and save it," Al said, now moving toward the bird.

"What, and take it to UC Med? See if they can put something back together, with enough pinions and thread?"

The bird was tossed with terrible force on the waves. "I can't watch," Al said, but he did. Mattie felt for the blue shoe in her pocket. She was sure of only one thing: The ocean smelled familiar to this bird; the ocean, the sand, and the sky were its home. She and Al would smell as comforting as wolves.

"Why shouldn't we do something?" Al asked.

"Because there's no fixing and there's no saving, Al. There's helping sometimes, but not this bird."

Mattie looked out toward the horizon. The bird thrashed in the foam and spray near the shore. It flailed and flapped and made it to the shore like a broken toy, and then began to flop its way toward a heap of seaweed and bulbs.

Al watched, fidgeting, trying to wash something painful off his hands. "I don't think either of us should go into town. This was a bad omen. I have a bad feeling about the whole thing."

Mattie watched the waves. "What's your bad feeling, Al?"

"My bad feeling is, maybe Daddy was involved with Abby somehow." He pulled at his nose like an old man. "I saw them on the beach here once. My friends and I had come out to drop acid, and sleep on the beach during a minus tide. We were hiking through the dune grass, and I saw Daddy sitting on a blanket with Abby."

"Are you sure it was them? Why haven't you ever told me?"

"Because it was so fucking weird. And I'm positive it was Abby and Daddy. Her hair was so distinctive."

"How old do you think she was?"

"Fourteen or fifteen."

"You should have told me that earlier, big brother."

"They were passing a bottle of wine back and forth."

"Did they kiss or anything? Or see you?"

Al shook his head. "They were sitting there. Drinking straight from a bottle. Daddy and a fourteen-year-old girl. I mean, what is wrong with this picture?"

Isa and the children were screaming for Mattie and Al to walk faster. They had constructed a house made mostly of stones, balanced one on top of another, a big flat rock on the boulder, a smaller one on top of that, nestly and balanced, lumpy and delicate all at once, solid and also full of motion, surrounded by a fence of twigs stuck in sand.

"That is so amazing," said Mattie, noticing how solid it looked. One little bump, though, and it would all tumble over.

She volunteered to drive into town to pick up lunch at the superette. The man at the butcher counter squinted at her.

"Mattie Ryder?" She looked more closely at the handsome man with the resonant voice.

"Yes," she said. "Do I know you?"

"Eighth grade, Del Mar School. William Allen."

"No way." But she could see that this was in fact Billy Allen, former classmate, a hoodlum in the Summer of Love. He'd been so short, the smallest boy in the class. But now he stood about six feet, and he was rumpled, nice-looking, with thick brown hair and glasses. She managed a half-smile and shook her head. Interest fluttered through her. Was this him?

"What are you doing here?" she asked.

"My old man owns this store, remember? That's him over there," and he jutted his chin toward the older man behind the register. "I saw you once, years ago. But I was too shy to say hello."

"Too shy to talk to me?" Mattie asked.

"You were with your husband and your boy."

"I have two kids now. And I'm divorced."

"So am I. Well, what kind of sandwiches do you want?" William was all business now, waving his hand over the lunch meats and cheese.

He had nice grayish eyes behind the glasses, and he watched her even as he spread mayonnaise and mustard on ten slices of bread.

"Let me ask you something," she said, partly just to keep a conversation going. "I grew up with Abby Grann. Her dad and mine were best friends. I was sort of hoping to run into her one of these days. I have something of her dad's I thought she might like to have."

William smiled. "Abby Grann. She lived out here until a few years ago. My dad always had a soft spot for her. She knew to come here when she was hard up. Hey, Pop." The older man did not look up from his newspaper. "Dad. Get your old carcass over here." He folded his paper and came over. "What ever happened to Abby Grann?"

"Who's asking?" He extended his hand.

Mattie shook it. "Mattie Ryder. William and I were in school together. I grew up with Abby. I've got something of hers to return."

"Well, in that case — Actually, I have no idea. But Noah still lives in the same old house, out past Marshall."

"Who's Noah?" Mattie asked.

"Her kid. He's the librarian here."

"How could she have a kid who's old enough to be a librarian?"

"She had him when she was young, in her teens."

Mattie's heart was pounding so hard she stopped flirting with William. "When is the library open?"

"Now, if you hurry. On Saturdays, ten till one."

She sat in the car trying to decide what to do. The children had to be really hungry by now.

She started the car and drove too fast through town, past the old depot for the North Pacific train, a curio shop, a diner, a boatyard, more cabins, a pasture full of cows, and then she saw the old library, squat, white, falling into disrepair, paint flaking, but with a new sign out front. Mattie looked at her watch. It was nearly one. The small parking lot was empty except for a white truck. She pulled into a space next to it, turned off the engine, and sat still. She rubbed the blue shoe in her pocket and looked out at the foggy day. You couldn't see much beyond the library; fog let you see only what it wanted you to see. After a while, the door of the building swung open, and a young man stepped out. He was a dead ringer for Neil Grann: tall, with thick chestnut-brown hair, glasses, and a broad, flat nose. In his hands was a book, which he read as he walked, held open on his palms like a hymnal.

six

William called the next night. Al was over, helping Mattie put the kids to bed, so she wrote down his number and promised to call later. After Al left, the house was quiet enough to call back, but before she did, she stretched out on the couch and held the cordless phone in her clasped hand. She closed her eyes to pray. Look, she said. I think You're aware that dating is not one of my strong suits. So please: Save me from the disaster of my own thinking.

She and William talked for half an hour. He was quite gregarious. Okay, she thought after she hung up, maybe he's not funny, like I was hoping, but he laughs when I'm funny. We can give him a partial credit there. Who'd have thought that little Billy Allen, in those pegged black jeans, who smoked at eleven and barely passed eighth grade, would grow to be a man so fluent in culture, in music and books, in politics.

They went out two nights later. They arranged to meet at her favorite restaurant. Things were made bittersweet by the fact that for the first time Isa wouldn't be able to babysit. No matter how well Isa appeared some days, Mattie felt that she could not be left alone with the children, not at Mattie's home, not at her own. Al and Katherine were staying with the kids.

William looked wonderful in the soft light of the Royal Thai. They shook hands and she looked at her feet. She wore her hair up, and as much makeup as she could without appearing to be wearing any. They ordered beers, and in the course of the meal two more each; she used hers to wash down the spicy Chilean sea bass. William was easy to talk to, was recently divorced, had never had children, was doing well financially. He gave her a quick teenage kiss on the lips when they said good-bye on the street.

In bed that night, she had a talk with herself. Let's go slow, let's keep this in the soda-shop stage for a while.

He called the next morning. "Can we have coffee today?"

"Sure," she said. Then she lied and said that she had been headed to Samuel P. Taylor Park — there was a redwood tree she liked to sit inside. Maybe they could meet for coffee there. Even as she spoke the words, she knew it was too intimate a setting for a second date. Oh well, she shrugged cheerfully.

She wore her clean hair loose, fanned out between her shoulders, over a long-sleeved black T-shirt with a scooped neckline. She had stuffed the blue shoe in her jeans pocket.

April was fragrant and full of whirling blossoms, and the clouds, though dark, were shot through with light, constantly moving and re-

186

arranging themselves — God the great scribble artist in the sky.

William brought lattes from the market in Lagunitas, and she led the way to the great family-circle redwood. Sunlight wafted in through a long oval slit in the wood, and the dust motes and tiny insects sparkled. She and William sat near each other with their backs against the tree, not touching, drinking their coffee. They were shyer here than they'd been at the restaurant. Mattie nervously touched the hollows and crevices of the tree like a blind person. William asked such good questions: What were the kids like? Ella was quiet and mellow and sweet, Harry took things more seriously. Who was Mattie's best friend? Well, she had two: Angela, who'd moved away, and Daniel, with whom she worked sometimes. How did she get along with her ex-husband? Oh, she said, pretty well.

She felt that she was hiding — but also that she'd been found. Spider webs hung from the bark like lace. He asked how her mother was doing, and she was afraid to say that her mother was spiraling downward, so she lied. "Slowing down a little. A little forgetful." "What about your father?" she asked. "Ned's great," William said. "He's still got all his wits about him. Working too hard, though." When sunlight hit the charred parts of the tree, they turned green, like the feathers of a grackle, iridescent. She and William kissed for a bit longer this time when they parted.

They slept together the next Friday at Mattie's house. The children had gone to Nicky's, and William arrived for dinner — roast chicken and asparagus, with wine, and then cupcakes that Harry had helped her make that afternoon while Ella slept. They ate and drank, resisting the pull as long as they could before tearing to the bedroom to throw off their clothes. He put his glasses on the bedside table, and took off his watch while she took off hers.

They lay facing each other, shyly at first. But he was a wonderful kisser, and they slowly began to investigate each other in the dark. He sculpted her body with his large warm hands and she opened her legs. He felt her delicately, as if he had lost something small and fragile that he wanted to find but didn't want to break when he did. The tension, the coiling inside her, was exquisite.

Afterward they lay entangled, and she put her face against his soft, furry chest. They talked quietly in the dark for a long time, drifted off, woke to make love again. It was all so lovely, but when she gave his head a gentle nudge when he began to kiss her belly button, he seemed to resist, and when he finally went down, it was just for a moment.

In the morning, when they made love again, he did not go down on her at all.

"It was wonderful, delicious," she told Angela after he had left. "I really like this guy.

Everything about him is terrific but — well. He's not heavily into giving head. Nicky loved it. Maybe I'm just spoiled."

"No you're not. You like what you like. And I tell you, it would be a real deal-breaker for me."

Mattie wondered: If you do the right thing for all the wrong reasons, does it count? If you stop sinning because something better has come along, does this reflect well on you in God's favor? If you finally stop sleeping with your ex-husband, who has a baby with his new ten-year-old wife, because someone cool and available has come along, do you get a partial credit?

She started talking to William on the phone twice a day, making a plan for the following weekend. Two days after they first slept together, he called from San Rafael to say that he was passing through on his way back home and wondered if he could stop by and say hello, and she said, "Yeah, why don't you stay for dinner?" and he said, "No, I just want to come by and flirt with you for a while."

He came by and they had a glass of red wine in the garden. Ella clung to Mattie like a drowning cat all through William's visit. But Harry seemed intrigued, asking William to play catch, and then signaled his approval by giving him a tour of his room. William stayed for dinner. He was so easy to be with, and looked at Mattie often with appreciation. She felt pretty again. It had been a while. The kids would not go to sleep. Mattie tucked them in at nine but they needed water, they needed to pee, and to talk, and by the time she got them to sleep, William had to leave because he was getting up at dawn to go fishing. She hated saying good-bye. She got out Nicky's movies.

It was hard to break the news to Daniel that she'd begun sleeping with William. She felt as if she were being unfaithful to him. Finally one day when he was over she managed to blurt it out. Daniel was putting up a white lattice wall between her house and the neighbor's. She was going to grow purple potato vines on it, partly as a privacy screen, partly for the beauty of a lavender curtain instead of ugly brown siding. Birds sang sweet liquid notes. From the far end of the yard she could hear Harry at Stefan's. They were building something in the backyard with two other neighborhood boys, Evan and Chris. Ella was at the park with a chattery new girlfriend from preschool named Pearl.

"So you know William, the guy I ran into at the Cove that day, when I saw Abby's son?" Mattie said haltingly. Daniel nodded. "He called, and we've gone out a couple of times, for coffee. I kind of like him."

Daniel, shoveling concrete into a posthole, grunted noncommittally. "Really." His face showed only the vaguest interest.

She glanced idly around. Tree swallows,

blue-black on top and white underneath, flew in and out of an abandoned woodpecker's hole in the cypress. She looked back at Daniel. His eyes were triangles, like a concerned clown's.

"What's the matter?"

He shrugged. "Have you slept with him yet?"

"Yeah."

Daniel plunged a dagger into his chest. "Oh, God," he exclaimed. Then he laughed at himself. "It's so scary that you like someone," he admitted. "We haven't had to share you — me, Al, and your kids."

Daniel let go of the post. It held. He pushed on it lightly and it didn't move. He threw his hands up. "So, fine! Go off with this corduroy guy." They sat on the ground to watch the swallows. He made the face of a furious child.

Her children were growing up fast. Ella would be dating soon. In the meantime, she made quiet art: people of clay; villages in the dirt outside, with twigs and pebbles for walls and bits of broken glass for tiled walkways; a small bone turned into a vase, upright in the dirt and holding a daisy.

Harry played loud inside; he got out his army men and drafted them into terrible battles. Sometimes all the soldiers were killed at once, pitched against the wall, kicked to every corner of his room. When he grew bored, he brought in bowls, which he set up at one end of his room and flipped playing cards into from the other end. His room was a disaster, army men and cards everywhere. He roughhoused with the cats and made them cry, squishing them like whoopee cushions, and Mattie yelled at him, afraid for everyone, the cats, Harry, herself.

And yet, one afternoon while she napped on the couch with Ella and the cats, she heard Harry come into the room and walk over to the couch, and felt him pull the covers up and tuck them in around her.

Mattie noticed how many secrets she kept from William, so that he wouldn't see her as someone with a lot of problems. She wanted him to see her as someone with just a few pieces of colorful carry-on luggage, instead of multiple body bags requiring special cargo fees and handling. What if he found out she'd been sleeping with Nicky until he'd come along? What if he found out about her father, drinking with Abby on the beach? What if he found out that her mother's mind was dissolving, and that she could no longer take care of herself?

"This is home for me, Angela," Mattie said on the phone. "I've held my breath my whole life, waiting for the other shoe to drop."

There was a silence. "God only has one shoe," Angela told her.

She missed Angela terribly, and called every other day. And she bitterly missed Marjorie.

She'd always felt safer with a dog, as if an armed intruder would back away upon seeing a panicky Cavalier King Charles spaniel. She heard noises in the night, in the garage, and when she poked her head into the garage, she imagined bony hands grasping her wrist. But when William called late each night, it quieted her. She was able to fall asleep more easily after their conversations. Angela offered the relationship her blessing over the phone, although Mattie believed that her approval was based almost entirely on William's not being Nicky. When she accused her of this, Angela said, "Yeah, well, but that's a lot."

It was one of those long golden May evenings warm enough to sit outside for a few glasses of wine, the light lasting longer now. The night did not close in on you. A soft breeze wafted through the garden, and they sipped a good California red, courtesy of William's father, and got a bit drunk. Mattie nearly told William about Isa, and Abby, and Noah, her tongue was so loose. But the night seemed too lovely for that kind of talk. She reminded herself not to sabotage the moment. She could see movement in the air all around her, could see that the wind had breath in it, a ripple, a warm exhalation. This month brought the sense of a light scarf being blown about, on the muscle of the wind. The scarf was long and loose and floating, and the light shone through it and it had its own color, and if you wrapped it and draped it just right around your neck, it could keep you warm.

They lay on top of the sheets in their underpants and T-shirts, kissing. Mattie felt his warm, sweet pony's breath on her and smelled his clean body. She felt like a teenager in love, radiating shyness and lust, and told herself not to expect too much, that expectations were premeditated resentments. But after ten minutes of the most wonderful kissing, he started licking her neck, and her breasts, and then her belly button, and she opened her legs for him to go on with his grazing. He moved slowly downward for a nice kiss, and she tried to hold his head down like a person in the movies who is drowning someone, but then he moved up and in a few moments slid inside her.

After they made love, she made grilled cheese sandwiches with sliced tomatoes. They drank wine and ate their sandwiches in bed. It was all fine, she insisted to herself. Sleeping together was heaven — to spoon, and sleep, and watch him sleep.

It felt so natural, so quickly, to put on her robe while he put on his boxers and T-shirt, and go to the kitchen together. One morning when she made coffee, she noticed that there were six messages on the answering machine. She hit the Play button.

"Al!" her mother brayed. "Al! Oh, for

Chrissakes, pick up."

"Why would your mother call Al here?"

"I guess she got confused and dialed the wrong number," said Mattie, putting ground coffee into the filter.

The second message began. "Al! For Chrissakes!" Isa shouted. "Jesus Christ on a crutch."

The third message delivered the sounds of Isa sobbing. "Mattie! Pick up. For Chrissakes! Jesus! Why won't anyone talk to me?"

William looked over. "Your mother seems a bit tense."

Mattie shrugged.

"Shouldn't you call her?"

"Oh, she's fine," Mattie said, a bit tense now herself.

Next up was Daniel, who'd left a message about how lonely he was feeling because Pauline was staying in the city overnight. He said he was thinking of building himself a balcony so he could throw himself off. Could she help him work on it today? Then Nicky had called to say they had forgotten Ella's bike helmet and so he'd be over in a minute, because they were going for a bike ride in Sausalito.

"Oh, no," Mattie groaned, feeling very rumpled and sticky and fragrant, like a bouquet of anchovies, while William ambled about in his boxers. "We've got to get dressed," she said. "Nicky's on his way over."

Right then the doorbell rang. They walked

quickly to the bedroom and put on some clothes. Mattie pulled her hair back in a rubber band, but no matter how she smoothed her face and tucked away errant hair, she looked moist and disheveled. "Just a minute!" she shouted, and William sprinted to the living room to plop down in a chair.

He picked up a copy of Harry's *Ranger Rick* and thumbed through it with a look of enormous concentration. Mattie opened the door. There was Nicky, holding her marvelous daughter, who was in glasses and floral overalls. He put Ella down, and she threw her arms around her mother's waist and pressed her face against Mattie's crotch, sniffing like a dog.

Mattie bent to kiss Ella. She turned slowly to look at William.

"Hi, Ella," he said. She looked back at him, puzzled, as if she could hear his voice but not see him yet. Nicky pretended not to be surprised, as William got up.

"This is William," Mattie said. "William? This is Nick."

William walked over as if he were about to be sworn in.

Soon they were spending every weekend together, sometimes at her house, sometimes at his. One Saturday when she was going out to visit him, Al asked over the phone if he could come along.

"Can't I go alone?" she asked. "I've waited so long for a romance."

"Nope. Mom said you *have* to take me with you."

William looked wonderful that day at the café in Point Reyes where they'd arranged to meet. A white T-shirt peeked above the top button of his denim shirt. She liked the tufts of gray at his temple, his wire-rimmed glasses. She liked his shy smile.

He and Al shook hands and stepped back to size each other up, visions from the past. "You look good," said Al. "It's great to see you."

"You too, Al. Can I drive?" William asked. "I want to take you the back way."

He drove along the old two-lane between Inverness and the beach at Drakes Bay. Al rode in the back, the chaperone. As they drove along, the scent of wildflowers and cows and salt from the ocean blew in.

Al tapped William on the shoulder. "Can we go by the Cove library later on, to say hello to Noah?"

"What is it with you guys and Noah?" William asked.

"Our dads were close," said Al defensively. "We grew up playing with Abby."

"Your dad was close to Neil? People say Neil was Noah's father."

"Oh, please," said Mattie. "That's ridiculous. That's like, small-town Peyton Place bullshit."

"People in town were never entirely convinced that he died a natural death. Or even, in Neil's case, a semi-natural death. There was some evidence that he OD'ed on medicine his doctor actually had prescribed for anxiety, to lower his blood pressure."

William shrugged. Mattie resisted the impulse to turn and gape at Al. All of a sudden William jammed on the brakes.

"Jesus," he said. "Did you see that?" He backed up, pulled off to the side of the road, and stopped the car, then reached for binoculars in his glove compartment. They got out and trooped to where the dirt road met the hillside, and sat down. William studied something in the hills below, a treeless green like Scotland, with a gray-flannel ocean reaching out to the horizon beyond.

When Mattie looked down, all she saw was a big pale rock. Then the rock moved. William handed her the binoculars, and through them she could see a tule elk, with broad antlers. She gasped and handed the binoculars to Al, who watched in silence. After a while, they noticed another, a rock that got to its feet, and then another, and another, and at some point they counted twelve.

They sat there immersed in the never-ending freight-train sound of waves below, and the birdsong, loud and varied as in a rainforest. Mattie looked from Al to William, savoring the moment. Elk moved slowly through the grass, and out of sight behind a hill below, making a crunching murmur as they walked away.

"I'd like to see a black bear," Al whispered. "I'd like to see some real nature now." Mattie laughed quietly.

"People look down and think they're just rocks," William said.

Al peered through the binoculars, smiling in the most menacing way. "But the crocodile spots them," he said. Mattie cracked up.

While they drove back to Point Reyes, William told them what he knew about Noah. Abby had disappeared after her father died. Yvonne Lang took care of Noah for a while, in an old house she'd bought for very little, just past Marshall. Then he went to live with some friends in Tomales, a boy he went to school with and the kid's parents. Abby tried to visit as much as she could, people said, but she was a mess. Maybe it was better in the long run that she was gone so much. People in the town filled in for her. Noah went to Sonoma State to study library science on a partial scholarship, the bulk of his tuition paid by private donations from people in town. Later he moved back into town, and lived in the house Yvonne had bought.

"But where did Yvonne live, then? What happened to her?"

"She had a heart attack a while ago," William said. "I haven't seen her in years."

Lewis was the one who let the cat out of the

bag, one night at Isa's. "I heard you have a new man in your life," he said.

"What!" cried Isa, sidling over. "You have a man in your life? Why don't I know about this?"

"Oh, I'm sorry!" Lewis said, realizing his mistake.

"It's brand-new. That's why I haven't told you. The only people I've told are Al and Daniel. I didn't want to jinx it. Did Daniel tell you?" she asked Lewis. He nodded miserably.

Isa looked confused and scared, pretending to be happy at the news, as if Mattie had announced a frightening diagnosis with, however, the likelihood of a full recovery. "Who is it?"

"Do you remember William Allen, who I went to junior high with?"

"No, no . . . William Allen." Isa smirked. "Not Billy Allen?"

Mattie sighed. "Yes. He used to be Billy, and now he's William."

"The little hoodlum in the black jeans?" Isa drew back.

"Oh, Mom. Don't do this to me. He's not a little guy anymore, and what if he was? And he doesn't wear tight jeans anymore, but what if he did?"

"But his father was in the Mafia."

"Oh, Mom," said Al. "For Christ's sake. His father's a grocer."

"He went to prison. Maybe he's a Mafia grocer now."

Mattie turned slowly to Al. "Can you do something with her?"

"Mom," said Al, putting his hands on Isa's shoulders as if to keep her from bouncing up and down. "Stop. You've gotten him mixed up with somebody else. Trust me. Ned has owned that grocery store forever."

"Fine. Whatever you say, Mattie. Where did you meet him again? What's it been, thirty years?"

"I ran into him at the Cove that day when we were there with you and the kids. At his dad's superette, when I went to get sandwiches. Believe me, it does not look like a gangland operation."

"Why didn't you say anything at the time?"

"I don't know," Mattie said. "There was so much going on."

Al drew a finger across his throat to get Mattie to stop talking.

"What do you mean, so much was going on? Waves? Waves were going on? The kids and I built a structure in the sand was going on? Hungry for lunch was going on?"

"God," Mattie yelped. "Can you pretend to be happy about this, for a second?"

"I am happy." Isa rolled her eyes. "Shrimpy little Billy Allen, with his Mafia father. Whoopee! Okay, I'm sorry, I'm out of line. But you have to admit, he wasn't a particularly memorable child."

"Mom!" Al shouted.

"He wasn't! He was — what's the word, Al? — sort of nondescript."

"Well, he's descript now," Al replied. "He's heavily descript."

Isa tried to looked pleased, clasping her hands together as if in prayer, but Mattie retreated from the kitchen. She walked down the hall into her mother's bathroom and sat on the toilet. Isa had been badgering Mattie for a year about whether she'd met anyone nice, and now she reacted like she was going out with John Gotti. Mattie dug her fingernails into her hairline, reveling in the pain.

"I'm sorry, my darling, my girl," Isa crooned. She was standing outside the bathroom door, wringing her hands, when Mattie finally emerged. "I'm a bad person. I don't deserve a wonderful daughter like you." Mattie said nothing. "Everyone should have a Mattie," Isa said. Mattie glared. Pictures of the family peered at them from both sides of the hallway, Alfred with his arms around Isa, in formal wear, in swim clothes; Alfred with his kids in his lap, with his arms around their shoulders; Alfred alone, smiling, smoking, holding a can of beer. Mattie heard the crisp rip of triangles appearing in his beer cans, up on Mount Tam, out at Neil's, she heard him opening a can of Coke for her; she heard her mother saying her name. She desperately wanted a Coke right now, opened with a church key, opened by her father. A can or a little-bitty bottle. Everything tasted better when your father was alive.

"Let's go back to the table," Mattie said gently. Isa's shoulders looked like those of a skinny child inside her bright paisley shirt. When they sat down, she reached for Mattie's hand. At first Mattie held it too tightly, and with disgust, the way you might hold the hand of someone else's monkey. But then she sighed, looked menacingly at her mother, raised her hand to her mouth, and kissed it.

It was all her fault when Mattie and William had their first unpleasant incident. He had called, trying to tempt her out to Olema with the promise of rock cod he'd caught off a boat at dawn that morning. She'd asked if he'd come to church with her and Daniel instead, then cook them rock cod for lunch. He seemed flustered. He wanted to meet Daniel, he said, but he really didn't like organized religion. Mattie promised there would be nothing too organized at her church, but still he resisted. She pushed a little harder, and he gave in.

When he arrived an hour later in a suit jacket and tie, she could tell that he was miserable. There was only cool distance. She apologized at once and asked if he wanted to hang out and watch TV instead of going along, but he pretended he hadn't heard her.

"It doesn't make sense for you to come if you'll be unhappy," she said.

"I already told you I didn't want to go, Mattie. Several times, in fact. But you insisted. So here I am, okay?"

Daniel was waiting for them on his porch. They walked up to meet him. He had beaded tubes on some of his dreadlocks now. He smiled rather shyly at William. They shook hands warmly, like people who had already spoken a number of times by phone. There were circles under Daniel's eyes, and when the phone inside rang, he excused himself and raced in.

"Hello?" they heard him say. "When are you coming home? Why are you still there?" He listened for a moment. Then he protested. "I'm going to church. I'll be home about one. . . . Of course with Mattie. Mattie and her new boyfriend. William. . . . Yes, he's right here. I'm looking at him!" He listened. "All right. See you then."

Daniel returned to the porch, and the three walked to William's car.

"I wish you were meeting me on a better day," Daniel said. "I hardly got any sleep last night. I can't sleep alone anymore."

He and William sat in front, talking easily. They seemed to like each other right off. They stopped to pick up Lewis, who was waiting outside, holding on to his walker. Daniel got out to help Lewis fold up the contraption. William caught Mattie's eye in the rearview mirror. He looked utterly flat to her, like a corpse who had

204

died with a resentment.

Old Mrs. Berry with her fierce walnut face and flowered hat greeted them in the narthex and handed them each a bulletin. Mattie felt proud to introduce her to the handsome man on her arm. Mattie, Daniel, and Lewis waved hellos to various members of the congregation as they walked to seats near the choir. Mattie sat between William and Lewis, with Daniel on the other side of Lewis. William stared ahead. Daniel rubbed his eyes. Lewis scanned the water-stained acoustical tiles, smiling as if Jesus were up there waving to him. Mattie reached for William's hand and he held hers for a minute or so. She felt furious with herself. Why had she forced him to come when he hadn't wanted to? But there was nothing she could do now. Buoy me up out of the fear, she prayed, and held her breath and felt as though she were in a big nickelodeon and if she could just pick the right tune, William and Daniel would begin to sway and swing, and everyone would be in harmony.

Mattie sat waiting for God to show her what to do. She turned to Lewis. His eyes were closed in prayer, so she closed hers too, and prayed out loud, softly, "Help me, help me." Lewis reached for her hand. "Don't let the devil steal your joy," he whispered. "Keep looking up."

She glanced at William, who looked as if he were being made to listen to a sermon in Latvian, and then at Daniel, who seemed barely awake, and she felt like someone had plugged her oxygen tube back in. From time to time William would make a sudden expansive gesture while whispering to Daniel, and maybe she was paranoid but it seemed a way of getting back at her, to show that he could be nice to people — just not to her. She didn't care so much anymore. The men seemed far away: she could have been watching them through the porthole of a quiet spaceship. Lewis was looking up, so she looked up too, over the heads of the choir members, nearly to the ceiling, where the notes hung above the singers like moths.

She had the family, including Lewis, over at the end of May for a garden party. "Casual, Mom, okay? Low-key. Quiche and salad." The week leading up to it was calm and pleasant. William was fun to be with, and even though the sex between them was not fantastic, sleeping with him, waking with him, felt terrific. No longer being even vaguely tempted to sleep with Nicky was even better.

She met William in Olema a couple of times, and he took her to places he loved — the Bear Valley Trail in Point Reyes for a hike, the Station House Cafe for popovers. Finally the day of the party came.

Mattie and Daniel had taken Lewis to church that morning. It was a warm, clear day, and the service was wonderful. The pastor told a story about a woman who asked her minister whether everyone she loved would be in heaven.

"What will make it heaven," said the minister, "is that you'll love everyone who is there."

The wisteria had gone nuts, as it always did in late springtime. In March it had looked gritchy and twiggy and crucified, disturbing the symmetry of the fence, and then it exploded into Oriental craziness, like a garish beaded curtain. The yard would have been a perfect setting for a garden party if it had not begun to drizzle.

So they moved the party indoors. She and William had a glass of wine before everyone arrived. Nicky had promised to return the children at four, before the party began, so they had the house to themselves. She did not want him to show up after the party started, because Isa could be counted on to be unpleasant. Nicky wasn't the point anymore. She'd asked Al and Katherine to pick up Isa and Lewis at four-thirty.

She and William made soup, tomato and mozzarella salad, and bread with the bread machine. Mozart played softly in the background on a boom box. By four-thirty, Nicky had still not come by. When Mattie called, her anxiety mounting, he answered the phone with great irritation in his voice. He and Lee were having a fight, and Alexander was screaming. Was there any way she could come get the children?

"No," she snapped. "I have people arriving. God damn it, Nicky. You promised." You *said,* she heard herself whine.

"Fine," he said, and hung up. Everybody at the party seemed to share his fine mood. Al's face had the cold, stiff look of someone who had been out on the bay too long. Isa came in on Lewis's arm. They had both dressed for a funeral. Lewis wore his black suit, and looked like her personal mortician. Isa had gone for broke, in a dark gray dress suit, dark gray heels, dark gray hat. It was definitely not a garden party outfit. It was rhino wear; JCPenney's Charging Rhino line.

But Isa suddenly called out, "Mattie!" so full of endearment that they might have been meeting at an airport in a distant city, and she waved. William and Daniel got to their feet.

Mattie took Isa's arm. "Mom?" she said. "This is William. William, this is my mother, Isa." They shook hands.

"I hardly recognize you," said Isa. "You've gotten so tall."

"Isa, you haven't aged at all," William replied smoothly. "It's good to see you again."

Everything about him obviously pleased Isa, because she grew girlish, giddy and animated. Mattie watched from the controls of her spaceship, studied her mother's face, overly made-up, paler than Mattie had ever seen, ghostly, with gashes of blusher on her cheeks, eyeliner around her eyes, brows scrawled on.

Isa seemed relieved to discover that William was nice-looking, polite, and tall. But in the blink of an eye, she started to sway and her eyes went out of focus, and she was a dazed rhino. She lifted her arms to Mattie the way Ella did when she wanted her mother to pull her out of the pool.

Everyone clustered around Isa to make sure she was okay, and the attention helped restore her. When the children finally arrived, Al met them at the door to thank Nicky for bringing them home — and to keep him from coming in. Mattie and Katherine put food on the table. Katherine had a knack for arranging things so they looked more beautiful; she served food inside wreaths of nasturtiums that she had picked in the garden, sprinkled a glitter of finely minced parsley on the salad, doodled a design in sour cream on the soup. William entertained the children. They were antsy and stuffed already from a late lunch of Lucky Charms and Coke that Nicky had fed them. William got out paper and drew them mazes.

William and Al reminisced about junior high, and William got Katherine to talk about her own school days — she had gone to a prestigious boarding school for girls outside Boston — but did not pay much attention to Mattie. Things could have been a lot worse. Isa had a second glass of wine and got too loud but not obstreperous. Lewis fell asleep briefly in his chair and started to snore. Ella had a stomach-ache, and spent twenty minutes on the toilet, straining, grunting, mooing with discomfort. At least she did not need Mattie to keep her company. From Harry's closed door came the steady thud of something being thrown against the wall, a black hole pulsing. Al and Isa got into a tiff about Al's weight, which was undeniably on the rise. Mattie endured. She did not drink much, and looked over at William now and then to see what he was making of her family: Al and Isa quibbling, Lewis snoring softly, the rhythmic Edgar Allan Poe thumps from Harry's room, Ella's terrible trumpeting from the bathroom. William seemed fine. This is my beautiful screwed-up family, Mattie thought, and now you have met them all.

Several days later, Mattie headed out to the Cove to return the favor. William's aunt Esther, his father's elder sister, was throwing a party at her house in Sebastopol. Her daughter, William's cousin Diana, had driven to the super-ette too, the plan being that William would drive everyone to Esther's. Mattie sought out Ned when she arrived at the store, and he told her how pretty she looked. She had pinned a gardenia to her hair, and wore a linen shift that matched her eyes. "William's in back," he announced, "picking out a bottle of wine." So she went to find him, and maybe neck for a moment or two.

"Hey, Mattie, come back here a sec," said Ned. She turned toward the register but stopped when she saw who was with him. "Noah" — Ned pointed at Mattie — "here's the woman I was telling you about, your mother's old friend." Noah's hair was shorter than it had been the first time she'd seen him. It fell only an inch or so past his ears. He had on a Mexican wedding shirt, worn jeans, scuffed huaraches. He looked up tentatively and pushed his wire-rimmed glasses up on his nose, appearing so much like Neil that Mattie's heart sank. Could it be that Neil had really fathered his daughter's child?

But then Noah smiled at her, and she stepped back, as the room began to tilt: this was Alfred's smile, this was her own father's smile. She stared into Noah's mouth, as if into a cave, at his big ivory teeth, slightly buck, like hers and Al's before their braces, like Harry's. "You okay?" Noah asked kindly, and she saw her father's mouth, and grabbed the little blue shoe in her pocket as if it were a sturdy handrail.

Noah called for Ned and reached out to Mattie as she started to faint. Ned called for William, who came out from the back room to greet her, only to find Noah and Ned holding her up, the three of them rooted to the old linoleum floor. "Oh, my gosh, honey. Are you okay?" William asked. "You stay right here. I'm going to get you some water." Noah and Ned shored her up. Mattie turned slowly toward Noah, whose eyes were hazel like Neil's, stricken behind the wire-rimmed glasses, but smiling her father's encouraging smile. He steadied her, and she felt a rummy floating pain, a sudden memory of her father's arms around her shoulders after an errant pitch had hit her in the head during a game of One Old Cat on the beach at Stinson.

Noah and Ned stood beside her, not holding her up exactly but spotting her, like coaches spotting a gymnast. All she could think was that she needed to get to a phone to call Al, but she remembered that William had said to wait right there, so she did. The smells of the store made her think of her grandmother's house, ancient, musty, and safe, where she could always find her grandmother's smile or her very familiar scowl.

Mattie reached out for the braid of smells, the floor, the parsley, the bread, and she held on. When William returned with a cup of water, Noah and Ned stepped back to let William take his place at Mattie's side.

seven

Mattie got into bed in a white nightgown, somewhere between bridal and baptismal. She felt like a Victorian, vaporish, consumptive. Luckily the kids were at Nicky's, so she could watch the news until Al arrived.

When he did, he hurried in and pulled the rattan chair up to where she lay under the covers. "Noah is our brother," she said, as if telling him something simple. Al studied her. "Daddy was his father. He has his teeth, exactly. Our teeth."

Al mulled this over. He went to stand at the window. He looked like someone with back trouble carrying the problems of the world. She thought he was crying, so she got herself out of bed and went to stand beside him. He was staring at the garden. They stood at the window with their arms around each other. Outside the sun played hide-and-seek through the rainclouds, dropping its light onto the grass and the garden, then ducking behind the gray clouds, bright, dark, bright, very dark, as if playing peek-a-boo with King Lear.

They spent the day in conversation, Mattie in bed, Al alternately at the window and slouched in the chair. He wanted to drive to the Cove and introduce himself to Noah right away, but

Mattie said no. What made him think they had the right to foist their need for discovery onto Noah? They went back and forth, Ping-Pong players defending their positions.

"I'm not doing anything until I know what to do," Mattie insisted.

"I need to verify this, though," Al said. "I'd like to see those teeth."

"So go see the teeth, then," said Mattie. "You can see him at the library on Saturdays."

Al worried his hands like a fretful infant. "Do you think Isa knew all this time?"

"Maybe, in some limbic way," Mattie said. "But let's not tell everyone else, Al."

"Nobody?"

"Just Katherine, for you, and Daniel and Angela, for me. Till we know what we're doing."

"What about William? You'll have to tell him eventually."

Mattie considered this, and realized with a start how little she wanted to share with William. "He lives in the same town," she said, "and he's a terrible gossip. So's Ned. He always says, 'Promise not to tell?' And Ned had some kind of friendly bond with Abby."

Mattie stayed in bed all Saturday with the cats and did not go to church the next day. She told Daniel she was coming down with something, and asked him to take Lewis to church. Daniel came over after the service with chicken soup from Whole Foods. "I'm worried about you. This is the first time you've missed church in I don't know how long."

"I told you, I'm coming down with something."

"I'm not sure I believe you."

"You won't believe what's true either," she said. And then she told him.

He looked at her as if he had not heard right. "What?" She told him again, and his face crumpled. He pulled his chair closer to the bed so that he could take her hands in his. He bowed his head, and held their hands together as if in prayer. "God almighty," he whispered.

He heated the soup for them, opened a can of mandarin oranges, and brought it all on a tray with the little blue shoe, which had been on the kitchen table. They lay together on the bed most of the day and watched old movies on TV.

"Your daddy had a big secret," Daniel said. "I can't imagine what that must have been like. My childhood was so different — me and my mom, and my iguanas, in our little apartment. Pretty curtains, toaster cozies, lots of plants, and cousins. But no dad. I always thought if my dad would come back, we'd be all right. But we actually were all right, more or less."

"Well, we had my dad around, but he had other women. I don't know how Al and I knew that, but we did. My dad was a very sexy guy — maybe he was rapacious, I don't know. So he never left, but he was never really there either."

"Is it okay to tell Pauline?"

"Of course. Go ahead, and tell her I wanted her to know."

Isa called late Sunday afternoon. She did not notice how quiet and weak Mattie's voice was. "Nobody loves me," she sobbed. "Nobody returns my calls. No one has called me in a week."

"I called you this morning," Mattie said. "I'm down with some sort of bug."

"You didn't call me. I waited by the phone all day."

"Mom. I called. And Al talked to you at Lewis's yesterday. Lewis made supper and took you downstairs to hear the Schubert quintet."

"Was that yesterday? Well. That doesn't get you off the hook."

"What hook!" Mattie shouted. "I called! I'm sick!" She hung up.

Isa called back an hour later. "Darling," she said, breathlessly, "Lewis says you weren't in church."

The children came home after dinner that night and seemed happy to find their mother in bed. The three cats lay beside her. Harry and Ella kicked off their shoes and crawled in, mauling the cats.

Mattie put the blue shoe, which she'd been clutching, on the nightstand, and hugged and kissed her dirty, marvelous children.

Nicky appeared in the doorway. "You okay?"

216

She nodded. "Can I get you anything?" She shook her head. Harry was thrusting papers at her. She reached for them. They were drawings of people, columns of numbers. "Mattie?" She looked up from the drawings. Nicky walked to a chair and sat down.

"What is it, Nicky?" she implored, reaching for his arm.

"Lee and I are expecting again."

"I'm going to have a little baby sister," Ella announced. Mattie turned slowly toward the sound of her voice. Ella's hair was clipped into sprouts with barrettes, fountains of sunlight. Her floral-frame glasses gave her the look of a secretarial kitten gone punk. Her nails were painted light pink, and then Mattie saw they had been chewed to the quick. Mattie heard Nicky say her name, but she reached for one of Ella's hands, which had been chewed at like artichoke leaves, with pricks of blood. Ella balled her hand into a fist.

"Oh, honey," Mattie said. Ella looked at her, beseeching.

"I'm going to name my baby sister Poem," she cried.

Mattie had chewed her nails too as a child, but not at five years old. She watched with a kind of grief in the next few days as Ella's habit took hold. She nibbled frequently and furtively at her nails, driving toward the vulnerable pink beneath. Mattie made herself not mention it.

She remembered the look of disgust on Isa's face when she first discovered Mattie's mutilated nails: Poor Isa, Mattie thought ruefully now, her son blowing things up in the backyard, her daughter eating her own hands, her husband up to God knows what, with who knows who, this poor damaged, betrayed woman who did such good work for so many. Mattie remembered looking up at her mother from behind the fan of ruined fingers, how it hid her mouth, kept her from saying the wrong thing. She remembered also the animal pleasure, the trance and satisfaction of grooming, the nibble, the salty bead of blood, pleasure right on the edge of hurt.

Couldn't you go back to twiddling your belly button? she wanted to ask Ella, but she didn't mention the nailbiting at all. The belly button had seemed so innocuous and tender, while the nailbiting made her cuticles bleed. Ella looked like she was slowly eating herself, trying to erase herself from the picture.

Days passed. Mattie scared William into staying away by coughing whenever he called. She didn't want to tell him the secret of Noah. Harry and Ella kept her company in bed. Ella colored in her Little Mermaid coloring books and Harry drew. His drawings were becoming more and more precise. He had already completed plans for a swimming pool submarine, a catapult, and a robot. The robot had two names, depending on his mood. When he and it were happy, it was Enon. When he was mad, it was Bruton.

On Thursday morning Mattie woke up, got the children off to school, and then did not crawl back into bed. This she considered major progress. When she was dressed, she tucked the little shoe into the pocket of her jeans. She recoiled from images of her father, spat at his memory. She saw him now as irredeemable, a proven pedophile, even as she remembered standing on his wingtips while he waltzed her around the room, even as she remembered being on his shoulders, dressed in a panda costume, walking through this neighborhood on Halloween, with Al bounding ahead, door to door, Alfred's hands holding her ankles firmly. Mattie felt a pang of anxious compassion for Isa: people must have known that Alfred was unfaithful. This was a town where telephone lines hummed with reports of affairs and divorces. They used to call it "wandering," when it was another couple, as in, "Charlie's wandering was always painful for Marcy." "Painful" did not do it justice. When Nicky had been unfaithful with those students, it had felt like the jungles of Vietnam inside Mattie. Isa, on the phone years before, would glow with horrified pleasure at news of fresh scandals and subsequent divorce, while elsewhere in town people must have been getting off on the gossip about Alfred. Had people at the Cove known about Abby and Noah? Had people in the town? Had Isa?

Mattie prayed about Noah, wishing she could welcome him into her family — she could call him Poem! Her children could have a brand-new uncle. But this would hurt them, set the mobile of their lives spinning and tangling.

She never left the house anymore without the blue shoe. She was getting a little funny, dissociated, dreamy. The color of the shoe reminded her from time to time of a turquoise-blue washtub she'd seen on an altar near Oaxaca, before she got pregnant with Harry. She and Nicky had been camping on a beach beneath the stars, and one Sunday morning they'd wandered into the nearest town, with its low-slung huts, depressed dogs slinking around, and people dressed in their finest. "*¿Iglesia?*" Nicky asked an old woman selling mangoes on sticks, bright as torches against dust, and she pointed up the road. Mattie bought a mango from her, cut into tiers like an artichoke. She carried it in front of her like the Olympic flame, and then she and Nicky sat on the steps of the church and ate it together as they waited for the service to begin.

Inside, during the mass, Spanish words and songs burbled over them like a brook. Midway through the service, the priest stopped and said something to his congregation that included an amused "*anglos,*" and people tittered and murmured. Turning to Mattie and Nicky, holding his hands to his heart, the priest said, in English, "One life, given for all." Nicky, who was not a believer, wept. The woman sitting next to him, who was clutching a coffee-stained paper napkin, tore it carefully and handed half to Nicky. On the altar was a turquoise-blue plastic tub, the kind you would wash dishes in if you lived in a tiny apartment. At the end of the service, the priest carried the tub into the congregation and pulled out a bright red rose, wet from water in the tub. He dripped the rose in the water again and again, and baptized both of them: Nicky and Mattie.

Mattie took Isa to the doctor the day before she and Al planned to go out to the Cove again. Everyone had called her with concerns about Isa that week. Lewis, close to tears, said that Isa seemed drugged with confusion. The woman at the front desk at The Sequoias informed that she had wandered away one night. The social worker who looked after the lower-income seniors, who said she was used to the fogginess and foibles of her charges, had reported something "really off" with Isa. "Also, she's incontinent. It could be a bladder infection," said the social worker. "I would take her to the doctor."

Isa was weak and cross when Mattie picked her up. In the car, she referred to William as Phil, and claimed not to have spoken to Mattie in more than a week. But in the doctor's office she was clear and animated, witty, coquettish. She remembered the name of the president, and the minutiae of that morning's major news stories. It was as if she had memorized the front page of the paper.

Al greeted Noah at the front desk of the library when he and Mattie entered, and Noah gestured pleasantly to a man reading in an easy chair, so that Al would know to speak quietly. "Are you okay?" Noah asked Mattie, and she nodded, cringing at the memory of having nearly fainted at the superette.

"I just had a little bug or something," she whispered.

"Good," Noah said, nodding. "Well, let me know if you need anything."

Mattie noticed Al trying to sneak a glimpse into Noah's mouth. But his full lips covered his teeth, so Al smiled awkwardly and walked to the fiction shelves. Mattie, who had covered her nose while saying hello, as if to stifle a sneeze, headed to history. She didn't want Noah to notice her nose — his father's nose — and yelp with recognition. Mattie spied on him through the stacks. Once they looked at each other at the same moment; he flushed, and looked down.

He had big puppy hands, which he raked through his shaggy hair and with which he palmed his face when he spoke. When someone needed a book checked out or a question answered, he listened without making much eye contact, staring off with a look of grave attention into the middle distance, nodding so the person knew he was listening. A skateboard was propped against the wall behind his chair. When he got up to help a patron find something, Mattie noticed that he had small, almost dwarfish feet for such a tall, lanky man; he was wearing battered running shoes.

Mattie sidled up to Al, who was spying on Noah through the space above the thrillers section. "Okay?" she whispered.

"He won't open his mouth."

She walked Al to the desk as if he were a child who needed help getting his first library card. "This is a great little place," she whispered to Noah. He smiled.

She reported everything to Daniel, who dropped by for a visit that night. He listened without interrupting.

"Your brother has little goat feet?" he asked, and she nodded. He drew back, grimaced. She smiled.

"Like a dwarf?"

Mattie nodded vigorously.

Daniel pondered this. "Like little hooves?"

"I miss you," William said when he called Mattie that evening. "Whatcha doing?"

"Oh, not much. Can you come over?" He did, and it was great to see him, to eat, and watch TV, and make love. She desperately wanted to tell him about Noah — but again, she didn't. He always had gossip about people they'd seen at the store or the beach, who seemed like lovely, ordinary people. She held the secret of Noah in her pocket, like the blue shoe, or a live grenade.

At church one Sunday, during the Prayers of the People, Mattie said out loud, "I'm asking prayers for my mother, Isa, who seems to have something wrong with her mind. I'm asking prayers for my children, whose father is having another baby with his new wife. I'm asking prayers for me and my brother, that we can come to know God's will. And I pray for a man named Noah." She said his name in public for the first time, in the grave and tender silence of church.

Lee was starting to show. Mattie saw her whenever she dropped off the children. She'd become more beautiful as her belly expanded. She still had the fake burr, but it was growing fainter. One Saturday morning when Mattie dropped the kids off at Nicky and Lee's, Ella clung to Mattie so tightly that Mattie had to pry her hands off her neck to set her down on the manicured lawn. "You're a big girl now," Isa would have scolded Mattie, if she, at five, had been so clingy; but anyone in his right mind could see that Ella was just a little girl. Alexander looked even more like Harry now. It was devastating to Mattie to see in another child the specific miracle of her son's own face. It pierced her.

★ ★ ★

Isa no longer showered daily. She smelled like wild onions — another thing stolen from Mattie: her mother's smell — African violets, tea, and almonds. Isa needed even more help now, four or five hours a week. Mattie and Al kept putting off dealing with it, though, hating to break the news to Isa, not to mention dreading the added expense. Lewis broached the topic with Mattie. He met her for a walk in front of The Sequoias. They went along the salt marsh, Lewis pushing his walker. "The good Lord will take care of Isa," he said. "But we must help too. I have fifteen dollars a week to contribute. That will buy one hour. You and Al must pay for two each. I have taken this to the Lord in prayer, and I have received my answer — five more hours of assistance per week." Mattie was amazed at his certainty and his initiative. His pants were flecked with food but his mind was unblemished. "Okay," she said. There were wren tits singing from leafy branches, red-winged blackbirds everywhere.

They hired a woman named Mai to help around the apartment, clean, do laundry, be there when Isa showered in case she fell. Mattie felt as if she had a new baby, someone to keep clean and safe from falling: Isa was her eternity, scrolling back to the womb and beyond, scrolling forward into God knew how many years of decline.

225

★ ★ ★

William came over every couple of nights, and he and Mattie talked a few times every day. Still she did not tell him about Noah. She had been tempted to, but a caution inside her persuaded her to hold her tongue. It gave her a sense of power to withhold the information, and the secret, in turn, hardened her heart against William's charms.

They pulled away from each other but didn't discuss the idea of breaking up. He receded periodically, like a tide; she waited for his return. She preferred to be with Daniel. William had a certain hostility toward women. He ogled the young, Mattie began to notice, and made fun of older women. He was friends with many women he'd been involved with, and believed that this reflected well on him, but would say bad things about them to Mattie. He sometimes mocked their taste in music, or mentioned their sexual incompatibility, as if this reflected well on Mattie.

But Mattie liked having a boyfriend. She also liked not sleeping with Nicky. William filled the bed; he was a talisman against her ex-husband. She liked having someone to hold hands with at the movies. She and William liked the same books, and music. They shared the same liberal politics, although he fancied himself more of a radical than she because he didn't even bother to vote. She liked talking with him on the phone. She liked obsessing less about Daniel.

Maybe William didn't have faith; maybe he didn't have that deep visible soul, was not, when push came to shove, her soul mate, like Daniel, or Angela, or Al. Still, he was usually good company.

Pauline called one night to say she and Daniel were going to see Mark Morris, how about a double date?

On the night of the performance, Mattie got all dolled up in her fanciest vintage dress. With Daniel and Pauline she had arranged to meet William in San Rafael. He was standing under a streetlight outside the Double Rainbow ice cream shop, handsome in a black wool jacket and white shirt. Pauline gave a whoosh of appreciation when Mattie pointed him out, and Mattie felt a wave of happiness in having a good-looking boyfriend.

They ate near the Marines Memorial Theatre. Pauline's skin glowed, and her hair was piled on top of her head, tendrils flowing out everywhere. "I love modern dance," she said. "Alvin Ailey most of all. I love how those long-legged dancers carry the line with the least possible interference."

"That's a great way to put it," said William. Daniel glanced at Mattie.

Pauline could seem so brilliant, so undepressed, Mattie thought. She watched her speak, noticed too how Daniel looked at her with pride. Glancing at William, she could see that he was mesmerized.

"Have you seen Mark Morris before?" Pauline asked.

"Never," William admitted. "But I know he's considered a genius."

"He is. But prepare yourself. He's — what's the word, Daniel?"

"Elephantine?" Daniel said.

"Don't be smart, darling." Pauline turned back to William. "He's a wild man. There are all kinds of body types you won't have seen onstage before — stocky women, dark and muscular men running to fat, maybe one or two with long legs and high asses, going bald, in drag."

"I can't wait," he said. "I've always wanted to see him."

But when Mark Morris came out alone onstage for the first dance, with his swirly, curly hair and paunch, hammy legs with feet that managed to point, William drew his head close to Mattie and whispered, "Good Lord!" She tried to focus on the dance: I am what I am, Morris seemed to be saying, and I am going to share what I am, revel in it, and maybe then you will be able to revel in you too. William looked skeptical and appalled.

"I'm a bad boyfriend," he said at the bar during intermission.

"No, no," said Mattie, "you're actually a good boyfriend."

"I just love ballet," he told Pauline. "So can you help me learn how to love Mark Morris?"

Pauline began speaking to William with showy passion. Daniel and Mattie ended up playing hangman at the bar. They exchanged secret glances, like bad kids. They drank cheap wine and she felt flirty. Maybe Pauline and William could fall in love, drink fine wine, and not believe in God together.

In bed with William that night, Mattie tumbled out with it: "Why isn't it exhilarating to you that while everyone is usually so busy creeping around politely, being thin and healthy, cleaning up messes before anyone can see them, here's Mark Morris celebrating messes and appetites and middle age and fat butts?"

"Maybe those aren't good things to celebrate," he said. She felt stung.

He seemed so constrained, so neatly trimmed, someone who'd been doing topiary with his soul all his life. They lay in the dark, dozing off. He smelled to her like an old iron heating up on an ironing board.

When Mattie went to pick Isa up for dinner a few nights later, she found her lying on the floor of her apartment. Her pants were wet.

"Mom!" Mattie cried.

The children gathered around, and Harry, who'd seen police shows on TV, started shouting for people to give her air. He threw open the windows.

Isa sat up as if nothing out of the ordinary

were going on. She refused to believe that she had fallen. It was simply that she had skipped lunch, and weakness had come over her, she explained. Mattie pulled her to her feet, and Isa went to look for her purse. "Mom!" said Mattie. "I don't think we should go out. I think we should have some nice soup right here." She knew that she was speaking slowly, as though talking to a half-wit. Isa pleaded, she'd been looking forward to going out all day. And so Mattie led her mother to the bathroom, purposeful, as she had once led her children to the toilet when they were potty training, and helped her wash and change into dry underpants and trousers.

At Denny's, Isa ate dreamily, her pinkie in the air. From time to time she looked up and around at the children, hunched over their drawings, puzzled by their presence here as if Denny's now let dogs sit on its banquettes. The circles of Isa's mind were breaking free and floating away, like stages of a rocket dropping away on blastoff.

"Could we have a neurologist examine her?" Mattie asked Dr. Brodkey over the phone the next day.

"Yes," she replied. "But I'd recommend that we put it off awhile. Once we open that door it's hard to get it closed again entirely."

"That door — what? — of having her diagnosed? Wouldn't a CAT scan give you more information about what's up? And what you could do to help her?"

"It's an expensive procedure," the doctor explained. "I'm not sure we can get it authorized."

"But she was on the floor when I got there. She's incontinent."

"All right, then. Bring her to my office again. Let's see what's going on."

At Dr. Brodkey's office, Isa was bright and warm, answering every challenge tossed her way — counting backward from one hundred by sevens, remembering the words to the national anthem and the name of the doctor's grandchild. By the time Mattie got her home and set out a simple dinner for her, Isa was all but speaking baby talk. Mattie put her in her easy chair in front of the TV, with a glass of cool water on the table beside her, the remote, her glasses, the phone, and some grapes to tide her over. Isa kept looking up at her as if she were a painting crookedly hung. "Is the thing with the — you know — the light in it working? Could you do the thing where you do it?"

After a brief interrogation, Mattie figured out that Isa wanted the TV on.

"I feel like we're falling down the rabbit hole," Mattie told Al the next time she saw him. "With Brodkey, she's totally lucid, and with us, she's like Shirley Temple on Quaaludes. I don't know what's real anymore. I think she's usually the way she is around us — confused. It's like the late, great Philip K. Dick

231

said. 'Reality is that which, when you stop believing in it, doesn't go away.' "

Mattie spent the weekend working with Daniel in the garden, planting tomatoes and building cages around them to keep the deer away. Pauline had gone off again, spending the weekend in the city at a film festival with friends. Daniel was distant, concentrating too hard.

"What do you think's going on?" Mattie asked finally.

"I don't know. If she wants to spend the weekend inside in the dark watching movies, fine. I want to be out in the sun. Maybe it's my imagination, but she pulled away from me when you and William started going out. Isn't that odd?" He dug a hole for a tomato plant. "Can I tell you something? Maybe you'll think I'm crazy. But I've been thinking about getting an iguana for a long time. Because I think an iguana would be good company."

"Oh." They stopped working and sat in the shade, swilling apple juice. "Did you just say you wanted to get an iguana?" He nodded. He'd had several iguanas as a boy. Pets were not allowed in the apartment where he and his mother had lived, but she'd let him keep iguanas. He'd had one named Flor and one named Andy. A month ago, he found a man selling iguanas at the flea market in Sonoma. "It's been a dream of mine lately, like other men might want a model train," he said, and Mattie nodded as if he was making sense now, really cooking with gas.

After church the next day, they drove to the flea market and purchased a year-old iguana, which Daniel named Otis. "How's Pauline going to be with this?" Mattie asked. Daniel shrugged. She herself was a little afraid of Otis. He was all ridges, green scales, lots of flashes of turquoise, bright eyes. The man at the flea market had sold Daniel a long glass box with a mesh top, which had an opening lined in tinfoil into which you could insert a heat lamp. On the way home they bought a collar and leash at a pet store; the man at the flea market had told them that iguanas like to go for walks on leashes.

Mattie could not imagine that Pauline would want or agree to an iguana. Maybe she would catch salmonella, which iguanas sometimes carry. Maybe she'd make Daniel pick between Otis and her, and he'd pick Otis — and Mattie. Perhaps Mattie could learn to love Otis. She hadn't considered reptiles pets before. Show me someone on the street with a boa around his neck, she thought, and I'll show you a very angry person.

They all drove to Daniel's and set up Otis's glass cage in the living room.

When Pauline came home the next day, her screams could be heard four houses away, according to Daniel. He showed up at Mattie's with Otis and the glass cage in his car. Harry was home from school by then, and he cried out with joy when he saw the iguana at their house.

"But I don't want an iguana either," Mattie said. Harry and Daniel stood begging like puppies.

"Please, Mama. Please, Mama."

"Please, Mat."

So she said yes, because she wanted Daniel and Harry to love her. This also gave her a good excuse to call William.

"Want to come over and see my new iguana?" she asked.

There was a long pause. "Okay," said William.

When he showed up that evening, there was much fuss and fascination with Otis. He was like a miniature dragon, a memento of prehistory.

Al could not believe she now had an iguana. He knew she was deeply afraid of reptiles. "Boy, you really do love Daniel, don't you?" he said over the phone. "Tell me all about the little bugger."

"Well . . . he's a very strange creature. He usually doesn't move or respond, except to have these terrible episodes from time to time where he tears around his cage like a balloon losing air, spewing these thin white ribbons of shit."

"Well, you gotta love that," said Al.

"He's like an elegant and vaguely hostile scrap of leather."

"Sort of like Mom?"

Mattie laughed. "Harry adores him. He says, 'Oh, *Otis,* you are such a *good* little iguana.' "

Otis brought the family closer together. So much was going on all at once — Noah's invisible presence in their house, Isa's deterioration, Lee's pregnancy. One day after Otis had a terrible episode, Harry came to sit in Mattie's lap while she read in her rattan chair. He'd watched Otis carefully after the outburst, he told her. She sat with him in silence. "I'm very worried about Otis," he said after a while, near tears. "I think he may have done something to his mind."

In between bouts of madness, Otis was as basic as it got: stare, stare, lie on hot rock, stare, sneak to other end of cage, stare. Mattie wondered idly if he might be a spy. She had heard a local comedian once say that he thought people with Down's syndrome were spies for God, and she wondered if Otis might be one too. She could not see a single redeeming quality in him, except that Harry loved him so. Maybe she just preferred pets who sucked up to you.

"I'm going to get an iguana for my boy when I grow up," Harry said.

"How do you know you're going to have a son?"

"Well, I want a boy," Harry replied. "I'd know how to work a boy."

Whenever Mattie went to the Cove to visit William, she looked for Noah too. Whenever she saw him on foot or on skateboard, she'd stop to watch him, like a stalker. She bumped into him at Ned's store and they said hello. She glanced into his basket and saw the makings for a Thai meal — noodles and fish sauce, lemongrass, a can of coconut milk, some tofu, red chilies, basil, some limes. Ned told her, "Whenever he goes traveling, he comes home and starts making the food of wherever he's been. When he went to India, he learned to make all their curries and flatbreads and dal. That's a beautiful child," Ned said. "I love that kid."

Noah was polite, careful, kind, and shy, easygoing, reserved. Mattie covertly watched him play basketball with some other young men one Saturday afternoon at the school on the edge of town. People gathered on the bleachers to watch them play; Mattie watched from her car. The men moved with balance and poise, like a street gang who had taken up ballet, but Noah was the most graceful of all. He could maneuver past other players, using moves he must have learned on the skateboard, fluidly darting and weaving, skating for daylight, parting the sea of crouching legs, faking with a move to the right so he could come in for a basket on the left.

She went to the library again with Al. Noah was at his desk, checking in books. He looked up and smiled nervously. Al walked off toward the biographies. Mattie lost herself in fiction. They watched each other watching him, over dusty spaces in the stacks.

Noah looked up at the two of them when they walked toward the door. Had they found everything they needed?

Al nodded. "What are *you* reading?"

Noah held up a paperback on his desk. *Revolutionary Road*, by Richard Yates. "It's my favorite book."

It had been a favorite of Alfred's too. Noah ran his fingers through his hair a number of times until it stood straight up in a tuft on his head. "I've never read it," Mattie said. Al picked up a long rubber band and began threading it across the fingers of both hands, as if making a cat's cradle.

"It's about loneliness," Noah said. "All these people in families, trying to connect and love each other, but they can't get it to work. It's about sad lies. You need to read it. Everybody should. It's the best book in the world."

So she and Al did. She read it with Noah and her father in mind. It was so great that it made her a little crazy.

Nights in mid-June stayed light forever, and were sometimes so warm you could hardly sleep, sometimes cold enough to require a blanket. Some nights Mattie went to sleep in a T-shirt and underpants, covered with a sheet, and woke to rising fog, the willows outside her window tossing like restless sleepers.

One morning when Harry and Ella were still at Nicky's, Mattie went in to plug in Otis's heat lamp. He looked more still than usual. He looked utterly dead. She wasn't positive, so she lifted the lid off his cage to nudge him, and realized she was too afraid to touch him.

She fetched some chopsticks and nudged him with them. He seemed to be in the later stages of rigor mortis. She cried out. She called Daniel and asked if he could come over right away to help her. Then she paged the vet. It was eight o'clock on a Sunday morning and he sounded tired. "I think Harry's iguana has died, or is dying," she said. He offered to meet her at the office.

Daniel showed up not long after. He picked Otis up and set him back down. "Boy, he's really dead. Poor Harry. Poor Otis." Daniel placed him in a shoe box through which Mattie had gamely poked some holes.

In the car they were silent, crushed on Harry's behalf.

The vet lifted Otis out of the box and set him on a towel on the examination table. Otis lay still, looking small and pathetic and touching, like a guy with a sunken chest other men would jeer at. The vet examined Otis on one side, then turned him over. Otis was on his back.

238

The vet put his stethoscope on Otis's puny chest. The steel circle of the stethoscope was almost wider than Otis. The vet closed his eyes and concentrated, as if he were Christiaan Barnard considering a difficult case. After a moment he admitted, "I don't actually know what I'm listening for. But he's definitely alive."

Mattie's heart leapt. "Really?" she asked breathlessly, hardly daring to hope.

"Shouldn't you take his temperature?" Daniel smiled meanly. The vet handed him the thermometer, and he drew back.

"Is this your first iguana?" Mattie asked.

"Yes." He stroked Otis for a while, then turned him over onto his stomach. Otis blinked, and looked around. He took one step, then another.

"Oh my God," Mattie whispered. "This is like being at Lourdes."

They sat side by side in front of Otis's cage, watching him as you might watch TV. Every time Otis moved, she and Daniel smiled, as though they were watching their baby sleep. "I'm so happy," Daniel said sadly. She saw that his head had dropped as if in prayer, and then she became aware that he was moving closer to her. She believed he might put his arm around her.

His arm was on the couch behind them, but his hand had moved. His arm hung in the air for an instant. Then he lowered it across her back. His hand cupped the round of one shoulder, the way a hand might cup the head of an infant, the fullest a hand could ever be.

"That was a beautiful thing you did for Harry," Daniel told Mattie. His hand was still on her shoulder. When he lifted it, she couldn't believe her shoulder hadn't turned to silver.

When William came over that night, he was in a state of testy exhaustion. Mattie felt metallic with PMS, lonely and needy. William swiftly disappeared into her bedroom to rest before dinner. Harry was pitching cards into a salad bowl in his bedroom. She left them both alone as long as she could, playing with Ella outside, helping her make a village in the dirt with acorns and pine needles, broken glass, bits of plastic. They paved the streets with patio gravel, and Ella made a campfire circle of pebbles, with torn red rose petals for flames, while Mattie worried about William. When she couldn't bear worrying anymore, she went inside to hear about his day. She stepped into her room, expecting to find him resting, but found him on the phone instead. When she caught his eye, he said into the receiver, "Just a sec." Then he looked up at her as if she were a salesperson. "Whatcha need?" he asked.

She told him she didn't need anything. In the hallway she heard him say softly, "So go on." She felt that something frightening was happening. She went back into her room and stretched out on the bed on her side, then stared at him plaintively, so he really had no choice but to get off the phone. He apologized to whoever it was, and promised to call back later.

Mattie asked, in a child's high, worried voice, "Who was that?"

William sighed. "I can't do this tonight," he said. "I'm too tired." He got to his feet while Mattie dug her fingernails so deeply into her scalp that she knew there were indents and maybe even blood.

"Don't go," she said with her eyes squinched shut. "I'm tired. I need to be with you."

"All I want," he said tersely from the doorway, "is to come here after a long day at work and lie down for a while. Talk to a friend on the phone, kick back. Then I'll want to be with you and the children, and help make some dinner, and catch up with you when we can be alone. Is that so fucking much to ask?"

Mattie took a series of rabbity breaths. "But you seem to be having this secret phone call."

"Secret phone call? Jesus." He sank into the chair cushions. "If I wanted to have a secret phone call, I wouldn't have it from your fucking bed."

She tried to hold it back, but the sentence cascaded out. "Nicky always did." William heaved another sigh. Desperation rose inside her, and she went to sit at his feet like a dog.

She put her head against his knees and held her breath, and after a long, long moment, he began to rub her head gently. Mattie's mind swirled with fearful scenes of his leaving and what a bad night it would be. He stroked her head and made sounds of exasperation, the way she did when Harry or Ella was up in the middle of the night, when she herself was desperate for sleep.

As in an epiphany, she suddenly saw the way to keep him here tonight, to have him drop all current charges. She said softly, "There's something I need to tell you." She took a breath and looked up into his worried face. "You're never going to believe this," she said. She tried to swallow what she was about to say, tried to think of a decoy. Please don't let me tell William, she prayed.

"How bad can it be?"

She groaned, and then she told him.

"*What?*" he said.

She nodded, miserably, so afraid he would be angry with her for keeping the secret from him. She covered her face with her hands and kept nodding. His face shifted from angry to concerned. He helped her to her feet. He put his arms around her and nuzzled the side of her cheek the way she did when her children were afraid, and a few moments later she began to feel a little better.

eight

Late June was supposed to be tender and verdant and mild, a cheerleader for summer. The promise of June was supposed to signal, "Oh, we're going to have such fun!" But May's winds, which were supposed to stop, never did. There were conditions from all the wrong seasons, mixed up together — too much heat one week, and when that passed, the fog returned, grim, gray, biting. Then it was glorious for a few days, mild and blue, until the winds of spring, and two days of rain. "Ha! I'm deep summer. Ha! Now a winter storm. Ha! I'm windy spring, whooo, whooo."

Life in June and early July mimicked the weather: wind, rain, glorious heat, fog, blue skies. Mattie had more money. Nicky finally made associate professor, with tenure and a raise, and could offer her three hundred dollars more a month. And Ned hired her to work for fifteen hours a week at the store at a decent hourly wage. She liked it there, stacking fruit, ringing up groceries when Ned stepped out, sweeping, freshening up the place in general, chasing dogs outside. Ned loved her, and she was fond of him, and she loved the way he smelled, like a blanket. He let her pick the radio station that played during the day, and so she could listen to NPR and get paid. Ned gave her groceries at a great discount. She overheard the latest gossip; everyone seemed to tell Ned everything.

Noah came in from time to time, and she would ask him about books. Then he would disappear for a while. There would be a substitute at the library, who never knew where Noah had gone. "Oh, you know how Noah is," she'd tell Mattie, gaily. Things with William were just barely okay. She wasn't in love with him any longer, and he wasn't in love with her. Still, she mostly liked having him around. She liked his looks, his relationship with his father, and the store, and she liked that because of him, she no longer slept with Nicky. It bothered her when she felt she was using William, but her conscience did not force her to give him up. She liked it when old friends saw her with him for the first time at the movies or a restaurant; Angela referred to him as Mattie's beard. Her children liked his presence in their lives too — he had the basics down: he could draw and play catch. He took Harry and his friends to macho movies that Mattie refused to see. Maybe it made the children feel more secure that their mother was capable of acquiring a nice-looking boyfriend. Whenever Mattie thought about breaking things off, she'd have a pleasant time with him, and she'd decide to let things ride a while longer.

Isa fell again, and Dr. Brodkey finally agreed

to schedule a CAT scan. When the results were in, Dr. Brodkey showed Mattie and Al areas of her brain that looked more like Swiss cheese than gray matter. Isa was definitely having infarcts, the doctor said.

"What an ugly word," said Al. "And what does it all mean?"

Dr. Brodkey pointed to spots on the X ray. "It means strokes big enough to knock out a small lake of brain tissue, called a lacuna. They leave behind dead brain tissue, which the body converts to scar tissue. So she loses mental ground. The good news," Dr. Brodkey said somberly, "is that it's not Alzheimer's."

"And that's good news because . . ." Al sounded skeptical.

"Because there are medications for what she has," the doctor replied. "We'll start her out on Coumadin, an anticoagulant. A blood thinner. Dosing can be tricky in the beginning, but we'll get it right. She'll need to avoid foods with vitamin K — like broccoli and spinach, because Coumadin is a vitamin K antagonist. Coumadin will help slow down the rate and frequency of these mini-strokes."

Having the children home during the day in summer was a mixed blessing. Mattie loved seeing them more, but she still needed time for housekeeping, shopping, gardening, and helping Isa, and for her work at Sears and the superette. She had taken a break from making sandwiches with Daniel and Pauline, as relations with Pauline were strained, but still her life felt dense, compressed. She set lower standards for housework, for everything she could. While this struck her as being the secret of life, it was a solution that drove William crazy. He'd shake his head impatiently at the cats sleeping on a pile of unfolded laundry on the couch; he'd turn pale when he found out that she'd accidentally left her car engine idling all day in front of the superette when she had raced in late, after dropping Ella off at day camp.

Harry lurked around the house, watching Otis, flipping cards across his room, begging rides to other boys' homes, needing this, needing that. It was like having a homeless person staying with her. I need money, I need food, I need a ride, I need you. Ella was usually busy with her art and dolls and her friend Pearl. She groomed the dolls endlessly, cooed to them, tucked them into her bed at night and then slept on a quilt on the floor so she wouldn't disturb them. She was trying very hard not to bite her nails, without success.

When Mattie heard Ella tell her dolls, "You'd be so pretty if you stopped biting your nails," she interrupted her: "Did someone tell you that?" Mattie asked, and Ella told her. Mattie called Pearl's mother and said she knew that her intentions were good but to please never mention the nails again. Mattie prayed for a solution to Ella's nervous habits; but she did not get an answer.

One Sunday night, when Nicky dropped the children off, Mattie noticed Ella's nails were painted with pink glittery polish, a good reason not to bite them. Ella preened. She did things so that her sparkly nails would show — picked things up ostentatiously with her forefinger, and washed her face with her palms so the beautiful nails might fan out, like someone with a new engagement ring.

Mattie called Lee the next day to thank her, and they actually fell into a comfortable talk. Lee was having a difficult pregnancy, with cramps and spotting and fear. Mattie heard herself say she would pray for Lee and the baby. Then she went off to Longs, and returned with five bottles of nail polish in shades from light pink to scarlet.

Isa had tried putting something that tasted like poison on Mattie's bleeding nails to keep her from biting them when she was little, but that had never helped. Maybe beautiful polish could do what aversion never had done. Ella actually gasped when she saw all those bottles of polish. Mattie bought polish remover too, a soft file, and cotton balls, and Ella immediately wanted her to apply a new color. Mattie buffed the nails, and smoothed thick cream into the ruined cuticles. They both blew on Ella's fingers, and she held them up to the sun until the cream had been absorbed. Then, wearing her reading glasses, Mattie applied a coat of rose pink. The smell was intoxicating. Ella waved her fingers, flapping them to let the polish dry, and because she could not contain herself. She resembled a baby canary trying for liftoff. But by breakfast two mornings later, she had picked at her nails, peeled the polish away in flakes. Mattie touched Ella's hands, and Ella wrung them like a widow. Later Mattie found her picking off polish while she talked to her dollies.

"Oops!" Mattie said. Ella looked down at her hands. "It's okay," Mattie told her. "Let's take off the old polish and try again, okay?" The polish remover smelled, and burned the nicks around Ella's cuticles. She cried out, so Mattie bathed her fingers in water and blew on them.

Ella wanted scarlet next. "I love these little fingernails," she said, studying the bright red. But they looked terrible.

As hard as they tried to settle into summer, new stresses sprang up: Harry punched Ella in the arm over some minor disagreement, or a trip to the swimming pool had to be postponed. The oldest cat was feebler every day, walking into walls and into the other cats. Ella's nails always found their way back to her mouth, and she'd scrape the polish off with her teeth and pick at the flecks.

One weekend Harry was to go camping with Stefan and his mother in the Sierra foothills, and Ella would have Lee and Nicky and Alexander to herself for the two days. Mattie helped her choose her prettiest clothes, and packed her swimsuit and her dolls and all her bottles of polish. Ella left hand in hand with Lee, looking back to smile at Mattie. When Nicky brought her home on Sunday, the polish on Ella's fingernails was so badly chipped that it looked as if they were bleeding from the nail bed, like silt rising to the surface in tiny ponds.

Mattie spent that whole weekend with William — one night at her house, one night at his. She had worried about Harry, afraid that harm would come to him, that he would drown or be bitten by a rattlesnake, or that he'd get homesick and want to come back early. William couldn't figure out where her mind was. She took advantage of this: it helped keep him on his toes. He seemed to appreciate her more when she grew inattentive. It was like having a boyfriend on easy credit terms.

Harry returned from the trip swollen with poison oak. Ella caught it, and it ringed her eyes. Lewis's son in Georgia had kidney stones, and Lewis had to fly down to care for him. Left to her own devices, Isa subsisted on broccoli, spinach — anything rich in vitamin K. There was no overt bad reaction, but slow deterioration followed. The children scratched their welts and sores. Mattie thought that locusts could not be far away.

★ ★ ★

The first time Mattie worked at the superette after telling William about Noah, Ned pretended not to know. He was shooing dogs out of the store when she arrived. They were not allowed in officially, but they sneaked through the gap in the warped frame of the screen door. Ned was always shouting at them. "Out, out," he was saying when Mattie stepped around him to go inside. She knew that later Ned would give the dogs' owners bones from the butcher counter; and the dogs would be back the next day.

Ned hugged her, and she stood toeing the linoleum. She put on her apron, saying to the floor, "William must have told you about my father and Abby, right?" She did not look up.

After a moment, Ned admitted, "Yes, he did. What a shock. I knew Neil and Yvonne — and your folks, in passing. And Abby. I always felt like I had to love Abby, because I didn't know if anyone else did."

Mattie nodded.

"Listen, honey," he said. "I don't know if this matters to you. But someone saw Abby yesterday." His face was going in and out of focus. "A couple at the bar last night said they'd seen her in the window of one of those huts next to Nick's Cove." Mattie took her apron off. "It was the smallest hut," he continued. "The one in the middle."

The pier next to the clapboard cabins looked

250

like an abandoned train trestle disappearing into the pinprick of perspective. There was no handrail, no pilings dribbled with pitch, no nothing on which to get your balance, just decomposing salt-rotted wood. It was all turning to dust. The deserted shacks sat on stilts a hundred feet away. Abby had been seen in the window of the smallest one, Ned had told her. Mattie shivered, trundled back to work, and returned a few days later with Daniel.

There were hundreds of sea gulls and sand-pipers when the tide was out, cormorants, mudhens, and mallards diving all at once so you might see three or four duck butts sticking into the air. The middle cabin, built like a boat, with a brave little prow to fend off the waves, was wedged between bigger cabins on either side, also ghostly and abandoned.

"I guess even ghosts need summer homes," Daniel said.

"There's something so sad about these cabins," said Mattie.

"All beach houses are sad when there are no kids digging in the sand outside," Daniel said. "You know what they remind me of? Ice-fishing huts in the Midwest, the ones they drag out on the ice. They cut holes in the ice and pull out tough, whiskery, inedible fish."

"Pike-ish things."

Neither spoke for a while. Mattie looked up into a dark, empty window of the smallest hut.

"I love this," she said. "I could live here. Could you?"

"I could live anywhere there's light."

Mattie felt an intoxication, of sea air and beer. "I could live wherever you were."

"I could live wherever you were," he said right back, and they looked into the darkness underneath the deserted restaurant to the left, Nick's Cove. "Living here must be like taking a journey twice a day," Daniel said. "Only it would be the water that journeyed. You would just sit inside, and the water would flow up to you, surround you. And hours later, the water would rush past you again, flowing back out to sea."

Mattie was in love with Daniel, of course; this was the X within the circle on her map: *I love Daniel.* It was wrong, he was married. But it was true. His friendship was an amulet. When she told him things she was thinking, about Harry or Ella, Alfred and Abby, rage against Isa and Lee, he said it back to her in language that showed he understood what she'd said. He had the time to hear, like a person who believed there was someone alive beneath the rubble of herself, who heard the soft sounds she could still make from the broken parts that had waited decades to be missed.

Mattie called Isa every morning and saw her

often, and she tried, God knows she tried, to bring love and patience to those visits. She thought of the words of Teresa of Ávila, who said, "The Lord doesn't so much look at the greatness of our works, as at the love with which they are done," and this sounded fine except when it came to Isa. There was so much stuff marbled in, all the memories of their lives together: years of anger and revulsion. Mattie had heard someone say once that we have everything inside us that Jesus has, only He doesn't have all the other stuff too. So she asked herself, If you're as loving as possible when you're with your mother, does it still count if there are other parts too — hands, for instance, trembling with rage?

Isa had lost ground but was holding her own in her compromised way when July began. One afternoon when Mattie was on her way to Safeway, it occurred to her that Isa might like to go shopping too, so on the spur of the moment, she called. Isa was instantly excited; she did need two things, she said, cat food and toilet paper.

Mattie drove by to pick her up. She let Isa putter and find her own pace and did not nudge and manipulate her into hurrying. Isa wanted to show Mattie things in her apartment that she was proud of, even though Mattie had seen them a thousand times: the view of Mount Tamalpais from her living room window; her huge, sulky longhaired cat. Mattie was watching her mother attentively. She had morphed into a new creation, no longer the ageless athletic activist but now a tentative old woman. There was something oddly birdlike about her, but also something more relaxed. She often had an air of radiance about her, the radiance of silver hair.

From time to time, Isa tipped over into full dither, though, just like that, her mind popping to the surface like a seal, goggle-eyed, "Here I am!" then disappearing into the waves, "Oops — good-bye."

Mattie felt happy to be with Isa and also pleased with her own patient helpful self. But when she said, "We really have to go now, Mom," she caught a look in her mother's eyes that made her wary. It was the craftiness she had been used to seeing in Harry's face when his toddler gremlins had risen to the surface. It was the look of somebody lying in wait, ready to pounce. Isa said, "Honey?" in this way she had.

"Yes?" Mattie asked rather squeakily.

"Why don'tcha go get my coupons?"

Mattie thought this over. "No," she decided. "Not the coupons. We don't have time. You just need a couple of things."

"Oh, honey, for God's sake," Isa said. "Go get the coupons!"

"I'm not going to. Once we get the coupons, forget about it. It'll turn into a shopathon."

So, with a look of exasperation, Isa went off

to get her own coupons. Mattie started to laugh. How bad could things get? Isa reappeared, beaming, innocent, adorable. She was Coyote Trickster: like a lot of old people on fixed incomes, she lived on the margins now, made do with very little, sneaked past her children's comfort zones, wreaked havoc with their need to control. She'd use her coupons, suck up her daughter's precious time, but she'd save a few pennies. Mattie did her Lamaze, pitiful shallow breaths as if she were giving birth to her own mother, or trying to crawl back inside her.

By the time they got to Safeway, Mattie saw she had barely half an hour before she'd have to pick up the children.

"Let me run in and get whatever you need," Mattie said.

"Oh, no." Isa shook her head. "I need to go in myself."

"Why? What do you need? Toilet paper and cat food, right?"

"I want to go in myself," Isa insisted. "I only like certain brands. Besides, I'm not an invalid."

A siren went off in Mattie's head: She's armed, Mattie thought. She's got the coupons in her purse, and she's just crazy enough to use them. Do not let her get out of the car.

"I'm pressed for time. Please let me run in," Mattie begged.

Mattie's pastor often said that we are Jesus'

presence here on earth and so we need to act like Him. Mattie thought about this, and squirmed. Would Jesus have let his mother get out of the car to buy toilet paper and cat food? Would he have been in a swivet because Mary had coupons in her purse? No. So they parked and Mattie helped Isa out of the car. They took baby steps to the line of shopping carts. When had her mother stopped being able to walk? The carts were jammed into one another. "Mom," Mattie said, "we don't need a shopping cart. Don't you just need toilet paper and cat food?"

Her mother turned to her, wild-eyed, her lips pulled into a tight smile. Mattie drew back, crying out silently, Where's my mother? What have you done with my mother?

Isa reached out to pat her arm. Mattie tugged at a cart, pushing the others back with one foot like a grumpy mime, until it finally came free. Sometimes having an elderly mother was like having a toddler, only you felt like attacking her more often. Breathe, Mattie whispered, there's still time. She fell in behind Isa.

Since she had a few things to pick up herself, Mattie told her mother where the cat food and toilet paper were. "Okay?" Isa gazed back at Mattie blankly.

Mattie got what she needed and went looking for Isa. She checked in the cat food aisle and the toilet paper aisle, and Isa was in neither. Mattie went to wait in the express line; now she had ten minutes left.

She noticed Isa in the deli section. "Mom," Mattie called to her impatiently. "Come on."

"Okay, honey," Isa said, and waved. Then she headed in the opposite direction. "Mom, come here!" Mattie called. She did not want to lose her place in line — now there were people behind her.

"I still need toilet paper." Isa's voice faded into Doppler effect.

Mattie looked at her watch. Then she looked as far away as she could, into the Siberia of the produce department. Isa was out there now, with her cart, next to two store employees. She appeared to be dealing cards to them. They took what she had dealt them and dispersed throughout the store, and Mattie realized that her mother was dispensing coupons.

She imagined a quick trip to the housewares department to buy a hammer. One blow should do it. She stood there quietly instead, refusing to lose her place in line with six people behind her. Also, if she bought one more item, she would no longer qualify for the express line.

"Mom," Mattie called as nicely as she could, as if admonishing a mischievous child, "come here." Isa tottered toward her with her cart, scanning for any clerks who might be returning to her with items from their scavenger hunt. She waved to Mattie again.

Mattie, now at the head of the line, let a woman go before her. Only if Isa came right then and still qualified for the express line herself would Mattie be on time to pick up the kids. There was nothing else she could do, so she prayed.

She prayed to see Isa through God's eyes, from the inside out. Nothing happened, that was too much of a stretch. So she prayed to see her through the eyes of a friend, the eyes of someone besides her overly critical daughter. Eventually she began to see her mother differently. She saw this gawky, tremulous woman with a badly pleated memory, working hard to keep living independently. She saw an elderly woman cadging coupons so she could pay her own way and not have to ask her skittish children for help. So Mattie stood in line as patiently as she could. She let six people go ahead of her. And by the time her mother popped back out of the waves to stand beside her in line, goggle-eyed and blinky, Mattie's heart was soft toward her again. Mattie knew this was not clinically a miracle, but it felt like one; or maybe not a miracle, but grace, if grace meant you went from small and hassled and full of hate, tapping your foot with impatience, to holding your mother's warm hand.

"Mom!" Mattie said, but Isa could hear in her daughter's voice that she was not mad. She turned to the man behind them and said, with her nose in the air and her eyes squinched shut, "This is my daughter," as if introducing him to the queen.

Mattie and Daniel picked up the broken glass scattered across the living room floor. She and Harry had been playing catch in the front yard when Ella, furious at being left out, had cried that she could play too; she grabbed the softball from her mother and pitched it through the window. Falling glass pierced the cover of Otis's cage, missing the iguana by inches.

Mattie wanted to charge a replacement window at Yardbirds right away, but Daniel argued for some time. He wanted to see if they could make the window larger. Daniel said God would provide the glass if they were patient. He had a feeling. " 'Your young will have visions,' " he said, quoting the prophet Joel, " 'and your old will dream dreams,' and your middle-aged will have occasional hunches. There's so much money in this county right now. Someone is preparing to remove a large pane of glass from their home. And we will put it in yours. In the meantime, let's staple up some Visqueen."

They stapled it to the outside frame. Harry manned the staple gun until Stefan came home. Then he took off to play. Mattie slipped him a dollar to let Ella tag along.

Mattie and Daniel took a break in the shade of the pear tree. She brought a Dos Equis for each of them and some fresh guacamole she had made. It was creamy and chunky, with lots of lime and salt.

She had spent twenty minutes at the health

food store that morning picking out perfect avocados, holding each in her hand as if it were part of Daniel. She closed her eyes at the store and daydreamed about a look she wished he'd give her. She remembered the weight of his hand on her shoulder. She felt the spot at the end of the fruit where it had been attached to the tree, and traced it with her finger. This aroused her, and she thought she must be going mad.

She felt stranger than ever these days. She sometimes found herself wanting to lean forward and smell Ned's neck, to sink her nose into his throat like a vampire. She knew Ned was a stand-in for her father, and it was unsettling for desire to come in on the same wind as disgust. She thought endlessly of Abby and Alfred together. She felt both weak and dithery, a little like Isa, and voracious and neglectful too, as Isa used to be. Mattie wanted to devour her children when she wasn't with them, but she could hardly tolerate their neediness when they were about. Ella clung to her like a starfish, and Mattie saw herself peel away her fingers as she and Al used to peel the arms of starfish off the boulders at Pelican Rock.

At Nicky's, only good things were happening. With his new salary increase, they were adding a room to the house. Mattie and Nicky had raised their two babies in the one room; but Nicky's kids were each going to have their own.

Lee's cramping had passed, and now she was glowing again like a night-light — the best of being womanly and young. Their big boy was heartbreakingly beautiful. Nicky got a Saab. They had their porch enclosed to keep the bugs off their perfect skin and lives. They hired a sixteen-year-old named Katie to come in the afternoons to take care of Alexander. On some Sundays she dropped Harry and Ella off at Mattie's, where, after the English garden and swing set at Nicky's, Mattie's family must have looked to her like trolls living under a bridge.

Nicky's house had Persian cats lolling about on Persian rugs.

Mattie had Otis.

He continued to stare off into eternity in his glass cage by the living room window, shedding and having his terrible episodes. The first time Katie came in with the kids and peered into the glass, Otis had a prolonged shit-spewing episode. She had said, "Oh, God!" with such disgust that Mattie felt a roar of corresponding shame.

But Harry redeemed the moment: "That's my boy," he enthused.

Isa was often at Mattie's these days, because Lewis was still at his son's in Georgia and she got lonely. She was antler-thin, and clearly not all there. Left on her own, she rarely put dinner together, although when she did, no matter how many times Mattie reminded her, she always included foods rich in vitamin K. She'd call Mattie to tell her. "Aren't I a good girl?"

"Mom," Mattie would sigh. "The Coumadin doesn't work if you eat foods with vitamin K."

"And you got your medical degree *where?*"

These pressures would have seemed more or less bearable. But then Mattie and Al had a terrible fight. They'd been getting along well, sharing in the help Isa needed, rattling along in basic agreement that for the time being neither would do anything rash concerning Noah and Abby. They agreed to let the shock of Noah's existence settle in, and wait until they figured out their next move. But one night Mattie told Al what Ned had said, that Abby had been seen briefly. Al surprised her by blowing up.

"Oh, shit, Mattie! You told Ned? Ned will've told everyone. Now everyone is going to say our father ruined Abby's life."

Mattie grimaced. She had somehow forgotten it was such a secret, because she'd so easily given it up to William. But she couldn't really explain the calculus of trading the secret for William's kindness. She was mad too that Al would question her judgment. "Ned won't tell anyone," she said haltingly. "And Daddy didn't ruin her life. He gave her Noah — which was the best thing that ever happened to her."

Al flushed. "You weren't going to tell anyone but Daniel and Angela. Now everyone knows but Noah. He'll know soon enough, and then he'll understand why we've been skulking around town like pedophiles."

"We aren't the pedophiles, Al. Daddy was."

Al sucked in his breath as if she'd punched him. Mattie knew the ground kept shifting under them both — first she insisted that Noah was a gift her father had given Abby, and in the next instant that Alfred was disgusting. But there wasn't time to sort it out. She looked for traction, to defend herself against the most unlikely enemy of all, Al.

"Oh, for Chrissakes, Mattie. It was the sixties," Al said, turning away from her.

"So it was okay to be a sexual predator in the sixties?"

"Listen to you. We don't even know what happened. What if she seduced Daddy?" he asked, glaring.

Mattie whistled, slow and accusing. "She was my age."

"That's not the point. The point is . . . Shit, the point is, the point is . . ." His cheeks were pink with emotion. He folded a bank receipt into a fan and did not look up. "The point is we had a deal. I only told Katherine, like we agreed, and you were supposed to only tell Daniel and Angela. We had an agreement. A plan. Now you're plowing straight ahead, all by yourself."

"So my boyfriend told his father. What is the big deal?"

"The big deal is that we had an agreement to do it together," Al said. "This is how it always ends up in our family, everyone just going off alone — doing whatever they feel like, and not honoring promises."

"I thought you wanted to welcome Noah into the fold."

"You said you wouldn't tell, and then you did."

"God, you sound like Harry," Mattie said. "What, are you going to go tell Mom on me now?"

"You're in the wrong, Mattie. Just admit it."

" 'It was the sixties,' " she sneered. Al got up and stalked toward the door. Before he slammed it, he looked back at her with Harry's fury, Ella's desolation. Then he was gone.

"Everything's just awful," Mattie told Daniel days later as they drove to church. He had agreed to drive Mattie's car, because she felt too shaky. "Al and I haven't spoken since the fight. Isa's barely functional. My car is falling apart, and I have no windows in the living room. It's Cannery Row at my house. Nicky has cats that cost more than we spend on groceries in a month."

Daniel listened. He stopped at a light and turned to her. "But Mattie," he said, "we have Otis!"

In church he put his arm around her. The pastor read from Psalm 42: "My soul is downcast within me; therefore I will remember you from the land of the Jordan. . . . I say to God my Rock, 'Why have you forgotten me?' "

Mattie wiped at her eyes.

The pastor started the sermon by singing "I Need Thee Every Hour," and the pianist followed with the sweetest descant before the congregation joined in.

Mattie tried to listen to the sermon but had trouble concentrating. What should she do about everything? Or anything? About one single thing? Then the pastor, as if reading her mind, said that it took time to know God's will; that even Jesus didn't arrive at "Thy will be done" quickly, or He wouldn't have spent so much time in the garden.

After the service, Daniel opened the passenger door for her. She picked up the Bible he always brought to church and turned to the psalm again. " 'As the deer pants for streams of water, so my soul pants for You, O God.' "

"That was so beautiful," Daniel said as they drove. " 'As the deer pants for streams of water.' " He pulled into the drive-through window at Blondie's, where he ordered three strawberry milk shakes.

They were late getting to Daniel's because they stopped by the side of the road to drink their shakes. Pauline was at the bedroom window when they pulled into the driveway. They got out of the car, and Daniel held up the third milk shake toward the window, as if raising a toast to Pauline. She disappeared from sight.

"Come in and say hi," Daniel insisted to Mattie. Pauline threw open the front door, gorgeous in a shift of coral gauze, an ivory moon and star hanging from a soft white cord around her neck. She held her arms out to Mattie. Stepping up for a hug, Mattie felt vaguely threatened. Pauline gave Daniel a warm kiss and ushered them into the kitchen, where bread was baking. By then Mattie was nearly asthmatic with terror. Pauline put her shake in the refrigerator while Daniel and Mattie sat at the table. Pauline put water on for tea.

"Have you and Al made up? I heard about the fight," she said. Mattie suspected this was meant to show that Daniel shared everything with her.

Mattie shook her head no, whispered, "Not yet."

"Well, everything's going to be fine," Pauline replied. Mattie nodded miserably, and then felt Daniel's foot nudge hers. It was not exactly footsie, but it seemed a steadying connection just the same, like her father might have made during conferences with her unhappy teachers. Mattie smiled into her lap.

"Have you read the latest Doctorow?" Pauline asked. Mattie shook her head. "It's fantastic. I can lend it to you if you want." Mattie felt a prick of suspicion.

"That's sweet of you. Thanks."

"It's by my bed," Pauline said. "Why don't you go get it?"

Mattie trudged up the carpeted steps as if an

angry parent were waiting for her upstairs. Daniel had offered to retrieve the book, but Pauline had needed him to open a jar of jam. The bedroom looked so beautiful, so simple. Daniel had done the carpentry himself, and Pauline had chosen and found the furniture and fabrics at secondhand stores. He had built window seats, and she had covered them with buttery-hued damask cushions and ivory throw pillows. You couldn't have such light colors with kids around, Mattie thought. You needed patterns, jungle fatigues. You couldn't have anything nice. Sunlight streamed through the windows. Mattie turned toward the sleigh bed. On it was a tray with two coffee cups on saucers, a blue Chinese bowl holding one strawberry and a lacy pile of strawberry leaves. The book was on a bedside table, beneath a pair of tortoise shell glasses.

Mattie walked slowly to get the book she no longer wanted. As she got close to the bed, she could smell the residue of sex. It smelled as if someone had just returned with a good catch, a hold full of bass on ice — bleachy, sweaty love. God, she thought, shaking her head and picturing Pauline: You got me. The comforter was sheathed in the palest blue. Mattie reached for the book; she felt Pauline rubbing her nose in the comforter: Mine. We are the ones, Pauline was telling her, we are the ones who make love.

Mattie limped downstairs to the kitchen with

the book. She stared off in the distance like Otis as she walked. Something inside her shifted; the veil parted for a second, long enough for her to realize something new. Pauline had sent Mattie to her room to put her in her place, but not because she was simply sadistic. She'd been afraid. Mattie wouldn't need to be put back in her place if she hadn't fallen out of it. Pauline was afraid that she was losing Daniel. She wanted him back. And she wouldn't need him back if Mattie didn't have him.

Mattie could not look at Pauline or Daniel when she stepped into the room.

They all made too much conversation while they had tea.

Mattie gave Daniel the blue shoe a few days later. They were in the middle of a heat wave, an Iowa July, deep watermelon days. She'd run into him at the garden store, where he was buying topsoil. It was sweltering. "What's this for?" he asked.

"I don't know," she said. "I just thought you might like it for a while."

Mattie and Al hadn't spoken in a few weeks. Lewis hadn't returned. Isa wept for him when she called Mattie, afraid his son would force him to stay in Georgia. What could Mattie say? Just that he'd return. "Come out to the pool with us, Mom."

"I can't wear a swimsuit anymore," Isa said stiffly.

Mattie laughed. "Yes, you could," she said. "You still have great legs. But wear a light shift, if you'll feel more comfortable. I'll pack a lunch and pick you up at noon."

She took her mother, Ella, Harry, and Stefan to the high school pool. They made a nest of towels under an umbrella for Isa. Mattie offered her a frosty can of apple juice before jumping into the water with Ella. From the pool her mother looked like an old sock monkey. Harry and Stefan disappeared into the shouting, splashing chaos of the deep end, while Mattie and Ella stayed where it was shallow. They had tea parties on the pool floor, the web of sun their tablecloth, holding their breath and imaginary teacups, pinkies extended, in the shimmering net of light.

One Friday afternoon when Mattie arrived at the superette to work, Ned whispered with an odd urgency that he and William had just spotted Abby. They'd been driving past the shacks early that morning, when they'd seen her sitting in the ice plant that grew near the huts, drinking from a brown paper bag.

"You won't tell anyone, will you?" Mattie implored, thinking of Al.

"Excuse me, Ned." A woman was taking him by the arm. Mattie turned to look at the Blondie's manager, Suzanne. "I need thirty

269

pounds of ground beef. You got that much in the freezer?"

"I think so," said Ned. "Don't worry," he told Mattie. "I'm not going to tell anyone." He walked off with Suzanne.

Suzanne linked her arm in his. "Tell anyone what?"

Angela listened to the whole story over the phone. "An electrical storm is building."

"Secrets get out, don't they?" Mattie said.

"I guess so. The truth seems to want to establish itself. It always eventually floats to the surface, like a dead body. Look at J. Edgar Hoover. The dresses — and Clyde — didn't come out till he'd been dead awhile."

Mattie laughed for the first time all day.

On a horrid hot evening in late July, Isa got on a bus one night, for no reason anyone later could discern, least of all Isa, and fell getting out. She ended up in the medical center at The Sequoias with a sprained ankle, badly bruised and deeply disoriented.

After she hung up with the nurse, Mattie called Al. He arrived with Katherine ten minutes later. It was a relief to see him. Katherine threw her arms around Mattie and held her. She wore a green knit cap. Her bangs were growing out in front of her eyes. She brought the children chocolate milk to distract them while Mattie and Al headed out.

Isa was asleep in bed. Through a curtain that separated the two patients, Mattie and Al caught a glimpse of an old black woman in the next bed. A chubby young Filipino nurse came in. Her name tag said "Esmerelda."

"Mommy's going to be okay," Esmerelda promised.

"How long do you think she needs to stay here?" Mattie asked.

"Mommy needs full-time care until she can walk again. If you can get a nurse, she could go home in a few days."

Isa woke up groggily but snapped to with a look of intense concentration. Then she took in the strange surroundings and burst into tears.

"Why am I here? Get me out! I'm perfectly fine. Oh, Mattie, please get me out!" But she wasn't going anywhere.

Mattie stopped by the medical center with Daniel the next afternoon. Isa was terribly agitated. "Jesus Christ, she and her family're driving me crazy," she whispered, indicating her roommate. "All these black yahoos." Mattie shushed her mother, horrified.

The roommate's family showed up at that moment. They greeted Mattie and Daniel like long-lost family and introduced themselves as the woman's daughters and grandson, and smiled with nervous good manners at Isa. She glowered at everyone.

Mattie was telling Isa how the kids were

spending their summer, when the other woman's daughters began softly singing "Leaning on the Everlasting Arms." It was beautiful at first, the daughters and the grandson singing, and Mattie closed her eyes to listen better. Then a harmonica started — it must have been the grandson. The sound was harsh and tinny, as if someone had started accompanying them on dental drill.

"Jesus Christ!" Isa exclaimed. "I told you — didn't I tell you?"

Mattie glanced inside the curtain in time to see the sleeping woman reach out a crablike claw and grip her grandson's wrist. Her daughters sang to her, and her grandson started playing harmonica again, and Isa cried out in pain, her fingers stuck in her ears, reminding Mattie of Ella. A look crossed the other woman's face too, but you couldn't tell whether it was recognition — whether this tinny accompaniment was getting through the sponge of her coma — or whether it was just terror at the calamitous noise: The drill! The drill!

When Nicky came by with the children that evening, Harry ran into the living room to play with his pet. He wailed in surprise. Otis was gone. He'd made a break for freedom. Mattie did what they do in the movies — she secured the area and called in a search party, Al and Daniel, who combed the house. Harry proposed holding an article of Otis's clothes for

Stefan's retriever to smell. But Mattie pointed out that Otis had no clothes.

"Otis has no clothes?" Harry asked sarcastically, and she felt she'd been trapped in an episode of *Perry Mason*, with Raymond Burr about to produce one of Otis's bathrobes or brassieres. Harry whipped out Otis's leash, with its tiny name tag. Stefan's dog sniffed it, and with Harry exhorting him, raced around for a while.

"Get that fucking dog out of here before he eats Otis," said Al.

"Don't swear at the children, Al," said Mattie.

When the excitement of the search was over, the real sorrow began. Part of Mattie was exasperated — this was an iguana. But loss was loss, and the children were inconsolable. They cried for Otis and all the other sad things in the world.

Harry locked himself in the bathroom. When he finally let Mattie in, his eyes were red and swollen. "Mommy?" he said. "God has stopped loving this family."

Mattie told him not to give up, that there was still hope, but that if Otis didn't return, maybe it was God wanting to give Otis his freedom.

"Otis will die outside, though," Harry said. "He's cold-blooded."

Mattie's heart may have been cold toward Otis, but it was so warm toward Harry. She promised they would find him.

"He's just a big heartbreaker," Harry cried.

Oh, Harry, Mattie thought, but secretly she hoped Otis would not come back. She fantasized about how much bigger the living room would seem once cleared of Otis's cage. She thought with a kind of moral righteousness about mothers in other countries who did not have the luxury of worrying about their kids' pets. Otis, with his hot rock and his lettuce leaves, was living more luxuriously than half of the world's children. And then she thought, What about dealing with this one boy's broken heart?

She imagined Otis staying outside all night, hugging his shoulders to his little chest, shivering. That got her down on her hands and knees to begin another search. She even went through Ella's Beanie Baby collection — maybe Otis was pulling a Hannibal Lecter, had hollowed out the chimpanzee and was hiding inside. She looked in Harry's closet and then, almost as an afterthought, went through his GI Joe trashcan. Otis was at the bottom.

Mattie called for Harry. He raced in joyfully, reached into the trashcan, and picked Otis up. Ella came in, clutching her chest like a *verklemmt* old auntie. Harry put Otis in his cage in the living room, and the three of them stood looking at him. He didn't move, didn't blink, just stared. Harry went to the kitchen for some lettuce, and stood over the cage holding a leaf like a bottle of milk for an orphaned newborn calf. Otis didn't move toward it. Harry refused to go to bed until Mattie promised to stay awake with Otis for a while. Otis did not move at all. She sat there holding a lettuce leaf, the two of them looking off in the same direction.

As she was staring into space, a feeling stirred in her. Her eyes had glanced off something that she should have paid attention to. The feeling was so strong that after she was sure Harry was asleep, she retrieved the GI Joe trashcan. But there was nothing special inside — wadded pieces of paper covered with Harry's precise and spidery figures, a red plastic car, food wrappers, dirty twine, punched-paper dots. Mattie looked at Otis again. He was looking at her. "Do you know what I'm supposed to notice here?" she asked out loud.

She clapped her hands to her mouth. Isa knew. Isa had known all along, not only that Alfred had girlfriends: Isa had known all along about Abby and Noah, and knew still, somewhere deep in the Otis part of her brain.

Mattie sat rocking, her head in her hands.

Everyone had known. The game had been to keep from knowing what you knew — and certainly never to say what might be true. If you let even a trickle in, it might wash you away. The game was to hope that everyone else would agree not to know what they knew too.

Mattie and Al used to go to the pier with their parents, when Nick's Cove was still a

275

thriving restaurant. Now the pier and restaurant were in near-ruins, but thirty years before, this had been a working pier. Commercial fishermen brought in their catch every morning, men would unload the rope-handled boxes full of fish from the boats, and someone from the restaurant would come by with a wheelbarrow to cart them off.

Mattie sat on the wet sand across from fog-shrouded hills rolling down to the bay, several hundred feet from the shacks, which balanced on spindly stilts like long-legged birds. Beneath them, on the beach at low tide, she could see the flotsam and jetsam that had flotted and jetted onto the sand — a mud-encrusted shopping cart, shredded styrofoam buoys, a yellow rubber glove.

Mattie kept her eye on the smallest cabin, the one in the middle, with the prow. The only sounds were the cries of gulls, the surf, an occasional car on the road up past the beach. Finally she noticed motion through the window, the flash of what looked like a ghostly old man, some kind of ancient mariner. He disappeared, and there was no more movement.

The smells of the low tide were very strong, swamp smells, and the water was deep baby blue. Patches of darkening sky broke through the fog. Mattie watched and waited and thought about the blue on the paint-can key. She wondered if Isa knew where that room was, the one Alfred had painted. Then Mattie saw the face again, small and obscure.

The face appeared ruddy and wrinkled. Mattie turned to see what the eyes would be seeing, a reflection of trees floating on the blue sparkling water. When she looked back to the shack's window, the face was gone. Then the window opened slowly, and the person inside tossed something out, something red, a bowl of reddish-gold paint, or a soup of tomatoes and saffron. The strands fluttered balletically in the air like prayer flags: long, thick reddish-gold hair. Abby, newly shorn, stood holding her face toward the sky.

Mattie leapt to her feet and ran as fast as she could to the cabin. She looked in the window but saw no one inside. She jiggled the door; it was locked. "Abby!" she cried. She knocked, pounded, looked again through the window, half expecting to find Abby surrounded by baby-blue walls. The weathered and battered walls were instead a dingy, uninspired white.

nine

On a cold morning in September, Mattie returned to the shack. She wanted to do right by Al, and give him time to let Abby's presence in town sink in, and then go out with him some afternoon. But school had started, and he could go only on weekends. When she asked if he wanted her to wait for him to go, Al said no, his presence might scare Abby away. Mattie thought he might be a little afraid of seeing her. She went by herself.

A storm was gathering. The gulls sounded like chimps, and over the roar of the wind and the surf, she could hear chimes. Standing on tiptoe and craning her neck, she could see through one of the windows. She could see a screened-in cold cupboard, where a buckled pack of tortillas perched between a brick of orange cheese and a pint of milk. Cut into one wall was a rectangle where a Murphy bed must have been hidden away. "Hello?" she called feebly, but all she heard was the wind and the waves, the gulls, the chimes, the bass beat of her heart.

She pouted and tried to think straight. Somehow, impossibly, Abby must be in here; maybe she was folded up inside the Murphy bed. Maybe she was hiding, feeling the way

Otis might feel when the three cats sat beside his glass cage and watched his every move, scheming and dreaming of lizard for lunch. Mattie turned and walked back down to the beach.

Gulls lined the pier, crabby and nasal, like Angela's uncle Irving. Mattie listened to them kvetch: "Oh, can it, Phil." "Jeez, my knee's killing me." The pilings supporting the pier were splayed drunkenly, dropping off entirely as the pier extended out to sea. Daniel once said it looked as if the pier had tried to take a long walk down its own short self. Should she call him from the pay phone? He could be out here in an hour. Meanwhile, she could keep Abby treed inside the cabin, like a possum.

But Mattie didn't call. She knew Daniel was preparing for a long vacation with Pauline. They would drive halfway across the country, to Michigan, where Pauline had grown up, staying in motels along the way. Mattie and Pauline were barely speaking, and when they did talk, the air was charged with tension. Mattie usually waited for Daniel to call. She'd had to phone the other day, though, and she prayed as she dialed that Daniel or the machine would pick up. "Hey," Pauline said lazily after Mattie said hello. "How you doing?"

"Good. Lots going on." She told Pauline briefly about Isa, and Pauline made clucking sounds of warmth and commiseration.

"How's that cute William?" she asked.

Want his number? Mattie wanted to respond. "He's good." Please, she wanted to cry, I'll give you twenty bucks if you'll put Daniel on. "He's terrific."

"You don't want to let that one get away," Pauline said.

Mattie laughed and rubbed her eyes with her free hand. "Is Daniel there by any chance?"

"Yeah, he's taking a nap. Let me have him call you back."

"Great," Mattie said.

"How'd you like that book I lent you?" Pauline asked.

Mattie looked back up at the shack, at the little ark. It was an embracing shape, the color of depression and old age, bleached out and neutral. It was the color of exhaustion, the color of old people who do not get out much anymore. Mattie turned away, toward the low hills across the bay. If only she could see that face again — Abby's face in the window, ghostly, distant. Mattie smelled seaweed, oyster shells, gulls.

All she could do was turn like a ballerina on top of a jewelry box, seeing now the tawny fog snuggling down into the dips of the hills, now the crossbeams under the deserted restaurant, now the pilings, peglegged and clubfooted, the gulls sitting sentry. The sloshing and lapping of the waves was so comforting, like someone helping a child fall asleep, shhhh shhhh shhhhh, and she could think only to keep turning slowly in the sand.

At the window where Abby had been, there was no movement, no shadow. Across the water, plumes of fog in several shades of gray, low and rounded like recumbent bodies, like the photos of nudes that resembled sand dunes. She could no longer remember, if she had indeed ever known, what Abby had to offer, but she knew only that when she herself was a teenager, gawky and always scared, sure that no one liked her, pining for her glamorous father, missing him desperately and calming herself with images of him out there saving the world, Abby had gotten his attention instead. And on one of those weekends when Mattie had been missing her father, imagining him in Washington, he'd been only miles from home, at some nearby hospital — maybe the one in Tomales where the ranchers' wives gave birth. Maybe there he watched his infant son emerge from a girl as young as his children, his soul-sick daughter, his alcoholic son.

Mattie imagined her mother back then, spinning slowly as she herself spun now in the sand — looking for her husband, for what they had had, for their future together, while he tiptoed away to Abby Grann. Maybe Abby was a green shoot that broke through the pavement of a marriage that was killing him. Mattie looked back up to the rotted pane where she had seen

Abby, the window old and clouded as beach glass.

The door of the shack creaked when Mattie opened it. No one was there, but the window was open, the window through which the red hair had been strewn. "Abby?" Mattie said softly. There were old moldy dog smells, and some milk going bad in the cold cupboard, Coke bottles on a counter with an inch of soda left, cigarette butts at the bottom. "Abby?" You could reach up and touch the ceiling. This was a home you could put on, pull down over your head like a serape, carry off with you. Mattie walked a few steps to the window, glanced down at the piling on one side of the shack, where dusty ivy reached from the earthy banks of the beach, flowing and twining into heaps of watery seaweed. The shack felt like a jail cell. In the middle of the back wall, on the shore side, was an incongruous little door that seemed to lead directly outside, ten feet above the beach. It had a rusty latch to keep it from banging in the wind. Mattie supposed there must be a closet, with a window, inside. Two posts, three feet apart, held up the ceiling in the middle of the room. Maybe there had been a door here once, and two rooms, but now you could walk through the door frame to nowhere and back.

Mattie crossed to the cold cupboard. If you looked through its screen, you could see crescents of beach. Beside the sink were a kettle on a hot plate, an empty box of Lipton's tea bags, and the last bag, drowned and tangled in its own string on its paper envelope. Mattie turned back and gave a tug to the small door, but it wouldn't open. She stood with her back against the door, rubbing her eyes. Maybe she had only imagined Abby. The face had looked so distant and dreamy at the window, as if she weren't really inside, as if she'd been superimposed on the glass. Mattie tugged again. There was some give, but the door opened only slightly. The gap closed suddenly, the door pulled snugly again, as if by a spring inside. Mattie tilted her head. She heard the weather-noisy sea, the wind, the gulls, the chimes — and she heard someone breathing.

She took hold of the latch and pulled it as hard as she could. The door groaned and opened. Sitting there, on her haunches, on top of a toilet seat in a most cramped space, clutching her knees to her chest, hiding her face behind a curtain of bangs, was Abby Grann.

Abby's hair, cut just below her ears, was dirty and matted. She wore the clothes of a beggar in a fairy tale — a long faded red cotton peasant dress, the hemline ragged and muddy above socks pierced by foxtails. Over the dress hung a shapeless Irish fisherman's sweater, sagging to her ankles, full of holes like a fishing net. Mattie thought of the Fisher King's queen in her raggedy guise, gathering herbs to take away the pain of his wounds that would not heal.

Mattie gasped and drew back, her nostrils flaring with all the smells that assailed her — urine and rust, and unclean breath, and cigarettes, and underarms, and dirty feet. Abby had covered her face with her huge hands, and had begun humming a tuneless song, like a child who believes that not seeing the parent means the parent cannot see the child.

After a long moment Mattie reached out and touched Abby's red cracked knuckles. Behind her was a tiny window, and a view of bay and hills, blue water, green hills, swaying trees, rolling fog.

"Abby, I'm Mattie," she whispered.

Nothing — no movement, no motion, no sound but the tuneless song.

Then Abby lowered her hands, and her face shone with an expression of ruined beauty. Her skin was fair, with roses in the hollows of her cheeks and red plaid blotches near her eyes. These were Neil's eyes, hazel, almost green, wreathed in black lashes, deep and bloodshot. Her mouth was Neil's too, long and full.

Eyes closed, Abby hummed. Mattie's heart hammered in her chest.

"I've been wanting to talk to you so long," said Mattie. Abby looked over her shoulder through the window with a direct view to the bay, to water no longer so rough. The wind had quieted and the waves were nearly smooth. The tide was rising; it would soon cover the pilings of the house.

"I want to talk to you about my father." Nothing, no sound from Abby but the tuneless song, and eyes that looked around without expression, landing on Mattie's gaze but not stopping, as if Mattie's eyes were windows she didn't have time to look through just now.

Abby was like an ostrich; if she just sat there long enough, maybe Mattie would go away. Mattie felt desperate. "I have a son too," she said in a rush, "a little boy named Harry, who looks like Noah. But he's only nine." Mattie sank toward the plywood floor, holding the door open with her knee.

Talking to Abby was like trying to lasso a fish, throwing out a lariat here and there: each time, fwap, it landed dead on the floor. Abby looked at her, her face tilted slightly like the man in the moon, and then stood. When she rose, Mattie stepped back. Abby slipped past her.

What was Mattie supposed to do, rush her, wrestle her to the floor, handcuff her? She felt her stomach drop. She'd expected that finding Abby would change everything, or at least change something. She watched as Abby shuffled out the door, down the dirt road toward the deserted restaurant. Mattie's vision began to blur with fatigue, the lack of sleep the night before, but also with exhaustion born of hopelessness. She shook her head to clear it, but words and thoughts flapped around her head. She let her head drop, and leaned over and slid down onto the plywood floor, made a pillow of her hands, and closed her eyes.

Mattie drove to the superette. When she arrived, Ned was closing for the night, ringing up his last two customers at the register. He unlocked the door to let her in.

"There you are. William says he hasn't heard from you in a few days. You coming tomorrow?" Mattie nodded unconvincingly.

She stood by awkwardly while the two customers paid, and focused on the rolls of fly strips festooning the superette. Ned locked the door behind the last customer, turned the "Open" sign to "Closed." "What's going on?"

"I just saw Abby Grann," she said.

"Oh, God. Well, let's go to my office." Ned turned off the lights and led the way. His thick rubber soles squeaked with each step.

The back room was crammed with produce boxes, some stacked and full, some flattened, some wedged between a desk and a chair. Ned pulled the chair toward her. He retrieved a pint of Johnnie Walker from the desk drawer, and poured them each a couple of inches.

Mattie told him everything about her encounter, and Ned listened. When Mattie was finished, he fished a pack of Lucky Strikes out of another drawer. He lit one and offered it to her. She shook her head. He closed his eyes and inhaled deeply, looking as if he was trying to recall someone's name. He rubbed his eyes. The smoke from his cigarette wafted toward the ceiling like a ballet dancer. She remembered an obscure line of Meister Eckhart's — about how, if the soul could have known God without the world, God would never have created the world. She thought now that if God could have given her Ned without her having to date William, she would not have had to date William. Her mouth opened slowly with an insight: It was wrong, she now realized, to go out with someone who simply filled a space meant for Daniel.

The children were asleep when Mattie got home. She related her adventures to Al and Katherine, who had come by to care for them. Katherine took Mattie's hand in hers. Her fingers were as long and elegant as a pianist's. Al barely spoke.

"What are you thinking?" Mattie asked him.

"It's just so sad, is what I'm thinking. I'm thinking about Mom, and what she's been through. What it would be like to have a husband who'd fucked a teenage girl. I'm thinking I wish I could save her." He gripped the hair above his forehead, and pulled it backward, as if he were trying to scalp himself. Katherine touched his arm. He turned to her. "You cannot imagine what it took for her to get that shrink in place for me. It meant crossing my fa-

287

ther, going against his will. It meant spending money we didn't have. It meant giving up what little free time she had, to work as an office temp — filing, typing memos! And then driving me to the therapist, and waiting till my hour was up. And I'm thinking, What do I have to give her now?"

"You're so loyal to her," said Mattie.

"But I'm annoyed with her half the time too."

"Yeah, well, she's annoying. But you're loyal anyway."

After Al and Katherine left, Mattie went to the kids' rooms to tuck them in. Harry, as always, slept with one leg on top of his blanket. Ella was on the floor beside her bed, where she had nestled her dolls. The bottles of nail polish were lined up on her bedside table.

The next morning, Mattie sat at the kitchen table with Daniel, drinking coffee, with Ella asleep in her lap. She and Daniel were saying good-bye.

"Oh, I don't really want to leave, Mattie. Too much is happening."

"Then why are you going?" she asked.

"I don't know how to get out of it. I have to do it, to save my marriage."

"You don't, really."

"Don't have to go, or don't have to try and save my marriage?" She shrugged. Daniel began to do origami with his shirttail.

"I hate to leave when you have so much

going on," he said. He reached into his pants pocket and pulled out the blue shoe, held it out to her on his palm the way you offer a sugar cube to a horse. Mattie pushed his fingers closed around the shoe, her hand covering his, cupping it so the blue shoe wouldn't run away.

She called William and told him she needed to see him. He said stiffly that he was sorry but he'd kind of figured things out for himself. He'd decided to save himself the trip. Mattie felt more hurt than she'd expected. She said, "Okay, then. Well, I guess I'll see you at the store," and he said, "Okay, then. Good. See you soon."

"He's in a rage because you initiated it," Angela told her later on the phone. "I'd push all the furniture up against the door if I were you."

"It's weird. The needle's not moving to the left or the right."

"The needles are moving all over the place, just not on the one dial you're staring at. There is serious movement going on inside you, with Isa . . . Abby . . . Daniel. How's Isa, anyway?"

"She's Otis part of the time, and George Wallace the rest," Mattie said.

Isa was so foggy and tired these days that Mattie and Al had had to hire aides for fourteen hours a day. Mattie had gotten a small line of equity loan on the house to pay for the extra help — an aide to be there at seven when Isa woke up, and stay all day, while trying to remain out of sight, because otherwise Isa would be unpleasant. Mattie had seen one afternoon how awful it could be. Isa was staring contemptuously at the aide, who'd been begging her to take a shower.

"Why don't you get out one of your voodoo dolls, and shower it instead?" Isa asked. She'd widened her eyes until they were nearly all white, like a demented voodoo queen. Isa was scared to death herself, Mattie saw, and getting meaner every day. She wouldn't shower, even with someone right outside the bathroom to help her if she fell. There was a rail, and a shower chair, but even those were not enough; she needed someone to hold her, hand her soap, help her rinse, yet she would not allow this. "Why don't you button your lip," she told the woman.

"Yes, ma'am," the aide replied.

Another aide, Lorraine, a heavyset African-American woman, had cooked Isa pumpkin soup and corn muffins, which she was finishing up one afternoon when Mattie arrived. "That looks so good," Mattie had told Lorraine, at which point Isa pinched her nostrils shut and held her nose in the air to show that she thought the food stank. Mattie's heart sank again. It was hot and humid, and a heavy smell of urine filled the place, because no matter how clean the aides kept things, there was urine in the sofa and the mattress. Mattie noticed pajamas in a bucket in the shower, and in another Isa's good-looking tailored trousers with three pairs of soaked underpants and Depends inside them.

The aides did the wash every day. Mattie brought rolls of quarters for them to use at the machines, and sat with her mother while they did the laundry. These were women Isa would have scrambled to support in her organizing years, women she would convince lawyer friends to represent pro bono, women whose children she would have clothed with shirts and pants her own kids still wore. Now she had turned into a caricature of the racists she had hated.

Mattie continued to pray for a miracle. Al had started tutoring a student two nights a week to help pay for the aides. Mattie had increased her hours at the store. The last time she had taken Isa in for a checkup, Dr. Brodkey found a bedsore on Isa's bottom, caused by her lying too long in her own urine. The doctor insisted that Mattie take a brochure to look at with Al, from a nearby nursing home, The Willows, that took Medi-Cal.

They read the brochure that night, miserable as could be. On the cover was the picture of an old man sitting on a bench beside his handsome, caring son. The man seemed to be shuffling even though he was sitting down, a look of wooden dignity on his face, his vacant eyes glittery. The hands in his lap at first seemed to be

291

in repose, but were undoubtedly gripped with fear like Isa's.

"I can't do this," said Al. "I'm sorry. I just can't."

"You can't look at a brochure with me?"

"I can't put our mother in a nursing home."

Mattie prayed even harder for a miracle.

Toward the end of September, Lewis came home. He was stunned by how much ground Isa had lost. He sat with her as much as he could, and called Mattie every few hours. The Isa who had come home from the medical center was simply not the same Isa who had gone in.

Harry was in fourth grade now, and there was at least an hour of homework every night, real homework. No matter how hard she tried, Mattie could not get him to sit down, do the work, put it away, dust off his hands, and reclaim any of the night. It was hopeless, she thought. He had no future. He would have to work at 7-Eleven when he grew up, helping people find the longer straws for Slurpees.

His backpack looked as if he'd stolen it from a wino. At bedtime on Sunday nights, he would announce, "I've got homework."

"Oh, Harry, why didn't you mention this before?" Mattie would say.

"God. It's not a big deal," he'd reply disdainfully. "Where do we keep our dowels, and cheesecloth?"

★ ★ ★

One evening, during a heat wave, Mattie drove out to Abby's shack. The day had been fierce and red. Mattie had been sitting at the kitchen table when she happened to look up and see the silhouette of a squirrel behind the curtain, racing across the sill, hunched and hurried as a spy. The next thing she knew, she had risen and gone to find her purse.

This time when Mattie walked up to the window of the shack, she saw motion inside. She stood at the door for a while, and finally knocked. Time passed. She did not knock again. Then Abby opened the door. She looked over Mattie's shoulder, but stepped back so Mattie could come in.

There was a chair now in the middle of the room, to the side of the doorposts. Mattie sat down. She knew not to look straight at Abby — so she glanced out to sea instead. Abby meanwhile circled the perimeter of the shack like a shark, as if spreading her scent to mark the place, while taking in what could be seen. She stopped in shadows with her back to Mattie. She was pale, a ghost in the house.

The teakettle whistled. Abby took two cracked thick coffee cups, ivory with a dark green band, and poured boiling water into each. She picked up a used tea bag, dunked it into one cup, then the other, and wrung it out before putting it on its wrapper.

Mattie got to her feet. It was seven-thirty.

The days were still so long in September. She usually loved this, the length of the light, because the big dark always came after. But she was scared to death this evening, to be inside Abby's timeless zone. She stood at the window nearest the sink. Abby did not seem to be intentionally ignoring her; she didn't even seem to see her. She was just making tea, adding sugar, and the last drops of milk from the carton in the cold cupboard. The sun was still out but not shining on them any longer. Abby handed Mattie a cup of tea. Her neck seemed nearly as wrinkled as Isa's. She sat with her back against the door to the tiny bathroom and lit a cigarette. They held their cups of sweet milky tea.

Abby had an awful voice, from the other side of the grave, like Otis played on the wrong speed. "I can't talk to you today," she said.

Mattie sipped her tea. "Okay. Then when? And how will I know?"

"I'll get in touch with you," Abby said.

"How?"

Abby thought for a long time. She blew out smoke as if cooling a burn. "Through Ned."

Harry had a night soccer game at school, and Al ended up coming along. Ella sat with Mattie and him in the bleachers, then squirmed away to play on nearby swings.

"Stay where I can see you," Mattie called. They watched Harry out on the field, strong and graceful, a natural leader, leading the charge, calling out encouragement, giving his all with every length, every kick. "All right, Harry," Al shouted, making a megaphone of his hands.

"How come you never had children?" Mattie asked rather abruptly.

Al reared back as if she'd stung him. "I didn't want them."

"How come?" Mattie asked.

"I don't like little kids. I love yours — but that's about it."

Mattie looked around for Ella, who was not far away, prowling the border of the playing field, walking in her own world along a chain-link fence lined with weeds. She was singing to herself, and when she looked up at Mattie, checking in, she had a glint in her eye. They waved to each other, and Ella turned away.

"I never knew that, Al."

"There are people who glisten when children are around, but not me. I love Harry and Ella, but it's partly because I always get to leave. I'd last four minutes if I couldn't."

"Yeah?"

"I would raise reptiles more easily than kids."

Mattie smiled. She watched her son run down the field with gangly grace, like a gazelle. Ella was still walking along the fence, singing her song, picking tiny daisies, lost in her world, right where she wanted to be, on the edge and at the same time so safe.

* ★ ★

Isa got much better after Lewis returned. He was often at her apartment when Mattie stopped by; she took him to church every Sunday.

But one day he called from the medical center. Isa had done what everyone kept nagging her to do. She'd tried to take a shower — but she'd fallen, and hit her head so hard on the bathtub that she'd be in the medical center for at least a week. Dr. Brodkey urged Mattie and Al to consider admitting Isa to the convalescent hospital until she got stronger.

"Neither of you can take care of her full-time, right?" the doctor asked them pointedly when they came to visit Isa.

Al and Mattie both shook their heads slowly, but while driving home he told her, "This kills me. I don't think I can do it."

"I understand."

"I know you do, but Mom gave up everything to get me help. So how can I even think of putting her away?"

"She gave up me, to help you." Neither could think of anything else to say. They drove along. Finally Mattie spoke: "Anyway, it's just until she's stronger."

"But what if she's never stronger?"

"We have to figure this out as we go. And I know this is the next right thing."

Several days later, Mattie was at the airport

to pick up Angela. Although Mattie had said, "Oh no, that's too much trouble," Angela had insisted on accompanying her and Al on a safari to The Willows. Now Mattie stood at the gate with Ella, watching as passengers filed off the plane. A vision in white appeared, in drawstring linen trousers and a flowing embroidered blouse. Above it all was Angela's face, rounder than Mattie remembered, beaming. Mattie felt as if the medics had arrived.

Harry had gone off to a sleepover, and the women had the house to themselves for once. Angela painted Ella's nails while Mattie cooked spaghetti, and then Ella did Angela's toenails. After dinner, Ella took Angela to each of her shrines, like the Stations of the Cross — the villages she had built in the dirt, a flower bed she and Daniel had planted, Marjorie's burial ground, and inside the house, the laundry room, which Mattie and Daniel had painted a soft, buttery yellow. Angela and Ella unfolded the futon there. They stretched out on it and lay gazing at the ceiling like people waiting for an eclipse. The three cats appeared. They stepped gingerly onto the futon, walked around for a while, then jockeyed for position on the soft throne of Angela's stomach. Later Ella snuggled between Mattie and Angela on Mattie's bed until she fell asleep, and Mattie carried her to bed. The women lay on their sides facing each other and talked all night, like homesick beings from another planet who had been living among earthlings far too long.

The director of The Willows was warm and sympathetic and hearty. He gave them a sales pitch and then left them in the waiting room. Big-band music played softly, and framed photos of 1940s movie stars covered the walls. Mattie imagined the chandelier descending from the ceiling, and the antique table rising, and the walls moving closer together, until she was squished like a gigantic breast in a mammogram.

"It's like he's trying to sell us a car," Al whispered.

"Boy, I tell you," Angela said. "No matter how nice it looks, it's all about urine. I can smell it from here." The odor was strong and sharp.

"You're so wonderful to come with us," Mattie told her. The big-band music played on. The director returned to show them around.

Mattie's heart sank lower with every step. This was an impossible place to put her mother — and it was as good as convalescent care got. It was a place inhabited by vacancy, she thought. You could hear the sound of vacant minds. The first woman they met was tall and elegant, and seemed still with it, until she started popping and peeping, as if answering the mating song of a whooping crane: Pop pop peep. Maybe this was what language sounded like to her, all pops and peeps. Several people were parked in wheelchairs in the hallway, staring. There were a couple of snappy, well-dressed women on a bench in one sunlit corner, and the director stopped to fawn over them, but Mattie couldn't help feeling that they were shills, that when the tour was over he would start talking abusively to them, or hustle them back to their main jobs in the kitchen or laundry room.

"Here we go," said the director, holding the door to a room marked "Activities," where four vacant people sat slumped over.

"Hello," the director called cheerfully, and two of the four looked up.

"Excuse me," Angela asked. "What would you call this activity?"

Mattie knew the answer; it was called sitting. And sitting was different from lying down near death. Sitting in community, in the sun, was different from lying down and staring at your own walls, which is what most people seemed to be doing here — except for the shills, and the popping-peeping woman, and the people in the activity room, actively sitting.

On the way out, they saw the old man pictured on the brochure. When they passed, Angela clutched at her heart and fanned herself. "It was him," she whispered, as if they'd come upon Paul McCartney.

Al and Mattie put their mother in The Willows a few days afterward, against her desperate will and their own. She sobbed. "It's just for a week," Al told her, "till you're strong again. I promise." Lewis drove with them and held Isa's hand all day, gently telling her again and again that she needed to be here just for a while. She held her nose. The Willows stank of people's urine, and it smelled of bad food going worse, left on trays, on nightclothes, in the hallway. Isa cried, she smoldered, she shrugged and flung hands off herself when anyone tried to console her. She looked over at a roommate who appeared to be dead.

"Why can't I come to your house, Mattie?" When Mattie couldn't answer, Isa wept.

Mattie cried too: "I can't take care of you properly. You need more than I can give you. You need to get strong, and then you can go home."

Isa sat in her wheelchair and wept some more. Mattie and Al exchanged anguished looks. Mattie felt she might faint suddenly, and had to sit down in the room's only chair. She could hear Al consoling Isa, promising that he would get her out soon, but Mattie wished he would shut up. Would Isa ever get her freedom back? Her mother stopped crying, and a puzzled look appeared on her face, as if someone was calling her from far away.

Mattie tried to visit Isa at The Willows every day. Al sat by her bed for an hour every evening

300

while she ate. Both of them kept up a stream of light conversation, pushing stories that might cheer her, mostly about Ella and Harry. But Isa slept much of the time and then woke crying. Sometimes she seemed not to mind being at The Willows, and she reigned bossily from her bed, complaining about what she called the room service. Other times she wailed for her old life. The nurses and orderlies were kind yet firm with her, and she grew fond of one in particular, a heavy young woman in her twenties with huge Scrabble-tile teeth named Adrianne, who called Isa "Missus" and watched tennis with her on TV.

In October, Adrianne announced that if the family could provide nursing care, Isa was ready to leave The Willows. Now new troubles arose. They had no plan B. Where would Isa live? Personal Care, the assisted-living program at The Sequoias, wasn't covered by Medi-Cal; board and care facilities were several thousand dollars a month that they didn't have. Nursing homes like The Willows would be paid for by Medi-Cal, and her apartment was subsidized by an HUD grant — so these were the two places she could afford to be. But while she couldn't live alone any longer, she wasn't ready for convalescent care.

Mattie wrote a note to God — "Help!" — and put it in a shoe box.

The heat came again, bright, rigorous overhead light. One Saturday, while they were on their way to the swimming pool, Mattie brought the children to visit Isa. The first two times they'd visited, Harry had cried about having to go. Mattie remembered when they'd all been able to go to the pool together. "Please, Harry," she told him, "seeing you will help her." She brought colored pencils and paper for them, but Harry was sullen and Ella equally wary.

They had to make their way past the old people who sat in the hallway like deserted rusty appliances. One woman did endless tongue-thrusts from her wheelchair. The children's eyes were wide open, huge, like shields. They were scared of the witchy old women in the hall who might clutch at them without warning. Harry pulled his arms in and took baby steps to keep himself safe. He did not leave anything out that might be grabbed or bitten or kicked by those bony, unearthly legs. In Isa's room, Harry and Ella leaned into each other, became one big squat body, so that the scary people could not break through and get in. They were Siamese twins, united for once, joined at their sides. But after fifteen minutes or so, Ella softened and went to sit beside Isa in bed and draw. Isa was at her best, happy and patient. Harry glowered and fidgeted and turned in the swivel chair while his untied shoes wobbled, threatening to fall off his feet.

They went to Isa's at breakfast time a few days later. She was in bed, eating, but she shouted in joy to see the children. She seemed better, stronger, more her old self. She let Harry work the controls of her bed. Both kids crawled in bed with her, one on each side. Ella played with the familiar flesh of her grand-mother's upper arm. Then Adrianne came in and clapped her hands, chop-chop; time to get Isa out of bed. So Mattie and the children wandered the halls and worriedly watched the old people do things nice old people were not supposed to do — play with food, moan, gape at things that weren't there. Grandparents were supposed to have looks of tender appreciation on their faces when they saw children; these people wore rubber Halloween masks of insanity and vacancy, their eyes rolling and weepy, their tongues thrusting, their fingers of bone.

Daniel called from a gas station in Idaho late one night. He and Pauline had been fighting — about nothing, he said, fighting about fighting. Pauline wanted him to go out and let her be in the motel room alone, but he couldn't stand the banishment.

"It's bad this time. Everything's gotten out of the burlap sack."

"Oh, Daniel."

"I'm so depressed, Mattie. But if I leave her, I feel like I'll go nuts."

Mattie was gladdened by the news, even as she listened to his pain.

"What would you do if you were me?" he asked.

She didn't answer immediately, because she could hardly draw a breath. It was the point of no return, and it was time. "I would come stay in our laundry room for a while, until I could figure things out," she said. "And I'd trust God. He will either calm the waters, or He will calm you."

Daniel was silent for a moment. "I feel like my mind is breaking up. I'll call again tomorrow."

And he did. He asked if the offer still stood.

"Yep," said Mattie. "We'll get the laundry room ready."

"Okay. But Mattie? I snore." He sounded congested.

"I won't be able to hear you from my room."

"What will you tell the children?"

"That you're going to stay with us for a while."

Again Daniel said he'd call back, and when he did, it was to say that Pauline had hit the ceiling. She'd told him that if he left now, it was all over. He hated himself for seeming weak, but he needed more time to think.

Mattie felt both crushed and a little relieved. Boy, that was close, she thought. There would have been no going back to what they had now. Still, she got in bed at noon and wept.

Later in the day, she called The Sequoias and asked about Personal Care. There were studio apartments with no doors or stoves or refrigerators, and people around during the day to help you dress, eat, take your medication. It was way beyond Mattie and Al's reach financially, unless they sold Isa's house. But then where would Mattie and the children live? Isa's Social Security check was twelve hundred dollars, Mattie and Al had each kicked in nearly five hundred for the aides already. But Mattie had to get Isa out of The Willows.

Every time she drove to the superette, Mattie hoped that Ned would take her aside to say that Abby had called. She kept thinking in a cracked way that the paint-can key came from a blue room somewhere, with money hidden away on which Isa could live. She expected Daddy still to have all the important answers. Al said, "Oh, honey," when she told him.

Lee had been ordered to bed for the last month of her pregnancy, so Nicky came by to take Harry and Ella out to dinner a couple of nights a week instead of keeping them on the weekend. Otherwise they were with Mattie all the time. Harry was withdrawn and angry about everything. He put chokeholds on Ella's dolls to upset her, and slammed them on the floor. He had a perpetual sneer now, usually regarding Mattie with mild contempt.

"Harry," she asked one day, "could you take the garbage out?"

"Doesn't look like it," he said.

Ella seemed more and more to be unfurling.

Her fair hair always escaped the barrettes and scrunchies intended to contain it. She chose clothes that no longer fit, or that wouldn't for a year, and trailed loose threads and bits of yarn, as though she'd unknit completely if you tugged at a thread to remove it.

One day when the phone rang, Mattie leapt to answer it, hoping it was Ned. It was Daniel, still in Idaho. "Okay," he said. "I'm driving home. Could I still stay with you a couple of nights?"

"Yes," she said.

Mattie started getting the laundry room ready for Daniel, and the kids agreed to help. She opened the window, made up the futon with her best sheets and comforter, put a low table beside it, with towels folded in a way that Harry said made them look fancier. Ella brought in flowers from the garden, and also taped some of her drawings to the wall. Harry organized pencils and a sketch pad on the table, a fresh package of dental floss, some moist towelettes, a glass for water. The cats arrived and plopped on the sunbeam that stretched across the futon.

Harry and Ella even went willingly with Mattie to The Willows that afternoon. Al was already there. He and the kids found a stray wheelchair to push one another around in. Mattie and Isa listened to the children's happy voices in the hall until Isa fell asleep. Mattie sat looking at a bottle of expensive lotion from

Paris, a brand her mother had always worn, which Alfred used to give her. She breathed in the smells, urine and decay, flowers and feet, toast and tea, breathed in the warm, eternal almond scent of her mother's skin.

Daniel called from Elko and again from Sparks. Each time she heard his voice, she figured he was calling to say he'd come to his senses, he had to drive back to Pauline. But he was still coming. "I'm going slow," he said. "I've been stopping to fish. I'm so depressed."

Mattie told him what her therapist had said once, that you should go only as fast as the slowest part of you could go. "Have you talked to Pauline?"

"No. She's said some things that are pretty hard to forget."

That was all he wanted to say. When she put the phone down, it rang again. She picked it up, sure that it was Daniel. But this time it was Ned.

The snap of a match, the smell of sulfur and then tobacco. Outside the shack window a burst of evening sun was burning through the fog. The leaves of the trees on the road tossed furiously. Mattie and Abby were drinking weak milky tea. The Murphy bed was unfolded, made up with white sheets and Mexican blankets.

"I really miss my dad," Mattie said. Abby had color in her cheeks now, perhaps from walking on the beach. But there was no light on in her eyes.

"I remember your father's feet," Mattie said. What an odd thing to say, but it was one true thing. "He had long, bony feet. Like flippers."

Abby looked at her as if she were speaking backward.

"Isn't that funny?" Mattie asked. "I can't always remember to turn my engine off when I get out of the car, but I remember that your father's second toes were longer than his big toes. And he had a five-o'clock shadow, like Nixon. He must have hated that."

Abby's face became cool and mean, her chin jutting with disdain. "He was such an asshole," she said.

"Who?"

Abby didn't seem to be about to answer. "My father."

"I thought you meant mine," Mattie said. Abby shook her head.

The waves crashed on the shore. The gulls cried. Mattie couldn't think of a thing to say. Finally Abby spoke. " 'Sometimes when I'm lonely, Don't know why, Keep thinkin' I won't be lonely, By and by.' "

"What's that?"

Abby scratched her head. It sounded like sandpaper.

"From a book of poems Alfred gave me for graduation. Langston Hughes."

"Graduation?"

"From eighth grade."

Mattie's stomach bucked, and she held her hands out like a beggar. "Tell me more. Please."

"I remember when he came to the carriage house where I was living, after I ran away from home. First he didn't believe my baby was his, but he was the only man I'd gone all the way with until then. He gave me money for an abortion and took me to the city to have it, but I got out of the car and ran away. He screamed 'You stupid bitch' at me in the streets. We were on Lombard. I remember we saw Al that day, right in the middle of fighting, on Lombard. Then Yvonne told him he *had* to help me, or she would leave."

There were vacuums in Mattie's heart, caffeinated, froggy. "What? What do you mean, she would leave?"

Abby cocked her head. "And what do *you* mean?"

"I mean, what are you saying? You make it sound like Yvonne was involved with my dad too."

"I don't know what you're saying." Abby picked tobacco off her tongue and scratched her head again. Now it sounded like a rodent trying to get out of a box. It sounded like the rats that had been in Mattie's walls. "Is this a joke?" she asked.

"Tell me what you mean! That my dad and Yvonne were together?"

Abby stubbed her cigarette in an abalone shell ashtray. "Of course they were together."

"But I thought she and your dad were the couple."

Abby knitted her brow. "They were too."

Mattie felt for the pulse in her neck, to see if she was surviving. It was a river of heartbeats. God, she prayed, God God God God.

The shack was almost dark, although the sun was still setting across the water. Abby got up and went to the toilet. She didn't close the door, and when she didn't come out, Mattie went to investigate. Red-faced, exhausted, Abby was hunkered down on the seat, the huge sweater down to her ankles. She hugged her knees to her chest, and her cheek rested on one knee.

Mattie had questions to ask her still, but she saw that the conversation was over for now. She walked through the ghostly door frame to the sink, rinsed out her cup, laid it on a paper towel to dry. She turned back to Abby and said to the half-opened door, "At some point down the road, I need to talk to Noah."

"No, you don't," Abby said after a long silence. "Leave the poor baby alone."

The bathroom door closed slowly. Mattie stood at the sink and hugged her own shoulders. The rising tide swirled and crashed around the pilings below the shack. Mattie was perched on the edge of a crevasse. She could hear the tide rushing past her on both sides of the house. The sea smelled strong, too strong. Everything smelled too strong. The lights of the town across the water glittered gold and distant as stars, while the sun lay flattened and red between the water and the star-filled night.

ten

The October sun shone on Noah's tall, narrow cabin on a rise in the middle of a field five minutes from the Cove. Mattie drove past. She knew even before she took the paint-can key out of her pocket that the flecks would match the paint of the house, although the hard sun glowing in the blue silk sky had faded it over the years. Oaks and bay laurels hemmed in the field. The house itself looked as if it had been set down in front of a blue studio backdrop, a house-shaped hole in the sky. Seeing Noah's truck in the parking lot of the library had emboldened her to drive out here. Ned had drawn her a map on a scrap of brown paper bag. She'd pushed it deep into her pocket, alongside the paint-can key and the little blue shoe. She wanted to tiptoe up to Noah's house and peek inside. But she was afraid to get too close. She rolled down the window and breathed the outside air. It smelled fresh and old at once, grandfatherly and green.

She drove closer. She couldn't imagine what the point was. This was ridiculous: he wasn't home, and she was going to be late for work. But the secret she'd been keeping all these years, without even knowing what it was, had made her feel like one of those people whose metal fillings picked up radio stations, tinny music that played inside their heads. And now she wanted the bad fillings pulled. A breeze rustled the shining limbs of the bay trees. Leaves fluttered, nervous and playful, gold, green. She thought of the limbs as Japanese dancers, now twining around one another, now giving one another room.

Mattie sat at her kitchen table with a cup of coffee several days later, tracing her lifeline with the paint-can key, thinking about the decisions she needed to make. What should she do about Noah, Isa, Daniel? The children were with Nicky. Daniel, who was staying in the laundry room, had gone to fix Pauline's car. He'd be back, and he'd feel melancholy. It was not exactly the romantic Hallmark fantasy Mattie had hoped for, to have a deeply depressed Daniel living with her, yet she liked having him around. The children adored him, and camped out in the laundry room whenever they could. He'd had a brainstorm too, persuading Mattie to let Ella get her ears pierced. And by God, Ella had stopped biting her nails so much. Now she endlessly twisted the posts in her ears instead.

Isa was back at The Sequoias. The aides had stopped giving her foods containing vitamin K, so the medicine could kick in, and it did: she stopped having strokes. But Mattie and Al played a shell game with the Sequoias personnel, to keep them from noticing that Isa was too frail in mind and body to remain where she was, in Independent Living.

Mattie sat at the table, obsessing, orbiting around herself. She was sick of her worried, hostile mind. It would have killed her a long time before, she felt, if it hadn't needed the transportation.

She realized with a start that the tables might be turned; she hoped Noah would not stalk her, or sneak onto her property, or fixate, or spy on her. She stared off into the middle distance and let her focus blur. Then she closed her eyes and sat as still as she could, waiting. She prayed, hummed idly. And something floated into her brain, a cellophane butterfly of thought, the most radical thought of all. She could tell the truth.

Mattie did a double-take, and her lips parted in a half-smile. What a concept! Tell the truth, and let go of the results. People sometimes called out to her pastor, "Say it!" Say what is *true:* tell Daniel, and even Pauline, that she was in love with Daniel, and hoped to be with him someday. Let Daniel and Pauline figure out what they wanted to do. Tell Isa that she was no longer strong enough to live alone. Here were her choices: The Willows, or Personal Care. Tell Noah that she was his sister; he could do what he wanted with that. She hoped he would want to be her brother. She felt she was standing on a snowy slope at Lake Tahoe, afraid and game at the same time, trying to get her balance and catch her breath, her lungs seared by the cold. So that is what I would do, she told the ceiling, as if it had been standing with its hands on its hips, waiting for her final answer.

She thought she'd start with Daniel, since he was closest, but when she went to knock on his door for dinner that night, she heard him on the phone with Pauline: "That is so crazy. That is so provocative. Because she and I are not sleeping together. That is not what this is about." Mattie felt crushed, and confused and angry: We're not sleeping together yet, she wanted to shout through the door. Then it *will* be what this is about. But then, maybe he didn't know he was in love. This was a fly in the ointment.

The next morning the phone rang at dawn. It was Isa, crying hysterically about a terrible fire at Mattie's.

"No, no," Mattie tried to reassure her, "maybe you dreamt it." But Isa did not believe her. "I tell you, Mom, I'm right here in my house, everyone's fine." Isa hung up on her.

When Daniel came out of his room, she told him what was happening.

"What are you going to do?"

"Yesterday I had an epiphany. I realized that all I ever have to do is to tell the truth, and let go of the results. That was my first inclination.

But now I'm leaning toward sedation."

"Sounds like a plan." Their eyes met briefly, and she thought about telling him that she was in love with him. But a moment later, unable to catch her breath, she thought, What were you *thinking?* and reached for the newspaper.

Lewis called later in the morning, asking breathlessly if everyone was okay. He had been awakened by a call from Isa. "Please try to convince her, Lewis, there is no fire," Mattie told him. Two hours later the receptionist from The Sequoias called: Isa was stopping people in the hall to tell them about the terrible fire at her daughter's house. Mattie drove over with some Valium. She gave them to Lewis, with instructions to dispense them to Isa whenever the obsession with the fire started up again.

The fear resurfaced every few hours for a week. Lewis ran out of Valium. Isa grieved for Mattie's lost photo albums and dead animals. The director of The Sequoias called a number of times, expressing worry about Isa's state, and Mattie lied and said that her mother was having trouble adjusting to some new arthritis medicine. She told the director she'd call Isa's physician. After Mattie had left a message for Dr. Brodkey, Lewis called her to say that Isa had struck at him in frustration. Mattie called Dr. Brodkey again, this time saying it was urgent. She left a message at Al's school, asking him to call the minute he could. She cleaned house while waiting. When neither of them called back, Mattie got in bed with the phone and a seven-ounce Hershey bar with almonds, and stayed there past noon eating chocolate. The doctor didn't call until dinnertime. By then Mattie had figured she'd rounded the corner to being a perfect size 14. At this rate, she'd be a 16 by Christmas. Maybe Sears would rehire her. Dr. Brodkey said she'd write a prescription for a sedative; she'd run out of other ideas.

Days passed in a blur. Mattie usually loved autumn most — the tang in the air, shorter days that brought with them the sense of deepening and rest. She loved the elegant light, the pumpkin and scarlet leaves. And she didn't even mind Thanksgiving. Everyone knew just what to do: You sat, ate too much, got stupefied. Then you cleaned up and everyone went home.

They had Thanksgiving dinner at Mattie's house. Daniel made a table extension out of plywood, which they covered with one of Isa's old lace tablecloths. Mattie roasted a turkey. Al and Katherine brought side dishes, Lewis fresh cranberry sauce, tart and lumpy and delicious. Katherine remembered a can of the jellied kind for the children. Isa seemed sedated, not speaking much, her eyes intelligent but her mouth frozen into a simulation of interest. It was easy, a series of conversations about the latest national news, town gossip, the children's school, Lewis's family. All talk of fires had been put out. They sat down, with Mattie and Daniel as heads of the table, and Lewis said grace. Everything was going well until Pauline called.

"Hey," she said to Mattie. "Have you already sat down to eat?"

"Yes, but just barely. What's up?"

"I need to borrow Daniel's car, to drive into the city. My starter's shot."

"Shall I go get him?"

"No, no. I've got a cab outside. I'll be over in ten minutes."

Pauline let herself in, flounced into the dining room, and gave everyone expansive hugs and kisses. Isa cried out with such joyful surprise to see Pauline that it might have been Bobby Kennedy who'd just walked in. Pauline pulled up a chair between Isa and Al, beaming at them both. "Hey, you," she said to Daniel.

She looked wonderful, luminous, her lush hair, now streaked with a few strands of gray, piled on top of her head, and held in place with black lacquer chopsticks. She reached out to touch Daniel's hand when he said something that pleased her — acting twinkly, coquettish, sarcastic, wrapped like a package in a deep-lavender pashmina. Daniel seemed happy to see her so buoyant, but not as happy as Isa.

"Oh my God, but this is marvelous," Isa exclaimed. Her face had pinked up. "Why haven't we seen you more?" Pauline shrugged, as if it didn't make sense to her either. Isa turned to

Mattie. "Has she ever looked more beautiful?" Mattie replied that no, she never had. "But I mean, this just makes our day, doesn't it, Mattie?" Mattie nodded, yes, it sure did. She smiled nicely at her mother, wondering if there was any vitamin K–rich food on the table with which to induce another stroke — just a small one, to make her stop talking.

When Pauline accepted a plate from Daniel, with samples of everything, Mattie's stomach tightened with unhappiness, and she excused herself to the bathroom. She checked herself out in the mirror before returning: she looked sweaty and dumpy from working in the kitchen. She splashed cool water on her face, powdered her nose, put on lipstick.

Pauline kept the conversation flowing, and flirted with everyone, Harry and Ella, Al and Katherine, Lewis and Daniel and Isa, everyone but Mattie, with whom she was overly cordial. Katherine was cold toward Pauline to the point of being rude, for which Mattie adored her. Pauline described in great detail some driftwood figures that had appeared overnight at Bolinas Beach, sculptures of beach musicians. She'd gone back twice to see them. The kids would love them. They made you feel wild and creative. Mattie sat feeling like Bartleby.

Isa brightened under the sun lamp of Pauline's attention. She spoke in complete sentences, in paragraphs even. She seemed to be tracking. She and Pauline held hands. Mattie imagined her own hands around Isa's neck, throttling her.

Pauline said her good-byes, and took Daniel aside. While Mattie turned to watch, Harry crawled loyally onto her lap. She nuzzled his head gratefully. Daniel looked as if he had a headache, and Pauline looked sorry, but she retrieved her black wool coat and put it on. Mattie rose to join them.

Daniel wiggled the car key off his chain and gave it to her.

"Good-bye," Pauline cried gaily. "I've got to go right now or I'll be late!" Daniel turned slowly toward Mattie, looking like a little boy who had just seen his only balloon float out of reach and head for the open sky.

A few days after Thanksgiving, Daniel sat Mattie down at the kitchen table and told her that he and Pauline had had a really good talk. "We spent a lot of Friday on the phone," he said. "I went and saw her yesterday."

Mattie's face would not cooperate with her wish to appear cool. She could feel her mouth purse like a child's, like Ella's, into teary disappointment. Daniel sighed loudly and shook his head.

"Are you going back?" Mattie's voice broke.

"I don't know what I'm doing, but this arrangement is making her nuts. It would make me crazy too, if she stayed with a man — even her best friend."

There was no sound in the kitchen but the hum of the refrigerator, the song of chickadees in the branches outside.

"I have to go pick up the kids from Nicky's today," she said abruptly. She left without looking at him.

Mattie stopped by Isa's with the children, and they stayed for dinner and watched TV with her. Mattie ordered in pizza and let the aide take two hours off. She wanted to go home, but delayed returning so that Daniel could stew in his own juices and indecision. By the time she realized that she was the one in the stew pot, and sped home, he was gone.

His things were still there, but he didn't call and he hadn't come back by the children's bedtime. Harry acted out, anxious and mean, rough with the cats, flicking their noses and laughing when they mewed. Mattie sent him to bed, lay down with Ella, and read her *Yertle the Turtle*. They heard Harry crying next door. Mattie softened. "Honey," she called. "I'll be right there."

She put down the book and tucked the covers around Ella's neck. They said a quick prayer, and Mattie kissed her. She put Raffi on the tape player, so Ella could listen as she drifted off. Then she went to see Harry. He was pressed up against the wall in the dark. She climbed in bed beside him and rubbed his thin back through his pajamas.

"Do you think he's ever coming back?" Harry asked in a quavering voice.

"Oh, yeah, I do. But honey, I don't know if he's really with us."

"Of course he's with us," Harry said. "He lives here now. He's ours."

"Oh, honey. He's actually still married to Pauline."

"Yeah, but he should be married to you."

"What makes you think so?"

"Duh. It's so obvious. She thinks she's so great." Mattie kissed her son, smelled the sweet skin. "Plus, she's got that big fat ass."

"Harry!" Mattie laughed. "Stop. We don't care what her butt looks like."

"I don't think I've seen such a big jiggly butt in my whole wide life."

This conversation cheered her up enormously. She stretched out on the couch and read until nearly midnight, looking up each time she heard a car pass, rearranging her face into expressions of sultry kindness. But when Daniel didn't come home by midnight, she got in bed and cried, as quietly as she could. She tried to cry herself to sleep, yet she stayed wide awake.

She imagined a murderer sneaking in the front door. She imagined Daniel coming home, walking into her arms, taking her teary face in his hands and bending to kiss her. She imagined Daniel and Pauline in bed, the intense sexual relief of making up. This pleasure might be reason enough to stay married. She took a sleeping pill with brandy, but it didn't help. It only impaired her, made it hard for her to walk to the bathroom for a pee. She looked at the demented woman in the bathroom mirror, and saw mug-shot numbers across her chest, after her arrest for stabbing Pauline and cutting off her head with a chain saw.

When had she started letting herself go? She needed a haircut, and a facelift. She needed to start dyeing her hair. Her wrinkles were deeper, her eyes exhausted. Finally she heard Daniel's car pull up, and his key in the front door. "Hi, kitties," she heard him say. He was thoroughly drunk, talking to the cats, slurring. She sighed with relief.

Pauline called the next morning when Daniel was still in bed. Mattie had brought him orange juice and aspirin and coffee first thing, settling into the kitchen herself with the paper.

"Let me ask you something," Pauline said. "How do you get this to come out right?"

Mattie thought it over. "I don't actually need to make it all come out right for everyone," she said. "Things sometimes happen, Pauline."

In the weeks that followed, Mattie was tired all the time from working at the store. When she got home the children fought, and she shouted at them and slammed doors; her mother called every few hours, again crying about the fire, and Mattie repeated tightly that there was no fire, that everyone was fine. But no one really was fine, especially her. She used to be sweet, able to tolerate so much more.

Now if people cut her off in traffic, she was ready to follow them home.

One afternoon she found everyone hiding from her in the laundry room. Daniel was in his beach chair, reading. Ella was sitting on the futon with her back in the corner, drawing. Harry was lying beside her, facedown, wearing swim trunks imprinted with sharks, and an orange plaid shirt with a collar. The cats were stacked up on Daniel's bookshelf, like opium users on dosshouse beds. Everyone turned to look at her as if she were armed.

"Hi, you guys," she said. "Don't you want some more light?" She flicked on the switch, filling the room with overhead glare. Ella shaded her eyes. Her nails were bleeding again. Harry ignored her. Daniel looked up fretfully. He had lost ten pounds in two months. She walked into the room and turned on the two reading lamps so everyone could see better, although none of them wanted to. "Harry," she said nicely, "you really can't wear sharks with plaid." Harry turned to Daniel.

"Mattie?" said Daniel, and got up to offer her his seat.

"I can't sit down," she said shrilly. "I've got a whole house to clean! While you all laze around like the gentry. What do you think I am, the

324

scullery maid?" She walked toward Ella, who dropped her sketch pad into her lap and put her bleeding hands in front of her face as if to fend off blows. "What are you doing, Ella?" she yelled. "Jesus Christ."

"Mom!" Harry shouted at her. She took a step toward him, not knowing what she might do; there was ringing in her ears and Isa's fire burned in her head, and she whipped around and hit the wall as hard as she could. Her fist went through the Sheetrock. The children screamed.

Mattie stood there, her fist hidden, swallowed up by the wall, surprised by how easy it was to punch a hole in Sheetrock. The room was silent except for the footsteps of the cats as they fled. Ella started to cry.

Daniel led her to the kitchen, where he made an ice pack for her hand out of a Ziploc bag. The children huddled in the doorway, as if she were dangerous. They looked like refugees.

"I'm having a hard time," Mattie said.

Daniel suggested he drop the children off with Nicky and Lee, but Mattie couldn't bear being the kind of mentally ill mother whose children had to be dropped off at their father's house after her episodes.

"But you are," Al pointed out when she called him from her bedroom. He laughed, and she did too.

Mattie and Daniel and the children hung out, uneasily, through the afternoon, and then, at sunset, they drove to Bolinas to look at the driftwood musicians on the beach. Mattie hated to admit it, but Pauline had been right. This was an astonishing creation, musicians jamming by a crumbling seawall. The sculptures were six to seven feet high, jaunty, exuberant, made of wood and whatever else had washed ashore in storms of the previous winter. They were elongated like Giacomettis. Wild heads and rolling eyes, skeletal ribs and round tummies, exploding hair, hands and fingers and instruments of hoses and ropes and twigs, eyes of juice-bottle tops, ratty pirate pennants.

The children shouted and screamed and raced around like dogs. A horn player blew a driftwood trombone, a pedal-steel guitarist and a bass player strummed kelp strings. All of them had twigs for toes, except the lucky vibe player, who wore mildewed boots. A mopheaded Rasta groupie with a tubular stoned look watched, and a coyote with a kelp mane howled with his head thrown back. There was a black marimba player, maybe singing harmony, with black zori hands and a kerchief of green fishnet. The drummer had an Amish broom beard, his chest the old foot liner from the floor of a truck. People milled around, pointing out details, laughing.

Someone eventually built a bonfire. Mattie and Daniel went to warm themselves, smiled at the other grown-ups. It was getting cold. Bottles of wine and flasks of brandy emerged from purses and pockets, and were passed around. Mattie and Daniel took sips of whatever came their way. "Where are the kids?" she asked.

"They're right over there," Daniel said, pointing down the beach. Her children were moving across the sand, gathering materials. Harry had a tangle of wire or fishing line; seaweed streamed from Ella's hands.

"My father would have loved this," she told Daniel. He nodded, and reached for the bottle that someone was holding out to him. "This is what it was like when I was a kid, with Al and Abby in Neil's backyard — meeting up with whoever was there to go take a look at what had washed ashore."

Food appeared — cheese, bread, apples. Daniel pulled a bag of M&M's from his jacket pocket, and people picked them from his cupped palm like Communion wafers. The children made a cat near the musicians, with wire whiskers, seaweed tail, red juice-bottle-cap nose, and green cap eyes, and Mattie felt restored by what two kids could make from a bunch of beach junk tacked to driftwood poles.

She had somehow kept neglecting to tell Daniel she loved him. Actually, he asked her not to: After Christmas dinner, when everyone else had left, and the children had gone to sleep, she believed she was getting the nudge from God; this was the night to tell him. It took a while, and a shot of brandy, and it took ignoring something inside her that seemed to be trying to flag her down. But sitting by the fire, with the tree lights on, she took a deep breath and said shyly, "I'd like to tell you something." Daniel looked sick. "Are you okay?" she asked.

"I'm afraid you're going to say something that's too interesting for me to handle right now," he said. So she shut herself off like a flashlight.

She asked God and Angela what to do. Angela came through as usual. "Can't you give the poor guy a break? He's clearly not doing very well. Can you imagine the laundry room as a hospital room? You wouldn't try to get someone to get it together, or get them to date you, just after they've been admitted. You'd take them as they are, and you'd do what you could to help." So Mattie tried. Her heart grew softer, some of the time. He was really a mess, losing weight, not sleeping. There was something egg-wet and spiky about him, like a newly hatched bird. She watched him in the garden with Ella, picking flowers or playing fairies, or persuading Harry and his friends to help paint cabinets. His being there, the intimacy of the day-to-day, the sounds of sleep and the bathroom, his late-night pain on the phone with Pauline. It began to extinguish her lust. She started fantasizing about making love with Nicky again, or William.

One night she blew up at Daniel after he'd been holed up in his room on the phone with

Pauline. "I've been waiting to call Angela all night!" she snapped. "Now it's too late!"

Daniel looked at the phone in his hand as if he had no idea how it had gotten there. He turned to her. "Do you want me to move out?" he asked quietly. "I think this is too hard on you. You have so much going on."

"No, no," she said, instantly mortified. "I'm sorry I'm being so ugly. I'm just not myself." But she was herself, and that was the problem. She had wanted to move outside the small flower bed of her old sweet helpful self, and had imagined stepping into a wild, overgrown garden of jungle flowers and exotic ferns. Instead it seemed that inside her was a septic field: it was disgusting. She was short with everyone, Isa, the children, Daniel. There was no end to the depravity of her thoughts now. She thought about killing her children, and the cats. She wondered how Otis would like to be put down the garbage disposal.

Mattie told Daniel that she really wanted him to stay, which she did. The next day he made a cinder-block bookshelf with three pine slats, as if to prove himself, and he brought some books from home. Mattie and the kids came to his room often, alone and together, plopping down on his bed where slanting afternoon sun lit the walls and the futon.

He bought a fan at the Salvage Shop. Mattie knocked on the door one hot day in January and stepped in. He was sitting on his beach chair with a book, while Ella slept, boiled and butterflied like a shrimp, on the futon. Daniel put his book on the floor. Mattie nudged Ella over and stretched out beside her.

"How you doing?" Mattie asked.

"I'm a cuckoo clock," he said.

"Yeah, you and me both." His dreadlocks were trimmed to just below his ears. He still had the most beautiful lips she'd ever seen, the palest pink. He tucked his hands under his thighs as if they had to be contained, as if they would lash out otherwise, or fly away.

Isa had become strangely quiet. Where had all that energy gone, all those memories and opinions, all that talk? She watched people talk now, and listened, beaming. Lewis stopped in to see her several times a day. He brought her snacks from the dining room under his coat: fruit, buns, slices of cheese, anything he could sneak out that didn't have vitamin K. He let her show him the shrine of Alfred every day, the photos in frames in the hall, and listened to the tour of their marriage again and again: Oh, here we are with baby Al! Here we are at the St. Francis Hotel, on our twentieth anniversary, just as in love as the day we met! Here we are at Mattie's graduation; here we're camping in Yosemite the year before Alfred died. Lewis sat by her bed while she slept, and he prayed or read the book of Psalms he carried with him everywhere. He made her walk every day down the halls of The Sequoias. "Oh for Chrissakes," she would grouse, but would walk with him for twenty minutes, as far as the Personal Care units — which she treated like a forbidden zone. Then she'd turn around and head for home.

Isa needed to move into Personal Care, that was clear. She regularly fell out of bed in the middle of the night. The aides put pillows on the floor to cushion her fall. Mattie called The Sequoias one day to ask if there were any rooms in Personal Care. "No," said the director, "but you can put her on the waiting list."

"And how much does it cost again?"

"Thirty-eight hundred dollars a month, with the special fund kicking in five hundred."

"That's great," said Mattie. "Let me get back to you on it."

"Where are we gonna get it?" Mattie asked Al.

"What are we coming up with now, with her Social Security, you, me, and Lewis?"

"Twenty-five hundred, total."

"That's not so bad. We're close. We only need eight hundred more."

"And who's going to tell her she has to move? You know there are no cats in Personal Care."

Al looked at her thoughtfully. "I think you should tell her."

"Maybe we should kill her, in her sleep."

"Okay," he said.

★ ★ ★

It was Al, not Mattie, who decided it was time to visit Noah.

Al called her one day and said, "I don't want to sound like a Nike ad, but why don't we just do it? Get it over with. Drive out to Noah's and say hello."

"Just like that?"

"Just like that."

They practiced their opening lines as they went out to the Cove two days later. "Hi, I'm Mattie," she said brightly.

"The tone is all wrong. You sound like a flight attendant."

Mattie lowered her voice to basso profundo, slow. "IIIIIII'm Mattie."

"Good. Very *Tales from the Crypt*."

"What do I say next?"

"What do you want to say?"

"I want to say, 'I'm Mattie, and this is Al. And maybe you know this already, but our father was Alfred Ryder too.' "

Al made a face of surprise, like a grown-up playing peek-a-boo.

"I'm Mattie, and this is Al," she tried again. "And the fact is . . ."

"What's the fact, Mat?"

"The fact is, we're . . ."

"We're Alfred's older children," Al said. "We never knew our father had another son until pretty recently. And that child turns out to be you. So we're Alfred's three children. We didn't know how to proceed, or what would be best, so we decided to take a chance and say these words to you."

"That was perfect," said Mattie, and repeated it. They drove past the library, which was closed, past the superette, where Ned's truck was parked in front. They flashed through the downtown area to the old two-lane highway to Marshall, toward Noah's house.

From the car, Al and Mattie watched Noah sitting on the front porch of the light-blue house. He was drinking a beer and reading the paper. They got out of the car and waved. He watched as they walked toward him, but he didn't wave back. There was a wicker basket beside him, and a fan. His hair was short, buzzed, dark. He wore a black T-shirt faded nearly to gray. When they got closer to the porch, they saw that the basket contained a grizzled basset hound.

Noah looked up with polite defiance when they walked up the steps. Mattie saw by the expression on his face that he knew who they were.

The dog opened its wino eyes, took them in, and fell back to sleep. There were succulents everywhere on the stairs, in cracked and broken pots, and a branch of a bay tree stretched over the railing onto the porch. The dog emitted a windy, comatose growl.

"That sure looks like an old dog," Al said.

Noah ran his hand back over his own bristles as if to push them off his forehead. He shook Al's hand. Mattie wondered whether she should say something obvious about the dog, so he would like her too.

The dry grass was cut back twenty feet from the house, a lion-blond brush cut, framed by the bay trees. Noah reached down to scratch the dog's ears. Mattie and Al continued up the porch steps, uninvited, and sat on the broad rail.

"Hi, Noah," said Mattie. "I'm Mattie. This is Al."

Noah looked at her skeptically. "We've met at the library."

Mattie closed her eyes and rubbed her forehead. All she had to do was get the first sentence out. Help! she prayed. She found herself saying calmly to her feet, "We're Alfred's older children. We never knew our father had another son until a few months ago. . . ." When she was finished there was silence, except for the crickets and birds, the rustle of leaves and grasses. Noah was squinting at her as though she had spoken in broken English. Then the dog opened its boxy jaws and bayed operatically, as though hearing grievous news.

Everyone laughed nervously. Al squatted beside the dog and petted it. Noah stared into his lap, and squeezed the tip of his forefinger as if trying to force a splinter to the surface.

"You are a handsome guy," Al told the dog,

scratching its rear. The dog yawned.

"I don't mean to be rude," Noah said. "But I have to leave soon. I have a gardening job."

"That's okay," said Al. "We just wanted to say the words out loud. We didn't know if you knew already, or if you'd care, but we came anyway." Mattie felt huge and ungainly, and drunk. When Noah glanced over, she threw her hands up in a shrug, as an old Italian might, accepting a compliment or condolences. The dog barely moved. "There's nothing like a good dog," Al said. "It's like having God around, isn't it? Is yours sick, or is he just old?"

"Both," Noah said. He squatted beside the basket and scratched the mottled silkiness of the dog's ears. Al continued to pet its haunches, seemingly oblivious to Noah. After a moment, Noah moved his head closer to the dog and to Al, and Mattie had to look away from the two heads bent over the dog. She saw in them her father at two ages. She started weeping, as silently as she could manage. The smells of hot golden grass, manure, oil from Noah's truck, and the dirty dog clotted in her throat. Noah and Al looked at each other, the silence stretched tight between them. Al smiled, tapped his crossed bottom teeth, their father's teeth. Noah instinctively touched his too. "God," he said.

"We have the key our dad used to open the can of paint that he painted this place with. Isn't that funny?" Mattie reached into her pocket, having meant to bring the key, but there was only the shoe. She curled her fingers around it, then took it out of her pocket.

Noah gaped at it. "Where'd you get that?"

Al said, "It was in the glove compartment of our dad's old VW."

Noah froze. Mattie held the shoe in her palm and waited. Noah reached for it gingerly, as if it were blown glass rather than rubber.

"We got this from a gumball machine at a Mobil gas station in Sebastopol."

"Who did?" Al asked.

"Me and my dad," Noah said. Kabooom — everything buckled inside Mattie, like a wood floor during an earthquake. Al's face went white, but he listened to Noah with a calm expression. "My dad," Noah had called Alfred, and even though this was why she was here, hearing it was a blow. He was *your* dad? But how could that be — he was *our* dad.

Al soldiered on. "Do you remember the day you got that shoe?"

Noah nodded. He turned it upside down to look at the tread, scraping grime off with his thumbnail. "The gas station was near where Yvonne lived. I remember the flying horse, the old Coke machine, the coldest Cokes in the world. My dad always gave me a quarter for the gumball machine." She shuddered: Kabooom again. "You could get Ratfink decals," he said, "or shrunken heads, but one day I got this stupid shoe. It came in a hard plastic bubble,

336

which I kept my tiny treasures in for a while. My dad used to give me tiny things. I collected them — little space dudes, dinosaurs, miniature locks."

"Do you still have them?" Mattie asked. He shook his head. He was pleasant enough to her, but warmer toward Al. Of course, Al was not flinching as if cannonballs were blowing up all around him. Noah looked at his watch. He handed the shoe to Mattie, but she was afraid that if she took it back, he'd leave.

"My dog died," Mattie blurted out, and horrified at herself, she began to cry again. No one spoke. Al got to his feet and put his arm around Mattie's shoulders. She wiped at her eyes.

"God," Noah said, "that's so sad. What kind of dog was it?"

"A Cavalier King Charles spaniel."

"Oh, that's a great breed," he said. She nodded miserably. Leaves rustled. "Can I keep the shoe?" he asked.

"What?" she said, as if he wanted her car.

"Could I have the blue shoe?"

"You mean, like to keep forever?"

"Jeez. Never mind."

She looked at the turquoise high-top in his hand, the rubber filigree shoelace. "I would need it back someday," she said.

Noah looked dubious. "Well, that would be okay." He held it like a ladybug that had landed in his hand. Then he thought for a moment. "I think I have something for you. I'll be right back."

Al nodded jovially, but clutched his chest when he and Mattie were alone.

"He's really warmed up to you," Mattie whispered.

"I'm his brother," Al whispered back. "He can look into the mirror of me."

Noah returned with a wooden box, a padlock on the hasp, a key in the lock. Mattie's eyes widened, and her mouth opened, like a contestant on a game show: here were the papers that would make them all rich, Alfred's stock certificates, or the insurance. Noah put the box on the porch near Al's feet and sat on the step nearby. Noah was close enough that Mattie could smell the sweat on his skin. They all stared at the box, as if what was inside would step out on its own in a moment. Al looked over at Mattie, and then turned the key. The lock popped open. He handed the key to Noah, wiggled the lock out, set it down, and lifted the hinge. Mattie held her breath as he pushed back the lid and then looked in.

Inside was a rumpled wallet, flat brown, lightly stained, a little dusty. Al reached for it, glanced up at Noah, and opened it. It was empty, except for a few coins that fell out.

Noah took the wallet from Al and held it up. "This was my dad's," he said. He opened it and shook it, so Al and Mattie could see there was nothing inside. He slid his fingers in a hidden compartment, paused for a moment, and pulled out a black-and-white photo. He observed it with reverence.

She knew the photo even before it came fully into focus. She remembered the day it was taken. She could remember the colors of their clothes. She remembered sitting on the hi-fi cabinet with Al, in new pajamas Isa had bought them at Montgomery Ward. Mattie's were a soft red Asian style with black frog clasps. Al's were flannel, pale blue with silver circles. He had a crew cut and his arm was flopped around her. They looked very grown-up for the camera, although she was about three and he about seven, a little younger than her own kids now. She and Al were somber children smiling for the photographer, urchins in nice new jammies.

Mattie looked up from the photo to find Noah watching her. He seemed so young, as if he were showing his parents a homework paper he'd gotten an A on. She raised her eyes to the sky. The day had grown humid, pearly gray. Noah bent to pick his dog up from the basket. He knitted his fingers together to hold the dog. Mattie reached forward to lift the lid of the box, wondering whether they had somehow missed something.

"That's all there is, Mattie. An old wallet of dad's. A photo. Some coins."

She turned to Noah. "Did you recognize us from the photo?"

"No," he said, "not the first times I saw you alone. But when you came into the library together — actually, after you left — I started feeling very odd, like in the Twilight Zone. And then I got this feeling, of knowing, even though I didn't know what I knew. Until I came home, and ended up digging out the picture. Then I could see who you were."

"Your mother never said anything about us?"

"No. My mother pretty much has her hands full, with herself," Noah said. "You can keep the picture."

"I'm going to leave you our telephone numbers," Al said. "In case you want to call. Do you have a pencil?"

"There's one by the phone, right inside the door." Al went in to get it.

Noah looked toward the door for Al. Mattie couldn't think of a thing to say. She idly peeled a piece of bark off the bay tree branch. There were veins of white rot on its underside. She wanted to show Noah, as she would show Harry or Ella: Look! Rot! It's the beginning of the divine process. You know why? Without rot, things don't get soft enough for anything to happen. She held the bark up to the space on the trunk where it had been, and fitted it back carefully. More awkward moments passed.

"How's Abby?" Mattie asked.

"I haven't seen her lately. She hasn't been around."

Mattie heard Al call her name. She got up

and went inside. He was pointing to a clipping taped to the wall above the phone. It was a story from the local paper, dated nearly a year before, recognizing Yvonne Lang for a large donation she'd made to the library where Noah worked, which would keep it open another year. The first paragraph referred to her as a former Marshall resident. There was a small photo of her: the big, beautiful, ageless earth mother had grown old. She looked like an ancient Russian nun, all wrinkles and creases, spokes emanating from around her mouth like sun rays, deep dark eyes hidden by folds of skin. Half of her face was in light, the other mostly in shadow, which created a sense of rest: without the shadow you wouldn't have seen the shape, the landscape of her face. The shadow told one kind of story, and the light, burning through the ravages of age, told another.

On the porch, Noah stood with the dog in the sling of his arms, fingers knitted effortlessly, big hands and dirty nails making a cradle for his dog. He laid the dog back in the basket with the easy motion of hands that knew what to do.

Al and Mattie sat at her kitchen table studying the photograph, trying to remember who the people in it were. The two children in pajamas had their best faces forward. They were sitting so close that the patterns of their pajamas merged. His arm was around her shoulders, and the fingers and thumb of his hand formed a circle as if he might be about to make a shadow animal, open the circle to make the coyote bark.

"We should have asked Noah where Yvonne lives," said Mattie.

"We can ask him another time. We would've sounded like the FBI." They both leaned forward over the photograph.

"All that effort to find a box, and all that's inside is us," said Mattie.

Al kept looking at the picture. "I never noticed your head was so large."

"I know, I look like a dwarf. And you're so handsome. We look like we're hoping someone will adopt us, don't we? We're so clean! And eager."

"You are so full of hope here, though," said Al.

"It's not hope. It's desperation. Here I am, Daddy! Daddy, here I am!"

"Look at our old eyes," said Al. "You look so tired. We look like little kids who've got that disease that turns you into old people."

"I didn't ever sleep."

"Why not?"

"Someone had to stay up on watch. Or the ship of us might have sunk."

"You look so calm here."

"You don't get adopted if you look too nervous."

★ ★ ★

One drizzly day at the end of January, after she had driven the kids to school, Mattie felt an unshakable desire to walk along the salt marsh near The Sequoias. It was not convenient — there was so much work to do around the house — but this was her only day off for the week. She parked near The Sequoias and got out of the car. There was a sweet moistness in the air. Something tugged at her sleeve, just as she turned toward the marsh. Let's go visit Personal Care, it said; it's time. I have to get home, she replied. Just come inside one minute. No, no, I have to think about this some more, she implored. Trust me, it said. But we don't have the money, she cried, and there aren't any beds. There will be, it said.

Maybe she was going crazy. But she made herself walk to the Personal Care entrance anyway. The young receptionist, Mia, wore her hair swept up into a bun, and a patient smile. Mattie told her a little about Isa. "You need to apply at the front desk," Mia said. "They have a waiting list for the rooms, but I could show you the units. To tell you the truth, winter is really hard on our residents. Flu, you know. People move on fairly frequently to nursing care. Has your mom seen the facilities?" The phone rang. "Just a minute." Mia took the call, then rerouted it to a social worker.

"My mother won't come in and check it out," Mattie said. "She won't want to move." The phone rang again. Mia patched it through to a resident's room.

"Sign her up. There's time to get her used to the idea. They all hate it at first, and then they all love it and forget about the old life. Hold on." Mia plugged the line from her headset into the phone grid. "Hi, Yvonne," she said. "Where are you?" Mattie watched and listened. "There's a Whistlestop bus at Safeway at noon. Can you wait?"

Mattie reeled. There were hundreds of Yvonnes. This couldn't be Yvonne Lang. Get a grip, she told herself sternly. When Mia was off the phone, Mattie told her she'd return for a tour another time. She went outside, started her car, and drove to the Miller Avenue Safeway. She pulled over near the bus shelter in front, where, wreathed in turquoise necklaces, Yvonne Lang sat, calmly reading on the bench.

Mattie recoiled, as if Yvonne had turned and pointed a bony finger at her. She was beautiful, a radiant old woman. A lavender sweater set covered her full breasts, and she wore flowing black pants.

Mattie pulled away from the curb so fast her tires squealed.

"Hi, Yvonne," she said into the phone that night, several times. Al stood beside her in the hall. "Hi, Yvonne," she practiced. Daniel had taken the children out for ice cream. She and Al looked at each other like kids making crank

344

calls. And then Yvonne said, "Hello?"

"Hi, Yvonne," Mattie said. "It's Mattie Ryder." There was silence.

"Oh, for God's sakes," Yvonne said, her voice trembling. *"Mattie."*

She met Yvonne the next afternoon in the sunroom of The Sequoias.

Yvonne had a pleasing, slightly crooked smile, rose lipstick, and a big, marvelous nose. She took Mattie's hand and gazed into her eyes. Mattie's heart was hard, pounding like an injury. Yvonne led her down the hall to her studio, holding on to her hip and limping as she walked.

They sat and faced each other in purple velvet chairs. There were no refrigerators, stoves, or doors in the Personal Care units, just one big room and a bathroom. The residents ate their meals communally. Yvonne had made mint tea with an electric pot, with a switch that would turn itself off if you forgot. She poured the tea into chipped antique cups. Sunlight shone through the curtains on the windows. Her dark furniture gleamed, with doilies on every surface, lace islands of agates, shells and feathers, keyhole limpets, sand dollars as big as your hand and as small as a dime, beach glass of all colors in tiny bowls.

Mattie sighed and tried to figure out a way to break the ice. "Why are you in Personal Care?" she asked finally. "You seem so fit."

"I've had two heart attacks, and six months ago I had hip replacement surgery. A unit opened here while I was convalescing." Mattie nodded. Silence descended.

"I take it you know about Noah, then?" Yvonne asked. A wave of fear passed through Mattie's chest. She nodded. "Abby, and me too — with your dad, I mean?" Mattie nodded again. She couldn't speak. "You know everything?" Mattie shrugged. Yvonne sighed with relief. "Thank God. I think if he'd lived longer, he'd have told you himself."

Mattie stared at Yvonne, desperately wanting her to keep talking. Instead, she sipped her tea. A grandmother clock tocked on the dresser. Mattie looked at Yvonne. Her skin was as old and dry as desert lands whose bones you could see. "Yvonne, please. Tell me everything anyway, all of it."

"All right." Yvonne set her teacup down with a trembling hand. It chattered like teeth on the saucer. "Your father and I fell in love the year you were born. I was living with Neil, but it was your father and I who always connected, deep down. Neil was a charming rogue, and brilliant, but your father was special — the kindest, smartest man I ever knew."

Mattie reached for her cup, and her hand shook so much that the tea sloshed into the saucer.

"We did the best we could. Our feelings were not convenient. I never tried to get him to leave your mother, and I don't think he ever would have." Yvonne fingered her necklace, the rock of turquoise that lay nestled in the deep hollow of her throat. "And Alfred had to share me with Neil. But I loved him. And he loved me."

"Did Neil kill himself? That's what William Allen thinks."

"Yes."

"How?"

"Pills and alcohol. He lost us all — me, your father, Abby — all in a day."

"How did he find out about you and my dad? And Abby and my dad?"

"Abby told him."

"Why do you think Abby told?"

"Because she hated him. And she loved your father. And she was crocked half the time."

"Was she the friend you found a house for, when you asked Neil to tell my dad you'd found a house for your friend? Run-down, needed some repairs?"

"Yes. Abby was six months pregnant, and your father for obvious reasons didn't have a lot of spare time to help her find a place to live. I rented it for Abby, and then the baby when he arrived. Later I bought it for a song, with the money Neil left me."

"Are you close to Noah?"

"I've helped out when I could. I took care of him for a while, actually. At first. I've seen him over the years. I felt like he had enough to deal with, as it was."

"Did my dad paint that house?"

Yvonne nodded. Mattie hugged her stomach, like a pregnant woman. The clock tocked, little birds outside sang, her heart pounded. A look came over Yvonne's face, as if she were trying to swallow aspirin without water and, caught in her throat, it was dissolving. Mattie reached for her hand as tears, diverted by her wrinkles, began to run down Yvonne's face.

Mattie began to cry too, and withdrew into herself. After a while, she heard a rustle, and felt a Kleenex against her hand. She took it from Yvonne and dried her tears. They sat together, gravely.

"Did he ever really work in Washington?" Mattie asked.

Yvonne nodded. "He was a consultant on civil rights before Congress, during the Kennedy years. He did some great work. But he could not abide LBJ. Of course, he continued to let your mother think he was needed in Washington, because it meant he could get away." She shook her head. "He did the best he could, and that involved lies, and other women, and a girl. There was no excuse for what he did with Abby. Still, things might have been different if someone had been there to protect him early on. But you know, no one was, and he never recovered."

"Protect him from what?"

Yvonne looked puzzled. "You know. From what happened. Because hurt people hurt other people. That's the way it works."

Mattie could not quite track what Yvonne was saying. "You mean that he hurt my mother because he had been hurt somehow? Or that he hurt you, when he slept with Abby?"

Yvonne stared back. "You said you knew everything," she said, her voice flat, wary.

"I know about you, and Noah, and Abby."

"But not about the garage?" Yvonne sighed. When Mattie looked blank, Yvonne cleared her throat. A door inside Mattie swung open, creaked. A roar of water, like a mill, and a ringing, tinnitus, in an ear about to become diseased by what it had yet to hear.

"There was a man, a neighbor," Yvonne said. "He must have been forty when Alfred was ten, when this started. He was a fireman. He lived down the block. He offered all the neighborhood boys candy bars and Cokes to come over. Not just your father."

"Uh-huh." Mattie remembered something about a fireman who'd been her father's friend when he was young. The man had been a hero. "Jerry?"

"Yes, that's right. Jerry Howard."

"Jerry Howard," Mattie said, the name returning like a fragment of dream.

"Yes. Are you okay? You're perspiring. Shall I get you some water?" Mattie fought back a wave of nausea.

"Okay," she said weakly. "Yes, please."

Yvonne got up, limped to the bathroom, and

returned with a glass of water. She watched Mattie sip it. "Well. The boys hung out in his living room talking, while he took them one by one out to the garage and gave them blow jobs. Alfred didn't think it was wrong. All the other boys did it too. It felt great. Then all of them stopped but Alfred. He thought it was a good deal, that he was getting as good as he gave. He loved the candy bars, the Cokes, Jerry. And his parents fought so much that he really hated to go home. I never got Alfred to see how harmful it must have been, or really even to talk about it much."

Mattie saw a confusion of people in her head: Neil and Yvonne; Abby and Al chasing her around with a hose on hot summer nights at Neil's; her dad at ten years old, reaching for a chocolate bar in a garage, an older man bending toward him; Yvonne holding out a candy bar too; all that fucking turquoise; her mother, with her bright blue eyes, holding newborn babies, Al and Mattie, Harry and Ella — and Noah. Mattie felt herself blanch. She had the most terrible thought.

"Did my mom ever see Noah?"

"Just once, by accident. Of course, that was all it took. She ran into Abby and Noah up at Kaiser."

"God." Mattie's chest felt crushed.

"Your dad had been dead for a little while."

"Was it obvious who the father was?"

"A dead woman would have known," Yvonne said.

Mattie closed her eyes. Currents of grief passed through her, and she breathed through each one, as if in labor again. It had been painful the first times she'd seen Harry's face in Alexander, and that had been *after* a divorce. How had Isa endured? Mattie had an urge to call her and see how she was doing, to try by a show of love and kindness to make up for all the pain Isa had borne — but it hadn't worked when she was a child, and it wouldn't work now. She stared out one of Yvonne's windows, covered with a lace curtain, at a blur of kumquat leaves. Beyond the tree, in the furry green distance, she could see her mother in the waiting room at Kaiser, mortally wounded not by the blast of the nuclear bombs she rallied against, not by a bullet fired by the gun nuts she marched against, not by the cancer she had feared, but by a child's beautiful features. Mattie squinted until she could see the child, and then her father at ten, no taller than Harry was now, walking along like Harry on his way to the school bus stop, his eyes brown and concerned, glancing around as he passed the hero fireman's garage, kicking at weeds, calling to the neighborhood dogs he knew.

eleven

Early morning was gray and fuzzy. Fog pressed against the windowpanes. Mattie sat next to Otis's glass cage in the living room. The little dragon had grown a couple of inches, and his skin was dull and hazy, a sign that he was about to shed. Harry, who had looked up iguanas on the Internet, announced that Otis needed to soak, and be rubbed with a lubricant too, to help the shedding process.

"That is not going to happen," Mattie told him.

"Jeez!" he said. "You'd only have to do it twice a day."

"You could do it, honey."

"You're so mean. Why can't you be a normal mother? A mother who wants her child to be happy?"

Ella sat nearby. She had done her own hair that morning, and the blond pigtails sprouted on top of her head like a space girl's antennae. Her pinkie dangled over her lip as she read a Dr. Seuss book. Mattie was working long days at the superette, and Nicky was not around much. Al usually hung out with the kids after school until Mattie got home.

Harry seemed caught in a web of fears. Mattie had taken him and Ella into town for ice cream one night, and they were eating sundaes at a table when two policemen who patrolled on bikes came in. Harry froze, as if he were about to be busted. His hands trembled, as though he'd just realized he was violating the terms of his probation by eating a caramel sundae.

The policemen, without being asked, stopped by and introduced themselves, and gave both children police officer trading cards with their own pictures and biographies. When Harry took his trading card home, new fears ignited. Now he was afraid of wrecking the card. When Daniel fished it out of the pocket of Harry's shorts before starting a load of wash, Harry went white — aware how close a call it had been, feeling more than ever the menace shimmering beneath the very things meant to shelter, protect, or clean.

Mattie told Harry she'd help him soak Otis later, but only if he'd be in charge. He snuggled up closer to her, gratefully. "If it was Jesus, wouldn't you help him soak his shedding skin off?" She nodded. He patted her. "It will make you happy to help Otis feel fresher."

They soaked Otis that night, and the next day his old skin lay beneath him on the floor of his cage like a bathrobe he'd stepped out of. Mattie watched him in his noble-lizard mode. He was no more responsive to her than to any of the rocks in his cage. She thought idly about pouring Drano over him. "How would you like that?" she asked. Otis didn't move. He gave her nothing to work with. If he was nervous, she would know how to calm him. If he was lonely, she would move in closer. But nothing, ever — only the A side, noble frozen lizard, or the B side, electric lizard, tearing around his cage, spewing shit. Sometimes he'd accidentally look at her, but she'd slide right off his eyes.

A lamp glowed on a corner shelf, a tender light reflected on the window so it looked like the rising sun. The real sun had still not risen. When the phone rang, Mattie did not get up to answer. It was probably Isa. Mattie half believed that her mother's subconscious was picking up signals about Yvonne's reappearance in Mattie's life. She closed her eyes as the answering machine began playing its recorded message. Thinking of Yvonne sent anxiety through Mattie's mind — not because Yvonne had slept with her father for twenty years, not because Yvonne had pulled back Alfred's bandages to reveal his sexual wound, but because Yvonne lived in the Personal Care units at The Sequoias, where Isa needed to live now too. Obviously, they couldn't live in the same place. Whoever it was hung up without leaving a message.

Mattie continued to sit beside Otis. She stared in the direction he was looking, woman and iguana facing southeast. Her mind spun around an ice rink, doing figure eights. Hi, Yvonne, she imagined saying into the phone.

Shall we get together and talk some more about you and my dad? Hi, Abby. Shall we get together and talk about you and my dad? Hi, Noah. Want to get together and talk about you and my dad? Maybe we could all get together and lay memories of him out on the floor like quilting squares. Then I could have my dad back.

The phone rang again, and the machine took the message. It was Isa, crying about a lost red dog. Mattie got up and answered. "Mom. Whose dog are you talking about?"

"My dog, for Chrissakes. God, Mattie. My little red dog. Have you lost your mind?" Mattie stared through the window. The lamp's light was reflected outside, oval, flattened, hanging in a homely, straggly tree. The tree was bald except for the explosion of needles at the top, like a skinny person with a cloud of hair, holding in its arms a lozenge of sunrise.

"Do you mean your cat, Mom?" Mattie asked.

There was the splutter of indignation. Isa hung up. Mattie's stomach turned to worms. She sat back down near Otis.

The phone rang again an hour later. It was Lewis. "I'm here with your mother," he said. "I think perhaps you should come over."

"What's she doing?" Mattie asked.

"She's going up and down the hall, accosting people, looking for her little red dog."

"But she doesn't have a little red dog,"

Mattie pointed out.

"Mattie, I think you better come on down," Lewis said. She'd never heard him sound so hopeless before. He mentioned that there might be a studio opening up in Personal Care soon, and they could move her. He told Mattie that it would break his heart — Isa's loss of autonomy, of her cat, and the view of the mountain. But Mattie worried only about how Isa could bear to see Yvonne again, daily, relive a lifetime's humiliation. It would destroy the marriage Isa liked to pretend she'd had. Please let her have a big stroke, Mattie prayed.

She called Dr. Brodkey. "Listen," the doctor said. "One of my older patients who has some of your mother's symptoms, although he has Alzheimer's, is responding to Prozac. I think it's worth a try."

Driving to the drugstore to pick up the prescription, Mattie found herself wondering: If the right medication could bring Isa back to her old state, bright, animated, bossy, and incredibly annoying, would Mattie want her? Would she want more years of the old Isa — to be talked to alternately as if she were the queen's eunuch and the Christ? Part of her hoped for her mother just to die, suddenly, soon. Another part of her hoped there were sweet memories for Isa still to come. Hope, as Augustine said, was costly. Lord, she prayed. You there? She saw Jesus' face, smiling, those

356

kind dark eyes. She gave him Harry's ferocious look of defiance: What if, she challenged, what if I give her a bunch of vitamin K foods? Broccoli! Liver! She paused for dramatic effect. *Kale.*

She had prayed for help, and now a pharmacy clerk was getting Prozac for Isa. Maybe it would help her mother perk up and quiet down. Maybe they could buy her a couple more seasons; then she could die in her sleep, in a bed in Personal Care. Mattie and an aide would have tucked her into bed the night of her death, called good night at the door before Isa sailed away. Mattie closed her eyes and imagined how sweet it would be to take that kind of care of Isa. "I think I want to be like a *ship's* chaplain," she exclaimed in a whisper. The clerk hummed loudly as she rang up the order. So I'm crazy! Mattie agreed. You could be busy crazy, or you could be crazy like religious people who worked in soup kitchens. This is the kind of crazy she wanted to be — soup-kitchen crazy, ladling out soup to people who felt like Otis on the inside, frozen, frantic, alien. She threw back her shoulders. I got it, she called silently to God while the clerk put the Prozac in a bag. I'm back! I'm a ship's chaplain now! The clerk gave her the bag, a receipt, and an encouraging smile. "You just take this exactly as prescribed," she said.

When Mattie arrived with the Prozac, Lewis

and Isa were sitting side by side on the couch in the living room, holding hands, looking grim and red-eyed. Their walkers were side by side too, like dogs ready for a nice walk. Mattie hugged her mother, who clung to her. Lewis's dark irises were spotted with old age and cataracts. The moles on his dark skin were multiplying, and light skin tabs spread like glitter, as if his face were a star map, a universe of planets. Mattie bent to kiss him, smooth the skin in the hollows of his cheeks. "Your mother was worried about a little red dog," he said. Mattie nodded. "But not anymore, right, Isa?" Isa nodded.

"I have a cat," Isa said, proud but shaky. The cat hid beneath the curtains, peering out as if Mattie might toss a grenade its way. The apartment smelled of urine — Isa's and the cat's. Mattie noticed a long, broad brown smear near the easy chair, like fingerpaint, too big to be the cat's. She got a sponge and cleaned the streak on the carpet.

"How did you manage to spill food under your chair?" she asked as she sponged up the shit. Isa looked amused, and pleased, and shrugged; her eyes were sunken and inflamed.

"Mom," Mattie said, after throwing away the sponge. "Mom, your doctor called." This was not the literal truth. "Your bloodwork raised a few questions." This was not quite true either; Isa had not had bloodwork. "She's prescribed a new medication. And she insists you move into

Personal Care for now."

"No!" Isa cried out. "No, I will die first."

"Isa," said Lewis. "Just till you're stronger."

"I'm not going anywhere! You can both go to hell!"

"Mom, now, be smart about it," Mattie said. "You'll still have an apartment — it's just down there at the other end of the property. You and Lewis can see each other every day, just like now. And someone will be there to help you get started every morning — help you bathe, give you your meds. And make sure you get healthy meals. Then at night they'll help you get ready for bed. They'll be there if you fall. I'm going down to Personal Care right now to see where you are on the waiting list, because we're taking the next bed." Mattie sounded more definite than she felt. She strode toward the door with a confidence she was not actually experiencing.

Isa had her fingers in her ears and was chanting in secular tongues. Mattie was desperate to win back her love and trust, but like Ulysses ignoring the sirens beckoning from the rocks, she walked on toward the door.

She went to Personal Care to talk to the director. There was now just one person ahead of Isa on the waiting list. Who, Mattie wanted to ask. Can I get a name and an apartment number on that? What was she going to do, trick the person into going out to the parking lot some night, and mow her down? She walked back to her mother's apartment not knowing what to expect or what to do. She had told a kind of a truth, although not one that lined up perfectly with the facts. Now she was going to trust God.

Her mother was clutching her cat and crying softly. Mattie stayed with her as long as she could before going to pick up Harry and Ella at school. "I promise you, Mom, it's going to be okay," she said. "Better than okay. Right, Lewis?"

"It's true, darling Isa." He stroked Isa's hair and brow like a longtime lover.

As she drove toward Ella's school, Mattie remembered a story the pastor had recently told, about a girl who was crying in the night. When her mother came to comfort her, the girl said she was too afraid of the dark to sleep. "But God's with you, comforting and protecting you," the mother said.

"But I need someone with skin on," the little girl said.

This is who Mattie wanted to be in the world: God with skin on, someone who would show up and listen, bring you a glass of water if you were thirsty. Al was God with skin on for Mattie. So were Angela, Daniel, Lewis, her pastor, her children. Isa wasn't, though. Isa was the scared, autistic parts of Mattie's mind, with skin on, the parts most needing the love that terrified them most.

Daniel had picked up pad Thai for dinner.

They ate on trays in front of the TV with the kids, something they rarely did. Yet they all seemed to want to be together, and still be left alone. Mattie tried to look at Daniel and the kids with ship's-chaplain compassion as long as she could. Then she noticed that Harry was eating like someone shoveling hay onto a flatbed truck, and Daniel was watching TV too intensely, acting like someone who'd had a lobotomy. Ella ate fussily, with her bleeding pinkie in the air, like Quentin Crisp. Out of nowhere, Mattie felt a rage, volcanic eruptions of frustration. She considered throwing all the trays against the wall.

She closed her eyes. Help me out of this mess! she prayed. She stared at the TV but saw nothing there, until finally she saw herself and Al at the table with Isa and Alfred, Isa starving herself down to a size 8, five-nine and one hundred twenty pounds, Mattie growing fat, Al stoned on LSD, and only Alfred seeming to enjoy his food, talking in his teacherly way about minus tides out at the Cove. Mattie used to eat the way Harry was eating now, and she saw that she was doing to Harry and Ella exactly what Alfred and Isa had done to her — pretending there were no shadows falling across the house like black fabric. Harry's were in the shapes of shadow puppets — of Lee, whom his parents had betrayed, whom he then betrayed by accepting her kindness; of Mattie, whom he blamed for the divorce; of Nicky's new children, who scampered and cooed while Harry worried and plotted like a hunchback prince: no wonder he had bad posture. Ella's shadow looked like Mattie's had, cast by parents who didn't love each other anymore, who had loved each other, though, until the daughter came along. Ella's father disappeared from her daily life when she was two. Her shadow was an echo where her father used to be.

Noah called Al one night, and after clearing his throat, hemming awhile, asked if Al had some pictures of his dad he could look at. "I only have a couple," Noah told Al. "I'd like one from when he was little. And one from when I would have been little. And maybe one when he was my age now too."

"Mattie has almost all our pictures," Al said. "Maybe we can we put together an album for you, and bring it out."

"I don't need an album," Noah protested. "Just a few pictures will do."

"But could we bring them out?" Al asked.

He told Mattie all this later, under the trees in his garden.

"He said we could come out?"

Al nodded.

"He didn't say, 'You can come out, but not your fat weepy sister'?"

"Wait — let me think." Al thought. "Nope, I don't think he said that."

Mattie felt stuck in a rut with Daniel. "How will I know when it's time to go to bed with him?" she asked Angela one night.

"You'll just know," Angela said. "You'll be afraid, but it will be like jumping off a low cliff into cold water. And then it will be wonderful once you're in."

Mattie fumed a bit; Angela could be so grandly reassuring. Hoping to get a rise from her, she asked, "How long did you and Julie go out before you went to bed?"

"You can't go by that." Angela laughed. "This is you, and Daniel, not even out of his marriage."

"Tell me anyway, Angela," Mattie insisted.

"Oh, I don't even like to think about it," Angela replied. "You know the old joke about lesbians: What do lesbians bring on the second date? A U-Haul. Let's put it this way: It didn't take as long."

Most nights after dinner, Daniel would put Ella on his shoulders and they'd stop by Harry's room to see if he wanted to come along for a walk. Ella liked to smoke the cold night air like a forties movie star.

Several nights after Noah called Al, when the moon was full and low in the sky, glazing the neighborhood with a eucalyptus light, Mattie took a surreptitious look at Daniel. He seemed different, more like his old self — not cheerful yet, but calm. She wanted to crawl into bed with him right then, to cry about Isa while he held her, lie naked in the dark with him and talk about Noah.

After the children had been bathed and put to bed, Mattie knocked on the door of the laundry room. "Come in," Daniel said tentatively. She stepped inside, closed the door behind her and leaned against it. He was sitting on the futon with his back to the wall. He put down his book and took off his reading glasses. She could hear night birds, the cats galloping down the hall, floorboards creaking, settling in for the night.

"You okay?" Daniel asked. "Want to sit down?" She looked at him and shook her head. "Are you okay?" he asked again.

"I don't know." She squinted at him. He looked away shyly. "Let me just say what is true." She swallowed, and looked off toward the window as if she had heard something down the street. "What is true is that." She gritted her teeth. He looked afraid. "What is true is that." She turned and said it to the wall. "I love you, Daniel." She turned again, to face him. Daniel looked at her with misery sketched on his face, and she saw that all she could hope was that somehow they would still be friends in the morning.

"I know how much you love me, as a friend, and that's wonderful, and I don't know why I had to tell you that I have romantic feelings for you," Mattie said. "I know you're slogging through a terrible time in your life as it is. And that best friends should never cross certain lines. And now I have." She looked at him apologetically.

He looked at her beseechingly. "So please, I'm sorry," she said. He shook his head. Glacial water poured through her stomach.

"You don't have to move, Daniel. I can deal with this. But I did need to say it out loud. That's all. No problem." Mattie waved her arms, sweeping it all away.

Daniel narrowed his eyes, as she had seen him do when he tried to read without glasses and the print of a book was fuzzy, before he held it two feet away and waited for focus. She wanted to step back a few feet, but she was standing against the wall.

"Mattie," he said, his voice full of sorrow.

She felt woozy, faint.

"Okay," she said. Her insides were humid and dusty and sick.

He crossed his arms across his chest and hugged himself. "Mattie," he said, and brought his hands forward, clasped like a child's in prayer. "Obviously," he began. "Well, obviously," he said somberly, "I am madly in love with you too."

Mattie was not sure that she had quite heard him right. "You are?" She had to look away before he nodded. "Wow," she said to the window. She sank to her haunches, blinking excessively, her mouth feeling the way it did after too much novocaine. She usually hoped to look more like Myrna Loy than an organ grinder's monkey when a man finally proclaimed his adoration. Daniel got to his feet. He stood, looking at her. Mattie tried to stand up, but her arms flailed out spastically. Daniel took her into his arms.

She was afraid to take a deep breath for fear she'd suck him right up. He buried his face in her hair and she could feel him breathing through his nose. "I just needed to tell you that," she whispered.

"Good." He whispered too.

She stepped out of his arms, and for something to do, she picked a bit of flug off his flannel shirt.

"Do you want to sit down?" he asked quietly. She nodded. "Do you want to sit on the bed, or on the floor?"

"On the floor."

"Okay." They sat down, leaning into each other like teenagers. She turned slowly to him, and found him poised to kiss her, an almost sorrowful expression on his face. The sound of footsteps coming down the hall made them pull back, but there was no time to put more space between each other before Harry barreled in.

"Is my mother in there?" he said. "What's going on?" he asked, drawing back.

"We were talking," Mattie said. "What's up? What do you need?" Daniel dusted off his hands as if they had been sitting in the road,

366

and Harry gave him a long, gimlet look. Then he turned to his mother.

"What's up?" said Mattie.

"I can't sleep. Could you come and rub my back?"

She came back to Daniel's room after Harry dropped off to sleep. She knocked softly, then poked her head in the doorway. Daniel was stretched out on the futon again, reading. "I'm going to go upstairs and go to bed by myself now, okay?" she said. "I'd like to take this really slow."

He sat up and smiled at her. "How slow?" he asked.

"I just don't want to botch this."

"So — will you be the project coordinator on this? Manning the speed dial?"

"Sort of." She crossed the room. They kissed for a long time. She opened her eyes. "I have to go," she said.

It was strangely sweet in the next weeks, like being Mormons, or Victorians. Mattie stayed out of the laundry room most of the time, to avoid temptation. But they kissed a lot and gazed into each other's eyes. When they were with the children, she sneaked glances at the nape of his neck like an old-fashioned Japanese girl. She looked down into her lap and actually blushed sometimes.

"Wait, why are we avoiding temptation?"

Daniel asked one evening.

"We're just taking it slow," she said. "Isn't this sexy?"

"I guess. But could we pick up the pace here at all?"

Pauline seemed to know that something had changed. Daniel did not always return her messages the same day she left them, and their late-night phone calls had been phased out. She phoned during the day to rage at him. She wrote Mattie hate letters. Mattie read the first one, and tore up most of the others. They gave her a sense of superiority, a sense of having won the guy for once: she was used to being the unsuspecting woman in the dark, or the daughter of the woman in the dark, the woman whom the man could not live without, but whom he didn't pick.

"You've got to tell her, Daniel," Mattie said one day. "It's cruel and unusual punishment."

He nodded. "I'll tell her tomorrow."

He was gone for two hours the next morning. Mattie's mind raced with images of Pauline doing her witchy magic with him, breaking the trance Mattie had cast. They would end up back in bed, as she and Nicky had done. They would end up back in love. How could he resist Pauline, so sexy, and so vulnerable? Mattie would die if he left her. She had to lose weight, that was the ticket: when all else failed, you could always diet. She would start tomorrow; in the meantime, she headed for the kitchen and opened a bag of Oreos. She poured herself some milk and sat down at the table, dunking one cookie after another into the glass.

Daniel came back shaken and wan. Mattie was stretched out on the couch in the living room, feeling like a boa constrictor digesting a small pig. Daniel sat at one end of the couch and lifted her feet into his lap. "That was the hardest thing I've ever had to do," he said. "I told her that I *hated* causing her pain. She looked at me disgusted. Then she lit up a cigarette. She's smoking again. That made me feel terrible. I said I wasn't in love with her anymore, and I wanted to be divorced. She blew a stream of smoke straight up like she was aiming for a hole in the ceiling.

"She asked me when you and I had started sleeping together. I said we hadn't yet. She said, 'Yet? *Yet?*' and did I expect her to believe me, and I said no, I didn't, but it was true.

"Then she said, 'But you two are in love?' And I said yes, we were.

"And she doubled over, like I'd kicked her stomach, and she cried."

A few weeks on Prozac visibly helped Isa. She was still on the quiet side, but she came across as calm, not delusional. She didn't even need her walker anymore. On sunny days, she and Lewis would walk along the path by the salt marsh. They worked together on jigsaw puzzles. They ate meals together; Lewis treated her to dinner in the dining room, or an aide would make them something simple to eat while they watched the evening news together in Isa's apartment.

One day in April, the director of The Sequoias called Mattie to say that a unit in Personal Care would be opening soon. Isa could have it if she liked. It might be months before another opened, and you got to turn down an offer only twice; then you moved back to the bottom of the waiting list.

Mattie and Al sat on a curb, contemplating this opportunity, in the parking lot of the high school where he taught. Al looked tired, older, his eyes wreathed in crow's-feet.

"What do we do?" Al said. "She's definitely better, since the Prozac."

"We should take the room. While she can still keep it together enough to get in. Once she's in, it'll be hard for them to kick her out."

"I just feel so wasted these days, too wasted to make this decision. You really think we should take it?"

Mattie nodded. "She's not okay anymore, Al, just sedated. She got shit on the floor."

Al grimaced. "Yeah, but are you going to put me away the first time I shit on the floor?"

Mattie bobbed her head.

"Can you tell her? I know I can't."

That night when Mattie went to say good night to Daniel, she knelt to kiss him and lingered by his bed. He leaned in close. "You smell like nutmeg," he said. She moved away, and sat down primly on the beach chair.

"I can't hold out much longer," Daniel told her.

"I just want to feel a little less crazy when we first go to bed. I don't want to be putting my mother in a facility the first time we make love. Oh, Daniel!" she said. "It's a facility! When you can no longer lock people out of your own home, that means you're in a facility. I'm about to put my mother in a *facility*."

Mattie woke with a start in the middle of the night. She had felt someone crawling into bed with her. For a moment she was scared to death — and hoped — that it might be Daniel. But it was Harry. He shook her by the shoulder; he had woken from a nightmare and couldn't go back to sleep.

"You scared me," she admonished. "My heart is still pounding."

"I dreamt a bad guy got in and was going to kill us," Harry whimpered.

"Daniel won't let anyone hurt us. And God is keeping watch over us."

"Don't you get it?" Harry asked. "God would never not let a burglar come in, if the man had picked your house to burgle. God has to let life do its ways."

The next day Mattie knocked on Isa's door,

and when no one answered, she let herself into the apartment with her own key. Isa was at the sink, washing dishes with great cheer, all but whistling while she worked like Snow White. She wore light pink lipstick, and her cheeks had a hint of color again. Her hands were in yellow rubber gloves. Hot water poured from the faucet. Mattie leaned against the stove. The house still reeked of urine, from the cat box, from Isa's bed. Newspapers had piled up everywhere, as had scores of direct mail, from every imaginable liberal political organization in the country.

"Where's Linda? Where's Frieda?" Mattie asked, looking around.

"I fired them all today," Isa said proudly. "I don't need them anymore. I am much better. I can take care of myself." She continued washing dishes, a tight smile on her face, now simultaneously Snow White and the Wicked Stepmother. In fact, she only appeared to whistle while she worked; underneath she was all shadows and schemes.

"Mom," Mattie said gently. "You're better, true. But a studio has opened up in Personal Care, and you need to take it."

Isa twirled around like a gymnast. "Don't you dare tell me what I need to do or not do, don't you dare!" She held out a steaming cup of soapy water, like a gun, her face red and enraged. "I will never go to Personal Care. You're not in charge of me. You go to hell."

"Mom!"

Isa continued to hold out the cup, menacing.

"I know I'm not in charge of you. But the director here is very concerned. They don't want you to stay in this apartment any longer — your neighbors worry too much."

"Get out of my house," Isa shouted, and flung the hot water into Mattie's face.

Mattie cried out as the water scalded her, and Isa did too, reaching for Mattie even as she pushed her roughly. Mattie splashed cool water on her face and neck. Isa bleated.

"God!" Mattie whipped around to face her, toweling herself off with a dishrag. Her hands trembled as she grabbed Isa by the shoulders and shook her like a dog shaking a kitten. Isa drew her hands in front of her face to ward off blows she must have thought were coming. Then Mattie pushed her roughly against the stove.

"You burned me," she said. "My face is on fire!" She walked down the hall to the bathroom, splashed more cool water on herself, and dried her face with a towel that smelled, sickeningly, of her mother. She could hear Isa's sniffles in the other room, but her heart felt cold and hard. Help, she prayed. She sat quietly, waiting. Her face stung. It was going to peel. She was going to look like Otis.

After a minute, she heard her mother's footsteps in the hall, and then a knock on the door. "Go away," Mattie said.

"I'm a mean mommy," Isa cried. She kept

knocking, and pleading, and weeping, and eventually Mattie opened the door. Isa was staring heavenward, eyes brimming with tears. She looked at Mattie with contrition. "I'm so sorry," she said.

Mattie allowed Isa to tug her into the living room. Isa sat down on the couch and patted the spot beside her. Mattie sat instead on the floor. For five minutes, Mattie listened coldly to her mother cry. Finally she scooted closer and brought her mother's bony leg down over her shoulder, and held her feet, as though she might be carried away if Mattie let go.

When the unit officially opened up at The Sequoias, Adele, the director, called Mattie.

"Oh my God," Mattie said.

"I know your mother loves her independence," Adele said sadly.

"She's going to hit the roof."

"She needs to move out of her apartment, whether she takes the studio or not. She's no longer consistently well enough to live alone. The studio is a lovely little space. I can't decide for you. But if it were my mother, this is what I would do."

"Can we have some time to make a final decision, my brother and I — and Isa?"

"Yes, of course. I can give you until tomorrow night."

When Al gently broke the news to her that

she would be moving, Isa sobbed and struck at Mattie. Mattie caught her by the wrist, and made noises of understanding and misery, and Isa pulled away and stalked off, tottering. Mattie and Al exchanged glances, but neither got up to follow. They knew where she was headed — down the hall to Lewis's apartment.

Half an hour later the phone rang. Mattie answered and Lewis told her they could come get their mother.

She was in Lewis's easy chair, and she would not speak to her children. She had been crying. Lewis stared off in Isa's direction with his hands clasped. "This is very hard for her," he said. Mattie and Al, at the door, nodded. "This is hard for all of us. We've been hoping this day would never come, and now it has. But Isa understands that she cannot live alone any longer. And she agrees to at least go look at the studio tomorrow. Right, Isa darling?" Isa nodded miserably. Mattie came and knelt at her mother's feet, and put her face in her lap. She heard Al's soft footsteps, and she knew he was standing beside them now. She turned and looked up at him as he placed his hand lightly on Isa's shoulder. Mattie closed her eyes, and after a minute felt her mother's bony hands reach for her. Having found Mattie's ear, Isa began to scratch behind it idly, as if Mattie were a cat in her lap.

The next day Mattie was walking with Isa hand in hand down the hall. I am asking for another miracle, she prayed. You did something pretty amazing with us yesterday, and now we need one more favor.

They passed the reception desk, where no one was sitting, and the dining room — all high rafters and beautiful wood, the sun shining through windows and skylights — where a few people were having late-morning tea. They passed the piano room, and then Mattie heard someone call her name — a grackle-voiced woman. She and Isa turned to the sound, and the elevator in her stomach flipflopped. It was Yvonne.

She was dressed in yellow linen, with turquoise wrapped around her neck and forearms. Isa was recoiling, squinting at Yvonne, visibly disturbed at this old woman reaching for them. Things swirled and swam on the murky surface of Isa's face, and then she gaped, and gasped with recognition.

"Tillie!" she cried.

Mattie turned to look at Yvonne.

"Tillie, Tillie," Isa repeated, drifting into Yvonne's arms. "I never thought I'd see you again!" Yvonne held her warmly, looking bemused, waiting for the joke to be explained. Isa stepped back to look at her, throwing her hands into the air. "I've never forgotten you, Tillie. Oh my gosh, where are my manners? This is my daughter, Mattie," she said. "Mattie, this is my old friend Tillie. From — jeez, I can't remember, we go so far back. Help me out here,

Tillie. When did we first meet?"

Yvonne tried to remember when she'd ever been Tillie. She shook her head. She couldn't seem to remember either. "Let me show you around," she said.

Every day Mattie and Isa walked to Personal Care to visit Yvonne. Isa's studio would not be ready till the weekend. Isa cried about her cat, but Lewis would take care of it, and she could visit every day.

It stormed on moving day, wild and fierce, the wind lashing the trees outside. Daniel and Al and a couple of their friends carried Isa's furniture down the long hall, out of Independent Living, and on to the back, to Personal Care. They loaded her boxes onto dollies and wheeled them away. Isa wrapped the last of her fragile mementos in tissue paper and boxed them. When she was done, Mattie and Al walked her to Lewis's, the cat in her arms. Mattie had already brought him cat litter, and the half-dozen bags of kibble that had turned up in various nooks of Isa's apartment. Lewis threw open the door for them, and they flocked inside, all four of them crying. The cat smelled Lewis's little dog and dove under the sofa and would not come out. So Mattie never had to take the cat out of her mother's arms.

Thanks in part to a crushed Valium that Mattie had put into her breakfast applesauce at

Dr. Brodkey's suggestion, Isa was remarkably docile as they came to the Personal Care reception area and checked in. Mattie had asked the receptionist to refer to Yvonne as Mrs. Lang, and so she did when she buzzed Yvonne's room.

Yvonne joined them for the trip to Isa's new room. Her bed, dresser, and TV, her couch with its antimacassars, her easy chair, her table and bookshelf were all there. So was the pousse-café of Isa's life: boxes of photos and clippings, of figurines and souvenirs, of schoolwork and art her children and grandchildren had done, of other treasures and medicine bottles. The rest of her things would be divided between Goodwill and Mattie's attic. The photos of Alfred that had hung in her hall all these years were stacked on the pine table.

Isa turned to survey her new surroundings. She looked at Yvonne, who was staring at Alfred's handsome framed face, and her eyes narrowed. Mattie held her breath. Then Isa sank to the couch. "Tillie," she wept, "come sit by me." She batted at Mattie and Al when they came close, said that they were traitors and that she hated them. Al looked at her with despair.

Isa studied Yvonne, beseechingly. A dark cloud crossed her face, and then curiosity, a striving to place this person; a moment's grief, and then blindness, Oedipus blinding himself so that he could go on; and then pride. "Tillie!" She held out her arms. "Tillie!" She pointed to her walls, her photos, her boxes of keepsakes. "Look at all my things!"

The next week, Mattie and Daniel took turns doing housework and helping Harry with his homework, then went to their own beds to read at night. This had been her salvation with Nicky — books that spirited her away without her having to leave. One night, after the kids were asleep, Mattie heard Daniel on the phone, gently and firmly telling Pauline that he *really* wasn't ever going back.

He was sullen and withdrawn at breakfast the next morning. That afternoon, Pauline called and told Daniel she had filed for divorce. Things had been a mess ever since. Pauline called constantly, and hung up when Mattie or the children answered, and she called in the middle of the night. She told Daniel she was going to move to the city, and was trying to get the house ready to sell. He urged her to move out immediately, so he could make repairs and fix the garden, but she wouldn't budge.

Mattie's mind spewed out fearful thoughts. She took extra hours at the superette, where the work and Ned's companionship calmed her. She loved the smells of the store, loved the dust that blew in through the broken screen door, that came in on dog paws, that you could never clean off the rough and ancient surfaces. In Ned, she felt that God had jiggled a dad out of the universe for her. She fantasized about making love with Daniel, but held back. Sex seemed so scary, now that she was close to getting what she thought she wanted. Love made your stomach ache. Left to their own devices, people were dangerous, and she was too; they were all marred, so scarred and scared. Her only hope was that she and Daniel would not be left to their own devices. Standing beside him singing in church, she imagined she was being held in someone's soft warm hands.

They spoke the same language. One night, sitting on Daniel's futon, near tears, she asked, "Why would a loving God take everything away from my mother?"

"I don't see that God is taking anything away from her," Daniel said. "I see Him taking care of her instead: it's her illness that has done all the taking."

The weather went crazy in late April and May, offering a few seasons in a few weeks: fog, then rain, and then a heat wave, an eerie autumnal snap, and then more rain. What the hell was that, people wondered, movie trailers for the whole year?

Daniel came to Mattie's room one night when she was already in bed.

"Come in," she said, putting her book down on her stomach.

He sat in her rattan chair. "Hi. You're the systems analyst on the sleeping-together project, right? The timing consultant?"

"Yes, that's right."

His hands were folded in his lap, as though he were about to ask a banker for a loan. She took off her reading glasses, and Daniel came more clearly into focus. He was not as thin as he'd been during the worst of his depression. He had color in his cheeks from working on a roofing job for the past three days. The light in the room was soft and low.

"What I want to know is," he said slowly, "how much longer do we have to wait?"

"I don't know," she answered. "I'm so afraid. I'm afraid if we're lovers, we'll ruin it somehow. And I'll lose you. So I don't quite know what to do."

"You could let me love you, which I do. If you gave me an approximate date, like say, June twenty-first, the summer solstice, when we could think about climbing into bed, that would be plenty for me. I'd mark off the days on the wall of my room, like a prisoner."

She took a deep breath. "How about an approximate time?" she asked.

He leaned forward in the chair. "Okay," he agreed.

She looked at her watch, pushed the button that illuminated it. She followed the second hand as it went all the way around, once. "All right, then," she said. "How about now?"

Daniel stayed in the chair, a little shocked. After a while he got up and came to sit beside her on the bed. She put her book and glasses on the table, and without taking her eyes off him pulled her nightie over her head. He rose slightly to kiss her, really kiss her for the first time, and without meaning to she crossed her arms in front of her breasts. He kept kissing her like in the movies, and then he laid his head on the blanket over her lap. She stroked his ropy hair and felt his breath light as a wing through the covers, and after a moment she turned off the lamp in case the children came in.

The children did come in, but not until breakfast time. Ella ran and leapt into bed between them, and scuttled into her mother's arms. Mattie was back in her nightie, Daniel in his T-shirt and boxers. They had been snuggled up together. Harry cried out, "What's going on?" as if he were Mattie's father discovering her on the couch with her teenage boyfriend. He put his hands on his hips.

Mattie sat up against the pillows. "Daniel and I love each other, and are going to be together now," she said.

"But what about Pauline, and what about Daddy?" Harry demanded. "And what about *me?*"

No amount of talking was going to make much of a difference, and so Mattie answered questions: No, he won't be your new daddy, Nicky will always be your dad. Daniel and Pauline are getting divorced. No, we're not going to have a baby. Yes, he'll move out of the laundry room. No, you can't get a puppy.

That night Harry and Ella both dawdled, stalled, whined, made demands, needed more water, needed still more assurances, needed to get up and pee, needed Mattie to stay with them until they were sound asleep, needed more water, needed to poop, needed to call their father. "No!" At that Mattie put her foot down. "You can call him in the morning."

"I need to talk to him now," Ella wailed.

"You can't keep us from calling our dad," Harry sobbed.

A few weeks later, after their nightly walk, after the children were showered and in bed, Mattie and Daniel sat in the living room reading. The cats milled around nervously, like armed guards, the children cried from their beds for favors, water, pees, company. After fifteen minutes of their pleading, Mattie went to Ella's room and sat on her bed. They whispered in the glow of the night-light. Ella had her baby finger in her mouth, and Mattie gently removed it. When she held it to the night-light, she saw that there were only two bloody spots, where Ella had groomed hangnails with her teeth. Even in the low light, Mattie could see new growth, white crescent moons.

Mattie went to Yvonne's one afternoon, when Al had taken Isa to the doctor. She simply wanted to sit with Yvonne in the

strangeness of it all. Also, now that she had
Daniel, she was missing her father with a new
fierceness. Yvonne came to the door in a black
velvet shirt, many strands of turquoise, and
flashy silver earrings that drew attention to her
aged face, as if to announce: Look, I'm a thousand years old and it's okay.

"Come on in. I've made some tea. And one
of the men down the hall brings me pastries,"
Yvonne said. "I'm not supposed to eat them,
because of my heart." The scent of cigarette
smoke hung in the air, although there was no
sign of ashtray, matches, or cigarettes. Sweets,
men, smokes. The sand in her hourglass was
running out, and Yvonne was savoring every
last bit.

A few minutes later they sat stiffly with cups
of peppermint tea and lemon bars. The hollow
in Yvonne's throat would have accommodated
a Ping-Pong ball. Would Mattie have that cave
under her chin one day, a balcony of turkey
skin above it? She should be so lucky. They
drank tea, ate sweets.

Yvonne stared off through the window, at
white roses on scrawny stems reaching up like
giraffes trying to peek inside. "I miss my fireplace," she said. "All crones should have a
hearth."

She was so beautiful and full of appetites,
and Isa was such a mess. And Mattie's father
was so dead. "My mother didn't know the first
thing about my dad," Mattie said at last.

Yvonne leaned forward in her chair. "Sure she did, Mattie. They were deeply in love for a long time. They couldn't think about how it would turn out when they got married — no one does — and if they had, they wouldn't have gotten to have you and Al."

Mattie gripped her forehead so that her fingernails dug into flesh. She felt Yvonne's hand on her arm, light as a cornhusk.

Mattie had thought that love would save her and make her whole. But instead she often felt worse, fragmented, crazier. She tried to plant seeds of mutual accommodation, letting Daniel be how he was and feel however he felt. She tried to plant what she hoped to sow. You couldn't grow tomatoes from apricot seeds. She'd start out fine, but then the way he pronounced a certain word might sicken her, or the way he scraped food back into his mouth with a spoon, like he was feeding the baby of his own self, would make her want to pull back.

She felt much less patient with Isa and the children too, and almost incapable of talking to Nicky or Lee about arrangements. She snapped more, spewed. Maybe she was getting Tourette's.

On bad days, Daniel's love smothered her. She couldn't breathe, and she couldn't talk to him about it, because she was afraid he would move out and she would die. Yet she couldn't stand his snores in the night, which woke her, or the way he waited for her to wake up every morning. One morning when the children were at Nicky's, she cried when Daniel started to make love to her, and asked him to please not touch her. Daniel was hurt, and pulled away, and when she wanted to snuggle up with him, he got out of bed and said, "I'm not an ATM!"

Then they both cried and were kind to each other all day long.

Early one Saturday morning, Mattie dreamt that she and Abby were swimming in warm ocean water, surrounded by baby kangaroos that floated and bobbed around them like dolphins, playing. Abby was smiling, young and gorgeous again. When Mattie woke up, she was laughing too, but by the time she told Daniel the dream, she'd started to think it was an omen — that Abby was dead.

"How do you get that Abby is dead based on that dream?" Daniel asked.

"Because I don't think she'll be happy again this side of the grave. I think she might have cancer or something, lung cancer from smoking."

"Call Noah and ask. Tell him you have photos of your dad for him."

"God, remember when I was just going to tell the truth? And trust God?"

"I know. What happened?"

"Well, it's like that old joke: It was going great, and then I got out of bed."

She called Al to ask whether he would mind if she visited Noah without him, and he said, no, not at all. Just as she was about to dial Noah's number, the phone rang. It was Isa.

"Hi, Mom," Mattie said. "How is everything?"

"You finally got your wish, Mattie, didn't you? You put me away." With that she hung up.

Mattie closed her eyes and rubbed them wearily. It was all fubar — fucked-up beyond repair. It was one of her father's expressions, enlisted-man slang. She smiled, looked up, whispered: Hi, Dad.

She called Noah at the library. "Hey. It's Mattie," she said.

"Oh, hey."

"Al said you wanted some photographs of Dad."

"Yeah," he said. The word "Dad" startled the both of them.

"I could drop some by today. I have to come out for work."

"Today's not a great day for me. I'm training someone."

"I could drop them off at your house while you're working, then," she said.

There was a pause. "You could?"

"Yeah."

"Wow. That'd be cool. You can leave them inside the front door."

"Okay. Is Abby okay?" Sheepishly she told

him about her dream.

"That's like the best dream anyone's ever told me," Noah said. "Thanks, huh?"

"But I thought maybe it meant your mother was in trouble." There was silence at Noah's end. "So your mother's okay?" she said weakly.

"A social worker from the county is helping her out now. It turns out she has diabetes, but the kind where you can just take pills. She got food stamps, and a couple of cats've showed up. She's basically a street person, you know, a street person with a home."

"Is there anything she needs that I could drop off while I'm out there?"

"A couple pairs of thick socks," Noah suggested. "The diabetes is bad for your feet, if you don't keep them clean, which she doesn't. If you get infections, you could lose a foot. That would be great. I mean, if you got the socks."

Where is my little blue shoe? Mattie wanted to ask, but she didn't, and in fact, she found out later when she stopped by Noah's house with the photos.

It was sitting on the table by the door, at the center of a cairn of white garden stones, the turquoise bold against the white. She picked it up and whispered, "Hello," as if they shouldn't be seen together. She took the photos of her father out of her purse and made a wreath around the stones and the little blue shoe, a garland of pictures of her father, as a baby, as a boy in a long-sleeved striped sailor shirt, scattering birdseed in Venice, in his Berkeley mortarboard and gown, and at the beach in Bolinas, sitting in the sand where the driftwood musicians now jammed, binoculars around his neck. There was a beer in the sand beside him, and he was waving to whoever held the camera. This one had been taken a year before he died. She looked at it for a long time before stepping back out into the bright spring sun. The light on the green hills was like powdered sugar on a cake, sifted through a doily.

Mattie worked all day at the superette and her feet ached from standing, but she drove to Abby's anyway, to deliver the socks and some food Ned had put together.

Abby opened the door to her shack, peering nervously through the opening; she was trying to keep a little white kitten inside. It was two months old or so, and looked like a cheaply made Siamese. She scooped it in and let Mattie step past her. Abby had dark bags under her eyes, a basketball of gut bulging out of her T-shirt. The T-shirt was tucked into her stretch leggings, like Tweedledum, and she wore an old blue watch cap; it was all Mattie could do not to offer a fashion consultation. Along with the ocean and mildew, the place now smelled faintly of cat box and urine, as Isa's apartment had.

There was plenty of milk and cheese and

eggs in the cold cupboard, and several bottles of medicine on the counter by the sink, the hot plate nearby, with the kettle on top, boxes and cans of food on the shelves. Mattie put her bag of groceries on the counter, then showed Abby the socks; she told her that Noah had asked her to bring them.

The kitten threw itself at Mattie's ankles, and she got on the floor to play with it, feeling grains of cat litter under her hands. She saw that there were kerosene lamps on the counter, and a wood-burning stove with its pipe set up. Abby got on the floor beside Mattie to play with the kitten. She looked like an alien encountering such a creature for the first time, simultaneously puzzled and charmed. She held a dirty dishcloth out for it to charge and whipped it away at the last second. They played with the kitten for a while. Abby's bare feet smelled awful. They looked horrible, dirty, the nails like a tree sloth's, the toes crossing one over another.

"Put on the clean socks," Mattie said. "You've got to keep your feet clean and warm." She was so used to bossing her mother that it seemed only natural to order Abby around too. When she handed her a pair, she realized that it wouldn't do any good for Abby to put them on her dirty feet. They would only press the filth into her skin. Could I get a partial credit, Lord, for just bringing them out to her? Mattie wondered. Nope, said Jesus, sorry.

The bottoms of Abby's feet were caked with grime, cracked with fissures in which Mattie could see grains of cat litter. She started to imagine herself washing them, and prayed, Please, anything but that. Yet just as Abby had peeled away the paper band around the socks, Mattie heard herself tell her to stop.

"You can't put those nice new socks on dirty feet," she said. "Let me heat some water." And by God, ten minutes later, Mattie was gently bathing one of Abby's feet in a salad bowl of warm soapy water, wiping the grime off her ankle and heel and toes with a dish towel and Ivory soap, working the cat litter out of the cracks in her sole.

On her way home that night Mattie drove to Bolinas Beach. She wanted to see the sand where her father had been sitting in the photograph. She did not really forgive him much, yet. The sun was setting golden-red, and the drift-wood beach musicians had survived the storms of winter, all still in place with their instruments, bleached and raggedy but ready to play. The pedal-steel guitarist especially seemed to have been on a binge. The musicians all belonged on this seaweed-tossed beach, Mattie thought. They were a part of it, as if someone had watered the dunes with a hose and they had sprung up from the sand. But something looked different now. And then she saw that a new member had joined the band, a singer, a huge black woman with a real tambourine, a skirt of tennis netting, and wonderful spatulate fingers — forks, spoons, and butter knives — radiant in the last of the sun.

twelve

It was dark and cold at daybreak. When she went out to get the paper at quarter to seven, Mattie saw brilliant stars low in the sky, right there for the touching. She felt the bracing chill and snap of autumn on her skin. Twenty minutes later, as she poured coffee for Daniel and shot aerosol whipped cream into cups of cocoa for the children, she watched the sun rise, dense and thick and deep murky gold. She looked over at Daniel, who was working on the crossword puzzle. Who could have imagined, four years ago, that the Evergreen rat man standing on her front step, staring at the ground and unable to kill her rats, would one day be pushing the sugar bowl across the table to Ella, without looking up from his paper? His dreadlocks were even shorter now, clipped to within an inch of his head. He had cut them during a heat wave in July. Ella was growing out her hair, and it was in an awkward stage; multiple rubber bands and barrettes restrained it. Her nails were short, with chipped black polish, and she wore new green harlequin frames that Lee had helped her pick out. The Junior Miss Junkie Rock Star look was the latest rage in first grade, which Ella had begun a month before. Harry's hair was spiky, styled with mousse every morning, all sticky, stiff fifth-grade cool.

When the phone rang, Daniel got up to answer it. Calls this early were often from Pauline, asking him questions about their house. They had tried for several months to sell it, but the real estate market had gone into a downturn, and they had decided to rent for the time being. Daniel was always kind to Pauline; she still hung up if Mattie or the children answered.

"Hello, Isa." Daniel sounded relieved and surprised. "What are you doing up so early? . . . No, this is Daniel. Al lives at his house. But Mattie's here."

"Hi, Mom," Mattie said. "What an odd time for you to call. What's up?"

Isa's voice often sounded flimsy these days, as if it might tear, like old rice paper. But this morning she was bursting with joyful news, her voice strong, and the problem was just that she could not quite remember the details. "Oh, Mattie," she said, stalling, "I've never been so happy."

"That's wonderful. But what's the news?"

"Oh, honest to Pete!" There were clicks and exhalations of frustration as Isa struggled to remember. "Tell me about you — what's new, darling?"

"Mom, call me back when you remember, okay? I'm getting the kids off to school right now."

"But this is very important! Can't you think what it could be about?"

"Good news from your doctor?"

No.

"Something to do with Lewis?"

No.

"Something to do with my birthday?"

"Oh, is it your birthday soon?"

"Mom, it's coming right up, October twenty-ninth! Remember? Angela's having that big party for me at Stinson Beach."

"Well, that's nice," Isa said, as if Mattie were rambling on. "But that's not it."

"Something to do with Tillie?"

"Yes, that's it," Isa said triumphantly. "Darling, Tillie and I want to marry!"

"Good Lord," said Al, when Mattie reached him on the phone at school that morning. "Mom and Yvonne are getting married?"

"I haven't confirmed this with Yvonne. But Mom thinks it's happening."

"Is our mom a lesbian? Will we have two mothers now?"

"I'll have to consult with Angela and get back to you on that."

Life was so strange, the weather shifting so often. There were warm, bright days, and days that were dark and quiet and cool. Now all Isa talked about was Tillie. Lewis was still her steadfast companion, with her for part of every day, but Tillie was now the object of Isa's desire. She continued to call Yvonne Tillie. No one — least of all Yvonne — knew who Tillie was, or if there had ever been a Tillie in Isa's life, yet in Isa's presence, everyone carefully referred to Yvonne as Tillie.

"What time is Tillie coming over?" Isa would ask Mattie with heat. "Shouldn't she be here by now? Lewis and I went to see her yesterday. She had *lemon* bars! And a new yellow shawl. Isn't she *beautiful?*" Mattie got sick of it. Maybe she was jealous, that Yvonne, not herself or Al, would be the object of so much passion from their mother. Sometimes when Isa talked about Tillie, she thumped her chest to show the beating of her heart, and looked deranged with love.

"Mom says that you and she are getting married," Mattie told Yvonne later that morning, as Yvonne made them cups of tea with her prisoner's coil. Mattie had stopped by The Sequoias to see Isa but dropped by Yvonne's first.

Yvonne shook her head; her necklaces clicked. Cracked-earth lines radiated from her mouth and eyes. "This is the first I've heard of it," she said. "But she's certainly latched on to me more lately. Every time she sees me, she cries out 'Tillie!' as if she'd given me up for dead."

"I wonder if way deep down she associates you with Alfred," Mattie mused. "So she gets Alfred back in the deal. He didn't love her the way he loved you. But now, because he loved you, she gets to experience all that love she was so hungry for."

Mattie rose to stand beside Yvonne at the window. "I know your father would want me to help take care of her, that's all," Yvonne said. "He would have tried to do it too, if he were still alive."

Mattie thought of Abby's ruined feet but said nothing. "So does this mean you're not going to marry her?" she asked. She meant to say it lightly, but she felt disappointment on Isa's behalf, among a welter of feelings. Yvonne shook her head no, and then walked with a hitch to one of her velvet chairs and sat down. Mattie followed.

Isa's studio was clean, the windows open to let out the sour air. An aide had come earlier to help her get dressed, give her medicine, walk her to breakfast, and throw the sheets into the wash while she was gone. Isa sat in her easy chair watching TV. When Mattie moved into her line of sight, Isa's face drooped with disappointment.

"Oh, I thought you were Tillie," she said.

"Won't you see her at lunch?" Mattie asked, a little defensively.

"Yes!" Isa thumped her chest like a primate. "Help me get ready. I need some rouge. Please, for once, do what I ask. Get me the rouge, and some lipstick." Mattie retrieved Isa's makeup from the bathroom, then stood beside her throne, a bitter lady-in-waiting.

She patted Isa's nose with the powder puff, stroked on blusher, painted her lips with the lightest pink gloss. Isa looked as expectant as Ella in front of the vanity mirror when Mattie daubed on the gloss. "Will they let us marry?" Isa implored.

"Shh, shh," Mattie whispered, handing Isa a tissue to blot her lips. "I'm not sure, Mom."

When Isa was ready, in black silk and the pearls Alfred had given her on their twentieth anniversary, Isa focused on waiting for his mistress to come get her for lunch, so intently that she was unable to talk to Mattie at all.

"What's it all about, Otis?" Mattie wondered, sitting beside the iguana late that afternoon. He stared, frozen, although his skin was made for the most sinuous movement, armored and flexible at the same time, like chain mail. She still felt an undercurrent of edgy fear in his presence, this glorious fire-breathing dragon shrunken to the approximate size of a carrot. He was a little like Isa, she realized, so quiet, but scary still in his sudden bouts of frenzy. She smiled. "Help me, Otis," she pleaded, but he didn't move, didn't blink. He might as well have been dead, already stuffed, except for the tiny pulse she noticed in his throat, flaring out with each breath. Mattie went to the kitchen for a lettuce leaf. When she lowered it into his cage, Otis darted across the bottom. She screamed, and Otis dashed back and forth, thin ribbons of shit spewing everywhere until he was done. Then he froze again, the quick and the dead in one convenient package.

Mattie sat watching him, then looked out the window, where an ice-blue sky unfolded, veiled with angel-wing clouds. In the tree branches she could see yellow, orange, rose, red, in lush, ecstatic leafiness. Daniel was off working with a contractor, helping to build a house in Lagunitas, near the hollowed-out redwood where Mattie and Daniel had sat together so long before. There were moments when she wished they could go back there, to the fresh beginnings. She had forgotten, while she'd been praying for a man, how hard it could be to live with someone — the seesaw of needs, the body's betrayals. The horrible way Daniel scraped cottage cheese from the corners of his lips into his mouth. That he ate cottage cheese at all. They so often needed opposite things. She wanted to be alone when he wanted to be affectionate. She'd coquettishly asked for a cup of coffee with hot milk in bed one morning, and that night he brought home an espresso machine they couldn't afford. She wanted to talk when he needed to be deeply silent.

But still, he was so endearing. Sometimes after he got ready for church he came to find her, and stood with his arms at his sides, like a little boy in his first suit from Sears. He taught

399

Ella to hammer nails with the best of them, taught both kids to sew on buttons, and to iron. He taught them to sing "Joe Hill," and to make cheese omelettes.

He'd also discovered Nicky's porno movies, and that had made her want to die — or to leave him. But he'd wanted to watch them with her. She threw them out the following day, as leftovers from her life with Nicky. She'd found a diary Daniel had kept ever since meeting Pauline. She read it greedily, then confessed. He was mad at her for a full day and part of a second. He discovered that she didn't keep track of the checks she wrote. She found out he didn't floss very often, and hadn't paid taxes one recent year. He found her old magazine photograph of the beaming Indian holy man with the parcel of rocks tied to his penis. It had been folded up and tucked in the drawer of her bedside table. She found him holding it in their bedroom. "What are you looking for?" she demanded. "You're like a narc."

Daniel kept looking at the picture, covering his crotch with his hand. "Ouch," he said. She finally smiled. "Why do you keep this?" he asked.

She sat on the carpet beside him and took the picture of the destitute, naked, crazy-looking Indian man. "Because he's doing something impossible and scary, and living through it," she said. "Look at the weight he's bearing — that's gotta be ten pounds of rocks dangling there. But he's saying to God, 'I'm Yours, and You will sustain me. Look how well You're doing!' "

Daniel kept his eyes on the picture. "That's how you make me feel too." He licked his lips, swallowed. "But I guess it's too early to talk about, like, the possibility of marriage, right?"

"Oh, for Chrissakes," she caught herself saying. "Way too early." Her heart raced and chattered like wind-up teeth.

"In the spring, we'll have been together a year," Daniel said.

She felt herself blush and concentrated on breathing in, breathing out. She covered her face with her hands. "So tell me exactly what you're asking," she said, through her fingers.

"I'm asking you if you would marry me sometime in the spring."

She felt his hand against hers. The cupped palm of her hand grew slick with tears. "I'll wear the rocks to the wedding, if you want me to," he whispered. They sat close together, heads averted. He nuzzled the side of her head, and she let herself cry, and then wiped her nose with the back of her hand. Daniel lifted his T-shirt to wipe her eyes and nose.

He was looking at her as if she were his own sleeping child.

"Well?" he asked.

She closed her eyes, smiling, and nodded. "I have to get back to you about the rocks," she said.

There was a crispness to the night. Daniel got the children to bed while Mattie sat outside wrapped in a blanket. She looked up at the stars and thought about her wedding in the spring. The smell of the earth in April would be so rich. You got the bursting soil and also what it was bursting with. And the golden evenings grew longer and the night did not close in on you.

She and Daniel told the children the news together the next morning over breakfast. "We're going to get married in the spring," Mattie said gently, and Ella clapped her hands to her cheeks. But Harry gave Daniel a fatherly sideways look. This Rasta bum wanted to marry his mother?

"Whatever," he said, and went to his room. Mattie followed. She found him sitting on his bed, flipping baseball cards into the trashcan. She stretched out on his bed, and eventually he lay down beside her.

"I thought you loved Daniel," she said.

She couldn't see his face, because they were looking in the same direction, but she rubbed his shoulder blades and listened to his ticker tape of worry.

"I *do* love Daniel. But what about Pauline? It's horrible for her," he said. "She used to be our friend. And then Ella's getting fat, you know. A boy at the pool teased her about her stomach. And Daniel has dreadlocks, so people stare at him already, and everyone's just looking at our family. And what about Daddy? What if Daddy and Lee break up? Daddy couldn't come back to us, because then us would also be Daniel."

This startled Mattie. She caught herself from reassuring him too quickly, making short work of his worries. "I know it's hard in some ways, because none of us knows what's going to happen," she said. That uncertainty now filled her like a cool compound slipping into her cracks and holes. "But won't it still be great? He's so good, and funny and sweet."

"But he's terrible at sports," Harry said. "He's not even good at catch. And he runs funny — no offense. I wish we had a regular family."

When Mattie went to tell Isa, she couldn't find her in her studio. She eventually found her at Lewis's, watching tennis on TV and eating lasagne. Mattie kissed them both, and pulled up a chair.

"I have some news for you," she began. "Daniel and I are getting married in the spring."

Isa recoiled, as though she had been shot. "What?" she demanded. "Are you out of your mind?" She glared at Lewis.

"That's wonderful news," said Lewis, taking Mattie's hands in his. "Will Pastor marry you? Will you marry at church?"

"Yes, to both, I think. We haven't discussed many details. But I'd like you to walk me down the aisle, Lewis." He clutched her hands to his chest. Mattie looked at Isa. Her mother had taken out her dentures and placed them on her plate of lasagne, as if she meant to expose her valves, to frighten them both back into submission.

"But will they let *us* marry? Tillie and me?" Isa cried. "Can't you for even one time in your life think about someone besides yourself?"

Lewis stared at Isa. Then he turned to Mattie, still clasping her hands, and bowed his head. "May I recite the thirteenth chapter of Corinthians in the service?" he asked. She nodded, of course. It was the "New York, New York" of the New Testament, but if Lewis wanted to recite it, that was fine by her.

Angela had gone all-out for Mattie's birthday. She had borrowed a house on Stinson Beach from her girlfriend Julie's cousin, rented umbrellas, tables, and chairs from Big 4, and set them up on the beach halfway between the house and the water. Julie had flown up that morning and picked flowers from the garden, to make bouquets for the tables. Shish kebabs were marinating in the kitchen, coals were ready to be lit under grills in the backyard. Angela had asked guests to bring side dishes and drinks.

People came from church, and the same old

friends from the didgeridoo party came as well. Noah didn't, even though Mattie had left a message on his machine inviting him. He'd called back two days later to say he couldn't be there — and asked if she could drop by for a beer some night after work. The next day, when she went to the superette, she found that Noah had left her a present, wrapped in the Sunday comic pages. She knew before opening it that it would be the little blue shoe.

Angela had called Ned to invite him, without including William. Daniel had invited a few guys from his construction crew, Al some people he and Mattie had gone to high school with. He and Katherine arranged to pick up Isa, Lewis, and Yvonne.

Mattie and Angela shopped for clothes in a vintage store the day before the party. Both now wore size 14. They chose dresses that were elegant and girlish but not totally frou-frou; they wanted something that was flowing and, as Angela put it, forgiving: "We're going to eat a lot, and we don't want our middles constricted," she said. Mattie selected a celadon-green silk dress, very simple and 1920s, a koan of a color, bright and light and muted at the same time — the color of a rice bowl. Angela bought a light-purple shift; she would wear a wreath of flowers in her hair. She bought an outfit for Ella from Hollywood — a miniature black velvet evening gown with puffy sleeves and pink rosettes, and a tiny purse. Ella filled the purse with Kleenex, a tube of pink lip gloss, and a medal she'd won in an art contest at school. Harry wore a gray suit from Mervyn's that Nicky had taken him shopping for, a clip-on tie, and a lot of styling gel to spike his hair.

Daniel wore his good suit, light khaki, debonair. He had the blue shoe in his pocket in the morning, but gave it to Mattie when it grew cold and windy later. She was having a bad brain day, worrying about the darkening weather, what kind of shape Isa would be in, whether there'd be enough food. When people began to arrive with food and presents, it seemed the ultimate miracle, to have good people love you, freaked-out, self-centered mess that you were.

Mattie greeted everyone, then walked across the sand calling for Harry and Ella above the roaring surf and the cries of the gulls. The kids had wandered far down the beach, and were tossing sticks into the waves. Ella's hair had come out of its clips, and her dress was falling off her shoulders. She looked like Courtney Love. Harry had gotten soot from a campfire all over his shirt. Mattie wanted to scoop them both up, hold them and smell their necks.

She had never imagined she could love anyone the way she loved her children. Elation and the cold air off the ocean filled her chest. "Come back to the party soon," she called, as a sudden wave sloshed over Ella's party shoes.

Mattie covered her eyes. It was so hopeless.

All she'd asked was for them to stay present-able for a couple of hours, and here they were, wet and covered with ashes and bits of sea-weed. Mattie shook her head. She walked quickly to Ella's side. "We'll put your socks in the dryer, darling." She held her, and looked out at the water. She thought of Daniel, and felt she had never been so happy. So why in the next moment did she see herself filling her pockets with rocks and walking into the waves like Virginia Woolf? She must have a screw loose somewhere. Oh, well. She breathed in her daughter's sweet, salty smells.

Ella wiggled out of her arms. "I want to go back to the water," she cried.

"Okay, sugarpie," Mattie said. Ella ran back to the shore. Harry waved to Mattie. She waved back, watched them for a minute more, and then turned back to the party.

She was still far from the tables when she saw Isa, Lewis, and Yvonne step onto the sand. Someone must have escorted them to the patio. They were walking on their own toward the ta-bles, two walkers parked on the deck.

Mattie tried to signal to Daniel, but he was busy talking to Ned. Isa, Lewis, and Yvonne, all dressed to the nines, limped and sagged along slowly. They were clutching one another, taking huge steps over tiny mounds of sand, preparing to step over pieces of driftwood. Please don't let them fall, Mattie prayed, even as she tried to keep from laughing. They looked like marionettes with strings of different lengths for each limb, or martians just now arriving on these shores, learning to use human feet for the first time.

Mattie began to move toward her mother, slowly, as when her children had taken their first steps and she had been across the room, too far to help before they fell.

But Lewis and Yvonne held Isa up, and Mattie understood with a rush of admiration that Isa had always kept moving forward, one foot at a time, no matter how hard it was, no matter how the sand shifted beneath her.

She looked up and saw Al approaching them from the patio. They smiled at each other, both walking as quickly as they could. Al wore one of his father's old corduroy jackets with suede elbow patches, and a white dress shirt unbuttoned at the neck. They got to Isa and her companions at the same time. They steadied Lewis, who steadied Yvonne, who propped Isa up.

The wind was howling, blowing sand around. Bright flags snapped in the breeze. It was so cold: people's skin would turn purple and they'd look awful in the photographs. But once Isa, Lewis, and Yvonne were safely seated, and a stream of people came to hug Mattie, everyone seemed suspiciously happy. Mattie half believed that in spite of mishaps and confusion and wind, the other stuff, the love, would overcome.

Katherine, in a white lace dress and flowing

rose scarf, had brought bubbles for the guests, and gave them out, to blow whenever the spirit moved them. And Angela had brought plastic leis: purple, pink, red, white, yellow, wacky and gloriously tasteless, like paper party hats. The children returned from the beach, hungry and dirty and petulant. Al got Harry to help with the shish kebabs.

Ella, overcome by the noise and windiness, began to cry, and when all else failed — hugs, and compliments, and chocolate — Mattie took a long, deep breath and gave her the little blue shoe to hold. "This helps me get through *everything*," she whispered, and Ella's eyes widened as she beheld the treasure in her hand as if it were a sapphire. She curled her fingers around it with determination, and put it in her cocktail purse along with her other valuables.

"Go sit with Isa now," Mattie told her, and Ella kicked a long, serpentine path through the sand to the tables. Isa sat regally at her table, wearing the elegant silk dress Mattie had helped her pick out. She had on so much makeup that even from a distance she looked like embalmed royalty.

The winds blew harder, but minutes before lunch was ready, they parted. Calm split them down the middle, pushed them apart like a muscleman. When guests reached the tables with their food, they stepped onto a balmy beach.

Lewis said grace for everyone. Mattie looked

off at the blue-green sea as he spoke, thinking about her father. In her mind, he was chagrined, so far away, alone. She turned away from him, sick with memories of Abby at ten in the yard at Neil's, Abby bloated now in the little house on stilts. Actions had consequences, Alfred used to tell his children. Boy, did they ever. "Amen," Lewis said. "Amen," everyone chorused. And then they all began blowing bubbles at one another.

The cascade of iridescence blew like musical notes of light; everyone was breathing out good wishes, frivolous and loving, evanescent and silly. Mattie and Daniel kissed. Angela threw herself into Mattie's arms. Ella rushed up, her purse hanging open, its contents dumped into the sand of the windswept beach, trampled over now by the guests.

"My little blue shoe," Mattie finally managed to cry in a mottled voice, just as Ella burst into tears with much louder despair: "My lip gloss! My art medal!" Angela bent down to console her, and they took off hand in hand to search the beach. Daniel nudged Mattie with a questioning look, and Mattie whispered, "She's lost the little blue shoe." Daniel turned toward the beach, the sand and dune grass between here and there, turned back to Mattie and shook his head. He took her hand and kissed it.

The weather shifted again. It was going to rain. Rain, on her birthday — all because Ella had lost the little blue shoe! Help me, Mattie prayed, I'm cuckoo. Help me, please, thank you, please, help me, thank you. Slanted rays shone through a darkening swirl in the sky, rococo castles and feathers and mare's tails in the clouds. Someone was pulling out all the celestial stops. It was so beautiful that Mattie could hardly bear it. She and Daniel walked past the table where Al sat with Katherine. Harry came and tugged on Al's sleeve. "How soon till you can play?" he demanded. Al smiled, and asked him softly, "Did you bring a ball?" And when Harry nodded, Al promised to meet him a little later down the beach.

The employees of Thorndike Press hope you have enjoyed this Large Print book. All our Thorndike and Wheeler Large Print titles are designed for easy reading, and all our books are made to last. Other Thorndike Press Large Print books are available at your library, through selected bookstores, or directly from us.

For information about titles, please call:

(800) 223-1244

or visit our Web site at:

www.gale.com/thorndike
www.gale.com/wheeler

To share your comments, please write:

Publisher
Thorndike Press
295 Kennedy Memorial Drive
Waterville, ME   04901